R.

DANCING TILL MIDNIGHT

Also by Rosie Goodwin

The Bad Apple
No One's Girl

DANCING TILL MIDNIGHT

ROSIE GOODWIN

headline

First published in Great Britain in 2006
by HEADLINE BOOK PUBLISHING

1

Cataloguing in Publication Data is available from the British Library

ISBN 0 7553 2983 X

Typeset in Calisto by Palimpsest Book Production Limited,
Polmont, Stirlingshire

Printed and bound in Great Britain by
Mackays of Chatham plc, Chatham, Kent

Headline's policy is to use papers that are natural, renewable
and recyclable products and made from wood grown in sustainable forests.
The logging and manufacturing processes are expected to conform to the
environmental regulations of the country of origin.

HEADLINE BOOK PUBLISHING
A division of Hodder Headline
338 Euston Road
London NW1 3BH

www.headline.co.uk
www.hodderheadline.com

*This book is for my Mum and Dad
with all my love.*

Acknowledgements

Nellie Goodwin (Ellen), 1915–2004.
Francis Harold Goodwin (Frank), 1919–1999.
Special thoughts of Aunt Ellen and Uncle Frank – who loved to dance.

Also of my dear friend Christine, who will always be sadly missed.

Thanks to the staff of Nuneaton Library, who are always so helpful with research.

And a special mention, and my thanks, to Viv and Sarah at Astley Book Farm for all their support.

As always, a big thank you to the lovely team at Headline and my agent Philip Patterson.

And lastly, this book is also for Matthew, and all the 'special' children everywhere, with all my love . . .

Prologue

Nuneaton, Warwickshire, 1950

'Now get down those stairs and do not *think* of coming out again until you have seen the wickedness of your ways. I can scarcely believe that you could even think of bringing such books into the house, you bad girl! All those disgusting women cavorting their half-naked bodies about in those filthy costumes!' Emily Westwood gripped her small niece's elbow and flung her on to the top step of the dark cellar.

'B . . . but Aunt Emily, it's only a b . . . book about ballroom dancing,' the terrified child whimpered.

'Ballroom dancing, indeed! I am shocked that your school would even *allow* such books to go into their library. Why – it's nothing short of *sinful*, the way those brazen women display their bodies. Now get down there and do as you are told or you will feel the cane again. Why you should want to fill your head with such wanton rubbish is beyond me. The only book you should need to read is the Good Book, as I've told you before. But then you always have had a bad streak in you, just as your father did – as I find out daily to my cost. No good will come of being attracted to all this glitter, you just mark my words.'

The tall grey-haired woman slammed the door shut and suddenly the child found herself in total darkness. A feeling of panic engulfed her. She stood for some seconds as her eyes adjusted to the deep shadows, listening to the footsteps of the woman recede, then cautiously she felt her way down the roughly hewn stone steps into the pitch-black cellar. At the bottom she sank to the cold floor and hugged her knees as tears shimmered on her thick lashes and slid from her huge dark eyes.

Grace Collins was ten years old, with long, dark brown hair that reached almost to her waist. She was small for her age, although she could clean a house from top to bottom as well as any of the women who lived in the neighbouring houses. She had no memories of her mother or father; they had both been killed during the war in the bombing of Coventry. All she could remember was living with her

1

aunt, who had never shown her so much as one ounce of love or kindness. Emily Westwood had taken Grace in following the death of her parents; the child supposed she should be grateful for this, and suffered all manner of guilt feelings because she was not.

They had moved to the house they lived in, in Oaston Road in Nuneaton, when Grace was just a baby, and had lived there ever since. It was a huge, rambling Victorian semi-detached house – and even at her tender age Grace knew that it could have been beautiful. But it wasn't, for her aunt did not believe in ornaments and what she termed 'fripperies', and so the house remained like her, cold and uninviting.

Formerly, Grace had been accepting, for she could not miss what she had never had. But lately she had begun to question her aunt's strict disciplinarian ways. The boys at school taunted her because of the way she was forced to dress, and the girls soon grew tired of trying to befriend her, for Miss Westwood would not allow her out of the house except to go to church or school. Even so, school was fast becoming the only bright spot in her life, for she had recently discovered the delights of the library, and a whole new world had opened up to her through books. She would read anything and everything that she could get her hands on, which was what had led her to her current predicament – having dared to bring home a book on ballroom dancing.

She stared longingly up at the only window in the cellar. Tiny, it was thick with grime and high up, out of reach on the far wall that bordered the cemetery beyond. The wind that was howling outside was throwing the driving rain against the glass as if it were trying to find its way in. The little girl shuddered as she thought of all the dead bodies that were so close beyond the window, and as her leg began to smart she touched it tentatively. As always, the weals that were rising from the beating she had just taken with the cane were high up beneath her skirt where they wouldn't be seen, and she winced as her fingers moved tenderly over them. No doubt this would mean yet another note from her aunt excusing her from PE at school, for the woman would not want it to be known that she had physically attacked her.

A movement in a far corner made her eyes stretch wide with terror, and she was just in time to see a thick tail follow a hairy body as it scuttled away into a deep shadow. Rats! She swallowed hard to stop the scream that rose to her throat, but then all was quiet again save for the sound of the driving rain. Think of something else, she told herself, and with an effort she turned her thoughts to the book that her aunt had confiscated. Soon her head was full of beautiful gowns that swirled as the women who wore them twirled gracefully around the dance-floor. *One day* . . . she sighed, and for a time the cold dark cellar was forgotten.

Chapter One

'Oh, come on. *Surely* the old witch will give yer one night off?' Norma Brambles said to Grace, but her friend merely grinned.

'If I so much as even *suggested* going dancing, I think my aunt would keel over with a heart-attack,' Grace snorted as she lifted a cheese and tomato sandwich from her lunch-box.

Norma, her friend and office colleague, sighed loudly. 'Christ! I don't know how yer put up with it. The silly old sod must think she's still livin' in the Dark Ages, instead o' 1960.' Norma bit into her own sandwich as Grace looked on with amusement twinkling in her eye. 'Why don't yer leave the mardy-arse old sod to it, an' get yer own place?' she went on through a mouthful of fish-paste.

Grace shrugged. 'It wouldn't really be very fair to do that, would it? After all, she did bring me up, and now that she's not well I owe it to her to look out for her.'

'Huh! Can't see why meself. She ain't exactly been good to yer, has she? I mean, no disrespect – but look how you're dressed fer a start. That style o' clothes went out years ago.' To emphasise the point, Norma ran her hand down her full skirt before patting her high bouffant hair as she studied Grace thoughtfully.

Grace glanced down at her own skirt, which she had painstakingly stitched by hand. She had made most of her clothes for as long as she could remember, under the watchful eye of her aunt who still insisted on choosing the patterns for them.

'Yer know, yer could be really glamorous if yer put yer mind to it,' Norma went on musingly. 'Take yer hair fer a start-off. Why do yer allus wear it pulled back into that tight little bun thing? I bet it's really long when it's loose, ain't it?'

Grace patted her hair self-consciously. 'It is long actually, but Aunt Emily thinks it looks neater when it's tied back.'

'That doesn't surprise me.' Norma rolled her eyes to the ceiling. 'I bet she's the reason why yer never wear make-up an' all, ain't she?'

Grace nodded slowly, then suddenly to her horror, Norma leaped from her seat and, after positioning herself behind her friend, started to take the Kirby grips from her hair. Within seconds it had fallen down her back in a thick, dark luxurious mass.

Norma sighed enviously as she took a hairbrush from her bag and began to brush it. 'Christ, it's criminal to keep hair like this tied back. Come on, let's have a look at yer face now, eh?'

Grace looked on with trepidation as Norma extracted a lipstick from her handbag.

'Right, now pucker yer lips like this – see?' She made a comical imitation of a pout as somewhat reluctantly Grace did as she was told. Next Norma waved a mascara block at her. 'Now, look down.' Spitting on the black mascara, she then furiously wiped a little brush up and down it before applying it to Grace's long lashes. 'Christ, I'd die for lashes like these,' she said. 'They just seem to go on for ever, an' you don't even need no panstick, 'cos yer complexion's perfect. Yer make me sick.'

Grace blushed, making her look prettier still as Norma stood back with her hands on her hips to survey her handiwork. 'A few new togs now an' you'd knock 'em dead,' she declared, and producing a mirror from her seemingly bottomless bag, she brandished it in front of Grace. 'See what I mean?'

When Grace glanced in the mirror she gasped with amazement, for she certainly *did* look different. 'Goodness me, I never knew I could look like that,' she breathed.

Norma nudged her in the ribs. 'It's your turn to take the wage-packets down to the shop floor, an' all I can say is, lookin' like that you'll gain yourself a few admirers. In fact, the poor buggers won't know what's hit 'em.'

The two girls were still laughing when suddenly the door swung open and Mr Jackson, the office manager, strode in. His eyes opened slightly with surprise as they settled on Grace, but then he tapped his wristwatch. 'Very well then, girls. It's two minutes to one o'clock, and this isn't a beauty parlour, you know. Let's settle down and get back to work, eh? The men downstairs will be crying for your blood if you don't have their wage-packets ready within the next hour.'

'It's all in hand, Mr Jackson,' Norma grinned cheekily, and nodding, the manager walked on and disappeared into his office.

'Phew, I thought we was goin' to get a roastin' then.' Norma took a seat at her desk, and Grace's heart filled with affection as she looked across at the girl who was the only true friend she had ever had. She'd been working in the wages office of Courtaulds factory for three years, and up until now had loved every minute of it. Mr Jackson was a firm, but fair boss, and since Norma had started there a few months

4

before, she had been a constant source of amusement to her. Grace never tired of hearing about Norma's various outings and boyfriends, although it did sometimes seem to emphasise the drudgery of her own existence. She was now almost twenty years old and had grown into a very beautiful young woman – a fact that, if anything, made her aunt tie her even more closely to her apron-strings. She had never been completely happy with Grace working in an office with what she termed so many 'loose' women, but it had been preferable to her going into a factory, and she certainly didn't complain when Grace tipped her wages up each week. Her aunt's heart condition seemed to have worsened since Grace started work, however, and it had a nasty habit of flaring up every time Grace so much as mentioned doing something of which Emily Westwood disapproved.

As she thought of her now, Grace frowned. Aunt Emily had never been easy to live with, but lately she was getting even grumpier, if that were possible. Strangely, her heart condition never seemed to stop her attending her many church functions and services, but then, Grace supposed that this was the only pleasure she had left in life now. No matter how hard she tried – and she *had* tried over the years – the girl couldn't seem to please her. Even now she still tried, although she knew deep down that it was futile. For some reason, despite all her best efforts, she had always been a great disappointment to her aunt, and this hurt her.

Until she had come to work at the office and met Norma, Grace had never fully understood what she had missed. Then, one day, Norma took her home with her in her lunch-hour. That was the first time that Grace met Norma's mother. Hetty Brambles, like her daughter, was a jovial, fun-loving little woman with a ready smile who had made Grace feel welcome the second she stepped through the door. She was a widow, and to make ends meet she sometimes took in lodgers. Their house, unlike her aunt's, was noisy and untidy, with a steady stream of visitors forever coming and going. And yet despite that, Grace loved every second of the time she spent there, for the easy, light-hearted atmosphere was one that she was completely unused to.

A tap at the small office door brought her thoughts sharply back to the present. Glancing up from her desk, she was just in time to see a tall, fair-haired young man pop his head round the door. When his eyes settled on Grace she saw a look of admiration flit across his face, and she felt herself blushing hotly – a fact that was not lost on Norma, who had to look away to hide her amusement.

'Is Mr Jackson in?' he asked politely, obviously just as embarrassed as Grace.

Nodding towards the other door, she replied, 'Yes, he's through there.'

'Ta, love.' The unfortunate young man almost tripped in his haste to be past their desks, and within seconds of tapping at Mr Jackson's door, he had disappeared inside.

Leaning across her desk, Norma grinned wickedly. 'I reckon as you've just got yerself an admirer there if yer play yer cards right, kid. That was Barry Swan. He works down on the shop floor. A bit of all right, ain't he?'

Grace scowled at her. 'Don't talk such nonsense, Norma,' she whispered.

Norma merely shrugged before turning her attention back to the Olivetti typewriter on her desk. 'Have it your own way then. But mark my words, you ain't seen the last of him unless I'm very much mistaken.'

Grace stood up abruptly and snatched up the tray that contained the workforce's wages, suddenly very keen to get out of the office before the young man reappeared. 'I'll just take these downstairs then,' she mumbled, and within seconds she had scuttled away, leaving Norma with a grin on her face that stretched from ear to ear.

Emily Westwood rose from her seat, and, ignoring the cane that was propped against the chair arm, walked across the kitchen past a sideboard that took up almost all of one wall. A great wooden monstrosity of a thing, it had been bought many years ago for its storage value, rather than its good looks, as had most of the furniture in this house. Even so, it was so highly polished that she could see her face in it, like everything else in the room. Emily insisted on cleanliness in all things. After all, cleanliness was next to godliness, and she would settle for nothing less – although, of course, it was usually Grace who saw to the polishing.

Emily resented the time Grace spent at her place of work, even though it was she herself who had insisted on the girl getting a job. 'Idle hands make work for the devil,' she had told her, and besides, the wage-packet she handed over each week more than saw to their basic needs. Some weeks, Emily was even able to save a little from it. She felt no guilt for not allowing Grace to keep any of her earnings. The way she saw it, her niece would only have frittered it away on make-up and clothes, as did the other girls she worked with. Her thin lips pursed in disapproval as she thought of them with their short skirts and painted faces.

Reaching a small, ornate writing desk tucked away in the corner, Emily ran her hands lovingly across the grain of the wood. It was the only piece of furniture in the house that had any value, and was in the Chippendale style with delicate, shaped legs. It had been in

6

Emily's family for many years, passed down from one generation to another. Opening the middle drawer, she looked down on the stack of neatly piled papers within, but then her fingers moved past them to a minute wooden knob in a far corner. When she pressed it, a tiny concealed drawer popped out and her face grew sad as she looked on the contents.

Slowly she withdrew a printed invitation to an engagement party. It was yellowed with age, and brittle to the touch, but as she stared down at the faded letters her eyes filled with tears. After a moment she returned it to its hiding-place before extracting a small leather box. When she sprang the lid open, a tiny solitaire diamond winked up at her from a thin gold band, and now the tears flowed freely as she was transported back to another time, a happier time when her future stretched before her, full of promise.

'I love you, Emily.' He stared down at her from eyes misty with desire. He was tall and dark, and so handsome that every time he so much as touched her she went weak at the knees. 'I need you so much,' he whispered into her hair as his hungry hands roamed up and down her back, but gently she pushed him away.

'Not yet, darling. Not until we are married. Only a few more months to go and then we will be together for always.'

He sighed with frustration as she straightened her skirts and moved away from him, and she felt a cold hand close around her heart.

'In a month I'll be going away to war. Why should we wait? What if I don't come back? Why are you always like this? Don't you have any feelings?'

'Of course I have, but it's not right to . . . well, you know – do that sort of thing before you have a ring on your finger.' She blushed just to think of it as he stood up and began to pace the room impatiently.

'In case you'd forgotten, you do have a ring on your finger and the engagement party invitations have already gone out. I shall only be allowed a day pass to come back for that. We may not even be able to have much time alone together, so surely—'

'No. I'm sorry, but it's out of the question. I will not be bullied into doing anything that isn't right and proper.' She folded her hands in her lap primly as he stared at her in disbelief.

'Sometimes I feel that I don't know you at all,' he said quietly, and eager to make up for some of the harm she feared she'd done with her refusal, she reached out and caressed his hand. He snatched it away as he turned and headed towards the door, pausing to look back at her just once. The expression on his face made her blood turn to water.

7

'Will you be calling round tomorrow?' Her voice held a note of pleading but his face remained cool.

'If I have the time.' Then with a curt nod he was gone, leaving her alone with a deep feeling of misgiving, twisting the diamond ring on her finger.

The sound of someone opening the front gate pulled her thoughts sharply back to the present. Glancing at the wooden mantel clock, she realised with a little shock that it would be Grace returning from work. Quickly, she thrust the ring back into the drawer before closing it and dropping heavily onto the nearest chair.

'I'm home!' Grace's voice echoed in the hallway, and the next second she burst into the large room that served as both a kitchen and a parlour. The fresh air had given a healthy glow to her flawless cheeks, and although she had drawn her dark hair back into its customary tight knot, a few strands had escaped to curl around her face in the wind. The sight of her niece looking so pretty and happy hardened Emily's heart.

'You are almost *ten* minutes late, young lady,' she glowered at her. 'Where do you think you have been?'

Instantly the smile slid from Grace's face as she stared into her aunt's bleak grey eyes. 'I'm sorry. There was an urgent letter that Mr Jackson wanted to go out tonight, so I stayed behind for a few minutes to finish it for him.'

'Huh! Let's hope your dedication is reflected in your wage-packet at the end of the week. Wait a moment – that isn't lipstick I see on your lips, is it?'

Emily's eyes narrowed to pinpricks as she stared at her niece, and Grace felt her hands begin to tremble.

'Of c . . . course not,' she stammered.

Emily sniffed loudly. 'Good. I don't want you turning into one of those painted whores you work with.'

'They're not whores,' Grace protested, shocked. 'My friends at work just like to follow the fashion, that's all.'

Emily bristled when Grace dared to answer her back. '*That* is a matter of opinion. From where I'm standing they are nothing more than painted ladies, and they will reap their just rewards, you mark my words.'

Knowing that it would be useless to argue, Grace decided to change the subject. Crossing to the deep stone sink to fill the kettle, she enquired, 'So how have you been today?'

Emily sighed dramatically. 'No better than usual. My leg is still paining me – I fear the arthritis is getting worse. I cannot walk at all without the use of my stick now, so of course, I have been unable to do much about the house.'

'Never mind. Now I'm home I'll be able to do some jobs after I've cooked our meal.' Grace smiled at her warmly, but the woman's expression remained stern, and as the smile died on her face, Grace set about preparing their dinner, which tonight would be potatoes, cabbage, carrots and lamb chops.

Much later that evening after Grace had tidied the house, cleaned the bathroom and done a pile of ironing, she sank down onto the hard overstuffed fireside chair as Emily took up the Bible and began to read aloud. Although Grace tried to concentrate, she felt her attention drifting as she looked around the room. Apart from their two bedrooms and the bathroom, this was the only other room in the house that was ever used, for her aunt said she was not prepared to waste money on heating. Even then the room was barely warm, for Emily would only use sufficient coal to keep the fire alight. Only once had Grace ever dared to suggest that it might be nice to have a fire in the winter in the pretty tiled fireplaces in the bedrooms. They were an original feature of the house and Grace loved them, but her aunt's reaction at the very idea of such a sinful waste of fuel had ensured that she never made the same mistake again. These days, she was resigned to the fact that in the winter she went to bed in layers of clothes to see her breath hanging on the air, for, as her aunt was fond of pointing out, the post office savings she had been forced to live on since caring for Grace were dwindling fast.

The only form of entertainment allowed in the house was the wireless, but even this was restricted to the News on the Home Service, *Woman's Hour*, which her aunt listened to every afternoon and church services, the *Hymn and a Prayer* every day at 10.50 a.m. and the special Sunday morning broadcast. Once, when Grace had bravely suggested that they might get a television set, her aunt had gone purple with rage and declared that she would have no new-fangled devices through the door. And so now, just as she did every evening, Grace was forced to sit through yet another of her aunt's Bible readings.

When at last it was over, Emily rose slowly from her chair and, leaning heavily on her cane, walked towards the door. 'I'm off to bed. Make sure that everywhere is properly locked before you retire, Grace. And I will have my cup of tea in bed in the morning before you leave for work. A slight lie-in might do my leg some good.'

'Of course, Aunt. Goodnight.' Once the woman had disappeared through the door, Grace gave a sigh of relief and pulled her chair nearer to the fire. Curling her legs up beneath her, she stared into the low, flickering flames. Norma and some of the other girls from the office were going to see Billy Fury perform on Friday night at the Co-op Hall, and she would dearly have loved to go with them. But she knew better by now than to even suggest it to her aunt, for it would merely have brought on one of her 'heart spasms' as she called them, and caused a row.

Her thoughts moved to the young man who had come into the office earlier in the day. What had Norma said his name was? Barry, that was it – Barry Swan. An unfamiliar fluttery feeling started in the pit of her stomach as she recalled the way he'd looked at her, and she found herself smiling. Most of the girls at work were already engaged to be married, or had a boyfriend at least, but she was never allowed out, except to visit the library or accompany her aunt to church. That was another strange thing, now that she came to think of it. More and more of late she'd noticed that, no matter how ill her aunt was, it never stopped her from going to her church meetings and services. A pang of guilt shot through the girl for having such wicked thoughts. After all, Aunt Emily had taken her in and brought her up after the death of her parents, so instead of questioning her, she should be grateful. Unbidden, a picture of Norma's mother flashed before her eyes. Why couldn't Emily have been more like Mrs Brambles – kind, jovial and considerate? Grace could never remember her aunt so much as saying a kind word to her, let alone giving her a kiss or a cuddle as Norma's mother had . . .

Sometimes, Grace wondered why her aunt had ever taken her in at all, for no matter what Grace did, it was never good enough to please her, and sometimes the woman's behaviour bordered on cruelty. Grace had lost count of the times she had been beaten and locked in the cellar. Gone without meals. Made to write out chapters from the Bible until her hand ached. Forced to sit in near-darkness, stitching away at the drab clothes her aunt insisted she wear. But what could she do? Her aunt had brought her up, and now that her health was failing it was up to Grace to stick by her.

Suddenly, a vision of Barry popped up again and she found tears stinging the back of her eyes. There was no point in even thinking about him, as her life was already mapped out for her. She would grow into a lonely old maid caring for her aunt, just as her aunt had spent her life caring for *her*. The thought was unbearable and she lowered her head and wept.

Chapter Two

As Grace stepped out of the factory, someone called her name and she paused and looked round. When she saw Barry rushing towards her with his handsome face wreathed in a smile, she gulped deep in her throat with shyness and wished that the ground would open up and swallow her.

'Hello! Off to do a bit of shoppin' in your lunch-hour, are you?' he asked.

She shook her head as she struggled to regain her composure. He was standing less than an arm's length from her now, and close up he was even more handsome in a funny sort of way. She supposed that his mouth was just a little too wide for him to be classed as handsome in the conventional sense, and his hair needed a cut, but even so, when he smiled at her a million butterflies started to flutter in her stomach.

'Actually, I . . . um . . . well, I was j-just on my way to the library,' she managed to stutter eventually.

He grinned cheekily. 'That's a coincidence – so was I. You don't mind if I walk with you, do you?'

Deeply embarrassed, she shrugged as he fell into step beside her.

'Do much readin', do you?'

She nodded and dared to peep at him from the corner of her eye. 'I do, I suppose. What about you?'

He laughed aloud. 'To be honest, no, I don't. An' I might as well admit I weren't really goin' to the library. I just wanted to get to know you a bit better, that's all. Am I forgiven?'

His laughter was so infectious that she found herself grinning with him as a million unfamiliar feelings flowed through her. It felt strange and curiously nice to be walking along with a young man beside her, and she wondered what her aunt would say if she could see her now. Worse still, what would her aunt say if someone she knew saw them together? As they turned into Queens Road she glanced at him shyly. She'd never had the undivided attention of a male before and wasn't quite sure what she should say. But she needn't have worried, for Barry was quite happy to do enough talking for both of them, and now that

11

he'd finally managed to get her alone he intended to do just that. Glancing down at his work clothes, he spread his hands by way of apology. 'Sorry I'm in a bit of a state. It's dirty work in the dye shop. I normally get changed if I'm gonna pop out, but I didn't want to miss you.'

She flashed him a smile that made his heart skip a beat. 'It's quite all right. With all those different colours splashed all over you, you could start a new fashion trend.'

He smiled back at her. She might be quiet – in fact, the lads on the shop floor had nicknamed her the Ice Maiden – but at least she had a sense of humour. He'd been hoping to catch her alone ever since he had spotted her in the office, for there was something about her that was refreshingly different. She didn't dress like the other girls in the factory, or the office for that matter. Nor did she plaster herself in make-up. But then, from where he was standing she didn't need to, for in his eyes she was easily the most beautiful girl he had ever seen. For weeks now he'd been trying to find out more about her as he plucked up the courage to ask her out. But up to now all his questions had drawn a blank because it seemed that she never went to any of the places where the other factory workers went. It seemed that she never went *anywhere* if it came to that; rumour had it that she lived with a maiden aunt who kept her a virtual prisoner. He found that hard to believe. After all, it was 1960. As he peeped at her again their eyes locked and they both grinned self-consciously.

'I ain't too good when it comes to chat-up lines,' he admitted, and his confession had the desired effect, for she seemed to relax a little.

They crossed Edward Street, and without thinking he took her elbow as he hurried her through the lunch-hour traffic. The physical contact made the colour flood into her cheeks and she was almost relieved when they reached the other side of the road and he released her. Her arm where he had touched her was tingling and she had the urge to rub it, but she was too embarrassed, so instead she walked on without a word,

Although it was only early in November, the Christmas decorations were already beginning to appear in the shops and Grace peered into the windows as they passed. Her aunt never even went to the expense of a Christmas tree so the girl had to make do with the shop displays instead.

Barry noticed her interest and asked casually, 'Like Christmas, do you?'

She nodded eagerly. 'Oh yes, I do, but my aunt doesn't believe in the commercial side of Christmas, so I'm afraid when I see all the decorations springing up everywhere, I'm like a child in a toy shop.'

She'd confirmed the rumours he had heard without even realising it, and he stared at her curiously.

'She wouldn't think much of our place then,' he commented. 'When me mam starts to put the trimmin's up she tends to get a bit carried away. It usually ends up resemblin' Santa's Grotto, an' by Christmas Day we're all sick of the sight of them.'

Her eyes sparkled at the picture he conjured up. 'It sounds wonderful to me. I've longed for my aunt to at least have a Christmas tree ever since I was a child, but as I said, she doesn't believe in all that. She's more keen on the religious side.'

Barry grimaced. 'I can't imagine Christmas without a tree. When me an' me brother were little, that were part of the pleasure of Christmas – puttin' the tree up, I mean. Me dad would take us down the market to choose one, an' then we'd all carry it home between us. Then we'd sit an' me mam would help us make the paper streamers for the ceilin'.'

She looked sad. 'It sounds lovely. You don't realise how lucky you are. My aunt doesn't even believe in doing a Christmas dinner. We usually go to church in the morning and then the rest of the day is just like any other day.' She clamped her lips shut as she suddenly realised that she was confiding in him. He was remarkably easy to talk to and seemed genuinely interested in anything she had to say, although she felt that she was perhaps being a little unfair. She didn't mean to paint a harsh picture of her Aunt Emily.

'So, where else do you go, apart from to church then?'

Shrugging, she answered, 'I don't, to be honest. Except to work, of course. My aunt isn't in the best of health at present, so usually what with working and keeping the house going I don't get much free time.'

He stared at her incredulously. 'You mean to tell me you never even have a night out with your mates?'

When she shook her head he frowned in disbelief. 'I ain't never heard anythin' like that before. Everyone should have a bit of leisure time. After all, you know what they say – "all work an' no play makes Jack a dull boy" – not that you're dull, of course,' he added hastily.

She smiled at his discomfort but was saved from having to answer when they reached the library steps. 'Well, I'd best go in then,' she said hesitantly.

He fidgeted from foot to foot. 'I . . . err . . . I could wait for you, if you like.'

She grinned shyly, although she secretly hoped that he would, then she tripped up the steps, aware of his eyes burning into her back.

13

When she came out, he was standing in exactly the same position as she had left him. As soon as she reached the bottom of the steps he took the heavy books from her without a word and they fell into step again.

They were almost halfway back to the factory before either of them spoke again, then it was Barry who broke the silence when he said tentatively, 'I don't suppose there's much point in me askin' you out, is there? Not if you don't go out much, I mean.'

She shook her head regretfully. 'To be honest, it would be difficult at present. As I explained, my aunt isn't too well and I'm quite busy. But . . . I do appreciate you asking.'

He masked his bitter disappointment with a smile, then had a brain-wave. 'Well, all right then. If you can't manage to get out at night, perhaps you could meet me in your lunch-hour? We could go for a stroll round Riversley Park an' eat our sandwiches there, or perhaps go for a coffee or somethin'. What do you say?'

She was almost beside herself with embarrassment now but had to admit the idea was very appealing. 'All right.' She nodded slowly. 'That would be really nice, thank you.'

He beamed like a cat that had got the cream, and when they arrived back at the factory he passed her the books regretfully. 'Right. I'd best get back to the grindstone, else the foreman will have me guts for garters. I will see you tomorrow though, won't I?'

She nodded, feeling happier than she could ever remember feeling. 'Yes, that would be really nice. Shall we say here at twelve o'clock?'

'It's a date.' With a final grin Barry hurried away, and trying hard to wipe the smile from her own face, Grace slowly climbed the stairs that led to the office.

Norma was waiting for her, with a big grin on her face. 'So, yer dark horse you. Just what yer been up to, eh?'

Grace flushed to the roots of her hair. 'What do you mean? I've been to the library like I said I was going to.'

'Huh! Took a bodyguard along an' all, from what I just saw from the office window. I told yer Barry Swan were sweet on yer, didn't I?'

Grace giggled. 'Actually, Barry just came along with me for the walk.'

'Ooh, Barry now, is it? Yer don't waste no time, do yer? Not that I can blame yer. Bit of all right, is that Barry Swan. I wouldn't step over him meself, between you an' me. So when yer seein' him again?'

Grace came back down to earth with a bump. 'The only time I can see him is in my dinner-hour, isn't it? Can you imagine what my aunt would say if I were to ask her if I could go out on a date?'

14

'But you're twenty years old, fer God's sake. Don't *ask* the miserable old cow, *tell* her. Otherwise she'll have yer tied to her apron-strings for the rest of yer natural.'

Grace knew that what Norma said was right, but even so she quaked at what her aunt's reaction would be if she were to ask her if she could go out with a young man. 'For now we've agreed to just go for a walk in our lunch-hours,' she confided to her friend. 'It's better like that. Then if we get on I might ask my aunt if I can go out with him one evening. He could perhaps take me to a dance? I've always wanted to go ballroom dancing right since I was a little girl. But not before Christmas.'

Hearing the wistfulness in her friend's voice, Norma nodded, for beneath her brash exterior she had a kind heart and felt sorry for Grace. 'Ah well, happen you know her best. But do me one favour, eh? Don't pass up the chance of a nice chap like Barry just 'cos you're worried what yer aunt might think of him. Yer don't get many decent blokes to the pound from what I've seen of 'em, an' Barry seems really nice. A bit quiet fer my taste, but decent like.'

'I'll remember that,' Grace assured her with a grateful smile, then the two girls bent their heads over their typewriters, although for some reason, for the rest of the afternoon Grace found it very hard to concentrate.

Grace floated home that night, but her happiness was shortlived, for the second she set foot through the door her aunt began to complain.

'Where have you been? Are you late again? I've been sitting here longing for a cup of tea for the last two hours.'

Grace frowned. The fire had recently been made up and the curtains had been drawn against the bitterly cold night. If her aunt was capable of leaving her chair to do that, then surely she could have managed to make herself a cup of tea?

Recently, Grace had begun to feel resentful towards her aunt, perhaps because she had glimpsed a way of life at Norma's that was so very different from her own. Now Barry had told her of his close-knit family too and she was beginning to feel that her aunt was unfair. She had never minded caring for the older woman and probably never would, but surely Emily could have allowed her a little freedom, and done a little more for herself?

Sighing heavily, Grace lifted the kettle and filled it at the sink. She was home – if it could be called that.

*   *   *

'So, are yer goin' to sit there grinnin' like a Cheshire cat all night then, without tellin' me what all this is about, eh?' Daisy Swan playfully swiped at her son's ear.

Feigning surprise, he looked up at her. 'I don't know what you're on about, Mam.'

'No? Well, what you been readin' the newspaper upside down for, this last half an hour then?' Her twinkling eyes met his and to her amusement, he lowered his immediately. Barry was no good at lying, especially to his mother.

He scratched his head as he sought for the right words. 'If you must know, there is sommat I've been meanin' to have a word with you about. You see . . .'

'Come on, lad, spit it out fer Christ's sake,' she joked. 'It's Christmas Day in four days' time an' I need to get the puddin' done tonight so as it can stand an' soak up all the brandy. You know how fussy yer dad is when it comes to his Christmas puddin'.'

If possible, Barry went an even darker red and it came to her in a flash: this was something to do with a girl – it had to be, for now she came to think about it, he'd been wandering around like a love-sick calf for a couple of weeks or more. 'Girlfriend on the horizon, is there?' she teased.

He grinned sheepishly. 'As a matter of fact, there *is* someone as I'd like you to meet, Mam. I were wonderin' if I could perhaps bring her home tomorrow lunch-time?'

Daisy's heart lurched. Barry had had a few girlfriends in his time, but never one that he'd wanted to bring home, so this one must be special. Strange though, for he seemed to have been staying in a lot of late, so when was he managing to meet her? Deciding that it was none of her business, she said, 'I reckon we can do better than that, lad. Why don't you bring her home for dinner tomorrow night after work? That way she could stay a bit longer. Get to know us, eh? I could cook somethin' special.'

'No, Mam.' He shook his head quickly. 'There's no need to go to any trouble, really. Grace doesn't go out much at night. She lives with an elderly aunt who ain't in the best of health, so most of her time is taken up with lookin' after her.'

'I see. Well, this young lady sounds too good to be true. But if she's so taken up with her aunt, where do *you* come in? I mean, when do you ever get any time together?'

Barry shrugged his broad shoulders. 'We don't get much chance to be together, to be honest, Mam. An' she *is* too good to be true. You'll see what I mean when you meet her. She's the nicest, kindest girl I ever met bar none, an' she's beautiful into the bargain – in looks as well as in nature.'

'Stone the crows, lad. This little gel sounds like a right catch. If I'm any judge I'd have to say you've got it bad.'

'You could be right there, Mam,' he admitted, and the feeling of sadness that had settled on Daisy Swan deepened. Barry was the last of her brood at home, the baby of the family and much loved. During his National Service in the Army she'd missed him, of course, but that was only temporary. Still, she told herself, she'd always known that one day he'd fly the nest too, just as his two brothers had and if it was going to happen then she should at least be grateful that the girl he had obviously fallen for sounded a decent sort.

'Right,' she forced herself to say cheerfully. 'Tomorrow it is, then. I shall look forward to meetin' her. Though it's a shame as yer dad will be at work an' won't have the pleasure.'

'There's always another day,' her son pointed out, and turning his newspaper up the right way, he switched his attention back to that.

Grace paused at the door as panic gripped her. Seeing her hesitation, Barry took her hand and squeezed it reassuringly.

'Don't look so scared, Grace. Me mam don't bite, you know.'

'I'm sure she doesn't,' she mumbled. 'It's just . . .'

Laughing, he opened the door and ushered her into a room that almost made her eyes pop out of her head. Everywhere she looked were little china ornaments. The furniture was dated, but highly polished, and there was not a single thing out of place. Seeing her expression, Barry grinned.

'This is what me mam calls the posh room,' he informed her in a hushed voice. 'It's only used on high days and holidays. Usually I have to get in through the entry, but seein' as you're a guest she told me to bring you through this way.'

When she nervously fingered the collar of her coat he winked at her and drew her forward. 'Come on, let's go in, eh? Mam will have the dinner ready an' if we don't get a move on we won't have time to eat it afore it's time to get back to work.'

Grace followed him through a door to where a well-made woman was busily laying a drop-leaf table that had been dragged into the middle of the room.

'Hello, love.' Her eyes moved on from Barry to Grace and she smiled at her. 'And you must be Grace. It's about time I met yer. I've heard enough about yer from this one here.'

17

Her tired blue eyes were friendly, and Grace warmed to her immediately.

'Right, now sit yerself down an' I'll get us all a brew before I dish the dinner up.'

She pottered away as Grace perched on the edge of a hard-backed wooden chair. As she looked around, she couldn't help but compare this room to the one they had come through. This room was also cluttered with cheap ornaments and vases full of plastic flowers, but it had a cosy, lived-in feel to it.

At the side of a tiled hearth was an old wing-chair that had seen better days. Beside it was a worn pair of men's slippers that Grace guessed must belong to Barry's father. On the other side of the fireplace was an old leather-look settee, on which a large black cat lay fast asleep. A teak sideboard took up almost the whole of another wall, its top cluttered with newspapers and discarded letters and dust so thick that you could have written your name in it. The smell of a cottage pie filled the room and Grace felt herself begin to relax. It was warm and homely, and somehow she sensed that she was going to like Barry's mother.

When Daisy bustled back in a few minutes later, balancing a tray full of old mugs in one hand, Grace was amused to see that she'd removed her flowered wrap-around apron and had brushed her tightly permed, faded blonde hair.

'I hope you haven't gone to too much trouble,' Grace began, but Daisy Swan silenced her with a flap of her hand.

'O' course I ain't.' She smiled at her. 'I've been lookin' forward to meetin' yer, love. Our Barry ain't never offered to bring a girl home to meet me before, so it's a bit of a red-letter day from where I'm standin'.'

When Grace shifted uncomfortably in her seat, Daisy reached across and patted her hand. 'Don't mind me. I've got a gob as big as a parish oven, as our Stan is forever tellin' me. But you're very welcome, love, an' you'll soon get used to me.'

She was right, for when Grace left less than an hour later, she felt totally at ease with her.

'Now you just make sure as yer come an' see me again real soon,' Daisy told her as she hugged her on the doorstep.

'Thank you, I will,' Grace replied politely, and then Barry took her hand and they hurried away down the street.

Daisy watched them go from the doorway. She had actually been half dreading the meeting, and yet now that she'd met Grace, her mind was at ease. The youngster appeared to be everything that Barry had said she was. A bit on the quiet side, and obviously very well brought up, but not in the least hoity-toity. And he was certainly right about her being beautiful, although she obviously didn't make the best of herself, the way she scraped her hair back so severely. Then there were her clothes. Well, they were a little old-fashioned to say the least, nor had she worn so much as a scrap of make-up. But those eyes – the colour of violets – and that porcelain complexion. She could see why Barry was so attracted to her, and had a feeling that she would be seeing a lot more of that young woman in the future. Turning, she went thoughtfully back into her little terraced house.

The second that Grace entered the kitchen she knew that something was wrong, for her aunt was sitting upright in her chair with both hands clasped on the head of her walking cane, her face like thunder. There was no welcome – just a stare from cold, glittering eyes.

Grace's heart sank into her shoes. 'I'm not late, am I?' she asked, nervously glancing at the clock on the mantelpiece.

Her aunt's head wagged from side to side as, taking off her coat and hanging it in the tall cupboard to one side of the room, Grace watched her from the corner of her eye. When she'd closed the cupboard door quietly, Grace went to stand in front of her. 'What is it, Aunt? Are you feeling unwell?'

'Huh! Would you really care if I were, girl?' Emily's voice was sharp.

Grace chewed on her lip. It looked as if she was in for a bad evening; she could spot the signs from a hundred paces. She felt her palms grow clammy. It was funny, but her aunt could still have that effect on her, even now that she was a grown woman. 'Look, if I've done something to upset you, could you please just tell me what it is? I break up from work tomorrow for Christmas and I'm really tired.'

Emily's thin lips stretched back from her teeth in a sneer. 'Should it not be *you* telling me something?' she spat.

Grace flushed. 'Such as what?' she dared to ask, and Emily threw back her head and laughed; a mirthless sound that echoed around the bleak kitchen.

'Such as what you were getting up to in your lunch-hour today, young lady. Don't think that just because I am a helpless invalid, news of your escapades doesn't reach my ears. I had a visitor this afternoon. A reliable visitor, who informed me that she had seen you out strolling with a young man today. Do you deny it?'

Grace's shoulders momentarily sagged, but then she raised her head and looked her aunt in the eye. 'As a matter of fact I *did* go out with a friend in my dinner-hour. Is that a crime?'

'That all depends on what sort of a *friend* this young man is. And if it is all so innocent, why have you never spoken of him?'

'Because, Aunt Emily, I knew that this was just the sort of re-action I would get.' Grace had rarely answered her back so boldly before and Emily felt her temper rising.

'How *dare* you talk to me like that, after I have sacrificed so much for you? Have you no decency in you at all? You have always been a difficult, ungrateful child, but to stand there and answer me back in such an insolent fashion is unforgivable.'

Emily snatched a tiny scrap of a lace handkerchief from her pocket and began to dab at her nose, but for the first time in her life Grace was unmoved. She found herself comparing her aunt to Barry's mother, the fussy, kindly lady he'd introduced her to just that lunch-time, and Emily did not do well in the comparison.

'I'm sorry if the fact that I have friends upsets you, Aunt. Unfortunately, there is nothing you can do about it.'

'Oh yes, there is. I *forbid* you to see this young man again. Do you hear me? He probably only wants you for your money—' Emily stopped abruptly as Grace glared at her.

'Oh, so *that's* it, is it? You're afraid that I might turn my wages over to him instead of you! I do hear you, Aunt – loud and clear. But this time I intend to go against your wishes, whether you like it or not.'

'You will not wish to go against me when I tell you what sort of family you are mingling with,' Emily cried as her temper mounted. 'I have it on good authority that the Swans are the lowest of the low. Why, apparently, the father is to be seen swaying back from the Oddfellows' Arms on a nightly basis, and the only time the family ever sees the inside of a church is for weddings, christenings and funerals. Is that *really* the sort of family you wish to entangle your-self with, when you yourself have been brought up decently?' Emily held her breath as she watched a wealth of emotions flit across her niece's face. Usually she could manipulate the girl to her will, but for some reason tonight it was proving to be more difficult.

Grace, meanwhile, was trying hard to contain *her* temper, and when she stared back at her aunt there was a determined jut to her chin that Emily had never seen before, nor ever wished to see again.

'No doubt it was Miss Mountjoy who told you all this, Aunt. She's the only one who springs to mind who professes to be a true Christian yet loves nothing better than tearing people to shreds. Well, you can tell Miss Mountjoy that in this instance she happens to be wrong, for I met Barry's mother today for the very first time, and shall I tell you something? I received more affection in one hour from that woman than I've received from you in the whole of my entire life.'

'Well, really, Grace, this is most—' Emily would have continued with her tirade but Grace cut her short in mid-sentence.

'I have every intention of visiting Mrs Swan again, Aunt. And now as I said, I'm tired, so if you'll excuse me I'm going to have an early night. I'm sure you can manage to get your own meal for just *once*.' Grace headed for the door as Emily's temper erupted, so much so that she rose from the chair and took a step towards her, forgetting all about her cane.

'Why – of all the *wicked* ungrateful girls! You are just like your father, bad to the heart. You will live to regret this day, you just mark my words. You will . . .' The rest of her words were unheard, for the door closed with a bang and she found herself alone with only the ticking of the clock to break the silence.

As Grace stamped away upstairs, a memory from her childhood came back to her unbidden and she felt herself break out in a cold sweat.

Grace cowered away from her aunt as the woman snatched the small black and white photograph of a smiling man and woman from her hand. 'Where did you get this?' she screeched, and the trembling child nodded towards the sideboard drawer.

'I . . . in there.'

The woman glared down at the photograph, and then to the child's horror began to tear it into shreds. 'There, that's the best place for them.' She flung the remains of the small picture into the fire, and as the flames licked around them she grinned with satisfaction. 'See? They are in hell now where they belong! That was your mother and father – did you know that? And they are both in hell now too and not before time. They were bad, wicked, and their seed is in you, so God has entrusted you to my care so that I can make sure you don't turn out the same way.'

As the woman stared down at the child's tear-stained face a feeling of satisfaction flowed through her.

'But, Aunt Emily, wasn't my mummy your sister? I thought sisters loved one another.'

The woman threw back her head and laughed. 'Oh yes, she was my sister all right. But how do you love a whore? She was bad, rotten through and through, and it is my aim in life to stop you from turning out the same way. Come, you must go to the cellar until you realise how wicked you are.'

As she clutched the child's stick-like arm, the little one began to struggle as panic overwhelmed her. 'Please, Aunt, no. I won't go in the drawers again. I promise.'

'Huh! Promises from the likes of you are like pie crusts – they are made to be broken.' The woman dragged the child, who was now crying pitifully, towards the cellar door. When she reached it she threw it open and pushed the little girl inside on to the top step of the flight of stairs going down into the darkness. 'There,' she spat breathlessly. 'Now stay in there and perhaps when I decide to let you out, you will be a better person.'

As the door clanged shut the child felt a warm flood seep down her legs and she bowed her head in shame. Not only was she bad, she was also dirty, and now no doubt when her aunt decided to let her out she would be punished for that as well. When her sobs eventually subsided she crept down the steep stone steps and curled herself into a ball where she cried herself to sleep.

Once in the privacy of her room, Grace began to tremble. Why did her aunt always feel the need to punish her so? It didn't have to be like this. They should have been close. After all, they were all the other one had in the way of family since Grace had lost her parents. Until, that is, she had met Barry. Now she wondered how much longer she could stand living like this under her aunt's tyranny.

Chapter Three

'Norma, I was wondering . . . if you're not going out during lunch-time and my aunt should call, will you . . . Well, could you . . . ?'

Norma looked up from filing her nails. 'Yer want me to cover fer yer again, is that it?'

Shame-faced, Grace hung her head. Crossing to the window, Norma stared down into the street below. 'I don't mind coverin' fer yer, yer should know that by now – but why should I have to? The wicked old bat has only started ringin' durin' yer lunch-hour to try an' catch you out. Fer Christ's sake, Grace, you're too old to be answerable to her. Why should yer have to lie?'

'You know why.' Grace's eyes filled with tears at the predicament she found herself in. 'I have never ever had such a bad Christmas as the one just passed. My aunt was like a dog with a bone, harping on about Barry all the while, until in the end it was easier to lie to her and tell her that I'd stopped seeing him.'

When Norma saw the abject misery in her friend's eyes she hurried over to her and gave her a hug. 'Yer know, I reckon it's high time as yer thought o' getting away from her. Me mam would let yer come an' stay at our place like a shot, I know she would if I asked her.'

Grace squeezed her hand gratefully. 'Thanks for the offer, I really appreciate it – and don't think that I'm not tempted because I am. But I couldn't leave my aunt. She's not well. In fact, since Christmas she seems to have deteriorated.'

'Huh! That's a coincidence, ain't it?' Norma quipped as she raised her eyebrows. 'Come on, Grace. You ain't no fool. Yer know as well as I do that the old sod is swingin' the lead to play on yer sympathy. She looks as fit as a fiddle to me.'

Grace had a sneaking suspicion that Norma was right, but even so she still could not risk making the break, for if anything should happen to her aunt she knew she would never forgive herself.

Thankfully, just then Barry popped his head round the door and she was saved from having to answer. 'Are you all fit then?' He smiled at her and suddenly she was smiling too.

'She's as fit as she'll ever be.' Norma winked at him suggestively.

'Mind you, if yer played yer cards right, yer could have the pair of us. I'm free most evenin's.' She giggled when Barry turned as red as a beetroot. 'Don't look so worried. I'm only teasin',' she assured him. 'Now get her out for an hour an' don't worry about nothin'. I'll hold the fort here.'

When the door closed behind them the smile slid from Norma's face and, crossing back to the window, she watched them emerge into the street from the factory below. She shook her head and sighed. Grace was caught in a trap, and yet she seemed incapable of getting herself out of it. On the two occasions that Norma had met Grace's aunt she had been totally unimpressed with her, and was also surprised to find that she wasn't as old as she'd imagined she would be. She was probably only somewhere in her mid-fifties, Norma surmised, though she tried to come across as someone twenty years older. She seemed a cold, severe woman, incapable of showing any affection to anyone. But she certainly seemed to have a hold over her niece, and Norma shuddered to think what sort of childhood Grace must have endured. Still, at the end of the day this was something that Grace was going to have to sort out for herself, so crossing back to her chair, the other girl continued with her manicure and tried to put it from her mind.

As they walked along Queens Road before taking the short cut through Fife Street, Barry peeped at Grace from the corner of his eye. It was Monday, which meant that he hadn't seen her for two whole days, and he was shocked at how much he had missed her.

Grace was like no other girl he had ever known. She was unspoiled, uncomplicated and beautiful, and he knew that he was falling in love with her. He had a sneaky suspicion that his feelings were returned although she had never said so, but what worried him was – where did they go from here? Apart from the precious time they were able to steal together between the hours of noon and one o'clock he never saw her, had never even been able to take her out on a date, which he knew was strange to say the least.

An idea had been forming in his mind over the weekend, and he decided that now was as good a time as any to broach it.

'Grace?' His voice was hesitant, and when she looked at him from her huge dark blue eyes it was all he could do to stop himself from taking her in his arms there and then in the middle of the street. 'Look, I don't want you to think that I'm tryin' to interfere or anything, but the thing is . . . Well, if you need a break away from your aunt you could allus come to stay at me mam's for a while.'

24

Far from looking annoyed as he had feared she would, her eyes twinkled with mischief and she grinned at him endearingly. 'This must be the day for offers. Norma just made me a similar one before we left the office. But really, you are both worrying unnecessarily. I'm fine, honestly. I can handle my aunt and she's not so bad, not really. Just set in her ways, I suppose.'

'Huh! You can make all the excuses you like for her, but I reckon she's plain unreasonable. I mean, look at us, Grace. Sneakin' about in us dinner-hours like we've got sommat to be ashamed of. What's so wrong in two young people wantin' to spend time together? Weren't she young once?'

'Of course she was,' Grace said quietly. 'I think the fact that she lost her fiancé during the war might have something to do with how she is now. It's sad really. I can only think that she must have loved him very much, for I don't recall her ever having anything to do with another man, not that she had much chance to. She took me in when my parents were killed, so I owe her quite a lot, don't I?'

'Well, yes,' he admitted grudgingly, 'but you shouldn't have to sacrifice your whole life for her. I mean, look at her attacks. Ain't you never thought it strange that she allus takes a turn for the worse when there's sommat as you want to do as she don't approve of?'

Grace chewed on her lip thoughtfully, and after a moment she nodded. 'I suppose you are right up to a point. I've thought the same thing myself recently. But what can I do about it?'

'You can stand up to her, that's what you can do,' Barry told her firmly. 'The longer you leave it, the harder it'll be – an' before you know it, you'll be an old maid like she is. Perish the thought.'

By now they were walking along St Mary's Road where he lived, and hoping to change the subject, Grace asked, 'Will your mother be in, Barry?'

'She should be.' He kicked at a stone grumpily, and now that they were in the quieter back streets she slipped her arm daringly into his. Instantly the smile returned to his face and he was still smiling when he fitted his key into the front-door lock and let them in. The first thing they saw was a hastily scribbled note propped up against an empty milk bottle in the middle of the table. Barry read it quickly and turning to Grace he grinned. 'Now there's a bit o' luck,' he said. 'Seems we've got the house to usselves for a while. Me mam's gone off shoppin' in the January sales.'

He came to stand in front of her, and as he looked down at her and took her two hands in his, a wave of love washed over him. In all the weeks that he had been meeting her, he had never done more than give her a swift chaste kiss on the cheek, but now the urge was on him to kiss her properly, and as she saw the need in his eyes, Grace's heart began to pound. She felt herself grow hot then cold.

'Would you mind very much if I kissed you, Grace?'

She shook her head slowly. 'No, Barry, I wouldn't mind. In fact, I think I'd like you to.'

His head bent to hers, and as their lips joined, his hands were fumbling clumsily with the clips in her hair – then suddenly it was free to fall in a shining cascade down her back. He ran his hands through its silky softness as his lips covered her face with kisses that set her pulse racing, and she clung to him as if he were a lifeline. She had never known the joy of human contact and was hungry for every second of this. It was almost ten minutes before they drew breathlessly apart, and she was full of wonder at the joy of it.

Barry's eyes were full of adoration as he stared down at her. 'Oh Grace,' he whispered. 'I think I've gone an' fell in love with you. You'll have to make an honest man o' me now an' marry me.'

Almost as if she had been doused with a bucket of cold water, the shock of his words brought her back down to earth. Pulling away from him, she started to collect her hairpins up. 'It's a little soon to be talking about things like that,' she mumbled.

His face fell as he bent to help her. 'Sorry, I got a bit carried away. But I meant what I said, Grace. I'd marry you tomorrow if you'd have me.'

She paused to look into his eyes and smiled sadly. 'Thank you for the compliment. But I'd rather take it a little more slowly, if you don't mind. You don't even really know me yet.'

'I know all I need to know. But if you want to take it slow, that's fine by me. I've got all the time in the world an' I don't mind waitin' for sommat as is worth waitin' for.' His eyes told her that he meant every word he said, and suddenly the world was a brighter place. Perhaps things would find a way of working out, after all.

'Christ, I thought you was never comin' back. You'll never believe what I've just seen – never in a million years.' Norma was pacing the office floor with a face like thunder, and Grace's good mood instantly evaporated as a feeling of dread settled on her.

'My aunt's been here, hasn't she?'

'Too bloody right she has, the bitter old cow. Walked in here bold as brass, she did, as if she owned the bloody place, with her nose in the air as if there were a dirty smell under it.'

'Oh no.' Grace sank heavily on to a chair. 'What did you tell her?'

26

'Huh! Don't worry, I told her you'd had to go down the bank in yer lunch-hour fer the boss, an' luckily Mr Jackson were out so she couldn't be told no different.'

Grace sighed with relief, but Norma was far from over yet. 'That ain't the worst of it. Wait till yer hear this, then. Come in here limpin' like a good 'un, she did, but when she left I watched her go from the window – an' guess what? There weren't even a *trace* of a limp. In fact, the wily old bugger walked off down the road as sprightly as a two-year-old, with her cane tucked under her arm. What do you think o' that, then? 'Cos from where I'm standin' I'd say as the old sod's havin' yer on good an' proper.'

Grace stared at her in disbelief. 'You must be mistaken, Norma. My aunt can hardly walk without her stick now.'

'That's what she wants yer to think, but I'm tellin' yer, I saw her wi' me own eyes. She's connin' yer, sweetheart, you just mark me words. Pullin' at the old heartstrings she is, an' sucker that you are, you're fallin' for it.'

Grace strummed her fingers on the desktop as she tried to absorb what Norma had just told her. Try as she might, she just couldn't accept it. Norma must be mistaken; her aunt had never so much as ventured from her chair for months without the aid of her walking stick. Oh, she'd guessed that Emily could do more than she did – but to be able to walk without her stick? Grace simply couldn't believe that she could be so deceitful. And yet, on the other hand, Norma was a good friend so why should she lie to her? It was all very confusing, but thankfully she did not have long to ponder on it, for just then Mr Jackson entered the office and both girls scuttled away to their desks.

At three o'clock when it was time for their afternoon break, Norma fell into step with Grace as they made their way to the works canteen for a cup of tea. 'So – what yer goin' to do then?' Norma asked without preamble.

Grace sought for an answer. 'What *can* I do?' she asked.

Norma sighed and rolled her eyes to the ceiling. 'What yer should have done ages ago, that's what yer can do. Yer should leave the old sod to it. Let her find someone else to skivvy after her an' leave her to stew in her own juice.'

'It's not that easy,' Grace protested.

Never one to mince words, Norma retorted, 'Yes, it is. Just tell her straight out you've had enough o' bein' under the thumb an' either she lets yer have a life o' yer own, else you're off. What's goin' to happen to yer if yer don't? Think of it – you'll end up a shrivelled old maid like she is.'

27

'She wasn't always like that,' Grace said in her aunt's defence. 'Once she was engaged to be married, but her fiancé was killed during the war.'

'Well, fair enough, I don't deny that must have been hard fer her. But even so, it don't give her the right to ruin your life an' all. Trouble wi' you is, you're too soft. Allus ready to see the best in people.'

By now they had reached the counter, and after getting two cups of very stewed tea, they carried them to a table where Norma proceeded to spoon sugar into hers as she said, 'I forgot to ask with the witch visitin' – how did the date with Barry go?' She watched with amusement as colour stole up Grace's neck and crept becomingly into her cheeks.

'Actually, it went very well. In fact . . . Well, to tell the truth, Barry asked me to marry him.'

'He what?' Norma's eyes stretched wide and she almost choked on a mouthful of tea. 'So – are yer goin' to, then?'

'Going to what?' Grace asked innocently.

Norma sighed in exasperation. 'Marry him, o' course. What do yer think I mean? It ain't every day a girl gets a proposal, yer know, particularly off someone as nice as Barry Swan. I'll tell yer now, I wouldn't mind bein' in your shoes. Barry's a really decent bloke, an' they're few an' far between nowadays. Take my advice an' snatch his hand off afore he has a chance to change his mind.'

Grace stared gloomily down into her tea. 'I can't do that, I'm afraid. I mean – for a start-off, we hardly know one another.'

'That's hardly surprisin', is it, seein' as how yer never rarely get to see one another? It just goes back to what I was sayin'. Yer need to put yer foot down wi' yer aunt. Make a stand – otherwise Barry might start to look elsewhere. Think about it, Grace. At the end o' the day he's only flesh an' blood, ain't he? He won't hang around waitin' for ever.'

Totally confused, Grace nodded. She knew deep down that Norma was right – but at the moment she could see no way out of the position she found herself in.

She was still depressed when she made her way home that night. Although it was only six o'clock, the pavements were coated in a thick layer of frost and it was all she could do to keep her balance. The town centre was busy with people returning home from work but she was so lost in thought that she didn't even notice them. She used the time it took her to reach Oaston Road to try and put her thoughts into some sort of order, but the more she tried the more muddled up she became.

On the one hand she had her aunt, whom she loved despite the fact that Emily was cold and seemingly uncaring. On the other hand there was Barry, who professed to love her. But did she love him? It was a question that she found difficult to answer. After all, what *was* love? If love was liking being near him and enjoying his company; if love was the tingling in her stomach every time he looked at her; if love was counting the minutes until they could be together, then yes, she supposed she did. But was love enough reason to turn her back on the person who had sacrificed her life to bring her up? She was so lost in thought that it was almost a surprise when she found herself at the turning into Oaston Road.

She hurried along until her home came into sight and couldn't help but compare it to the neighbouring houses. Many of them had been updated and looked warm and inviting, but her aunt's house was still almost the same as when it had been built, lacking many of the labour-saving devices that were now available. Too afraid to ask outright, Grace had been hinting that they should get one of the twin-tub washing machines that were becoming so popular, but Emily wouldn't hear of it, and eventually Grace gave up trying. So every Saturday morning she had to wash the coloureds in the bath before boiling the whites in the copper. Then they all had to be rinsed in the sink before being taken into the yard to be fed through the great old-fashioned mangle. It was a time-consuming exercise and Grace dreaded it, although she had long since accepted that this was how it was always going to be. Her aunt was religious in her routine and expected Grace to be the same.

The information Norma had given Grace at lunch-time had knocked her for six, and the girl was still trying to come to terms with the fact that her aunt could be so devious. Surely Norma must have been mistaken! It was months since Grace had seen her aunt take so much as a single step without the aid of her walking stick, and yet Norma was insistent that Emily had actually waltzed off down the road with it tucked under her arm.

By now she had arrived at the front gate of her home – but was it really home? Had it ever been a home or merely just somewhere to exist? More and more of late, Grace was realising that she had never really lived. She had never been allowed to, her aunt had always seen to that. No doubt tonight Emily would go into a torrent of abuse following her visit to the factory. The girl's shoulders sagged at the thought of it. Lunch-time had been so wonderful with Barry. In fact, now when she thought back to the time they had spent together it took on an almost magical quality in her mind. But it was time to come back to reality and so, squaring her slight shoulders, she walked up the path and inserted her key in the lock.

As soon as Emily heard the front gate she hurried to the fireside chair and sank down into it. When Grace entered the room she flashed her a feeble smile and all the bad thoughts Grace had harboured against her vanished into thin air.

'What's wrong, Aunt? Are you feeling unwell?'

Emily stifled a smirk of satisfaction as she heard the concern in her niece's voice. 'I'm rather afraid I am, Grace. I think I may have overdone it a little today. I felt so much better this morning I actually ventured out for a walk. In fact, I even called into the office to see you during your dinner-hour. But by the time I got home I was feeling completely worn out so I'm afraid I haven't even managed to prepare the vegetables for the evening meal, or put the brisket in the oven.'

'Oh, don't worry about that. I can do it now I'm home. You just sit there until you feel better.' Grace crossed to the stone sink in the corner of the room and as she began to slice some carrots, Emily watched her suspiciously. Grace was so gullible, she always had been, and Emily knew that she only had to feign illness and Grace would be at her beck and call.

'*That girl* in the office informed me that the manager had sent you out on an errand in your lunch-hour. I hope you had time to eat your sandwiches,' she said innocently.

Grace kept her head bent over the task in hand so that her aunt would not see the guilty look on her face. 'Yes, that's right. I had to nip out to the bank. I must have just missed you.' She hated lying but she knew that there was no alternative, for if her aunt were to discover where she had really been, then all hell would be let loose.

'Mm, well . . . I can't say that I'm keen on the riff-raff you are being forced to work with. *That girl* was made up like a painted lady. I really can't see why she needs all that muck on her face. But then, the lower classes always tend to overdo everything.' She sniffed loudly, and Grace sensed another argument brewing.

'Aunt, I've told you before. Norma is actually a very nice person with a heart of gold. She would do anything for anybody. She just likes to keep up with the fashions, that's all.'

'Huh! Call that bird's nest on her head and that tight skirt she was wearing fashion, do you? Well, *I* think she looked as if she would be more suited to standing on a street corner than working in an office. Not that my opinion counts, of course. I've served my usefulness to you now, haven't I? Now that I've worked my fingers to the bone to bring you up and keep a roof over your head, I suppose soon you'll be sticking me in an old folk's home and getting on with your life.'

As she saw Grace's chin set Emily quickly changed her tack. 'Of course, I wouldn't blame you if you wanted to get rid of me. I know I must be a terrible burden on you.'

Her voice was heavy with self-pity and immediately Grace's kind heart was won over. Barry's kisses were still hot on her lips, but how could she leave her aunt now? She was the only family Emily had left, and if Grace abandoned her she would be all alone in the world.

Tonight she had intended to stand up to her aunt and tell her that from now on she wanted to be allowed to go out at least one night a week, but the woman looked such a pathetic figure, huddled in the chair, that Grace didn't have the heart to do it. Pushing all thoughts of Barry firmly to the back of her mind, she said reassuringly, 'Don't be so silly, Aunt Emily. Of course I wouldn't put you in a home. Not that you're old enough to go into one of those places.'

'I'm old before my time because of illness and all the worry I've had having to raise you all on my own,' her aunt whined, and as Grace lifted the heavy saucepan and carried it to the stove, she missed the smile that played across her aunt's lips.

Much later that night as she lay in bed in her sparsely furnished bedroom, Grace allowed her mind to return to the time she had spent with Barry. He had actually asked her to marry him and the thought was tempting to say the very least. Barry was kind and gentle and handsome – everything she had always imagined a good husband to be – but what chance was there for them with her aunt, who would not allow her to so much as even mention his name? Hot tears burned at the back of her eyes and trembled on her thick lashes before spilling down her cheeks. She still wasn't sure that she loved him, but what she *was* sure of was that with him, she could be happy. She would have her own home and one day, she hoped, children. Children on whom she would shower affection, children who would never be starved of love as she had been.

In her mind's eye, Grace conjured up a picture of a beautiful cottage with roses growing round the door and two happy children playing in a garden that was full of flowers and laughter. But then, almost as quickly as it had come, the image faded and in its place was a little girl cowering at the bottom of cold stone steps in a dark damp cellar. Shuddering, she pulled the blankets and eiderdown more tightly about her, and then at last, exhaustion claimed her and she slept.

In a bedroom farther along the landing, Emily Westwood lay staring up at the cracked ceiling high above her head as hatred coursed through her. Of late, she had seen a marked change in Grace, and she didn't like it one bit. Thankfully, Grace had the same kindly nature as her mother had possessed, which meant that Emily was able to play on her finer feelings. Unfortunately, Grace also looked like her mother, even more so as she blossomed into womanhood. She was now incredibly pretty, although she seemed to be oblivious to the fact. But how much longer would that last, now that the likes of Barry Swan were showing her attention?

Too agitated to sleep, Emily swung her long, stick-thin legs out of the bed and began to pace the bitterly cold bedroom as her voluminous cotton nightdress floated around her. Her grey hair had been combed into two long plaits that hung down her back, and her face, as she thought of her late sister, twisted with malice. Oh yes, Mary might have been beautiful, but she had betrayed Emily. She had been a whore with the face of an angel. Still, she had got her just rewards when a bomb blew her and her fickle husband to smithereens during the war. Better still, she had left behind her a child, a daughter who had borne the brunt of her mother's unfaithfulness; a child of whom Emily had no intention of letting go. Her revenge was not yet complete – *nor would it ever be for as long as she drew breath.*

Chapter Four

His deep brown eyes were hungry as he stared down into hers and she had the sensation of drowning in their depths. 'Grace, we can't go on like this.' Hearing the note of desperation in Barry's voice, her heart contracted.

'I know,' she muttered miserably, and yet, what alternative was there? Her aunt seemed to be getting worse, although for the first time ever, she was now being almost civil to Grace. Barry seemed to read her thoughts, for he tilted her chin to make her look at him again.

'Don't let her fool you, sweetheart. She's only being nice to you 'cos she has an idea you're about to take off. She'd chain you down if she could, but you mustn't let her. Look at us – snatching what time we can in our bloody lunch-hours. It ain't much at the end o' the day, is it? What I mean is, if you'd only stand up to her she'd have no choice but to let us see each other. I love you, Grace, an' I know I said I'd wait, but I don't know how much more of this creeping about I can stand.'

As she saw the misery etched on his face, guilt flooded through her. Sensing her turmoil, Barry drew her back into his arms and she nestled against his shoulder, enjoying the feel of his warm body through his thin workshirt. In forty minutes they would have to leave the sanctuary of his home to return to work, and then she would not see him again for two whole days, for today was Friday. This week for some reason it troubled her far more than it ever had before. When she was with Barry she could laugh and talk of silly inconsequential things, which only seemed to make her existence at home all the more unbearable. Even when his mother was present, the atmosphere was relaxed and happy, and Grace was fast coming to feel like one of the family. But that must surely come to an end soon, for as Barry had just told her, he was becoming tired of the lies and subterfuge. Her eyes filled with tears at the thought of losing him and instantly he was full of remorse.

'Aw, Grace.' He stroked the dark silken hair that was lying like a shining cloud about her slim shoulders. 'Sorry, love. I never meant to upset you. We'll find a way round it, you'll see. In the meantime, let's not spoil the bit o' time we do have, eh?' His lips came down on hers, warm and tender, and Grace felt herself responding.

'Won't your mother be back?' she asked breathlessly.

He grinned as his lips roved across her face. 'Naw, not before tea-time at least. She's gone shoppin' again in the sales with me aunty, an' when them pair get together they can shop for England.'

She relaxed and, basking in the heady, unfamiliar male smell of him, she gave herself up to the moment. When his hand closed across her breast she shivered at the unaccustomed feelings that sprang to life, and although she felt vaguely uneasy she did not stop him. His hand moved on and she lay back against the hard sofa as his kisses grew more demanding.

'Come on, let's go up to me room.'

Grace stared into his eyes for the merest of seconds as she wrestled with her conscience, and then unresisting she allowed him to lead her towards the stairs.

'Where the bloody hell do yer think you've been then? You're nearly an hour late back from yer lunch-break! Mr Jackson's doin' his nut in there,' Norma hissed.

Blushing, Grace hurried across to her desk. 'Sorry. I . . . um . . . Well, I just got held up.'

'Held down, more like.' Norma grinned, taking in Grace's dishev-elled appearance at a glance. 'Come on, spit it out. Yer know yer want to tell me really.'

'There's nothing to tell,' Grace whispered, keeping one eye on the door that led into Mr Jackson's office. 'Barry and I, we . . . err . . . we got delayed.'

Norma covered her mouth with her hand to stifle her laughter. 'Aw, come on, yer can do better than that. I ain't fell off a Christmas tree, yer know? You look like the cat that got the cream. Still, I won't push yer for details now. Yer can tell me all about it at break in the canteen.'

She returned her attention to her typewriter, and relieved, Grace did the same, as she tried to put her thoughts into some sort of order. It proved to be much easier said than done, but one thing she was sure of – her life would never be the same again. Now, somehow, she *must* find the courage to tell her aunt all about Barry. She owed him that much at least.

'Ah, here you are then. A little late again but then I suppose we need not argue over half an hour. *I've* prepared the vegetables for dinner.' Her aunt smiled at her niece as if she had accomplished some great feat.

Grace hung up her coat and crossed to the fire to warm her hands. It always unnerved her when her aunt was nice to her; she had learned long ago that there was usually some underlying motive.

'Have you had a pleasant day, Grace?'

'Same as usual,' the girl shrugged warily.

Her aunt nodded with satisfaction. 'Good. I was thinking we might go down to the Church Hall this evening, as they are having a whist-drive for charity. The vicar's wife has organised it and I thought it might make a pleasant change.'

'If it's all the same to you, Aunt, I think I'll give it a miss. I got some books out of the library today on my way home from work and I rather fancy curling up in front of the fire with one. It's awfully cold outside. In fact, the frost is thick on the pavements already.'

Her aunt's lips pursed with disapproval. 'I find it quite sad that you would rather fill your head with silly nonsense than support your church, Grace. But then, if you have made up your mind I don't suppose I shall be able to change it. You have always had a stubborn streak, as I have found to my cost – and lately it seems to have gotten worse. Still, I dare say I shall manage on my own somehow. I just hope my stick doesn't go from beneath me, if the pavements really are as bad as you make out.'

Grace felt a flicker of guilt but instead of giving in as she usually did, this time she stood her ground. 'The choice is yours, Aunt. Personally, I think you would be far better to stay in by the fire, particularly as you've been complaining all week about how tight your chest is.'

At the hint of sarcasm in her niece's voice, Emily flushed. 'Actually, it is feeling a little better tonight so I think I might risk it.'

Grace nodded as she crossed to the cooker to turn on the gas rings beneath the prepared vegetables and check on the shoulder of pork that was cooking in the oven. 'As you wish.'

Emily frowned. There was something different about her niece lately that she could not quite put her finger on. She had grave suspicions that Grace might still be seeing that young man from work and so she had made it her business to find out a little more about him. She watched Grace closely for her reaction as she said casually, 'Do you ever see anything of that Barry Swan now?'

Keeping her eyes averted, Grace replied, 'Why do you ask?'

'Well, I was speaking to Mrs Cavendish after church last Sunday and she happened to say that she knew of the family, that's all. Apparently they are – what can I say – quite common by all accounts, just as Miss Mountjoy once informed us. He, the father that is, goes to the pub almost every night, but then I suppose you couldn't expect much more from the likes of them.'

Grace was trying desperately hard to control her temper; her voice when she answered was quiet. 'I didn't know it was a crime to go out and enjoy yourself, for God's sake!'

'Grace, really. How *dare* you take the Lord's name in vain! Whatever are you thinking of, girl?'

Grace leaned heavily on the edge of the sink as she tried to answer politely. 'I'm sorry if I've offended you, Aunt, but I really cannot see what the habits of Barry's family have to do with you, me, Mrs Cavendish, Miss Mountjoy or anybody else for that matter. And in answer to your question, yes, I *do* still see Barry at work. He happens to be a very nice young man and I consider him to be a good friend.'

'Huh! Just so long as that's all he is. You wouldn't want to tie yourself up with his sort of riff-raff.'

Grace rounded on her furiously, unable to control her temper any longer. '*That's it!* I'm going to my room. For someone who professes to be a Christian, I have to say you leave a lot to be desired, for it seems to me that you are never happier than when you are pulling someone to pieces, and that goes for your snooty church friends too. So if you will excuse me, I think I prefer my own company. You can get your own damn tea.' As she stamped past her aunt, snatching up her library books on the way, Emily caught her wrist.

'Grace, you will stay here. Do you hear me?' Emily's voice was as furious as her own, but for the very first time Grace stared back at her defiantly and her voice when she answered was ominously quiet.

'Let *go* of me right now. I am not a child any more and I will not tolerate your bullying for another second.'

Emily dropped her hand as if it had been burned and watched in shock as Grace strode away, slamming the door to behind her. The woman turned to stare into the fire, her features tight with hatred. So, the little bitch was finally finding her feet, was she? No matter. Emily would put a stop to it if it were the last thing she did. Her sister's child had not suffered enough yet, nor would she have done so for some long, long time to come.

'Grace still ain't allowed out at night then?' Daisy smiled at her son affectionately as she placed his dinner in front of him on the darned linen tablecloth that covered the fringed chenille one beneath.

'No, she ain't, Mam.' He sighed. 'And to tell you the truth, it's getting me down a bit now. I mean – where are we going? What's the use in only being able to see each other at work? Grace is a young woman now, old enough to have a family of her own, but for some strange reason she seems to be tied to her aunt's apron-strings.'

'Happen you shouldn't knock that, lad. There's nowt wrong with havin' family loyalties. It just goes to show what a lovely girl Grace is. You mebbe need to give her a bit more time, that's all.'

Barry nodded distractedly as he ran his hand through his thick fair hair. 'I know you're right, Mam, but it don't make it any easier. Why won't her aunt let her have a life?'

'I dare say the woman has her reasons,' Daisy replied wisely. 'We all have a cross to bear, so try an' be patient. Things will come right in the end, you'll see.'

When he hung his head, her heart went out to him. She loved this son so very much – well enough to know that in Grace he had found his soulmate. She had never seen him so besotted with a girl, but for now all she could do was stand by and pray for his sake that her prophecy would come true.

Once in the privacy of her bedroom, Grace began to pace the floor like a caged animal. The room was bitingly cold, so much so that her breath hung on the air, but her temper was such that for now she was beyond feeling anything except the sense of injustice that was raging through her.

Crossing to the window, she stared out across the cemetery that backed on to the house. As a child she had feared the place, but now she sometimes almost envied the souls that were laid to rest there. Their suffering was over whilst hers continued. A full moon was riding high in the sky and the gravestones, some of which were leaning drunkenly, looked as if they were reaching up to try and touch it. The frost on the ground was sparkling like shattered diamonds, and slowly her shoulders slumped as her temper ebbed away.

Her thoughts moved back to the time she had spent with Barry today, and her heart began to race. She could still feel his lips burning on hers and her body trembled as she recalled his hands moving across it. She knew that, according to her aunt, what they had done without being married was a sin, so why then did she feel so good about it? For the first time in her life she had felt loved and wanted, and she would never forget that feeling for as long as she lived. During their afternoon break, Norma had tentatively told her of a new contraceptive pill that had just become available from the doctor, and from some special family-planning places. It seemed incredible to think that taking just one small tablet a day for twenty-one days a month could prevent an unwanted pregnancy, but she would never dare to visit the doctor's and get it on prescription. Grace shuddered at the very thought. What would happen if her aunt ever found the pills? Or worse still, if the doctor ever informed her that Grace was taking them?

An owl suddenly took flight from the shelter of one of the tall yew trees in the cemetery and she watched enviously as he flew gracefully into the sky to be silhouetted by the moon. He was free to come and go as he pleased, whilst she was a virtual prisoner in her aunt's home, trapped by her feelings of gratitude for what the woman had done for her. But what *had* she done for her, apart from offer her a roof over her head when her parent's had died? Thoughts of her mother and father brought tears of regret stinging to Grace's eyes. She had been little more than a baby when she had been orphaned, and the only real memory she had of her mother was the lovely smell of the lavender scent she had always worn and a kind voice. How different her life might have been if her parents had lived. But then she realised, just as she had a million times before, that it was no good living for what might have been. All she had was her aunt, and with that she had to be content.

Dropping into a chair, she lifted one of her library books and began to turn the pages, enjoying the wonderful photographs of ballroom dancing scenes that filled the pages. All the major dances were illustrated there, step by step, but Grace already knew at least half of them off by heart, for she often practised with an imaginary partner in her cold room at night, and had for as long as she could remember. On one page was a couple dancing a foxtrot, on the next another couple dancing a tango. These were followed by pages of couples dancing the Viennese waltz, the cha-cha, the quickstep and the waltz, the women floating visions in dresses made of pearls and sequins fit for a queen.

Slowly her worries drifted away as she and Barry took the places of the people in the book in her mind's eye. She could see them both clearly, twirling round the dance floor as he looked adoringly down into her eyes. Something overwhelmingly powerful was calling to her from the pages, and she knew that this was the world where she truly belonged. If only she could be allowed to dance she would be happy. Soon she had lost herself in the glamour of it all, just as she had taught herself to do over the years. Eventually she came to the last page and regretfully closed the book.

After a time she yawned and made her way along the narrow landing where she hastily changed into her nightclothes in the chilly bathroom. Once back in her bedroom she clambered supperless into bed. An early night would do her good, especially if she could dream of dancing with Barry. But she didn't dream of him. Instead she was transported back in time as her eyes closed.

This school report is quite unsatisfactory. I have to say that I am most disappointed in you, but then I suppose by now I should expect no more. You are worthless, just as your mother was before you. What do you have to say for yourself?'

Grace shrank away from the piercing grey eyes and began to tremble as her aunt crossed to a cupboard and took a cane from it. 'I'm sorry, Aunt. I'll try harder next term, I promise.'

'Huh! Empty promises, that's all that ever spills from your lips. Spare the rod and spoil the child, that's what I say. Perhaps a little taste of this will ensure that you try harder.'

The child bit down on her lip as the woman moved closer, but then miraculously, a knock at the door made her pause in her advance. Throwing the cane hastily back inside the cupboard, she moved quickly to the curtain and peeped around it. 'It's Miss Mountjoy,' she said. 'Open the door immediately, Grace, and remember your manners. Children should be seen and not heard.'

'Yes, Aunt.' Obediently, the child hurried down the hallway to admit the visitor before rushing away to put the kettle on. There was no elation, for she knew that the visitor had only gained her a reprieve. The punishment would still be administered later when she had gone, and then it would probably be ten times worse. The thought made her feel sick but still she kept a smile fixed to her lips as she showed Miss Mountjoy in to see her aunt.

'Such a polite child,' the woman simpered, and Aunt Emily smiled, a smile that did not quite reach her lips.

'I like to think I have done right by her,' she muttered humbly, and Miss Mountjoy immediately began to sing her praises, just as Emily had hoped she would.

'I think you deserve a medal, my dear. After all, were it not for you, the poor child would have had no one after she lost her parents, God rest their souls. What an excellent pillar of society you are. An example to us all.'

Emily bowed her head modestly before such praise. 'It was my Christian duty,' she said, basking in the glory her friend was bestowing on her.

Grace kept her own head bent across the bone china tea cups as she warmed the teapot, wondering how Miss Mountjoy would have reacted, if she could only have known what her aunt was really like: What would she have thought if she could see the scars on Grace's backside that never seemed to heal before some more were administered? What would she have thought if she could have known how many nights the little girl was forced to sleep in the cellar with the rats? And what would she have thought if she could have known how many times her stomach had rumbled with hunger until she was forced to beg for food?

Grace sighed. There was no point in even thinking about it, for Miss Mountjoy would never know. No one would, only herself and her aunt.

Chapter Five

'Come on now, keep your chin up. We're in this together. The old dear can't bite, you know, an' it ain't the end of the world.' Barry smiled at Grace reassuringly as they stood at the front gate of her home. But still she trembled; he had no idea just how formidable Emily Westwood could be. This could well be the end of the world, or at least, the end of the world as *she* knew it. Still, there was one thing he was right about. They had no option but to face her, and the sooner it was over, as far as she was concerned, the better.

'All right then. I'm ready now. Let's get it over with.' Smiling bravely, she squared her shoulders and allowed Barry to lead her up the path. Grace's heart was in her mouth, but her face when she opened the door was calm. 'This way,' she said as she led him down the long hallway. He followed obediently. Grace had to stifle the urge to grin as she suddenly likened them both to lambs going to slaughter, but then she controlled herself with an effort and opening the kitchen door, she looked at her aunt who was sitting in the fireside chair.

'Ah, Grace, there you are. I was just about to—' Emily stopped abruptly as she saw Barry and a frown creased her brow. 'You should have informed me that you were bringing a visitor home.' Her voice was as cold as ice, and as she stared at Grace disapprovingly, the girl visibly shuddered.

'I . . . I'm sorry, Aunt. I didn't plan to, but there's . . . Well, there's something that Barry and I need to talk to you about.' The words came out in a rush.

'I see. In that case you'd better take a seat, young man. I trust this won't take too long. I have made plans for both myself *and* Grace this evening.' Emily motioned Barry to a hard-backed chair that stood at the side of a large oak table and without a word Barry sat down as Grace fidgeted nervously with her hands.

'Well, what is it that is so important?' her aunt snapped.

Suddenly Grace was speechless, and sensing her distress Barry rose from his seat and quickly crossed to her side. 'The thing is, Miss Westwood, Grace and I have something to ask you. That is . . . *I* have.'

As Emily saw his arm slide protectively around her niece's waist a flush of annoyance rose to her cheeks, and it was all she could do to remain civil to him and not order him from the house there and then. 'Then I suggested you hurry up and ask, young man.'

'Very well.' He flashed Grace a reassuring smile and drawing himself up to his full height, he again turned his attention to her aunt.

Just as Grace had warned, he was finding Emily Westwood very formidable. Even more so than anything he'd had to deal with in combat training during his time in National Service. But even so he never once considered leaving without finishing what he had come to do.

'The thing is, Grace an' I . . . Well, the long an' short of it is we want to get wed an' I've come to ask if you'll give us your blessing.'

For a second Emily Westwood sat so still she might have been cast in stone, but then her eyes glittered dangerously and her mouth began to work, although for some moments she was so furious that no sound issued from it. Colour seeped into her cheeks, then to Grace's horror her rage erupted, all seemingly directed at Barry.

'How *dare* you come into my house and make such a ridiculous request? Why, my niece would never even consider marrying someone like *you*. She has been brought up to mix with decent company, not your sort of riff-raff.'

Something inside Grace suddenly snapped, and now her fear evaporated like morning mist and her rage was equal to her aunt's.

'Oh, but I *would* consider it, Aunt. In fact, it's what I want more than anything in the world. Barry is *not* riff-raff, but I'll tell you now, even if he were I would still marry him, because nothing could be worse than spending the rest of my life here with *you!*'

The colour that had stained Emily's cheeks drained away until she was as white as a sheet. To Grace's horror, she then clutched at her heart. The girl was instantly contrite as she flew to her side.

'Oh Aunt, I'm so sorry – I never meant to upset you, but you must have known that one day I would want to lead my own life.' The older woman brushed her away. 'Grace, I beg you to consider what you are proposing to do. You could do so much better for yourself.' Emily's eyes fastened on Grace as if she had forgotten that Barry was still in the room. 'Just think what sort of a life you would have, living with someone like *him*.'

'I will have a good life, Aunt – you just wait and see. But I'll still come and visit you, as often as you like.'

'I will *not* see. You will marry this . . . this Teddy boy . . . over my dead body. Whatever has come over you, girl? Have you taken leave

42

of your senses? Now ask him to leave immediately and tell him that I never want him, or his sort, to darken my door ever again, and then perhaps we might try to pretend that this unfortunate incident never happened.'

Grace sighed, as rising she went to stand next to Barry again. 'I can't do that, Aunt. I intend to marry Barry with or without your blessing.'

Deciding to try another tack, Emily began to cry pathetically.

'You can't do this to me, Grace. Why – if you leave me, how shall I manage? You're all I have in the world. And anyway, without you there will be no mon—' She stopped abruptly as Grace's face hardened.

'No money, is that what you were about to say? Well, don't worry, Barry and I will see that you don't starve, if that's what you're concerned about. But I do intend to marry him.'

'You will do no such thing, *do you hear me?*' The crocodile tears dried up as if by magic and now the woman's eyes were flashing with hatred again. 'I am still your legal guardian, and as there are some months to go until your twenty-first birthday, you cannot marry without my permission.' She smiled smugly, but Grace stood her ground.

'In that case I shall have to wait, shan't I? But be sure that as soon as my birthday is past we *will* be married. We have to be, you see . . . because I'm going to have a baby.' Had she hit her aunt full in the face, Emily could not have looked more shocked than she did now.

'My God! Is this some sort of a joke, Grace? If it is, I have to say I find it in very poor taste.' Emily watched appalled, as Barry drew her niece protectively towards him, and in that instant she knew that this was no joke, nor was it remotely funny.

A shocked silence descended on the room as Emily struggled to digest the news that Grace had just thrown at her, but then she snarled, wagging a shaking finger at her, 'Go to your room and pack your bags *now*, this minute. I will not have a whore living beneath my roof for one second longer. Nor will I allow a bastard into my home.'

'Aunt, please. There's no need for any of this. We can work through it. You'll like Barry if you'll just give him a chance. I'm not a whore, nor is the child I'm carrying a bastard. How could you say such a wicked thing?' Grace was openly crying now, but the older woman remained unmoved.

'Go to your room and pack, and then I pray that I need never set eyes on you again. After all I have done and sacrificed for you, *this* is how I am rewarded! Still, I should have known that all my efforts to make you into a decent person would be in vain. You are your mother's daughter through and through. She was a whore as well. And just as she was punished, so shall you be – you just mark my words. Now go and pack before I send you away with nothing. As for *you*,' she pointed an unsteady finger at Barry, '*get out of my house this instant.*'

His eyes as he stared back at her were as cold as hers. 'I shall leave with Grace and not a second before,' he said steadily. 'And don't think that sending her away like this will be any sort of a punishment, because I can assure you, from where I'm standing, you'll be doin' her a favour! If I were in her shoes, I wouldn't be able to get away from a wicked old sod like you quick enough.'

It was all Emily could do to keep her hands off him, and they balled into fists of rage at her side as she stamped across the kitchen to the table. Grace's mouth gaped in amazement as she saw her aunt move so quickly without the aid of her walking stick. She knew in that moment that everything Norma had ever said about her faking her illnesses was true. Her aunt had played on her sympathy and used her.

It was the final straw, and with a strangled sob she fled up the stairs to collect together her few measly possessions. Once in the privacy of her bedroom she leaned against the door for some seconds as she tried to regain her composure. Her eyes strayed around the sparsely furnished room and her emotions were mixed as she realised that this was the last time she would ever enter it. Would she be sorry to go? She was not sure. Until she'd met Barry she had never been shown so much as an ounce of affection, but did she really love him enough to marry him? The questions whirled around in her head even as she became aware that it was useless to ask them. Her aunt was ordering her from the house. It was too late for questions now.

Wearily, she crossed to her wardrobe, and after removing a battered suitcase from the bottom of it, she began to pack. Soon, all that she owned in the world was crammed inside. Pausing at the door to look back at her room for one last time, she then slowly descended the stairs.

Her aunt and Barry were standing exactly where she had left them, glowering at each other with open dislike, and her footsteps slowed as she walked towards him. She stopped suddenly to stare at her aunt beseechingly. It felt wrong to be leaving like this. Even now, after so much had been said, all it would have taken was one kind word and Grace would have forgiven Emily Westwood anything. She frantically searched her aunt's pale face for a glimmer of kindness or affection.

'It doesn't have to be like this, Aunt Emily. Can't you *please* find it in your heart to forgive me?' Tears trembled on her long dark lashes, but her aunt was unmoved by her obvious distress.

'It can be no other way, and no, I can *never* forgive you. From the second you walk out of this house you will be dead to me, and you will never see a penny of your inheritance, I shall see to that. You have made your bed and now you can lie on it, but be warned, it will bring you no joy. One day you will pay for your wickedness, just as your mother paid for hers.'

The tears spurted from Grace's eyes to roll unchecked down her cheeks, as Barry gently took the suitcase from her hand. He couldn't help but notice that it weighed very little, seeing that it contained all she owned in the world, and a wave of anger washed over him.

'Come on, love. You're wasting your breath. Let's be gone, eh?' He took her elbow and steered her towards the door, but still she hesitated. Everything was happening too fast.

'Shall I come and see you when we've both had time to calm down?' Her voice held a note of hope but her aunt quashed it with her final words.

'Were I to pass you in the gutter I would not stoop to help you. Now *go*, or I may not be responsible for my actions.' Her shaking finger pointed towards the door, and as the couple walked down the chilly hallway she followed them closely. Once they had stepped through the front door she slammed it resoundingly behind them. Grace jumped and her eyes when she looked at Barry were empty. He dropped the case and gathered her into his arms.

'Don't cry, love. You did your best. I reckon that bloody woman has got a swingin' brick for a heart. Take me word for it, you're better off without her.'

'But where will I g . . . go?' Grace stuttered through her tears.

He laughed softly. 'Why, you'll come home with me, you daft ha'porth. An' the day you're twenty-one, we'll be wed. Now come on, I think I can guarantee a better reception at my house than we got here.' And so he led her away from her home for the last time.

'Hurray, put the flags out. I were just goin' to send a search-party out for you, lad. I thought you'd got lost. Your dinner's just about to become a burned offerin' . . . Hey up, what's this then?' Daisy Swan asked when she saw Grace's tear-stained face behind Barry.

He pushed her gently before him into the room and instantly Daisy's face was a mask of concern as she saw the girl's distress.

'Why, darlin', whatever's the matter?'

45

Shamefaced, Barry hung his head. 'I'm afraid Grace's aunt has kicked her out, Mam. An' the long an' the short of it is, it's all my fault.'

Daisy frowned, deeply perplexed. 'Oh, and how's that then?'

'Well . . .' Barry shuffled from foot to foot as Daisy looked at him inquisitively. 'The fact is, Grace here, I mean, me an' Grace are going . . . Well, we're going to have a baby.'

Grace was too ashamed to look at the older woman. For a minute there was nothing but silence, until Daisy asked pointedly, 'Have yer told your aunt?'

Grace nodded as fresh tears sprang to her eyes.

Daisy sighed. 'Well, happen yer couldn't really expect her to shout it from the raffers, love. But it's early days yet – she'll come round, you'll see. It won't allus be dark before six. In the meantime, what do you intend to do about it?'

'We're goin' to get wed, of course,' Barry interrupted.

Daisy nodded. 'That's fine by me. And in the meantime there's an empty bedroom upstairs going begging. You're welcome to it, love. Now come on, let's get a cup of tea inside yer. You look like death warmed up. Move over, Stan, and let Grace get by the fire – she looks perished to the bone. As for you, our Barry, the blame – if you can call it that – don't rest all on your shoulders. It takes two to tango, as I'm sure Grace here will agree.'

Barry's father, who was an older version of his son, hotched good-naturedly along the settee and Grace quietly took a seat as Daisy bustled away to put the kettle on. She looked around the cluttered little room so different to the home she had just left. Every available space was crammed with ornaments and there were so many cushions on the chairs and settee that she could barely squeeze herself on, and yet there was a homely air about it that her own home had sadly lacked.

Stanley Swan, who up to now had said little, patted her hand comfortingly. 'Don't fret, love. As the missus quite rightly said, things will work out. This place might not be the Ritz, but you're more than welcome to share whatever we have, an' between you an' me you could have done a lot worse for yourself than our Barry. He's a good lad. Heart as big as a bucket, as you'll discover. You ain't the first to find themselves in this situation, an' no doubt you won't be the last. At the end o' the day, it's hardly a hanging offence, is it?'

Tears started afresh at so much kindness. They seemed to pour out of Grace as if she were a bottomless well. Perturbed, Barry looked on until at last it seemed that there were no more tears left to cry.

46

They finally slowed as Daisy pressed a large mug of tea into her hand.

Much later that evening, Daisy showed her upstairs to a small bedroom.

'This were our Ted's room, Barry's older brother, before he got married. It ain't posh,' she apologised as she clicked on the light, 'but I think you'll find it has everything' you need – an' if it ain't, just shout up.'

Grace looked around the cosy room. In one corner stood a large wooden wardrobe and next to it was a single bed with a cosy blue eiderdown on it. On the opposite wall was a chest of drawers, with a couple of model aeroplanes on it, and at the window hung pretty curtains. Faded linoleum covered the floor, broken by a neat bedside rug.

Daisy saw the girl's eyes flood with tears again, and she wrapped her arms around her.

'Come on now, that's enough. I've put a hot-water bottle in to warm the bed, an' I hope you'll be nice an' snug. A good night's sleep an' you'll feel different again in the morning, I guarantee it. No doubt our Barry will be along in a minute to say goodnight so I'll leave yer to get changed, but I'm in that room there if yer should want me. Goodnight, love.' She pottered away along the landing, and so began Grace's first night away from home.

'Blimey, what happened to you? Yer look bloody awful.'

'Thanks, Norma.' Grace grinned wryly, but then they both turned their attention back to their typewriters as Mr Jackson strode through the room. The second he had disappeared back into his office, Norma swivelled her chair around to stare at Grace enquiringly. 'So, come on then, what's happened? An' don't say nothin' 'cos I wouldn't believe yer.'

Aware that Norma would not be satisfied until she knew the whole story, Grace started to explain in a hushed voice.

When she had finished, Norma whistled softly. 'Stone the crows! Who would have thought it, eh? Yer could knock me down wi' a feather. Why the bloody hell didn't yer get yerself off to the doctor's fer the birth control pill, like I told yer?' Before Grace could answer, Norma flapped her hand at her. 'Don't even bother answering that – just tell me what you're going to do now.'

'Well, as I said, I'm staying at Barry's at the minute, but I'm hoping that once my aunt has calmed down a bit and got used to the idea, she'll let me go home until the wedding.'

'Huh, I wouldn't bust a gut waiting for that to happen if I were you,' Norma commented bluntly. 'I reckon there's about as much chance o' that ferret-faced old sod softening as there is of hell freezing over.'

When Grace's face fell her voice became soft. 'Now don't yer dare start blartin' on me. You'll have old Jackson out of the office an' then we'll both be out on us arses on top of everything else.'

Grace blew her nose noisily and managed to compose herself as Norma stared at her incredulously. 'I don't mind admittin' you've knocked me for six, gel. I never knew you had it in yer. Yet saying that, I did have me suspicions, I suppose – but then I thought, No, not our Grace. Still, they allus say the quiet ones are the worst, don't they? An' you've certainly landed yourself a catch. I don't mind telling you, if it weren't you as Barry had been seeing, I'd have set me cap at him meself, yer jammy bugger. What's it like, living at his mam's?'

'Well, it's a bit like Piccadilly Circus after my aunt's house,' Grace informed her. 'Barry's two brothers and their children are in and out all the time but they're all very friendly. Ted, the oldest, looks just like Barry – or perhaps I should say Barry looks just like him?'

'Mm, pity he's spoke for then,' Norma teased.

When a grin hovered at the corner of Grace's lips she winked at her cheekily, and with her curiosity satisfied for now, she turned her attention back to her work, content to wait for their break for the rest of the details.

The next three months passed pleasantly for Grace as she settled into Barry's home. For the first time in her life she felt wanted, and she began to look forward to the visits from his brothers and their families who all accepted her as if she had always been there. Then life got even better. It was Norma who suggested that they should start to go ballroom dancing once a week and Grace tentatively put the idea to Barry. When he openly admitted that he had two left feet and readily agreed to her going with Norma, she was almost beside herself with excitement, for it was what she had always dreamed of.

'Well, yer certainly can't turn up at a dance in *them* togs,' Norma declared as she eyed Grace's outfit scornfully. 'They're as old fashioned as the hills, an' besides – they fit where they touch now you've got a little bump showin'. I reckon we ought to have a day out in Coventry an' get you rigged up at the C&A.'

Once again, Barry happily agreed that it was a great idea. He had never been fond of shopping, and was only too happy to press some money into Grace's hand and send her off with Norma.

The day out proved to be a great success. As Norma sifted through the racks of clothes, Grace couldn't remember a time when she had enjoyed herself so much.

'Now, how about this one?' Holding a pretty blue velvet smock dress trimmed with tiny pearl buttons and a pretty lace collar, under Grace's chin, Norma grinned with satisfaction. '*That* suits you down to the ground. You're lucky smock dresses are in fashion an' the colour's just right for you,' she said admiringly. 'O' course, when the baby is born we can see about getting you a *proper* ball gown. But there ain't no rush fer that. Yer need to learn yer steps yet.'

Grace, who seemed to have a smile painted on her face, nodded in happy agreement as Norma went on with her search.

By the time Barry met them off the bus in Harefield Road both girls were loaded down with bags. He chuckled. 'Crikey. It looks like someone's been having a good time,' he commented as he relieved them of their shopping. 'Come on, let's get you home and then you can do a fashion parade for us.'

Grace was only too happy to oblige and everyone nodded their approval as she showed off her purchases.

Once the new dresses had been hung in her little wardrobe, Norma turned her attention to Grace's hair. The severe bun which Grace still wore for work now spilled loose about her shoulders in all its shining glory, and when Norma presented her with a Rimmel lipstick that she had treated her to, Grace felt as if she would burst with happiness.

On the night of the first dance, Barry walked her into town where she met Norma. It still felt very strange to be allowed out after dark but, looking very pretty in the new blue dress that perfectly matched the colour of her shining eyes, she felt wonderful. As Barry looked at her he almost wished that he'd agreed to dance with her, but he kissed her goodbye, told her to enjoy herself and promised to be there to walk her home at the end of the night. Then together, she and Norma made their way to Courtaulds Ballroom, where Grace's dream was fulfilled when she stood and stared in awe at the women in brightly coloured dresses twirling round the dance floor to a live band on the arms of smartly dressed partners.

'Right, are yer ready fer this, then?' Norma asked as she ground a Woodbine out in an ashtray on one of the tables placed around the dance floor.

Grace nodded eagerly as she followed Norma onto the floor. 'I'll lead then,' Norma told her. 'I ain't got much choice in this tight skirt. Just follow me.'

Despite the fact that she had never been allowed to go to dance classes after school like some other girls, Grace had practised secretly in her bedroom whenever she could, in constant fear of her aunt finding out. So she wasn't a complete beginner as Norma had presumed, although she found that doing the steps to music made a thrilling difference.

They had barely done one circuit when Norma peered at her inquisitively. ''Ere, I thought you'd never been to a dance before? How come yer know all the steps?'

Grace giggled. 'I used to practise in my room at my aunt's,' she confided, and then she gave herself up to the sheer pleasure of being at a real dance for the very first time.

Under Norma's guidance, she was soon showing a natural rhythm that surprised them both. By the end of the night there were stars in her eyes, which Barry teased her about when he picked her up. She was positively glowing.

'So, you enjoyed it then?' he asked good-naturedly as he tucked her hand in his arm, a big smile on his face.

'Oh yes.' Grace sighed dreamily as she thought back to the feelings she had experienced as Norma swept her about the dance-floor. 'Barry, it was wonderful. Can I go again?'

'Of course you can. As often as yer like,' he promised and Grace fleetingly felt so happy that she was sure she must have died and gone to heaven.

As a special treat, Barry took her on a coach trip to Stratford-on-Avon, where they visited Shakespeare's birthplace and Ann Hathaway's cottage, and together they also visited Coventry Cathedral and many of the local places of interest she had always longed to see. She was shocked to find that there were so many beautiful places to visit in Warwickshire – virtually on her own doorstep – for she had rarely glimpsed much more than the inside of a church. Barry's parents lavished affection on her, and Daisy could talk of little else but the new grandchild that Grace would shortly present them with. And yet – through it all, the girl found that she was still not totally happy, apart from the nights that she went dancing, when she could lose herself in the magic of it all. Each day she found herself waiting for the postman before she went to work, sure that today she would receive a letter from her aunt, but each day she was disappointed, and as the weeks passed her sense of rejection from the only family she had ever known increased.

As her twenty-first birthday in June approached, Grace noticed that her waistline was thickening. By now she was almost five months' pregnant, and one evening in May as they were sitting at dinner, Daisy broached the subject of the wedding.

'So.' She forked a large portion of mashed potato into her mouth as she looked across at the two young people in front of her. 'Have yer given much thought as to where yer might like to get wed?'

Barry nodded enthusiastically as he grinned at Grace with love shining in his eyes. 'As a matter of fact we have, Mam. We thought we might just have a quiet register office do an' then slip off to Chapel Saint Leonards for a few days. There don't seem much point in splashin' out on a big do under the circumstances, not while we're savin' for a house.'

Daisy nodded. 'I suppose you're right, though you could have saved a bit more if you didn't both insist on payin' board. It's a shame as Grace won't get to have a white wedding. She would have looked a fair treat in a long frock, and I can't see her aunt being too pleased with it not being in a proper church.'

'I don't think it will really matter to my aunt where I get married,' Grace said miserably, pushing the food around her plate. 'I doubt she'll come anyway.'

'You don't know that, not until you ask her,' Daisy pointed out.

Grace shook her head. 'Well, we'll soon find out. Barry and I are going to buy some wedding invitations tomorrow and then I thought I might pop round to see her and hand-deliver it.'

Personally, Daisy felt that she would be wasting her time, but wisely she didn't say so. 'That might not be such a bad idea,' she said tactfully instead. 'You've got to break the ice some time, an' what better way of doing it than to go and personally invite her. She's had time to simmer down now and yer never know – she might have had a change of heart. Stranger things have happened.'

Grace nodded slowly, wishing she could believe that, and for the rest of the meal the subject was dropped.

Three nights later, Grace hovered uncertainly at the front gate of her old home. The wedding invitation was gripped firmly in her hand and although there was a chill in the summer air she found that she was sweating. Barry had offered to come with her, but Grace had stood firm and told him that she preferred to go alone. Now, however, she was having second thoughts and wished that he were there. Still, it was too late for regrets and so, taking a deep breath, she opened the gate and strode up the path. She tapped tentatively at the door, and within seconds she heard her aunt's footsteps echo hollowly in the hall as she approached the front door.

'Grace!' Her voice registered surprise as she saw her niece standing on the doorstep, and just for a second she looked uncertain as she glanced quickly back over her shoulder. Fixing a false smile to her face, she held the door wide. 'You had better come in.'

Grace swallowed her confusion as she followed her aunt's ramrod-straight back along the hallway. She had expected to have the door slammed in her face or a torrent of abuse at the very least, but the reception she had received, if somewhat frosty, was civil at least. Perhaps Daisy had been right. Perhaps her aunt had forgiven her after all. Grace's hopes rose, but when she entered the kitchen she found herself confronted with Miss Mountjoy, whose expression was stiff.

'Well, Emily dear, they say if you talk of the devil he will be sure to appear. I think I should leave now. I'm sure you two will have a lot to talk about.' The tall, grey-haired woman rose from her seat at the table and began to work her long thin fingers into her gloves as she smiled at Emily sympathetically. 'Now, my dear. Please remember that you have not been at all well, and remember also that there *are* some of us who care about you.' She glared at Grace as she made for the door and Grace shrivelled beneath her gaze. Her aunt limped slowly to the door after the guest had swept past Grace with not so much as a backward glance, and as Grace stood there feeling like a naughty schoolgirl their voices wafted along the hallway.

'I really don't know *how* that girl can have the audacity to show her face after all she has put you through,' Grace heard Miss Mountjoy say. 'No doubt that boyfriend of hers has thrown her out on her ear and she has come grovelling back to beg you to take her in. But be strong, Emily. You have sacrificed far too much for that ungrateful girl already, so stand firm and think of yourself for once.'

'I will try,' Emily replied in a martyred voice.

Grace rolled her eyes at the irony of it all. In all the years she'd lived with her aunt she had never known her to think of anyone *but* herself – however, she was here to mend bridges if that were possible, so she clamped her lips together and waited for her aunt to join her.

She heard the front door close after all the necessary pleasantries had been dealt with, and then her aunt's footsteps came tripping along the hall floor, the limp forgotten. Pausing in the doorway, her eyes swept Grace from head to foot, taking in at a glance the shining hair and the short skirt that she was wearing. The false smile slid from her face.

'Just look at the state of you,' she sneered. 'You look like a lady of the night. *His* choice of clothes, no doubt.'

'Actually, Aunt Emily, the clothes were my choice – and I'm sorry if you don't approve of them,' Grace said steadily. 'But I haven't come here to talk about clothes. I've come to bring you this.' She held the small envelope at arm's length, and after a second, as Emily's curiosity got the better of her, she snatched it from her hand. After tearing it open she hastily read it, then peering through the thick lenses of the glasses perched on the end of her nose, she stared at Grace with contempt.

'*So*, on top of everything else you now intend to go through with a farce of a ceremony in a register office?' Her voice was incredulous, and Grace found herself flushing.

'We . . . we thought under the circumstances it might be more appropriate,' she explained hesitantly.

Emily crumpled the invitation and flung it into the fire. 'I should have expected no more from you. After all, you could hardly wear white, could you? Not when you are carrying a bastard inside you . . . But a register office! Why, you will not even be decently married in the eyes of God.'

'That's rubbish, Aunt. This is the 1960s, not the Dark Ages. Of course we'll be married. And I came here in good faith to ask you to attend. I thought we might go shopping for my wedding outfit together as well. You're the only family I have and it would mean the world to me.' Her anger had flown, to be replaced by sadness, but Emily just stared back at her unmoved.

'You are indeed your mother's daughter, and her bad seed has been passed on to you and no doubt the bastard you are carrying. I should have known that all my years of sacrifice were in vain, but it is over now. Go, and live in sin, and may you *never* know a moment's peace.'

Grace felt as if her heart was breaking but she could see that she was wasting her time and so slowly she turned and walked away as tears streamed down her cheeks.

Daisy looked up from the shawl she was crocheting. 'Barry, sit down, will you, for Christ's sake!' she said, exasperated. 'You'll wear a bloody hole in the carpet at this rate. You've been up an' down the room like a cat on hot bricks since the second Grace left. She'll be back soon enough.'

Barry ran his hands distractedly up and down the side of his jeans. 'Sorry, Mam. I'm a bit on edge. I wish I'd gone with her now. God knows what sort o' reception she'll get from that wicked old bag!'

'Grace can look after herself, lad – she'll be fine. An' I reckon as this was something she needed to do on her own. It's best that you didn't go, so sit down and try to relax.'

Barry sat down heavily next to her and picked up the *Mirror*. It was almost half an hour later when he heard someone open the entry gate. 'That will be her now.' He was at the kitchen door before Daisy could stop him, and Grace fell into his arms the second he opened the door.

'She's washed her hands of me. I've got no one in the whole world now,' Grace sobbed.

Barry cradled her to him. 'That's not true, love. You've got me, and the rest of us Swans, and soon we'll have a baby of us own. She never deserved you, anyway. You have to put the past behind you now. You've done all you can as far as your aunt's concerned, so let that be an end to it or she'll destroy the rest o' your life.'

Grace sniffed and looked up at him admiringly, thinking how wise he was. He was right. From now on, Barry would be her world.

They were married on 13 July 1961 at Nuneaton Register Office, within the Council House in Nuneaton town centre. Grace looked beautiful in a smart princess-cut dress and matching jacket in a pretty shade of blue that exactly matched the colour of her eyes. Norma had gone with her to choose her outfit, and together they had looked at some weird and wonderful designs. However, Grace had stood her ground, insisting that she didn't want anything too fancy, and today her choice came into its own, for it was stunning in its simplicity. In her hair she wore a rosebud of palest pink to match the flowers in her bouquet, and as she stood next to Barry before the registrar, his eyes shone with pride and love.

The wedding was a simple affair, with only Barry's brothers and their families, his parents and Norma present. Daisy cried copious tears, and sniffed loudly into a large white handkerchief that Stan handed to her. When it was over, they left the Council House and stood outside on the steps to have some photographs taken on Barry's father's old Kodak camera.

Grace kept a constant eye on the shoppers who hurried by, hoping for a glimpse of her aunt, but she was sadly disappointed. And then, amidst a hail of confetti, the couple walked the short distance to Trent Valley railway station to catch the train that would take them on their honeymoon. It was done. Grace Collins was now Mrs Barry Swan.

Chapter Six

'Come on, Wendy. If we don't hurry, your dad will be in from work before we are.' As Grace lifted a small red coat from the back of the chair, five-year-old Wendy pulled a face.

'Aw, Mammy, can't we stay just a *bit* longer?'

Daisy laughed as, taking the coat from Grace, she held it whilst her granddaughter shrugged her short arms into it. 'Come on now, me darlin',' she coaxed. 'You can come an' see me an' your grandy tomorrow again if you're good. You don't want your daddy to come home to no dinner now, do you?'

Wendy pouted, but stood still as Daisy slipped her warm woolly bonnet over her fair hair before tying it securely beneath her chin.

'There now, you'll be snug as a bug in a rug in all that lot. Now let's get Simon wrapped up, eh?' She turned to her grandson and went through the exact same procedure with him as Wendy looked solemnly on. At three years old, Simon was the double of his father at that age. Both Daisy and Stan spoiled him and his sister shamelessly, although they would never have admitted to it. They could not see enough of them and totally adored them, just as the children adored them.

Grace grinned at the two solemn little faces as Daisy fished in her purse for some change for them.

'There look, here are some pennies to buy some sweeties on the way home. But only if you're good, mind – and you're not to eat them till after dinner else your mam will be after me with a shotgun.'

The children giggled as Grace ushered them towards the door, pausing to kiss their grandad on the way.

'Night, night, Grandy,' they chorused, and he patted their heads affectionately. At the door Daisy gathered them to her for a final hug, and then turning her attention back to Grace she looked at her with concern.

'Are you sure goin' back to work ain't too much for you, love? It's a lot to take on, you know, on top of lookin' after the kids and doing the house up.'

'I'm fine, Daisy, honestly,' Grace said cheerfully. 'It's only part-time, and I was really lucky to get my old job back. I have to admit I'm quite enjoying it up to now – it gives me a break out of the house. Mind you, the office is not the same without Norma.'

Daisy nodded understandingly. 'Well, wherever she is, knowin' Norma, she'll be missing you too. Fancy her marrying an Army bloke and taking off like that, eh? Where is it they're living? Germany, ain't it?'

'Yes, it is, and they're having the time of their lives if her last letter is anything to go by.'

'Ah well, that's somethin' then,' Daisy remarked philosophically, as Grace accompanied the children onto the pavement directly outside the front door.

'I'll see you tomorrow morning then, love, when you drop Simon off on your way to work, eh?'

Grace waved goodbye and as the door closed she grasped the children's hands and began to march them along St Mary's Road. As they approached the abattoir, a large lorry swung into the gates in front of them. Through the open back, Wendy could see some cows straining their noses through the slats that ran from one end of the lorry to the other. She frowned at them curiously.

'Why are they taking the cows for a ride in a lorry, Mammy?' she asked, and just for a second Grace was lost for words. How could she tell her five-year-old daughter that the poor beasts were being delivered for slaughter? Unbidden, her mind slipped back to herself at almost the same age as Wendy was now, asking her aunt the very same question, and a cold hand closed around her heart as she remembered.

'Why are the cows going for a ride in the lorry, Aunt Emily?' Grace, who was walking primly at the side of the straight-backed woman, gazed up at her innocently.

The woman stared down at her. 'You stupid child,' she said harshly. 'Why do you think they are in the lorry? They are going to be slaughtered, of course.'

'What does slaughtered mean?' the little girl had dared to ask, and a cruel gleam appeared in the woman's eyes as she answered.

'Don't you know anything? It means they are going to be killed, shot, have their throats cut, or whatever it is they do to the filthy beasts.'

'But why?' Tears sprang to the child's eyes at the terrible picture her aunt had conjured up.

The woman sighed impatiently. 'Well, where else do you think your meat comes from? It doesn't grow on trees, you know.'

*The child felt vomit rise in her throat and quickly averted her eyes
from the gentle-eyed creatures in the back of the lorry. And there and
then her childhood began to slip away from her. She had just learned
a lesson she would never forget. Life was cruel, and so was her aunt,
and it would be a long, long time before she ate meat again.*

'Mammy, Mammy.' The child tugging gently on her hand dragged
Grace's thoughts sharply back to the present, and she shook her head
to rid herself of the terrible memories.

'Look, it's really cold. Let's hurry up and get home into the warm,
eh?' She felt guilty avoiding the child's question, but rather that than
rob her of her innocence. Hopefully, by the time they got home
Wendy would have forgotten all about it.

They moved on and when they came to Abbey Green, Grace gripped
their hands as she steered the children across into Manor Court Road.
They took the short cut through Fife Street and soon they were in
Queens Road, the main street that ran through Nuneaton town centre.
A misty rain had begun to fall and Grace shuddered, hoping that the
fire would still be in when they got home.

By the time they turned into Marlborough Road where they lived,
Simon's steps were dragging. He would certainly take no rocking off
to sleep tonight, Grace decided, and soon they were at the gate of
their little terraced house.

She and Barry had bought the house almost four years ago, and
ever since then they had worked on it ceaselessly, furnishing it from
second-hand shops and any bargains they came across. Grace had
made all the curtains herself from material bought at the rag market
in Birmingham, and now at last the house was beginning to take
shape, although money was always tight to say the very least, which
was why Grace had decided to go back to work part-time. As she
inserted the key in the lock and let them into the small front room
she was pleased to see that the fire, although low, was still burning.
She took the children's coats and hung them in the cupboard under
the stairs, then after settling them with some crayons and colouring
books at the table, she made the fire up and went into the kitchen to
prepare the dinner.

She was nearly ready when the back door opened and Barry walked
into the kitchen. As he crossed the room to drop a loving kiss on her
cheek, she immediately saw that he looked tired. She sighed. Barry
had left his job at the dye shop at Courtaulds some two years ago
and moved to The Sterling Metals across town to work in the fettling
shop there. The work was hard and the hours were long, but he never

57

complained. In fact, he did every bit of overtime that he could to bring a little more money in. The only problem with this was that most nights he was so tired that he had usually fallen asleep before Grace had even had a chance to get the children to bed, which meant that she spent most evenings with nothing but the television set they rented, or her sewing for company.

As he washed his hands at the deep stone sink they had inherited with the house she saw with concern that they were almost raw from the hot metal he worked with all day.

'They look sore. You ought to put something on them,' she commented, but he brushed this aside.

'Ah, there's nowt wrong with them. You can't expect no more with the sort of job I do,' he replied good-naturedly, then gesturing towards the front room, he asked, 'Kids in there, are they?'

Grace nodded. 'Yes, they are. You could get them to the table for me if you wouldn't mind. The dinner's almost ready.'

He swung away to do as he was asked and Grace smiled as she heard the kids squeal with delight when they saw him. Barry was a good father and a good provider, he was also a good husband, and yet . . . Why did she still feel that something was missing from her life? Annoyed, she pulled her thoughts away from the direction they were heading in as guilt flooded through her. There were lots of women who would gladly step into her shoes, she had no doubt, even if Barry was a little . . . she searched her mind for the right word. 'Boring' was the only one that sprang to mind and her guilt intensified. But what more could she expect? He spent every hour he could at work, trying to provide her and the children with the things they needed. Any spare time was spent in renovating the house, so how could she expect him *not* to be tired?

Angrily, she grabbed the potato masher and took her frustrations out on the potatoes she was preparing. The mince for the shepherd's pie was browning nicely, and the apple crumble was filling the kitchen with its spicy smell. Should they have custard or a small tin of evaporated milk with it? And the water was boiling for the cabbage to go in. All other thoughts disappeared as Grace kept an eye on the cooker.

Much later that evening, when she had tucked the children into bed and read them their favourite Noddy and Big Ears story, she collected the holiday brochures she had picked up that day and took them downstairs to show Barry. A little bubble of excitement began to form in her stomach. As yet, the children had still never had a holiday or even seen the sea, but this year, now that she was working again, she hoped that they might be able to manage a few days away. Her hopes were dashed the second she entered the front room, for there was Barry with his feet stretched out towards the fire, fast asleep. As she stood over him and looked down on his slumbering features, a wave of sadness swept through her. Leaving him to his rest, she dropped the brochures onto a small table at the side of the chair and made her way to bed for an early night.

'So, are you all set for tomorrow night then?' As Christine Ryan burst through the back door like a breath of fresh air, Grace looked up from her sewing machine and smiled at her. It was an old Singer model, with a treadle, and as Grace took her foot momentarily off the foot pedal a deafening silence descended on the room.

Christine was wearing a pair of hot pants that left nothing to the imagination, and the beehive hairdo she sported was so high that she appeared at least six inches taller than she actually was. Christine was Grace's neighbour, and over the years they had lived near each other they'd become firm friends.

'I can't say as I am all set to be honest, Chris,' Grace said regretfully. 'Or perhaps what I should say is, I am, but I don't think this dress is going to be.' She looked down at the yards and yards of tulle in front of her.

Throwing herself into a chair, Christine grinned. 'Aw well, that's the least o' your worries. Personally I think you're mad to even *think* of tackling something like that – I know *I* certainly couldn't. Still, if it ain't done in time you could always borrow something of mine to wear.'

Grace almost shuddered at the very thought of it but smiled politely. 'Thanks for the offer, Chris, but I'm sure I'll get it done. I hate anything to beat me, and if I stick to the pattern I should be all right. If not, I do have other clothes I can wear. It's just that I fancied a proper ballroom dress, and they're so expensive in the shops I thought I'd have a go at making one myself. Luckily I got the material for a snip from the rag market when I went to get the curtains for Simon's bedroom, so even if I end up making a mess of it, it won't be any great loss.'

'Huh, I can't see you doin' that.' Chris sighed enviously as she fingered the silky material. 'I've never known anyone as nifty as you when it comes to a needle an' thread. Your Wendy has got more dresses than any other little girl I know, and the smocking you do on them is first class.'

Grace warmed to the compliment and rising from her seat, she went to fill the kettle at the sink as Chris watched the children playing in the garden through the window. It was early summer and a glorious sunny day with the sun riding high in a cloudless blue sky.

'I bet there'll be a few turn out tomorrow,' Chris commented, and Grace nodded in agreement. Barry had reluctantly taken on the role of her dance partner for a time when Norma got married, but he had long since given up taking her, claiming that he felt awkward and didn't really enjoy it. Luckily, Grace had since met Chris and they had teamed up, and now went together, leaving Barry quite content to take care of the children and slumber in the chair.

'I have to say, I prefer the dances at Saint George's Hall to the ones at Courtaulds ballroom, although it would be better still if I had someone tall dark an' handsome to twirl me around instead o' you,' Chris teased.

Grace carefully measured two spoons of tea into a heavy earthenware brown teapot. 'Well, sorry I can't do much about that, not unless my Barry or your Dick suddenly develop an interest in dancing. I'm afraid you'll just have to make do with me.'

She strained the tea into two mugs and carrying them to the table placed one in front of Chris who immediately took a noisy slurp of it. Grace was well aware that there were those in the street who considered Chris to be what they termed 'common', but Grace found her highly amusing and had become very fond of her; she really looked forward to their evenings out together. In fact, they were the highlight of her week, for when she was dancing she had the sensation of being someone else, not a boring housewife who had seen very little of life, but someone glamorous and adventurous who could be anything she wanted to be. Chris, on the other hand, was always more interested in the men who hovered at the edge of the dance-floor, and loved nothing better than the attention they bestowed on her as she flirted shamelessly with them. Still, as Grace had quickly found out, there was no harm in her and she was actually very happily married. She just liked to escape from the humdrum reality of being a wife and mother for one evening a week, which was something they both had in common.

'Will you be going on holiday this year?' Chris asked now as the sounds of the children's laughter floated through the open window.

'It doesn't look like it up to now,' Grace said regretfully. 'I did get some brochures to show Barry a few months ago, but then I thought better of it. Come to think of it, I don't even know where they went now. Not that it matters. I decided that it wasn't fair to ask him. He already works all the hours God sends to try and get the house done up, and I didn't want to put him under any more pressure.'

'Mm.' Chris nodded. 'Me an' Dick are hopin' to get a caravan down at Skegness for the week in the Coventry fortnight, but whether we can afford it or not is another thing. Me oven's gone on the blink – the bloody thing. Only works when it's a mind to, so if Dick can't repair it that will be our holiday up the swanee, and all 'cos we'll have to get another one.' She glanced around the small room admiringly. 'You know, Grace, I don't know how you keep this place as you do with two little 'uns rampaging about. It puts my place to shame an' I've only got the one.'

Grace beamed at the compliment. Although everything in the room was second-hand, it all shone like a new pin and she was proud of it. Just then Wendy burst in and threw her sweaty little body into her mother's arms.

'I'm hot, Mammy. I want a drink, an' Simon does too.'

Chris drained her mug and stood up. 'Right, I'd best get off. I've work to do and I'm sitting here like a lady o' leisure. I'll see you tomorrow night.' Leaving a waft of Avon perfume in her wake she drifted from the room as Grace turned her attention to her daughter.

'Stone the crows, gel. You look a million dollars.' Chris gaped in amazement at the picture her friend presented in her new dress, and Grace blushed as Barry added his compliments to Chris's.

'She does, doesn't she? You just make sure as no one runs off with her for me, eh?'

'Huh, there's fat chance o' that, love. They'd have to get past me first,' Chris retorted. Barry grinned as he looked at her standing next to his wife. They made an unlikely pair, for although Chris was not unattractive, as far as he was concerned she couldn't hold a candle to Grace. There was something about his wife that set her apart – the way she held herself, the way she spoke, the way she walked. She had been a very pretty girl when he first met her, but now she had matured into a stunningly beautiful woman, and every day he thanked God for her.

He kissed her cheek and smiled, a smile that held all the love he felt for her. 'Now you have a good time an' watch what you get up to, eh? Looking like that, I'm not so sure I should let you out.'

Laughing, she threw a light coat around her shoulders as she made for the door with Chris closely following. 'Don't worry, love, I'll behave. I always do, as Chris will tell you. I'll see you later.'

He crossed to the front-room window and watched with amusement as the two friends trooped down the street together, arm-in-arm. There was Grace in her glamorous dress with its soft tulle overskirt over layers and layers of stiff net petticoats, while beside her Christine wobbled along on ridiculously high-heeled shoes in a tight little mini-skirt that was almost indecent. Still, his wife was happy, he thought to himself, and as long as she was happy, so was he. Hopefully she would be happier still when she saw the surprise he had in store for her on Saturday. Contented with his lot, he sat down to read the newspaper and see what was on the television, but in minutes he was fast asleep.

The two women wandered in leisurely fashion along Queens Road and into Bond Gate to the entrance to St George's Hall.

'I've got a feeling we're in for a good night tonight,' Christine remarked happily as they climbed the steep steps that led upstairs to the ballroom. They took their coats to the cloakroom and hung them up, then after visiting the ladies to make sure that their lipstick was in place, they entered the ballroom. The band was warming up on a stage at the end of the room, and after getting themselves a drink from the bar, Chris scanned the sea of faces waiting for the music to begin.

'Blimey, cop a load of *that.*' She dug Grace so viciously in the ribs that she almost spilled her drink.

'Steady on, Chris. Cop a load of what?'

'Him over there, look. Phew! I wouldn't mind bumpin' into him in a dark alley.'

Grace followed her friend's eyes until they came to rest on a tall, dark-haired man whom she had never seen there before. 'I suppose he is rather attractive,' she admitted grudgingly.

Chris almost choked. '*Rather attractive!* Why – you must need bloody glasses. He's blummen gorgeous! I'll tell you now, I'm havin' a dance with him tonight if it's the last thing I do.'

To Grace's embarrassment the man suddenly glanced their way, and when he saw them looking at him he flashed them a brilliant smile. Grace quickly averted her eyes, and much to Chris's amusement blushed a deep brick red.

'Now look at what you've gone and done,' she hissed. 'He must think we're giving him the eye.'

'Well, we are, ain't we?' Chris chuckled, totally unphased by her friend's discomfort. At last the music started and the two women took their places on the dance-floor for a waltz. They had done a couple of circuits when suddenly someone tapped Grace on the arm. Coming to an abrupt halt she found herself looking up into the eyes of the handsome stranger.

'May I?' he said politely.

Grace wished that the floor would just open up and swallow her, but not wishing to be impolite she nodded graciously as Chris scowled and left the dance-floor. Within seconds she was being whirled around in the strong circle of his arms. When she finally dared to look up at him she found him smiling at her with ill-concealed amusement.

'I hope I haven't upset you by asking you to dance?' His voice was deep, and as she looked into his twinkling blue eyes, she found herself smiling back despite her sense of embarrassment.

'Of course not . . . You dance very well.'

'So do you. You have a natural sense of rhythm. Do you come here often?'

They both laughed at the old tried and trusted cliché and Grace felt herself begin to relax.

'Fairly often. My friend and I go dancing every Friday night, but sometimes we go to the Co-op Hall, or Courtaulds ballroom.'

'In that case then, I shall have to start coming more often too,' he teased, and then they gave themselves up to the joy of dancing perfectly in step. At the end of the dance he delivered her back to Chris and bowed gallantly. 'Thank you. It was a pleasure to dance with such a beautiful woman who is so light on her feet. I hope you will do me the honour of dancing with me again – later in the evening, perhaps?'

Grace blushed and nodded.

'Smooth-talkin' bugger,' Chris muttered, and more than a little put out she turned her attention to her Cherry B.

Much later that evening as they were walking home Chris peered at Grace from narrowed eyes. 'Well, that were a waste of time, weren't it? At least from my point of view. I spent half the bloody night standin' on the sidelines like a bleedin' wallflower while Casanova swept you off your feet!'

'Now, now, Chris,' Grace giggled. 'If I didn't know you better I would think that was sour grapes.'

As Chris's unfailing good humour returned she laughed and slipped her arm through Grace's. 'Well, come on, fair do's – I saw him first and then you went and hogged him all night.'

'I did no such thing,' Grace retorted indignantly.

Chris tittered. 'I'll tell you what. Invite me in for a cup o' your lovely Camp Coffee an' I promise not to tell on you to your Barry.'

'Oh Chris, you are totally incorrigible. You are most welcome to a cup of coffee, but I assure you there is nothing to tell. It isn't a crime to dance with someone, is it?'

'Huh! That all depends on *how* you were dancing, an' *who* you were dancing with,' Chris giggled, and arm-in-arm the two young women went on their way.

The next morning, Grace woke to the sound of a bird singing outside the bedroom window, and she stretched lazily. As her mind drifted back to the evening before, she found herself blushing, as she thought of the tall, dark handsome stranger she had danced with. Instantly she felt guilty, and reaching across, she felt for Barry. His side of the bed was empty. Frowning, she pulled herself up onto her elbow to see that his clothes were gone from the back of the chair, where he had left them the night before.

Sliding from the bed, she shrugged her arms into an old candlewick dressing-gown and hurried along the narrow landing. After peeping in at the children to make sure that they were still asleep, she made her way downstairs, but there was no sign of him. As Grace put the kettle on, she tried to remember if he had told her the night before that he was working overtime, but she dismissed that idea almost immediately, for even when he did go out early, Barry always brought her a cup of tea in bed before leaving for work.

After making herself a drink she got the children up, and fed and dressed them. But still there was no sign of her husband, and the first little feelings of unease began to squirm in her stomach. This was most unlike Barry. In fact, she could never remember him disappearing before. He was solid and dependable, a little too much so sometimes, and she worried that something must be wrong. She turfed the children out into the garden to play while she slipped away to get dressed, and it was as she was coming back down the stairs that he suddenly appeared, with a grin on his face that stretched from ear to ear.

'Right then,' he said, before she even had a chance to ask him where he had been. 'If *madam* would care to step this way, I think I might have a little surprise for her.'

Taking her elbow, he manhandled her to the front door, then clapped his hands over her eyes as he manoeuvred her through it. 'Now, no peepin' till I tell you. Do you promise?'

She nodded solemnly, feeling the air in front of her as he led her blindly forward.

'Right. You can look now.'

Opening her eyes, she blinked in the bright sunshine before staring open-mouthed at the motorbike and sidecar that were parked at the kerb.

'But . . . what . . . whose is this?'

'It's ours, love. Do you like it? It's a Triumph Thunderbird 650cc motorbike, and the sidecar is a Busmar – all coachbuilt, mind. None o' your cheap rubbish.'

'But how did you manage to afford this?' she gasped.

He lowered his eyes guiltily. 'To tell you the truth, it ain't *completely* paid for, not just yet. I got it on the never-never, but I saved up over the last few months an' paid over half off in deposit. You see, it were like this: I found them holiday brochures you left lying around some months ago, and it got me to thinking. It ain't right that the kids ain't never seen the sea, and you deserve a holiday and all. But when I got round to pricing holidays up, I knew we'd never afford it in a month o' Sundays – not with the train fares an' the cost of a boardin' house and whatnot. So I decided if I got us some transport of us own, it would work out a lot cheaper. I couldn't afford a car an' this were the next best thing. An' that ain't all – I've made some enquiries and I've found out that I can hire a tent from the Scouts for ten bob. There's this bloke I work with who's given me the address of a farm down in Chapel Saint Leonards who will let us camp there for a pound a week. So – the long an' the short of it is, Mrs Swan, you, me an' our nippers are off to the seaside. What do you say to that?'

For a second she was so choked that she could only stare blankly at him. Then, as he took her in his arms: 'I say that you must be the kindest man I've ever known,' she whispered softly, and he sighed contentedly.

'How long has it been since I told you that I loved you, Mrs Swan?'

'Ooh . . . not since last night.' She stared admiringly at their new mode of transport.

'Well, I'd better remind you again then. I love you, Grace.'

'I know you do,' she said softly, and in that moment, more than anything in the world, he longed to hear her say it to him, for she never had, although her actions told him that she did. *Still,* he consoled himself, *one day she'll say it. We have all the time in the world.*

Chapter Seven

'Lord love us. You couldn't squeeze another bean in there.' Chris, who was standing on the pavement, watched Grace try to cram some towels into the back seat of the already overloaded sidecar. Wendy and Simon were squashed into the front seat with huge grins on their faces, and even Barry, now that they were about to set off, looked slightly bemused.

'She's right, love,' he piped up. 'If you cram much more in we'll never even get to pull away from the kerb. It's a sidecar, not a double-decker bus, you know. An' we're only goin' for a week – we ain't leavin' home.'

Grace grinned at him apologetically. 'Sorry. I suppose I have got a little carried away. But are you quite sure we've got everything?'

'I reckon you can safely say we have. Everythin' but the kitchen sink, that is. Now come on, put your crash helmet on an' hop on the back, else it'll be time to come back before we get there.'

Grace obediently pulled the heavy helmet across her shining dark hair and climbed onto the back seat, and as Barry revved the motorbike up she clung to him for dear life.

'Bye, Chris, see you next week!' she shouted. She would have liked to wave to her friend, who was laughing so hard that tears were rolling down her cheeks, but she was too afraid to let go of Barry. Then they were off and she closed her eyes as the houses whizzed past them.

It was almost dinner-time when they turned into the farm field that Barry's friend had recommended to them in Chapel Saint Leonard's, and Grace heaved a sigh of relief as Barry pulled the motorbike to a halt. The children fell out of the sidecar in a frenzy of excitement, and whilst Barry went to see the farmer's wife, Grace leaned heavily against the side of the bike, sure that she would never walk a straight line in her life ever again.

When Barry returned they unloaded the tent from the back of the sidecar and then spent the next hour and a half trying to erect it. At one stage Grace had visions of them having to sleep under the stars, but at last they managed it. It was as Barry was hammering in the tent pegs that the farmer's wife appeared. She was a buxom, red-faced woman with an easy smile and Grace liked her immediately.

'Ah, so you've managed it then. Good. Now you little ones, you see that big barn over there? If you go inside you'll find some nice fresh hay, an' if you bring a few armfuls back to your mam she'll be able to make you all a bed as is fit for a king.'

Needing no second bidding, Wendy and Simon scampered away as fast as their little legs would carry them while Grace smiled at the woman gratefully.

'Thank you very much indeed. That was very kind of you.'

'No trouble at all, me dear. I want you all to have a good holiday. I just popped over to tell you how the land lies so as you know where everything is. Over there' – she pointed to the left-hand side of the farmhouse – 'is the outside toilet, an' there's also an outside tap there. Just help yourself to water, an' should there be anythin' else you need, just give us a shout. The sea is two minutes down the road, near Chapel Point, and I can near on guarantee that the kids will love it. Their first holiday, is it?'

When Grace nodded, she beamed and the two women stood side by side and watched with amusement as Wendy and Simon staggered back towards them with their arms full of hay.

'Right, I'd best get on an' leave you to make the beds up. Have a good day now.'

'We will,' Grace said, then she and the children dragged the hay into the tent amidst much laughter.

Meantime Barry unloaded the rest of the sidecar. When he was done he stood back and scratched his head in amazement. It seemed impossible that so much could have been packed into such a small space. At last the camp met with Grace's approval, so then Barry set up a small primus stove, and after he had filled it with paraffin, Grace fried some bacon and made them all sandwiches, which the children wolfed down as if they hadn't eaten for a month.

'It must be the sea air,' he laughed as he stared across at his wife, who resembled something very close to a scarecrow, and she grinned back, enjoying herself already.

In no time at all they had filled a bag with a bottle of Kia-Ora orange squash, a flask of tea, sandwiches and towels, then they headed to the beach, where the children whooped with delight at their first sight of the sea. Barry bought them each a colourful bucket and spade at the beachside café, which they immediately used to bury him with. He endured it all good-naturedly until they tired of that and went splashing off into the waves. Shaking the sand from his body he rolled over to look at Grace, who was watching the children's antics with a broad smile on her face.

'Are you happy, Mrs Swan?' he asked.

'Very much, Mr Swan,' she replied. And she was.

By Wednesday evening when they tucked the children onto their hay mattresses, they were all as brown as berries, and Barry and Grace were more relaxed than they had been in a long, long time. They sat on the grass outside the tent, revelling in the feel of the warm evening breeze on their tanned skins, staring up at a starlit sky. Funds were running low, but luckily the children's demands were few; they were quite content to play with their buckets and spades on the golden sands or frolic in the sea, so Barry envisaged them being able to stay for the rest of the week. They had lived on chips from the nearby chip shop, or anything that Grace could fry or warm up on the small primus stove, apart from liberal amounts of ice cream, and Grace felt almost like a different person.

She adored her children with a passion, and had always determined that they would have all the love that she had lacked as a child. As she stared across at Barry she wished with all her heart that she could feel the same about him. Oh, she was more than fond of him, of that she was sure, but still there was the lingering doubt that she had married him for all the wrong reasons, the fact that she had been carrying Wendy being one of them. She hated feeling as she did; she was well aware that Barry deserved better, and she did try to be a good wife and hoped that she succeeded. But still she had never as yet openly told him that she loved him, for she was still not sure that she truly did, although she could not have wished for a better husband. She felt his eyes on her now and dismissed the thoughts she had been indulging in, thankful that he could not read her mind.

'It's a wonderful evening, love.' He reached across and squeezed her hand, loving her with all his heart, just as he had since the moment he first set eyes on her. She nodded and smiled back at him as a wicked little gleam shone in his eyes.

'Do you reckon the little ones will have dropped off properly yet?'

When she realised his intentions she blushed prettily. 'I should think so, judging by the amount of snoring coming from the tent.'

'Right, happen it's time we hit the sack an' all then. I reckon all this moonlight has put me in a romantic mood.'

She giggled as he playfully slapped her bottom, and as he held the flap of the tent aside she scrambled in on all fours ahead of him.

*   *   *

They woke the next morning to the sound of rain slapping against the tent. The wind had picked up as well, and when Grace felt the ground, her hand sank into wet grass. The children were still fast asleep, luckily high off the ground on their hay bale mattresses.

'Barry, *Barry*!' Her voice was urgent as she shook his arm, and as he roused, another particularly strong gust of wind rocked the tent.

'Bloody hell.' He was instantly awake and knuckling the sleep from his eyes. 'What the hell happened to the weather? Come on – get the kids out of here quick. It feels like the tent is gonna come down on top of us.'

Not needing to be told twice, Grace snatched Simon into her arms as Barry grabbed Wendy, then they were out in the rain, still in their nightclothes and running towards the nearby barn. Once inside they stood breathlessly, staring out at the storm, their wet nightclothes moulded to their shivering bodies.

Barry sat Wendy down on the nearest hay bale and scratched his head in bewilderment, just as the farmer's wife, Mrs Roe, appeared round the corner and ran into the barn to join them.

'Nice weather for ducks, ain't it?' She grinned.

Barry sighed. 'I can't believe this, Mrs Roe. It were lovely when we went to bed last night.'

She chuckled. 'Ah well – what you have to remember is, this is the coast, lad. It's only a flash storm, so no doubt it will be over as quick as it started.'

'That's as mebbe. I just hope the tent will hold up to it, that's all.' Barry looked across the field with concern as the tent whipped at its guide-ropes as if it was trying to escape.

Suddenly, to his horror, there was a loud crack and the tent folded in on itself before their very eyes to fall in a soggy heap on the ground.

'Damn,' Barry cursed softly. 'It looks like the main pole's gone. If it has, that's the end of our holiday for sure.'

At his words both Wendy and Simon began to cry and the kindly woman's heart went out to them. They were lovely children – a lovely family, in fact – and she had enjoyed seeing the children having so much fun. It was more than obvious that they were holidaying on a very tight budget and she hated to think of it ending like this for them.

'I'll tell you what,' she suggested. 'There ain't no point looking at the worst till this lot has blown over, an' in the meantime you'll catch your death of cold if you stand here much longer. Come with me an' we'll go into the farmhouse while I make you all some breakfast, eh? Then when the storm is over we'll see what's to be done.'

Barry and Grace smiled at her gratefully as they each picked up one of the children and followed her back out into the lashing rain again. As they entered the homely kitchen, which seemed huge to Grace in comparison to her own, a large black and white Border Collie rose lazily from the hearthrug, and with his tail wagging pottered over to the children who were instantly absorbed in playing with him.

In no time at all Mrs Roe had cooked them a breakfast fit for a king, and Wendy and Simon tucked in as if they hadn't seen food for weeks. Barry kept glancing out of the window and seeing his concern, Mrs Roe said, 'Stop frettin', lad. There ain't no problem been invented yet as can't be got round. I think I've already come up with a solution, but sitting there worrying won't solve nowt, so eat your breakfast while it's hot.'

Under her watchful eye, Barry did as he was told, and when the meal was finished, Grace helped Mrs Roe wash the breakfast pots up and transfer them to the most enormous dresser she had ever seen. By then the rain had slowed to a drizzle and the wind had dropped considerably. During the next half hour, just as Mrs Roe had predicted, the sun came out and the wet grass began to steam under its warming rays.

'Right.' The farmer's wife kicked off her slippers and slipped her feet into a pair of well-worn Wellington boots. 'Let's go and have a look at the damage, eh?'

The dejected family trooped obediently after her, and when they reached the tent, Barry lifted the soggy canvas and wriggled underneath it. He appeared seconds later with the main pole in two halves in his hand. 'That's it then. We can't re-pitch the tent without the main pole. It looks like we'd better start to pack up an' head for home.'

'You'll do no such thing, Mr Swan. Like I said back in the kitchen, I reckon I've come up with an idea that might solve your problems,' Mrs Roe told him with a wide grin on her face. She pointed towards the barn they had sheltered in earlier.

'You could put your tent back up in there an' tie it up to the rafters. That way you won't need the pole, and you'll be out of the weather an' all. What do you say?'

Barry was speechless that someone they had known for so short a time could show such kindness to them, and so Grace answered for him.

'That would be wonderful, Mrs Roe – if you're sure you don't mind, that is.'

'I wouldn't have offered if I minded, now would I? So come on, kids. Help your mam an' dad get all the stuff across now.'

Wendy and Simon were thrilled at the prospect of staying another few days and immediately started to gather together anything they could carry and take it to the barn. In less than an hour they were all set up again, and although the tent did look somewhat comical suspended from the rafters, it was more than adequate accommodation once more. In fact, Wendy insisted that it was even better than before and rolled about on the hay in delight. By now the sun was once again suspended in a cloudless blue sky and it was hard to imagine that such a short time ago they had found themselves in almost gale-force conditions. Mrs Roe supervised the whole setting up of the camp like a Sergeant Major, and then content that the family were comfortable again and that she had done her good deed for the day, she pottered away.

Wendy and Simon were climbing up and down the ladder into the hayloft above them, and suddenly as the funny side of the situation struck him, Barry started to laugh until the tears rolled down his cheeks.

'There's one thing, love,' he gasped. 'We won't forget this holiday in a hurry. No one back home will believe us when we tell them we ended up campin' in a barn with the tent tied to the rafters.'

His laughter was so infectious that soon Grace was laughing helplessly too, and the holiday that had almost turned into a disaster was saved.

On Thursday morning, Barry piled them all into the sidecar and took them on a trip to Grimsby docks, where they bought fish caught fresh from the sea, which Grace fried for their tea. And then, on Friday, he took them to visit Ingoldmells and Skegness.

The children were obviously enjoying every minute, and Grace was sorry when Saturday morning arrived and it was time to pack up and go home. Barry stared at the amount of luggage he had to somehow cram back into the sidecar. 'I'm sure we've got more than we came with,' he complained.

Grace chuckled. She looked tanned and relaxed, and he thought he had never seen her looking more beautiful. At last the packing was done, and he sat the two children in the sidecar as they said their tearful goodbyes to Mrs Roe.

'Now you be sure to come again next year.' She smiled as she waved them away.

'We will,' Grace called, as she clung to Barry with one arm and waved goodbye with the other. And then with a roar and a belch of smoke from the motorbike's exhaust pipe, they were off.

*   *   *

Within seconds of them pulling up outside their little terraced house in Nuneaton, Chris was hurrying out to meet them, carrying a bottle of milk. 'By heck!' she exclaimed, as Grace removed her crash helmet and she saw her tan. 'You look like you've been on a Caribbean cruise, yer jammy bugger. No need to ask if yer had good weather, is there? You're as brown as a berry.'

Grace and Barry exchanged an amused glance. 'Well, we did have *one* minor hiccup,' Grace admitted, 'but we'll tell you all about that when we get inside. I could kill for a cup of tea and I'm sure I've gone bandy-legged from sitting on the back of the motorbike for so long.'

She opened the sidecar door, and Wendy and Simon spilled out onto the pavement, proudly clutching the sticks of rock they had bought for Chris's little daughter.

'Where's Jenny?' Wendy asked.

Chris nodded towards her house. 'She's inside with her dad. Go on into her, if yer like. I'll stay here an' help your mam an' dad unload this lot.'

The children scuttled away and Chris shook her head in bewilderment as Barry began to unload the unfortunate tent and the luggage from the back of the sidecar.

'God above, it's a miracle as the bike ever managed to pull this lot,' she muttered, and lifting a case she humped it into the house, close on the heels of Grace.

While Barry was unpacking the rest, Grace put the kettle on as Chris sank onto a kitchen chair. She glanced across her shoulder to make sure that Barry was out of earshot, then leaning towards Grace she whispered, 'You'll never guess who I saw last night at the Saint George's Hall?'

Grace frowned. 'I have no idea,' she said with a shrug of her shoulders.

Chris chuckled. 'Only that nice bit o' stuff as chatted yer up a couple o' weeks back. He made a point of coming across an' asking where yer were.'

A vision of his handsome face sprang to Grace's mind. If truth were told, she had thought of him more than once, and it was quite a shock to hear that he had been enquiring after her. Nonchalantly she measured the tea-leaves into the teapot.

'Is that all? I thought you were going to tell me something interesting.'

'Huh! If he ain't interestin' then I don't know what is! I wish it were me as he'd took a fancy to. I tell yer, I'd give him a run for his money. Quality he is, off the top shelf if I'm any judge. Well-spoken, good looking', an' not short of a bob or two neither if I ain't very much mistaken.'

'That's all as maybe, Chris,' Grace snapped, 'but in case you'd forgotten, I happen to be a happily married woman.'

'Is that so?' Chris grinned. 'Well, sorry I mentioned it then. From where I'm standin' I thought you'd be flattered. I mean, no disrespect, but you and Barry are hardly a match made in heaven, are yer? What I mean is, you're as different as chalk from cheese. Barry's common like me an' the rest of them that lives round here, while you . . . Well, it's as plain as the nose on your face that you were brought up proper like.'

Grace gritted her teeth as memories of the childhood she had endured at her aunt's hands flooded back. 'Sometimes things and people are not what they appear, Chris, and I can assure you I am quite happy with my life as it is. So now, if you'll excuse me, I think my husband may need some help.'

As she flounced from the kitchen Chris realised that she had upset her. She hadn't meant to. After all, what had she said that was so wrong? And why, whenever she tried to probe into Grace's past, did she clam up like a shell?

'I suppose she has her reasons,' she told herself, and after rising from her chair, she smoothed down her Crimplene mini-skirt and followed her friend outside.

Chapter Eight

Grace put the cover over the Olivetti typewriter and tidied the papers on her desk into a neat pile then, glancing at the clock she quickly collected her coat and hurried from the office. The last week since they had arrived home from holiday had passed in a blur as she caught up with all the washing and ironing and ploughed through the massive amount of work that had accumulated on her desk. Here it was, Thursday already, and unless she hurried she would be late collecting Wendy from Fitton Street School before going on to pick Simon up from his grandma's.

She nodded at the other girls who were still busily typing as she passed, and soon she was outside in the warm summer afternoon, enjoying the feel of the sun on her face. Within minutes she was at the gates of the school with the other mums, waiting for the bell that would herald the end of the school day. Within seconds of it ringing, the huge double doors at the entrance to the school swung wide and children of all shapes and sizes began to pour through them. In minutes Wendy appeared, her school satchel swung haphazardly across her shoulder and her fair hair bouncing around her head like a halo. She looked hot and flustered, but at sight of her mother her face lit up as it always did. Grace felt a wave of love wash over her. Wendy was a lovely little girl, confident and happy, not at all as Grace had been as a child, and Grace thanked God for it. The one good thing that had come from being brought up by her aunt was her determination that her own children would never feel unloved, as she had. Wendy ran to her on her stocky little legs and flung herself into her arms, and Grace kissed her soundly before taking her hand and leading her away.

'We went on a nature walk in Riversley Park today with the teacher,' Wendy informed her happily. 'An' then 'cos it was so hot she took us through to the Pingle Fields an' let us take us shoes an' socks off an' have a splodge in the paddling pool.'

'Really? That must have been nice.' Grace smiled indulgently. 'But how did you dry your feet?'

'We ran round on the grass in the sun.' Wendy grinned. 'But the

74

trouble was, Patsy Hall stood on some glass an' Miss had to take her to the hospital. They had to put some stitches in her foot with a big needle, an' now she can't come to school till she's better.'

'Oh dear, that was unfortunate,' Grace said solemnly, and Wendy's head wagged in agreement. They walked on and turned into Edward Street in silence as Wendy pondered on her friend's misfortune, but soon she was smiling and chattering happily once again as her mother listened to her childish prattle.

Simon was playing in the garden with his cousin when they reached Daisy's house, so after discarding her satchel Wendy ran out to join them as Grace sat down to enjoy a cup of tea with Daisy.

'Had a good day, have you, love?' Daisy welcomed her.

Grace nodded wearily. 'Not bad, but I can't say I shall be sorry when it's over. I would never have believed how much washing could mount up in a week. I'm still trying to catch up on all the holiday stuff, and on top of that I'm really busy at work too. Still, at least I've got my new twin-tub washer. Honestly, Daisy, you really should get one. It certainly saves having to drag the copper and the dolly tub out.'

'Huh! The copper an' the dolly tub have allus been all right for me,' Daisy sniffed. 'I can't be doin' with all these new-fangled devices meself. Besides, I don't get that much washin' now there's just me an' the old man at home. How did yer manage to afford that anyway? You ain't had one o' them bloody Barclay credit cards they've just brought out, have yer?'

Grace giggled. 'No, Daisy, I haven't. I saved up for it out of my wages. But it's strange to think that now you could pay for something with a bit of plastic though, isn't it?'

'Strange ain't the word for it, but then that's progress I suppose.' Daisy carried two steaming mugs to the table and they lapsed into silence for a time as they sipped at their tea, before Daisy asked, 'Off dancin' tomorrow night, are yer?'

Colour flooded into Grace's cheeks as a vision of her handsome dancing partner flashed before her eyes. 'I doubt it,' she muttered. 'I haven't really got time this week, I've got too much to do at home, and I've still got to get to the Co-op to do the food shopping.'

Daisy frowned. 'Then you should make time. You deserve a break come Friday. God knows you work hard enough through the week.'

'Well, I might give it a miss this week anyway. To tell you the truth, I feel guilty sometimes, going off and leaving Barry in alone.'

'Don't know why you should.' Daisy told her, as she kicked her slippers off and wriggled her toes under the table. 'It was his choice not to go. You know what our Barry's like by now. Likes his own fireside too much, that's his trouble. But that ain't no reason for you to miss out. You know what I allus say – what don't get done today can wait till tomorrow.'

Grace looked down quickly so that Daisy would not see the flicker of amusement that she was unable to conceal. Looking around the cluttered, cosy little room, it was only too obvious that Daisy had never been a slave to housework, as the layers of dust testified. Strangely she found herself envying her, for she herself *was* a slave to routine, no doubt from the strict upbringing she had endured at the hands of her fastidiously tidy aunt.

'We'll see,' Grace replied, knowing that it would be useless to argue.

They finished their tea and rising, Grace crossed to the open back door to shout for the children. She had started to collect their things together when they erupted into the room.

'Come on, you two, it's time we were off,' she said. 'If you're good I might take you for a walk along the canal on the way home.'

The children nodded without argument at the promise of the treat ahead, and after kissing their grandma goodbye and waving to their cousin, they all set off. Grace walked them down Manor Court Road and on up the Cock and Bear hill, where they climbed down the steps by the bridge to the canal towpath. A colourful barge was sailing along, and its wake sparkled in the sunshine. Wendy released the children's hands and they ran on ahead of her as they tried to keep up with the barge, waving furiously at the man who was steering it. He waved back with a broad smile on his face before disappearing around a bend. The children's footsteps slowed and when Grace caught up with them they walked on together in silence for a time until she suddenly pulled them to an abrupt halt.

'Sssh, look over there and stand very still,' she whispered. Immediately the children's eyes followed her pointing finger. Almost directly opposite them on the other side of the riverbank was a fat old water rat, and as the children watched fascinated, he cleaned his whiskers, as if he had all the time in the world.

'What is it, Mammy?' whispered Simon, totally enthralled, but before Grace could answer him the rat looked up and stared directly at them for some seconds. Obviously not liking what he saw, he waddled to the canal edge and plopped almost soundlessly into the water, before diving and disappearing from sight.

'Oh, I wanted to take him home!' Simon wailed, but luckily just then, Wendy, who had run on ahead, squealed with delight again and pointed excitedly to a gap in the hedge.

76

Hurrying to catch up with her, Grace saw her disappear and yanked Simon, who was complaining loudly, along behind her. When she reached the spot where Wendy had dived through the hedge she saw the cause of the child's excitement.

'Look, Mammy, look!' Wendy was hopping up and down. 'All the flowers in the field have been painted gold! Can we pick some and take them home to put in a jamjar?'

The buttercup field, that stretched away as far as the eye could see, was a truly wonderful sight to behold.

'You know, these flowers are magic,' Grace whispered, and immediately she had the children's rapt attention. 'If you pick one and hold it underneath your chin like this,' she picked one and held it to Wendy's chin as the child stretched her neck as far as it would go, 'if the colour reflects on your neck it means that you like butter.'

Simon giggled and plucking another flower, he demanded, 'Now try me, Mammy.'

Grace held the flower beneath his chin as Wendy burst into an infectious fit of giggles. 'These flowers tell lies, Mammy. That one said Simon liked butter, and he don't like anything much at the minute, 'cept for chocolate. Grandma said all his teeth will go black an' drop out if he don't start to eat proper food soon.'

Simon launched himself at her and they fell onto the soft carpet of buttercups as he strongly denied her statement. Grace smiled. What Wendy had said was not far from the truth, for Simon was going through what Barry termed as his 'picky' stage at present. Still, she didn't want their play to turn into full-scale war so she hoisted them up one at a time and stood them on their feet, as Simon glared at Wendy resentfully.

'Now then, you two. That's quite enough of that, thank you very much. Well behaved children do *not* fight.'

Simon glared at his sister and stuck his tongue out as a last parting shot.

'They do not stick their tongues out either, Simon,' Grace scolded.

Wendy grinned smugly. 'No, they don't, else the ducks will come along an' peck it off.'

'*Right!* You have exactly two minutes to pick some flowers if you want to, and then we have to get home to get your dad's tea. Now go.'

Somewhat sullenly the children began to gather the buttercups on the perimeter of the field, and thankfully by the time they had finished, their good humour had returned, and they all continued along the towpath.

Soon, the Cat Gallows Bridge came into sight. The children were tired and sweaty by then and the flowers they were clutching in their hot little hands were beginning to wilt in the late afternoon sun, but Grace encouraged them on as they scrambled up the bank that would take them away from the canal and on to the road that would lead them home. As they turned into Marlborough Road they saw Jenny and her mother walking some way ahead of them and instantly their tiredness was forgotten as they ran on ahead to join her. Chris waited until Grace had caught up with her, and they fell into step, smiling at the children's antics ahead of them.

'Phew, it's been a scorcher today, ain't it?' Chris commented, as she wiped her damp hair from her brow.

Grace looked at the short flowery skirt and halter-neck top her friend was wearing. 'I'm surprised you could feel hot in that outfit,' she teased. 'If there were any less to it, you'd be had up for indecent exposure.'

'Well, you know what they say – if you've got it, flaunt it. I don't know why you don't take a leaf out o' my book. It's a crime to hide a figure like yours. You must be roastin' in that frock you've got on. Why don't you come round an' borrow a few outfits?'

Grace didn't want to hurt her friend's feelings, so she tactfully replied, 'I really don't think I could do them justice like you.'

Chris chuckled before asking, 'Are we off out dancin' tomorrow night then?'

Immediately, a picture of the tall handsome stranger who had swept her expertly around the dance-floor the last time they had gone out entered Grace's mind again, and she said hastily, 'No, I don't think so, not this week. To tell you the truth I'm still trying to catch up on all the washing and ironing since we got home from holiday and I'm not really in the mood.'

'Huh! Don't be so damn borin'. You know how you love to dance, an' you'd be in the mood by the time we got there. I thought we might try the Co-op Hall this week for a change.'

Grace pondered on what Chris had said. For no reason that she could explain she had no wish to see the stranger again. But then, if they were going to a different venue there would be very little chance of that, so where could the harm be?

'All right,' she agreed eventually. 'I'll see you about eight o'clock tomorrow night.'

'That's more like it. You're on.' Chris grinned, and after saying her goodbyes she disappeared up her entry, leaving Grace to continue on to her own home.

*   *   *

'So, are you off out tonight, love?' Barry planted a kiss on the top of Grace's head as he passed her. She was sitting at the kitchen table smocking the bodice of a dress she was making for Wendy. She shrugged. Although she had told Chris she would go, as the time approached to get ready she was having second thoughts.

'I did tell Chris I would,' she admitted, 'but to be honest, I'm not so sure that I want to now.'

Barry frowned. It wasn't like Grace to miss the opportunity of a dance, for she loved it. 'What's wrong? Are you not feelin' so good?'

'Oh no, it's nothing like that,' she assured him. 'It's just . . . I don't know really, I suppose I'm not in the mood.'

'That's not like you, love. You usually love to go, an' it would be a shame to let Chris down if you've promised. Go on, get yourself upstairs an' make yourself beautiful – not that you ain't already, o' course. It will do you good after all the work you've got through this week.' Secretly, Barry was relieved that Grace had found a dancing partner in Chris. Despite all of Grace's greatest efforts, he had found in ballroom dancing an art he could not master.

She placed the intricate piece of needlework she was working on onto the table. 'I suppose you're right,' she said reluctantly. 'It would be a bit naughty to let Chris down now, so if you're sure you can manage here I'll pop up and get ready.'

She hurried away up the steep narrow staircase, and when she re-appeared almost an hour later, Barry let out a low whistle of appreciation. She had washed her hair and brushed it until it shone like silk, and the smart box jacket and princess-cut dress she wore suited her to perfection. She looked tanned, sophisticated and elegant, and once again, as he had many times before, Barry found himself thinking what a fortunate man he was, and wondering what a woman like Grace had ever seen in him.

Chris was right on time, and as always, the difference in style in the way the two women were dressed was marked. Chris was wearing a dangerously low-cut top and her skirt was so short, Barry hoped that she wouldn't have cause to bend over. Her hair was piled high on her head in the usual backcombed beehive, and her face was so thick with panstick make-up that it appeared to have changed colour. Even so, Barry greeted her politely at the door and kissed Grace affec-tionately.

The two women set off, enjoying the feel of the cool evening breeze on their skin, and soon they were climbing the stairs to the Co-op Hall ballroom.

Chris's eyes scanned the crowd as they made their way to the bar that ran all down one side of the room, and as Grace continued on to get the drinks, she stopped to have a word with someone that she knew.

Grace ordered the drinks and was just about to pay for them when someone gently took her elbow. Starting, she looked up and grew flustered as she found herself staring straight into the eyes of the handsome stranger.

'Allow me.' He took a wallet from the pocket of his perfectly cut jacket, but Grace protested quickly, 'No really, I'll get them.'

A twinkle of amusement appeared in his eyes. 'Please, I insist.' He handed the barman a ten-shilling note and Grace looked around desperately for Chris as he waited for his change. With a gallant little bow he lifted the glass and placed it in her hand.

'A Babycham for madam, and this Cherry-B must be for your charming friend. As she seems to be otherwise engaged at present we may as well go and find a table. I'm sure she'll join us when she's ready.'

Before Grace could protest, he lifted Chris's drink and began to weave his way through the tables, leaving her no choice but to follow him. She cast a last desperate glance across her shoulder, but Chris was still deep in conversation and oblivious to her mounting distress. There was something about this man that she found deeply disturbing, although she couldn't quite put her finger on what it was. Perhaps it was something to do with the fact that he was devastatingly handsome, or the way he looked at her. She wasn't sure; she just felt uneasy about being alone with him.

He came to an empty table, and after placing the drinks down, he courteously pulled out a chair for her. Almost as if he could sense her unease, he smiled at her disarmingly.

'I hope you don't mind me turning up like this. I must admit I went to the Saint George's Hall last week and was disappointed when your friend informed me you were on holiday.'

'Was it Chris who told you we would be coming here tonight?' she asked. When he nodded she made a mental note to scold Chris on the way home.

'Yes, it was actually, although before you go jumping to conclusions I think I should explain that my intentions for asking were purely honourable.'

She raised her eyebrow questioningly, and he grinned.

'The thing is, Grace – it *is* Grace, isn't it?' When she nodded he went on. 'The thing is, I've been thinking about you a great deal since the last time we met and there's something I'd like to ask you.'

Grace gulped nervously as he smiled and went on: 'I was wondering – have you ever thought of dancing semi-professionally?'

'Why . . . no, I haven't to be honest,' Grace stuttered in amazement.

'Then I find that a great shame.' He sighed. 'You are totally wasted in venues such as this. It's been a long time since I've had the privilege of dancing with anyone who was remotely as good as you. My wife, Cheryl, and I used to dance together until last year. Unfortunately, she had a riding accident and since then has been forced to retire from the dancing circuit, which is why I was so thrilled when I came across you. You see, I would love to get back into competition dancing again, but obviously until I find a worthy partner, that will be out of the question. Would you be interested in partnering me, Grace?'

Relief rushed through her. So he hadn't been trying to seduce her, after all. He was merely interested in her dancing ability. She had the urge to laugh. 'Well, I have to say, Mr . . . ?' she said.

'Golding. Philip Golding.' He held out his hand and Grace shook it politely.

'What you have asked I consider to be a great compliment. The only problem is, it could prove to be quite difficult, although I admit the idea is very appealing. You see, I have two small children and a home to look after as well as working part-time, so Friday night is the only evening I come out.'

'That needn't necessarily be a problem.' He waved aside her concerns as he explained, 'The thing is, it would be quite some time before we were polished enough to enter competitions. In the meantime, we could consider Friday nights to be our practice nights. And then, even when I considered we were ready to enter competitions, they could be where and when to suit you. So – will you at least give it some thought?'

'Yes, I will.' Grace smiled, and at that moment Chris appeared at her elbow, grinning like a Cheshire cat.

'What's this then? Settin' your cap at my mate again, are you?' she joked to Philip.

'No, I'm not, as a matter of fact – as I'm sure Grace will inform you. My intentions are purely honourable. And now, ladies, if you will excuse me I shall go and get us all another drink, and then Grace, I hope you will do me the honour of dancing with me.'

'I would be delighted.' Grace smiled.

Chris's mouth gaped open in amazement. 'So what the bloody hell is all this about?' she demanded, as Philip weaved his way through the tables towards the bar. As Grace quickly explained to her, her mouth gaped even wider.

'Well, I'll be a monkey's uncle!' she exclaimed, and poking a finger into her beehive hairdo she scratched her scalp. 'Shame though, ain't it? The fact that he don't fancy you, I mean. Here were me thinkin' he were tryin' to pull you, an' all he wants to do is dance with you. What you goin' to do?'

'I'm not sure yet,' Grace told her truthfully. 'I'd like a little time to think about it, and I'll have to see how Barry feels about it, of course, before I reach a decision.'

'Mm, that's true. Mind you, knowin' your Barry, he won't much mind one way or another so long as his dinner is on the table. What I mean is, he's a lovely bloke an' he obviously adores the very ground you walk on, but he's a bit . . . what shall I say . . . stuck in his ways?'

'I suppose he is,' Grace admitted, but then Philip returned to the table as the band struck up a lively foxtrot and before she could blink he was whirling her around the dance-floor.

During the interval they returned to the table, and when he had replenished their drinks they began to chat and get to know one another a little better.

Grace found herself liking him more and more as the evening wore on. Between dances he told her that he owned a garage in Meridan where he sold quality second-hand cars, which explained why his hands were smoother than hers.

She couldn't help but compare them to Barry's, which were so covered in cuts and blisters most evenings that he could hardly bear to put them in water. But then she was forced to confess that he was totally different to Barry in all ways; he was so smart that he looked as if he had just stepped out of a tailor's window, whereas Barry never seemed to look even remotely tidy, even when he was dressed in his Sunday best. Philip was remarkably well-spoken too, and it soon became apparent from things he told her, that he had received a very good education. The interval passed so quickly that it felt as if they had only just sat down when the band struck up again. He led her onto the floor and they began to dance a tango as he whispered instructions into her ear.

'Left foot to the side, that's right, now to me . . . perfect.'

Grace looked around the room across his broad shoulder. Chris, who was more than a little disgruntled at the fact that she'd had her nose pushed out, was now chatting happily to another woman who lived in their street, so Grace gave herself up to the joy of dancing with a man who seemed to float on air. It finally came to the Last Waltz and Grace relaxed into her partner's arms as he guided her effortlessly around the floor, enjoying herself far more than she cared to admit.

When the dance ended and Philip led her from the floor, he beamed at her appreciatively.

'That was wonderful – you really are a natural. With a little bit of coaching you could outdance the best.'

She flushed with pleasure at the compliment. She loved to dance, but to dance with a man who loved it as much as she did was a real bonus.

'You will think about what I asked you, won't you?' he urged.

She smiled. 'Of course. I said I would, but now if you'll excuse me I'd better go and look for Chris or she'll think I've got lost.' Her eyes scanned the room, but there was no sign of her.

'Perhaps she's in the ladies' cloakroom,' Philip suggested. She nodded and hurried towards it. Just as she drew near Chris appeared with their coats slung carelessly across her arm.

'We're goin' to need these,' she told her. 'I've just been an' stuck me head out the door for a bit o' fresh air and it's rainin' bloody cats and dogs out there.'

'In that case, you must allow me to give you both a lift home,' Philip offered immediately.

Grace shook her head, shyly. 'There's no need for that, really. A bit of rain won't hurt us.'

'You speak for yourself,' Chris objected loudly. 'I'm tellin' you – it's bucketing down, an' I for one will be very glad to take you up on your offer.'

Knowing that she was outnumbered, Grace followed them meekly. Once they reached the entrance she saw that Chris had not exaggerated, for it seemed that the heavens had opened and the rain was bouncing off the pavements and running down the drains in torrents.

Pulling his raincoat across his head, Philip told them, 'Wait here. The car is just around the corner – I'll pull it up to the door for you.' Without another word he disappeared into the rain as Chris took a Woodbine from the packet in her coat pocket and lit it. Inhaling deeply, she grinned at Grace.

'Well, this ain't a bad way to end the night, is it? Bein' chauffeured home, I mean. I wonder what sort o' car he's got?'

She didn't have to wait long to find out, for shortly a shiny red Jaguar pulled up at the kerb. She almost choked with shock. 'Good heavens above! That must be worth more than me house,' she gasped, and as a mark of respect she tossed her cigarette into the gutter before clambering into the back seat.

Grace climbed into the front and the smell of the new leather upholstery filled her nostrils. 'This is a wonderful car,' she said admiringly.

He laughed. 'Well, I do own a garage, as I told you. You'd hardly expect me to be driving round in an old banger, would you? It wouldn't be much of an advert for my business. Driving cars like this is one of the perks of the job.'

Chris was so awed with the car that for once she was temporarily speechless and so when Philip looked at Grace enquiringly, she told him, 'Marlborough Road, please.'

They made the short journey in silence and he dropped Chris off at her door first before continuing the short distance up the road to Grace's. When he pulled up behind their motorbike and sidecar in front of their small terraced house she felt that she would die of shame, but Philip made no comment as he reached across her to open the door.

'Until next week then.' His voice held a note of hope, and she smiled at him as she stepped out into the rain. Then he was gone as the sleek car pulled away from the kerb with barely a sound, and she stood for some moments and watched, until the tail-lights disappeared around a bend in the road.

Chapter Nine

'So, we're in a BMW tonight then, are we?' Grace said as she climbed into the gleaming blue car. 'I never know what you're going to turn up in next.'

Philip smiled back as she settled into her seat. 'And I never know what I'm going to be driving from one day to another. I have a rather fast sales turnover.'

'Really? That surprises me,' Grace commented. 'I can't imagine that there would be that many people who could afford cars like this.'

'Oh, you'd be amazed,' he replied good-naturedly. 'There are lots of buyers looking for quality cars.'

Grace looked at the sumptuous upholstery and she sighed. In all the weeks that she had been practising with Philip, he had hardly ever picked her up in the same car twice. Seeing her look of amusement, he asked, 'What's so funny?'

'Nothing, really. It's just that I was thinking what a far cry your cars are from my husband's motorbike and sidecar.'

'Ladies should always travel in style.' His eyes locked momentarily with hers and unsure as to how she should answer, Grace hastily looked away through the window.

'Philip thinks we might be up to entering our first competition soon,' Grace told her mother-in-law as she sipped at her tea.

Daisy peered at her across the rim of her mug. 'Does he now? Well, you've certainly had enough practice.'

Detecting a hint of criticism in her voice, Grace frowned. 'You don't approve of me dancing with Philip, do you, Daisy?'

'Well, it ain't exactly that I don't approve, it's just . . . Oh, I don't know. It just seems a bit weird that you're spendin' so much time with him, that's all. Still, I suppose if our Barry is happy about it, then there's nowt to worry about.'

'There isn't,' Grace assured her. 'Barry knows that Philip and I are nothing more than dancing partners, and because he doesn't like dancing himself he's happy with the arrangement. If Philip's wife hadn't had her accident, he and I would never have teamed up.

Apparently they were really well-known on the dancing circuit. They even danced in a formation team in the Tower Ballroom at Blackpool once.'

'You don't say.' Daisy was clearly impressed. 'So where's this competition he's thinkin' of enterin' you in then?'

'It's at the Locarno Ballroom in Coventry at the beginning of September.'

The excitement was back in her voice and Daisy sighed. This Philip was a good-looking bugger accordin' to Chris, who she had bumped into in town just the day before, and a bit of a charmer too, from what she had heard. Still, Grace was a sensible girl and not one to have her head turned easily. Had she been able to choose a wife for Barry, Daisy could not have wished for anyone better than Grace, for she had developed into a wonderful wife and mother, and so hopefully the niggling doubts she harboured about her relationship with this other man would prove to be unfounded.

'Ah well, love. At the end o' the day we're all entitled to us little bit o' pleasure in life. Personally I can't think o' nothing better than a night out down at Fife Street Workin' Men's Club playin' Bingo wi' a glass o' stout in me hand. But then, it's each to his own, an' if you enjoy dancin' then it shouldn't be denied you. Just think yourself lucky as you've got a husband who ain't got a jealous bone in his body. There ain't many as would be as easy-goin' as our Barry, God bless him.'

'I know that, Daisy,' Grace replied seriously, but then she giggled. 'To tell you the truth, I think he's quite relieved that he doesn't have to take me dancing any more. Barry will turn his hands to most things around the house, but I'm afraid when it comes to dancing I had to almost drag him out of the door.'

'You don't need to tell me that,' Daisy chuckled. 'Takes after his dad for that. He's a pipe an' slipper man an' all. Though the difference is, Barry allus says as he *can't* dance – but that ain't strictly true. Between you an' me I think he's just too knackered half the time to be bothered. He loved to dance when he were a child. His dad on the other hand has got no sense o' rhythm an' two left feet. Still, as you say, he more than makes up for it in other directions an' I suppose it's the law of averages that we can't all be good at everythin'.'

As Grace smiled across the table at her, her eyes were full of affection. In the years since she had known Barry, Daisy had become the mother she had never had, and there was nothing that Grace would not have done for her, although her aunt's rejection still pained her. As she thought of her now, tears stung at the back of her eyes. Emily

86

Westwood had been true to her word and had never so much as acknowledged her since the day she left home.

Once, when Wendy was just a baby, Grace had almost bumped into her in the town centre. She had been pushing Wendy in her pram and as her aunt drew level with her in the marketplace, Grace had slowed, hoping to show off her lovely baby daughter. But her aunt had merely glared at her before walking stiffly on with her nose in the air. Grace's humiliation had been all-consuming, and that evening she had flung herself into Barry's arms the second he walked through the door and sobbed as if her heart would break. When she told him the reason for her distress his temper had been awful to behold, for he literally shook with rage.

'You don't need the likes o' that wrinkled-up old prune,' he had raged. 'You're better off without her. Our little family will want for nothin', not if I have to work every hour's overtime there is goin'. At least this way we ain't got nothin' to thank *her* for.'

Grace was fully aware that he was perfectly right, and yet the hurt still remained, buried deep inside.

Her thoughts were pulled abruptly back to the present when Wendy tugged at her sleeve.

'Mammy, don't forget I have to get home an' get changed for Jenny's party.'

Grace rose quickly from her seat. 'It's a good job you reminded me, sweetheart. I'd forgotten all about it. Come on, both of you, get your coats on and we'll be off.'

Obediently the children ran to fetch their coats just as their grandad appeared through the back door.

'Ah, just in time, eh?' Stan was filthy from his shift down the pit, and his false teeth shone brightly from his black face. 'Here you go then.' Placing his snap box down on the table, he fumbled in his coat pocket and produced two shiny sixpences from his pocket with a flourish. 'Get yourself some sweeties on your way home.' He tossed them into the air and the children caught them expertly.

'Thanks, Grandy.' He grinned at the affectionate term they always used for him. It had sprung from when Wendy was just a baby and could not pronounce 'Grandad', and it had stuck ever since.

Grace shepherded them towards the door. 'Thanks for having them, Daisy. I'll see you at the same time tomorrow.'

'You will that, love.' Daisy bent to plant kisses on the two small heads and then they were gone.

Turning to her husband, who was washing the worst of the soot from his hands in the sink, she said, 'You know, Stan, you can call me a worrier if you like, but I can't say as I'm altogether comfortable with this arrangement our Grace has got with this Philip chap.'

'Why's that then?'

She shrugged. 'I can't say for sure. It just don't seem right somehow, for her to be gallivantin' about while our Barry is sat at home. She must have mentioned that Philip at least a dozen times while she were here today.'

Stan threw back his head and laughed. 'Eeh, woman, I reckon you look for things to worry about. Our Grace ain't no fool. She's got her head screwed on. There's nowt wrong with her goin' dancin' – she loves it an' she don't ask for much else. Anyway, why is it a problem all of a sudden? If I remember rightly, it were you as were encouraging her to get out and about a bit more not so long ago.'

'I suppose you're right,' Daisy admitted reluctantly, but underneath the doubts persisted.

When Barry got home from work he found Grace up to her elbows in soapy water, washing the dinner pots at the sink. Just as he always did he crossed to her and kissed her gently before taking his coat off. It was almost seven o'clock and he looked tired. He had been at work since six that morning, as he had every single day that week. As he sank down at the kitchen table she dried her hands and slipped her oven gloves on before getting his meal from the oven where it had been keeping warm. Crossing to the table she put it down in front of him and said tenderly, 'You look tired. Why don't you finish work at the normal time tomorrow instead of doing overtime?'

He shook his head. 'Naw, you know me, love. While it's there for the takin' I'll do it. I know you've got your eye open for a new wardrobe for Simon's room, an' the extra money will mean that we can get it all the sooner. Where is the little monkey anyway?'

'He's in the front room watching the television, and Wendy is round at Jenny's birthday party. I shall have to nip and fetch her back soon or I'll never get her up for school tomorrow.'

Lifting his knife and fork, he began to eat his meal as his eyes followed Grace around the room. Lately if possible she seemed to have grown even more beautiful. There was an air of confidence and a glow about her that he had never seen before, and he could only imagine that it was because she was finally fulfilling her dream of becoming a ballroom dancer. He had raised no objections when she had asked him if he would mind her becoming Philip Golding's dancing partner, and she had given him no cause to regret it. And yet . . . He tried to analyse his feelings. Deep down he had a sense that she was distancing herself from him – not intentionally, but he could feel the gap widening between them all the same. And was it really any wonder? He better than anyone knew that Grace was far above him in all ways. She was beautiful and intelligent. Well-spoken and kind, whilst he . . . He was just an ordinary working-class bloke with no great gift to speak of, and no airs and graces. Philip on the other hand was everything that he envied. He was tall, dark and handsome, wealthy and well-spoken, with a way about him that could have charmed the birds off the trees. Barry had met him on more than one occasion when he had either picked Grace up in an impressive luxury car, or dropped her off after a dance. Each time he saw them together it shocked him to see what a handsome couple they made, and yet in all fairness, Grace seemed totally oblivious to the fact and had never given him one single reason to feel as he did.

'Barry, Barry.'

Her voice made him start, and glancing up he saw her standing at the door with her coat on.

'Sorry, love. I was miles away,' he apologised.

She grinned. 'I gathered that. Will you keep your ear open for Simon? I'm just going to pop to Chris's and get Wendy from the party.'

'Course I will.' He smiled at her gently and satisfied, she slipped out of the back door. When she reached Chris's front gate, the party was still in full swing and children were swarming everywhere when she entered the house. Chris looked a little harassed to say the very least.

'Phew, come on through to the kitchen for a cuppa,' she beckoned. 'We'll leave these little monsters to it for a bit. Another ten minutes and their mams should start to arrive to collect 'em. I'm tellin' you, as God's me judge, never again. They've all but wrecked the bloody house.'

Grace stepped over the remains of a fairy cake that had been trodden into the carpet, and followed her friend into a kitchen that closely resembled a bombsite.

'Look at it,' Chris wailed as she stared round at the mountain of dirty pots. 'I'll never get this place back to scratch, never in a month o' Sundays.'

'Of course you will,' Grace assured her, and began to collect the pots and carry them to the sink as Chris put the kettle on. Soon she had the bowl full of hot steamy water and as Chris ran off to try and keep some sort of order as parents began to arrive, she started the washing up. Methodically she worked her way through the pile and when Chris returned almost twenty minutes later she stared around the almost tidy kitchen in amazement.

'How the bleedin' hell did you manage that in that time?' she gasped.

Grace chuckled. 'Organisation, Chris – you should try it some time.'

'Not on your nelly. I'd rather live in organised chaos, thank you very much. Never have been too keen on all this domestic stuff meself. Still, each to their own, eh? That's what I say. Now I reckon you've earned that tea.' She reboiled the kettle and mashed a large pot, and carried it through to the middle room. The remaining children were sent into the front.

'That's better.' Chris sank into a chair and kicked her shoes off as she stretched her aching feet in front of her. 'Never again,' she vowed. 'I would never have believed that such small people could make *so* much noise. But that's enough about that. How are you doin' now-adays? I never get to see you much since Lover Boy swept you off your feet.'

'That's not fair, Chris,' Grace objected, still feeling more than a little guilty that she no longer went to the dances with Chris. 'You know he's not my Lover Boy, as you so crudely put it. Philip and I are dancing partners, nothing more.'

'More fool you then.' Chris winked cheekily. 'If I were goin' dancin' with him he'd get more than he bargained for. Not that my Dick would let me go in the first place. He ain't as easy-goin' as your Barry.'

'Yes, well, Barry knows that he has nothing to worry about. Both Philip and I are happily married to other people, and that's the way it will stay.'

Chris slurped her tea noisily. 'Who you trying to convince, mate – me or yourself?' When she saw the stain of annoyance rise in Grace's cheeks she hastily changed the subject, and from then until Grace left some minutes later the subject of Philip was not raised again.

It was much later that evening when Barry and the children were all fast asleep in bed and she was locking up for the night, before Grace allowed herself to think of the conversation again.

Why had Chris said such things? After all, her relationship with Philip was nothing more than a dancing partnership, as she had been quick to point out. *But was it?* For some time the mere sight of him had set her pulse racing, and more and more of late she found herself comparing him to Barry. She leaned heavily on the table as her chin drooped to her chest. Perhaps her feelings were running away with

90

her a little? But then, Philip had always behaved as a perfect gentleman and as long as it stayed that way she saw no reason why she should deny herself the pleasure of his company. When she was in his arms and they were floating around the dance-floor she could pretend that her life had always been that perfect. Her disciplinarian aunt, and her humdrum life faded away for just a time. So where was the harm in that? Convinced that all was as it should be, she made her way to bed and climbed in beside her snoring husband to lie staring into the darkness.

Grace settled back into the luxurious leather seat and sighed contentedly. Then: 'Is something wrong?' she asked, as she saw that Philip was not his usual cheerful self.

He shrugged. 'Oh, just a few problems at home.'

'Oh dear, nothing too serious, I hope?'

'To be honest it's the wife,' he blurted out. When he saw the look of shock on Grace's face, he continued, 'I don't usually mention my personal life, Grace, as you know. But I feel if I don't talk to someone soon, I shall go mad.'

'Then talk to me,' she offered instantly. 'We are friends, aren't we? And sometimes it helps to get things out in the open.'

He pulled the car into the kerb and they sat in silence for some minutes whilst the driving rain lashed against the windscreen. Eventually he raised his troubled eyes to hers and asked softly, 'Would you mind very much if we didn't go dancing tonight? I'm not in the mood, to be honest, and I don't think I would do you justice.'

'Of course I wouldn't mind,' Grace told him, and without even thinking she reached across and squeezed his hand. 'Nothing can be that bad,' she said softly.

He shook his head in denial. 'Don't you believe it. Look – I'll tell you what, I'll go and find us a nice quiet pub somewhere, and if you're sure you don't mind lending an ear I'll tell you all about it.'

She nodded slowly, suddenly not so sure that this had been such a good idea after all, but not wishing to offend him. He drove through the town and up Tuttle Hill towards Mancetter in silence. When they came to the Anchor Inn he pulled the car smoothly into the car park and after helping her out, he took her elbow and hurried her inside out of the rain. The pub was quite busy, but he managed to find them a window seat overlooking the canal. After making sure that she was comfortably seated he strode away to get the drinks. Grace glanced around nervously. It felt strange to be sitting in a pub with someone else's husband, and she suddenly regretted not asking Philip to drop her off at home. After all, what if someone she knew were to see her and tell Barry? What would he think? By the time Philip arrived back at the table she was looking almost as miserable as he was, but he smiled at her gratefully as he sat beside her.

'I appreciate this, Grace. Thanks for making the time.'

She pushed aside her unease and flashed him a brilliant smile which, could she have known it, made his heart leap in his chest.

'It's quite all right.' She smiled, sipping at her drink and shuddering.

He laughed. 'Sorry about that. I hope you like it – it's a brandy and soda. It's such a filthy night I thought it might warm you up.'

She looked at the drink apprehensively, but once it had burned its way down her throat she began to relax a little. 'What seems to be the problem then?'

'Ah.' He scratched his head, his handsome face a picture of misery. 'I'm afraid things are not going too well with my wife at present. In fact, to be honest, I don't know how much more I can take. Since she had her accident she's changed so much I hardly know her any more. Nothing is ever good enough for her. She has everything a woman could ask for – a big house and someone to come in and clean it for her. Both of our children are at university and she has her own car, and yet all she does is moan about everything and nothing.'

His expression was so wretched that Grace's heart went out to him. 'Have you tried talking to her and asking her what's wrong?' she asked softly.

He nodded. 'Of course I have, but to tell you the truth, Grace, I think she's simply fallen out of love with me. In fact, I wouldn't be surprised if she didn't have someone else.'

'Surely not!' Grace was so shocked that her eyes almost started from her head.

'Oh, it wouldn't be the first time, believe me. And every time it happens I always swear that this time I *won't* take her back. But then she comes crawling back with her tail between her legs and I always forgive her.'

'Oh Philip, that's awful. I'm so sorry.'

He looked into her eyes and said, 'The only awful thing about it is the fact that I didn't meet and marry someone like you. I wonder if Barry knows just what a lucky man he is.'

Grace blushed furiously as she looked away from his wonderful blue eyes. Sensing her unease, he wisely changed the subject, and when they had finished their drink, he asked, 'Would you like another?'

'No, thank you. I think I ought to be getting home now.' Her head was spinning and she felt happy – giggly, in fact – as he helped her into her coat.

In no time at all he drew up outside her small terraced house. 'Here we are then. I'm sorry I spoiled the night, but thanks for listening.'

She smiled at him, and he watched as if mesmerised, as the street-lamp played on her long silky hair.

'Anytime, and you didn't spoil the night. Goodnight, Philip.'

He watched her walk up the dark entry then accelerated away from the kerb as a smile played on his lips.

'Barry, wake up, I'm home.'

Blinking, Barry pulled himself up from the chair. 'What time is it?' he asked sleepily. When Grace told him that it was almost ten o'clock, he frowned. 'What you doin' home this early?'

She looked at the untidy lock of hair that had fallen across his brow, and his workworn hands, and tried desperately to push away the picture of Philip that was floating before her eyes. A feeling of panic engulfed her. 'Barry,' she said, almost desperately, 'I want you to take me to bed and make love to me.'

He was so shocked that for a second he was speechless. Grace had never, not once in all the time they had been together, ever made the first move. In fact, sometimes he had the sinking feeling that she only endured the sexual side of their relationship for his sake. But now that she had, a feeling of joy overcame him, and in an instant he was on his feet, wide awake and leading her towards the stairs door.

'Only too happy to oblige, Mrs Swan.'

He gripped her hand and pushed her before him up the stairs, and once they reached the privacy of their bedroom she began to pull her clothes off and fling them haphazardly about the room. Suddenly she longed to feel his hands on her body. When she stood naked before him, he gazed at her in awe. She was so beautiful that she took his breath away. Her lips were parted temptingly as she waited for his kiss and as he crossed to her she felt him harden against her. There was an urgency about her that had never been there before. An urgency that longed for everything that was familiar and dear. Anything that would take away the frightening feelings that coursed through her as she thought of Philip.

Barry laid her gently on the bed and as his lips roved across her body she waited for the tingling sensations that would surely follow in their wake. But although she waited and waited, there was nothing. She arched herself towards him, longing to feel him inside her and closed her eyes in anticipation. But when he did thrust into her, unable to restrain himself a moment longer, it was not his face she saw behind her closed lids, but Philip's.

'Love me!' she cried, as she tried to push away the image, but even as Barry's passion mounted, it was Philip whom she longed for, Philip she longed to be with.

Her passion died, as quickly as it had come, and suddenly all she wanted to do was curl up in a ball in the darkness and cry. Barry shuddered as his passion reached a climax and then it was over and he rolled off her to lie panting at her side.

'I love you, Grace,' he whispered, and when there was no answer his heart was heavy. If only she would say it, just once.

'Get some sleep, you've had a long day,' she murmured. Within minutes she felt him relax and soon his soft snores echoed around the room. A feeling of sadness overcame her as tears spilled onto her pillow in the darkness. What is happening to me? she asked herself, and the answer came back all too soon. *You're falling in love with Philip.* No! She tried to deny it. I'm Barry's wife and I love him. *But do you?* the persistent little voice niggled. *Do you really love him? Have you ever loved him? Or did you simply marry him to escape your aunt?*

The very idea was unthinkable. Creeping from the bed she dragged on her old robe and made her way downstairs, where she paced the small living room restlessly. Suddenly the comfortable little world that Barry and she had created looked set to crumble, and as she glanced at the home that she had always considered to be her palace, she saw it for the first time as it really was, nothing but a mismatch of second-hand furniture and worthless objects. Cheap home-made curtains hanging at the windows, equally cheap linoleum on the floor that no amount of polishing could improve on.

Had she waited, she might have met a man like Philip, a man who could provide the sort of life she had never known existed, a man who could set her heart racing with a single touch, for had she not in marrying Barry, exchanged one prison for another?

No, I *do* love Barry, she tried to convince herself. I have everything a woman could wish for. A home, be it ever so humble, a loving husband, and two beautiful children. I married him because I wanted to. Philip is just a friend, and that is all he will ever be.

So why then did her heart not agree?

Wearily she crept up to bed where she tossed and turned at the side of her husband until the first cold fingers of dawn washed the sky.

94

Chapter Ten

As Grace climbed into Philip's car a week later, she sensed an air of excitement about him. Smiling, she turned in her seat and waved to the children who were watching her from the window then looked back at him as he pulled away from the kerb.

'Well, something has certainly put the smile back on your face,' she joked. 'You look like the cat that got the cream. Have you and your wife managed to sort out your differences?'

'No, no, it's nothing like that, but it's something that I hope will make you smile too when I tell you about it.' His eyes were twinkling with mischief and she was intrigued.

'So come on. Tell me what it is and don't keep me in suspense.'

His good mood was infectious and she found herself laughing in anticipation.

'Right, I will then. It's like this, you see. I just happen to have found out about a competition we should enter.'

'You mean the one at the Locarno in Coventry next month?'

He shook his head impatiently. 'No, better than that. It's at the Tower Ballroom in Blackpool next Saturday and I *know* we could walk the floor with the prize now, so what do you say?'

'It's . . . utterly out of the question,' she stuttered. 'In case you'd forgotten, I happen to be the mother of two small children. I can't just leave them at the drop of a hat.'

He took his hand briefly off the steering-wheel to wave aside her objections. 'This is next Saturday we're talking about, and it's in *Blackpool*, not Timbuctoo. If you want to become known on the dancing circuit you have to be seen at the right venues, which means making the odd sacrifice. Surely Barry could cope with the children for just *one* night?'

'One night! You mean a *whole* night?' Grace was even more shocked.

'Well, of course one night. We would have to travel down the evening before to be sure of getting there on time. Barry could manage, couldn't he?'

'I . . . I suppose he could,' she muttered, somewhat reluctantly. 'But that's only if he wasn't planning to work on Saturday. Sometimes he does overtime if it's going and I don't think he'd be too thrilled at the prospect of having to miss that.'

'Couldn't their grandparents have them overnight then?' Philip seemed to have thought of everything, and Grace had to admit that she was tempted. After all, it would be her very first competition. But then would it really be such a good idea?

'I suppose I could ask them,' she replied, although she still had grave reservations. 'That is, if Barry agreed to me going, of course.'

'Brilliant!' He beamed and for now the subject was dropped.

Grace found it hard to concentrate that night as he whirled her around the dance-floor. The more she thought of it, the more she longed to go to Blackpool.

Much later in the evening he smiled at her as they sat outside her house in his car. 'So, will you ask Barry then?'

Taking a deep breath she nodded. 'Yes, I'll ask him. But how does Cheryl feel about it?' She knew from things he had told her that his relationship with his wife had gone from bad to worse over the last few weeks, but she was not prepared for what he said next.

'I'm afraid Cheryl and I have decided to separate. We will still live in the same house, in different rooms, for the sake of the children for a time. But to all intents and purposes our marriage is over.'

'Oh Philip, I'm so sorry. How awful for you.' She took his hand as he smiled sadly.

'It was entirely her choice. I think she has someone else, as I believe I confided to you some time ago, but there's nothing I can do about it. These things happen, I'm afraid.'

She was lost for words as she tried to contemplate how awful it must be for him, but then remembering the time and knowing that Barry was waiting up for her, she put her hand on the door handle.

'I shall have to go in now, Philip. But I will talk to Barry and if he agrees I'll get in touch with you.'

'Here, I'll give you the garage number. You can reach me there.' He fumbled in the glove compartment for a minute before handing her a card, and she slipped it into her handbag.

'Right, I'll go and put it to him. But I'm making no promises, mind. If he doesn't agree with it then as far as I'm concerned, that's the end of it.'

'That's fair enough. You can but try. I'll keep my fingers crossed and hope to hear from you.'

She waved as he pulled away and turning, she squared her shoulders before going to face Barry. As usual, he was fast asleep in the chair at the side of the fire. She sighed. Why couldn't he be more like Philip? Charming, handsome, and fun to be with. When she shook his shoulder gently, he looked up at her from red-rimmed eyes heavy with sleep.

'Hello, love. Had a good night, have you? I've missed you.'

'I have had a good night, as it happens – something really exciting has happened. Philip thinks we're ready to enter our first competition now, but that's where the problem lies. You see . . .' With the words tumbling out of her mouth she began to explain and when she had done he scratched his head in bewilderment.

'You mean to tell me you want to spend next Friday night in Blackpool with this here Philip?'

'I wouldn't have put it quite like that. I would be there for the competition, and if we're a pair I could hardly go without a partner, could I?'

He saw the longing in her eyes and his heart sank. He wanted to tell her, *No, you're not going. You belong here with me and the children.* But he loved her so much; it was hard to deny her anything.

'It would all be very open and above board, I assure you,' she rushed on breathlessly. 'And just *imagine* dancing in the Tower Ballroom.'

Personally he could think of nothing worse, but he knew how much Grace loved to dance and could see that it meant a great deal to her. 'Well, I suppose we could manage it one way or another,' he said, somewhat grudgingly.

Her whole face lit up. 'You mean I can go? You're really going to let me go?'

'Of course I am. You should know by now that you can wrap me round your little finger, woman. There ain't nothin' as you ask for as I wouldn't try an' get you.'

'Oh, Barry!' She leaped onto his lap in a completely uncharacteristic manner and covered his face in kisses as he chuckled with delight and made the most of every second.

'Here, steady on, gel. If this is how you're goin' to behave I'll be sendin' you off every week.'

She laughed and, jumping from his lap, she began to do a comical little dance around the room.

'Keep that up, an' you'll be doin' your ankle in, an' then you won't be goin' nowhere,' he teased, but nothing could spoil her delight at the prospect of the competition ahead.

She was still chattering away happily as they got ready for bed and he listened to her indulgently, thinking how beautiful she was when she laughed. She lay awake long after he had gone to sleep, her mind

97

full of the coming weekend. And then suddenly the first problem reared its ugly head and she came back down to earth with a bump. What would she wear? The only ballroom dress she had was the one she had made from the material she had bought at Birmingham rag market. It was pretty enough in its own way, and she prided herself that it was well-sewn. But she had no doubt that it would look positively cheap compared to the dresses that the other competitors would be wearing. Still, there was no chance of buying one; the gas bill had just dropped through the letterbox, and on top of that, Simon was desperate for a new pair of shoes. She sighed into the darkness, but then her spirits rose again at the thought of the adventure ahead and she finally fell asleep with a big smile on her face.

'Do you really think this is such a good idea, our Barry?' Daisy's face mirrored her concern as she stared at her son across the table. It was a cold blustery Sunday morning and he had taken the children for a walk and called in to see their grandma while Grace prepared the Sunday lunch.

'Grace don't ask for a lot, Mam,' he pointed out. 'An' I thought the break might do her good. She ain't goin' till I get home from work on Friday an' she'll be back Saturday night.'

'That's as maybe, lad. But he's a good-lookin' bugger, that Philip, from what I've heard of him, an' Grace is a beautiful young woman.'

'Yes, she is beautiful, Mam, an' she's also my wife. I'd trust Grace with me life if need be. If I feel all right about it, why can't you?'

Daisy swiped a lock of her frizzy hair from her creased forehead. 'I don't know what it is, but I've just got a bad feelin' about it. Why don't you get off your arse an' take her dancin' again so as she don't need another partner?'

Barry almost choked on the mouthful of tea he had just swallowed. 'Aw, give us a break, Mam.' He grinned. 'You know as well as me that I can't dance to save me life. I was never cut out to be a Fred Astaire.'

'Only because you've allus been too idle to learn. Grace, as you quite rightly say, don't ask for a lot, an' God knows the poor gel has had enough to put up with in her life, what with bein' brought up by that vicious old brute of an aunt of hers. An' let's face it, she jumped out o' the frying pan and into the fire when she married you, didn't she, 'cos life ain't been exactly easy for her, has it?' When he opened his mouth to protest she held her hand up. 'I don't mean to call you, love. Far from it. You've been a good husband and a good dad. What I mean is, you've never been exactly flush with money, what with trying to buy an' furnish your house on a shoestring and one thing and another. Grace is lookin' for a bit of excitement in her life, an' I think she finds it in her dancing. Trouble is, from where I'm standin', this here bloke who she's took up with is in a different class to us. He can show her another way o' life – and what happens if he turns her head? I mean, at the end o' the day, Grace is a lovely gel, but she's only flesh and blood, and she has her weaknesses just like the rest of us. Why don't you think about goin' with her again? With a few lessons under yer belt I've no doubt you could dance wi' the best of 'em.'

By now Barry was red-faced with rage, partly because he knew that what she said was true. He scraped his chair back from the table so fast that it almost overbalanced and slammed his mug down. 'I think it's time I was makin' tracks, Mam, before you an' me fall out. I know you mean well, but I'm afraid for once in me life I'm goin' to have to ask you to mind your own business.'

Before Daisy could say another word he strode into the front room with a face like thunder to collect the children and left, slamming the front door resoundingly behind him.

Daisy bit down on her lip as tears pricked at the back of her eyes.

Stan, who had listened to the whole of the exchange from behind his newspaper, sighed. 'You made a right cock up o' that, didn't you, love?'

'I suppose I did,' she muttered miserably. 'But I never meant to upset him.'

'Then happen in future it might pay you to keep your mouth shut, woman. You should know better at your age than to try to interfere between husband an' wife.' Seeing her deep distress his tone softened. 'Look, love, don't go whippin' yourself. What's said is said an' there ain't no takin' it back, but our Barry is a mild-mannered man. It will all be forgot the next time you see him, you mark me words.'

'I just hope you're right, Stan,' she muttered, but the deep feeling of misgiving remained.

'Well, all I can say is you must have the luck o' the Irish. I can't see my Dick lettin' me go swannin' off to Blackpool with a bloke for a dirty weekend.' Chris grinned mischievously as colour washed Grace's cheeks.

'It's not like that at all, Chris. You should know me better than that by now.' Grace looked deeply offended, and not wishing to hurt her feelings, Chris apologised.

'Sorry, mate. You know me, I've got a gob like a parish oven. I were only teasin'. I'm still jealous though, you jammy sod. What you goin' to wear anyway?'

Grace, who could never stay angry for long, grinned ruefully. 'It will have to be the dress I made, won't it? There's no way I can afford to buy one, so I'll have to make do.'

'Huh! No doubt you'll still knock spots off half the women there anyway. You could look good in a sack, you could.' Chris swirled the tea-leaves round in her mug as she watched Grace ironing. 'So where will you be stayin'?'

'I've no idea,' Grace admitted. 'I rang Philip at work to tell him that Barry had no objections to me going, and he told me to leave all the arrangements to him. I suppose he'll book us into a bed and breakfast somewhere.'

'Wish it were me.' Chris sighed enviously. 'Have you ever been to Blackpool before?'

'Never.' Grace smiled.

'Ah well, you're in for a right treat then. There ain't nowhere in the world like Blackpool. Me an' Dick went there for us honeymoon an' we had the time of our lives. I couldn't go on any rides round the Pleasure Beach though, 'cos I were up the duff with our Jenny at the time, but there's so much to do there you hardly know what to do first.'

'Such as what?' Grace was intrigued and seeing that she had a captive audience, Chris went on.

'It's hard to know where to begin, to be honest . . . There's the Illuminations, for a start. Ah, wait till you see 'em – seven miles of 'em from end to end there is. An' then there's Madame Tussaud's Waxworks, an' the trams.'

'I doubt I'll get to see much,' Grace told her. 'We'll be in the Tower at the competition all day Saturday, so we'll probably only have a couple of hours on Friday night to look around. Not even that if the traffic is bad, and then we'll be starting for home as soon as the competition is over.'

Chris glanced at the clock and rose hastily. 'Christ, I didn't realise it were that time. Dick will be in for his tea in half an hour an' I ain't peeled a single spud yet. I'd best be off, an' if I don't see you again before you go, have a good time, but don't do anythin' I wouldn't do, eh?'

Grace giggled. 'That gives me plenty of scope, doesn't it?'

Chris laughed as she disappeared out of the door, and for a moment Grace became still. The day after tomorrow she would be going and she could still hardly believe it. She was looking forward to it far more than she cared to admit, but her excitement was tempered with guilt at the thought of leaving Barry and the children, even if it was only for one night. She had no qualms about being alone with Philip. He had always behaved impeccably and she had her own feelings well and truly under control. Weeks ago she had been forced to admit that she was attracted to him, but her commonsense had prevailed. She was a married woman, and although Philip's marriage may not have been made in heaven, he was a married man. There was no one and nothing in the world that meant more to her than her husband and children, and so for their sake they could never be more than friends, not that Philip had ever so much as intimated that they should be. Theirs was purely a dancing partnership and so far as she was concerned, that's all it would ever be. In a happy frame of mind she began to prepare the tea.

'Now are you quite sure as you've got everythin'?' Barry asked yet again. He was standing on the pavement with Simon in his arms and Wendy at his side as Philip loaded Grace's case into the boot of his car.

'You've already asked me that at least a dozen times,' she teased him. He flushed as Philip came round to open the passenger door for her.

Barry had come home from work early so that she and Philip could make an early start, and had even pressed some spending money that she knew they could ill afford into her hand. Before she even got there she knew that she would probably spend it on gifts for the children, but the kindly gesture had touched her all the same.

'Now are you quite sure that you'll be all right?' she fretted.

Now it was his turn to grin. 'You've already asked *me* that a dozen times an' all.'

Grace bent and kissed Wendy, who was looking dangerously tearful. 'You be a really good girl for Daddy, eh? And if you are, I might bring you something nice back tomorrow.' Wendy was instantly in a better frame of mind as Grace turned her attention to Simon. 'And you be a good boy too and you might get a present as well.' Now it was Barry's turn, and aware that Philip was watching them she pecked him self-consciously on the cheek.

'I'll see you tomorrow then.'

He nodded as she slipped into the passenger seat.

Philip came round the car and shook his hand. 'Don't worry, Barry. I'll take good care of her.'

'You'd better.' Barry looked him straight in the eye, and Philip

101

climbed into the car and started the engine. Then they were off and Grace turned to wave at her family standing on the kerb, feeling suddenly as if she was leaving them for ever. When they disappeared around a bend in the road, she took out a handkerchief and sniffed noisily.

Philip grinned. 'You're only going for one night,' he pointed out with a hint of amusement in his voice.

Grace nodded. 'I know – but I've never left them before.'

'I'm sure they'll be fine, and once we get there you'll be enjoying yourself so much I doubt you'll even think of them.'

In her wildest dreams, Grace could never imagine a time when she wouldn't think of her family.

Looking at him, she asked curiously, 'How does your wife feel about you going?' Instantly she could have bitten her tongue off as the smile slid from his face and he became solemn.

'My wife couldn't give a damn if I never went home again. I actually asked her if she would like to come with us, but she almost bit my head off.'

'I'm so sorry, Philip. I take that to mean that things are no better then?'

'Better, huh! They're going from bad to worse. She doesn't even come home half the time now. Too busy with her fancy man, no doubt. Still, I suppose I shouldn't expect any more. It's not the first time and no doubt he will go the same way as all the others eventually.'

Grace was appalled at the picture he conjured up and felt desperately sorry for him. 'Why do you put up with it?' she dared to ask.

He shrugged. 'The kids, I suppose. Even though they're not at home half the time, I like them to know I'm there for them even if their mother isn't.'

'You're such a good man, Philip,' she whispered admiringly.

His good humour returned. 'I'll tell you what, we've got this far so let's just go and enjoy ourselves, eh?'

Her spirits lifted as she returned his smile and a little bubble of excitement tempered with a lot of nerves filled her. 'Do you think we stand any chance in this competition?' she asked.

He nodded enthusiastically. 'We're going to wipe the floor with them,' he prophesied confidently. 'It might only be an amateur competition this time, but you never know who's there at events like this. If we were to be recognised by the right people, we might even get signed up to join a professional formation team and then the sky's the limit.'

She leaned back in the luxurious leather seat to enjoy the ride, and the wonderful smell of his expensive after-shave, so different to the smell of grease and oil that she had come to associate with Barry as she slowly began to relax. They talked of this and that, and Grace expressed her concerns about how worried she had been about the children ever since Myra Hindley and Ian Brady, now known as the Moors Murderers, had been sentenced to life imprisonment for the murder of two children and a teenager earlier in the year.

'For weeks afterwards I hardly dared let them out of my sight,' she confided. 'I mean, can you imagine anyone being evil enough to do that to innocent children?'

Philip raised his eyebrows and risked taking his eyes off the road for a moment to frown at her. 'Grace, will you *please* stop worrying about the children! Barry is perfectly capable of looking after them for just one night. We're supposed to be enjoying ourselves.'

Grace grinned guiltily. Philip was right, but it was hard to just switch off. Even so she deliberately kept the conversation light from then on and studiously avoided talking about the children or his wife for the rest of the way.

They did the journey in just under three hours, and at almost six o'clock they were cruising along the Golden Mile. It had been a pleasant journey and Grace had discovered that the pair of them had a lot in common. They liked the same music, the same food, not to mention their mutual love of ballroom dancing, and he was easy to talk to. Her eyes sparkled like a child's as she stared out of the car window at the bright lights.

'Oh Philip, I never in my wildest dreams imagined that it would be anything like this,' she gasped.

'Wait till you see the hotel I've booked us into then,' he said.

For an instant she frowned. 'I hope it isn't anywhere too expensive.' Her voice was filled with concern.

'This is my treat, as I told you before we came, so just sit back and enjoy it. We should be there soon.'

Grace did as she was told as they drove past the swarms of holidaymakers. Brightly lit trams ran back and forth the length of the sea-front, disguised as rockets and spaceships and all manner of weird and wonderful contraptions. Everywhere she looked there were children with wide smiles on their faces, clutching candyfloss and hot dogs, as their harassed parents hauled them along in the biting wind. Groups of teenagers in scanty outfits sporting Kiss Me Quick hats were laughing and having fun, and she found herself being caught up in the atmosphere of the place.

103

They were driving towards the North Shore when Philip suddenly indicated and turned into the car park of a large hotel on the front. Grace stared at it incredulously. It was big and imposing and looked very, very expensive.

'We're not staying *here*, are we?' she asked in amazement as he drew the car to a halt.

He nodded with a big grin on his face. 'We most certainly are, madam. My motto is, if a thing's worth doing it's worth doing well. So come on. If we hurry we should still be in time for dinner.'

Grace was suddenly very aware of the cheap off-the-peg outfit she was wearing as Philip came round to her side of the car and opened the door with a gentlemanly bow. He offered her his arm and as if he could read her mind, he leaned towards her and whispered, 'You look absolutely stunning, Grace.' He said it with such sincerity that a little thrill rippled through her as she linked her arm through his and climbed the imposing steps to the foyer of the hotel.

If anything, the inside was even more impressive than the outside and Grace began to feel a little out of her depth. Huge crystal chandeliers hung from elaborately carved ceilings, and the carpet was so thick that she felt her feet sinking into it as they approached the desk. Philip gave their names as she stared about her in awe, and then the next second a liveried porter was leading them towards a mirrored lift. When it stopped on the first floor she followed Philip along a seemingly endless corridor as he peered at the door numbers. 'Ah, here we are. This is your room, Grace, and I'm right next door.'

He placed the key in the lock and turned it, then threw the door open with a flourish as she stepped past him into the room. For a second she stood rooted to the spot as her mouth dropped open in amazement. It was truly the most beautiful room she had ever seen, the sort of room she had only ever glimpsed in magazines and fairy stories. The walls were a soft rose pink and the carpet on the floor, which was a slightly deeper shade, was as thick as the one in the foyer and stretched from wall to wall. At the windows hung heavy chintz curtains and there were matching ones hanging from a canopy that framed the bed with its matching bedspread. Fresh flowers in beautiful cut-glass vases stood everywhere she looked, and as she walked slowly further into the room their perfume met her.

Philip watched her with an indulgent smile on his face. She was so overcome that she hardly knew what to say. 'Oh Philip, it's . . . Well, it's just . . .'

'I hope you are trying to say that the room meets with your approval,' he joked.

'Oh, much more than that. Why, it's absolutely beautiful.'

'Good, I'm glad you like it. Now, I'm going to slip off to my room and get changed for dinner. The porter should arrive with your bags any minute, so shall we meet downstairs in the dining room – in, say, half an hour?'

She nodded fervently, feeling almost as if she had been transported to another world, and he left her to explore her room in peace.

The second he had gone she crossed to a door, which she found led to an en-suite bathroom, and again she was totally awed. The bathroom was decorated in much the same colours as the bedroom. Every single wall was mirrored from floor to ceiling, making it appear much bigger than it actually was. Enormous fluffy towels were draped across the side of an ornate bathtub and she had the urge to throw her clothes off there and then and dive in. But she didn't because there was still far too much to explore, so she hurried into the bedroom again and went to stand at the window. The sight that met her eyes almost took her breath away.

Below her, the Illuminations stretched away as far as the eye could see, and beyond that a silver moon hung suspended above a black velvet sea. On the horizon, she could see ships with their lights twinkling in the darkness and she felt as if she could have stood admiring the view all night. But just then there was a tap at the door and a porter appeared with her luggage. He placed it down for her whilst she fumbled in her purse for a tip and then he left and she knew that she had better get ready for dinner.

After quickly unpacking she decided to wear a little black dress she had made herself some time ago. It was very plain, but the material was good quality, so she hoped that she would not look too out of place amongst some of the women she had glimpsed when they entered the hotel; women who she dared to guess would spend more money on one outfit than she had on her entire home-made wardrobe. She washed and changed quickly and then applied the minimum amount of make-up and brushed her hair till it shone like silk. Taking one last appraising glance at herself in the mirror she knew that there was no more she could do, so with some trepidation she took the lift down to the elaborate dining room.

Philip was already there waiting for her. When he saw her he rose from his seat and looked at her admiringly. Many of the women at the surrounding tables were dripping in diamonds and gold. He was quick to notice that although Grace wore no jewellery whatsoever, apart from her plain gold wedding band and her modest engagement ring, still she managed to outshine them, and the glances

105

of the men as she approached the table assured him that they felt the same.

He pulled her chair out for her and looked at her in the glow of the candle that stood in an ornate silver candlestick in the middle of the table.

'No one would ever believe that you had been to work, looked after two children, and then travelled all the way here tonight,' he told her sincerely. 'You look as fresh as a daisy.'

Grace smiled becomingly, thinking that with his slicked-back dark hair and his wonderful blue eyes he looked like an older version of James Dean. The table looked wonderful and she was suddenly glad that her aunt had taught her impeccable table manners, otherwise she might have been worried about the vast amount of silver cutlery laid out before her.

A waiter approached and handed them two beautifully printed menus, but Grace was more than happy to leave the choice to Philip, assuring him that she would be happy with anything he cared to order, which he did with a flair that told her he was used to being waited on. The wine flowed like water, and somewhere in the middle of the meal Barry and the children and their humdrum life suddenly seemed a million miles away, and she determined to make the most of every minute of what was fast becoming a magical interlude.

Chapter Eleven

'The night is young, so what would madam care to do? It seems a shame not to make the most of it.' Philip's eyes twinkled suggestively, and as Grace leaned back in her chair she felt herself responding to his light-hearted mood. As the tiny diamond engagement ring that Barry had bought her caught the light from the candle in the centre of the table, guilt momentarily coursed through her but she pushed the feeling away. She didn't want to think of Barry right now.

She was comfortably full from the delicious meal they had just eaten, and as she had consumed far more wine than she had ever drunk in her whole life before, she was feeling uncharacteristically flirtatious.

'What would sir suggest?'

He tapped his chin. 'Mmm, now let me see. We could go to a show, or perhaps you would rather see the Illuminations properly? Or we could hop on a tram and go the whole length of them right from the North to the South Shore if you liked.'

Grace nodded eagerly, suddenly feeling like a child that had been let out of school early. 'Ooh, yes, please. I'd love to do that.'

'Right. In that case, we ought to pop up and get changed into something warmer. Blackpool can be quite nippy at the best of times, and if you go out in that dress, as becoming as it is, you just might freeze to death, or catch your death of cold at the very least.' He walked around the table and helped her from her seat.

'Oh dear,' she giggled, as she swayed unsteadily. 'I must have had more wine than I thought.'

'And why not indeed? You are here to enjoy yourself, my dear, and the odd drop of wine never hurt anybody.'

'I don't know about the odd drop,' Grace replied, eyeing the two empty bottles on the table. 'I think I had far more than that.'

He took her elbow and steered her through the tables towards the foyer. 'So what? Tonight is yours to do as you will. Just let your hair down and enjoy yourself. You'll be back to reality all too soon.'

They passed beneath the sparkling crystal chandelier as he led her into the lift that would take them upstairs to their rooms, slipping his arm around her slim waist to steady her as it rose. Once alone she rummaged through her wardrobe. Fortunately she had packed a pair of bell-bottom trousers, and she slipped into them and pulled a warm jumper over her head. Then she hurried to the mirror and brushed her hair and applied fresh lipstick and was ready to go. Philip tapped at the door within minutes, and when she opened it he looked her up and down appreciatively.

'I really don't know how you do it. It doesn't matter what you wear, you always look beautiful.'

She flushed happily at the compliment, enjoying herself far more than she cared to admit and relishing Philip's full attention. Somehow he managed to make her feel that she was the only woman in a room – the only woman in the whole world for that matter – and she liked it. He held her coat as she shrugged her arms into it and then followed him from the hotel and out into the chilly evening. Within seconds the wind had whipped her hair into a mass of shiny dark tangles and her cheeks were glowing. She had to bend to walk against the wind and when Philip offered his arm she tucked her own into his gratefully as he towed her along. They came to a tram stop and she hid behind him, feeling incredibly small behind his solid broad back. When the tram arrived he pushed her up the steps before him and she sank gratefully into the nearest window seat as he squashed into the one beside her. When his arm slid along the back of the seat she made no complaint. After all, she reasoned, he was only trying to get his best view of the lights as he leaned across her. And then she gave herself up to the magic that had entranced millions of people before her, and home and Barry, and even the children were forgotten for now.

The tram dropped them at the South Shore, and as Philip helped her down from it her eyes flew to the Pleasure Beach. Everywhere she looked was teeming with people, all laughing and happy, and her light-hearted mood increased even more.

'Would you like to look round the fair?' he asked, following her eyes. When she nodded eagerly he good-naturedly led her towards it. On the way they stopped at the first shop they came to and Grace bought some brightly coloured sticks of Blackpool Rock, then they headed for the Pleasure Beach again. Without thinking she caught his hand and dragged him towards the ghost train.

'Oh Philip, could we go on this? I've never been to a fair before and I've always wanted to go on a ghost train.'

He threw back his head and laughed. 'I don't see why not. Although if you don't like it I don't want you blaming me.'

'Oh I won't,' she hastened to assure him, and so they joined the queue. Once seated in the car she was not quite so brave, and as it started up and swept them towards the dark entrance she clung to his arm and buried her face in his shirtfront, revelling in the clean masculine smell of him. He laughed and urged her to open her eyes just in time for a vampire to loom at them out of the pitch-black. She squealed and hid her face again and did not surface until they had come back out.

'Well – that was a bit of a waste of time,' he teased.

Shame-faced, she looked back at him. 'Sorry. It seems I'm not quite as brave as I thought I was.'

'Let's see if we can't find you something a little tamer then,' he said indulgently, and taking her hand he hauled her through the crowds until they came to the Big Dipper.

'Now we *must* have a go on this,' he told her, as she stared at it with some trepidation. 'No one should come to Blackpool and not have a go on the Big Dipper.'

Her knees began to tremble as the queue took them ever nearer to the front, and then a young spotty-faced assistant was strapping them into the car and it was too late to change her mind. Once more she closed her eyes as the car climbed the steep incline, but right at the top she opened them briefly to see Blackpool spread out before her and it took her breath away. Then they were hurtling down the other side and she opened her lips and screamed at the top of her lungs, causing Philip to laugh uncontrollably.

After the Big Dipper they went on the bumper cars and so many other rides that Grace lost count of them until finally she dragged Philip to a halt and begged, 'Could we *please* sit down for a minute? My ribs ache from so much laughing, and my poor feet are killing me. I'm afraid whoever designed these wedge shoes didn't intend them for walking.'

Instantly he was the perfect gentleman as he took her elbow and steered her through the crowd to the outskirts of the fair. 'Of course we can. We'll get out of here now if you're sure there's nothing else you'd like to go on? Let's go and have a drink somewhere.'

The noise of the fair receded as they crossed the road and walked slowly along the front, and soon only the sound of the waves crashing on the shore could be heard.

'Oh Philip, this is just perfect.' Grace sighed contentedly as she stared at the sparkling black waves far out at sea. He hooked her arm through his again and smiled down at her.

'I have to admit I was just thinking the same thing.' His face suddenly became sad and she stared at him curiously.

'What's wrong?' Her voice was gentle.

He shrugged. 'Why couldn't I have married someone like you, Grace? Someone who appreciated the simple things in life.'

When she raised her eyebrows, he looked out at the choppy waves and went on, 'My wife would never be seen dead in a place like Blackpool. It would be nowhere near grand enough for her. Even the hotel we're staying at wouldn't come up to her standards. Nothing is ever good enough for her, although I've tried so hard to please her over the years.'

Grace stared at him as a wave of sympathy washed over her. Philip's wife sounded awful and yet he was such a kind, generous man.

'Perhaps things will get better,' she suggested falteringly.

He shook his head as they turned and crossed the road, and he led her towards the entrance to a hotel.

'No, things won't improve now. I've had to face the fact that my marriage is over. We can't all be as lucky as you, Grace.'

By now they were inside the hotel and ever the gentleman, he led her towards a seat before hurrying away to get some drinks. When he returned she eyed the glass he placed in front of her doubtfully.

'It's brandy. I thought it might warm you up,' he told her.

Grace sighed. 'I'm not so sure I should drink it. I had rather a lot of wine at dinner and if I drink that on top, you might have to carry me back to the hotel,' she pointed out.

A wry grin played around his lips. 'I can think of far worse things I might have to do,' he said huskily.

Grace lifted the glass and sipped at it, coughing as the fiery liquid took her breath. They lapsed into silence for a while, and then she looked up to see Philip watching her intently.

'You know, Grace, you're a bit of a mystery to me. What I mean is – I've partnered you for some time now and yet I know very little about you at all. You don't often say much about yourself.'

Grace shrugged self-consciously. 'Perhaps that's because there's very little to say. Compared to some, I've led a rather boring life.'

'Mm – that could well be a matter of opinion. You've obviously had a good upbringing. What I mean by that is, the way you talk and conduct yourself tell me that you were brought up in a rather upper-class background.'

Grace laughed bitterly. 'If you can call being brought up by a maiden aunt who believed that to show a child any tenderness or affection was a failing then I suppose I was.'

When he raised his eyebrows questioningly she looked away as she

110

thought back to her childhood. 'I shouldn't have said that,' she said quietly. 'I suppose I'm being rather unfair and ungrateful. My parents were killed in an air raid during the war when I was very young, and my aunt took me in.'

'Did you not get on?'

She felt colour rush into her cheeks. 'My aunt was . . .' She struggled to find the right words. 'I suppose it wasn't really a matter of getting on. My aunt was very strict and believed that children should be seen and not heard.'

'I see.' He watched her intently for a moment before asking, 'So how did you come to meet Barry?'

She glanced at him curiously. 'Why do you ask that?'

'To be honest, I can't help but notice that you seem to be . . . rather different. What I mean is, Barry is obviously a very nice man but if you don't mind me saying, you seem to be rather ill-matched.'

Grace glared at him indignantly. 'Barry, as you say, is a very nice man. In fact, he was the very first person to ever show me any love or affection.'

'Ah!' Something in the way he said it infuriated her all the more.

'If you are thinking that's why I married him, you are wrong,' she told him hotly. 'I married Barry because I *love* him, not because I wanted to escape from my aunt.'

He held his hands up as if to shield her off. 'All right, all right. I had no intention of upsetting you. Although I have to say, it sounds like you're trying to convince yourself, not me.'

Grace stamped to her feet and snatched up her coat, ignoring her unfinished drink. 'I think it's time we were getting back to the hotel, don't you?'

Instantly he was on his feet, his face contrite. 'Oh Grace, I've offended you. I'm *so* sorry. I suppose because my own marriage is such a mess, I can't see any good in anyone else's. Please forgive me, I wouldn't hurt your feelings for the world.'

He looked so genuinely upset that her temper dissolved instantly. 'It's all right. No offence taken. I think I'm touchy because I've had a drop too much to drink.' But underneath she was far more disturbed than she cared to admit, for his words had hit a raw nerve.

They walked back outside and she was glad of the wind that defied conversation. Philip stepped to the kerb and after hailing a passing taxi he hustled her inside. The short ride back to the hotel was made in silence, as Grace began to question herself. Why had she reacted so strongly to what Philip had said? Could it be that she and Barry really *were* a mismatch? Did she *really* love him? And if she did, then why had she never ever once told him so? With the amount of alcohol she had drunk, the questions whirled around in her head finding no satisfactory answer, and by the time the taxi drew into the hotel car park her light-hearted mood had disappeared and she was suddenly tired and wanted only her bed and solitude.

Philip paid the driver as she hurried up the steps out of the coastal wind. Once inside the warmth of the hotel he nodded towards the bar.

'How about a nightcap before we hit the sack?'

She shook her head. 'No, thanks, Philip. I've had a lovely time but I'm ready for bed now. I want to phone Barry before it's too late.'

She saw the disappointment on his face, but he offered no argument. Instead he simply led her towards the lift and stood silently at her side as it rose to the first floor. Once outside her bedroom door he took her hand and kissed it. His eyes were gentle as he smiled at her.

'I'll see you in the morning then. All bright-eyed and bushy-tailed hopefully at breakfast.'

She nodded and without another word he inclined his head and strode away to his room next door to hers.

Once inside her own room she suddenly felt a need to hear Barry's voice. Of course there was no chance of that, for they didn't have a phone at home. But what she could do was ring Chris, who had promised she would pass any messages on. After fumbling in her bag for the number she crossed to the telephone that stood on a small ornate table and dialled the number with shaking fingers. Within seconds, Chris's voice came on the line.

'Hello.'

A wave of homesickness washed over Grace as she pictured her friend at home in Nuneaton. 'Hello, Chris. It's me, Grace.'

'Bloody hell, mate – what you doing phoning me when you're with Lover Boy?'

Grace grinned. 'Behave yourself, Chris. Lover Boy, as you call him, has gone to bed and so will I in a minute.'

'Well, that's more like it, gel. Never waste an opportunity, that's what I say.'

'Oh Chris,' Grace giggled, 'I shall be going to bed *alone*, I can assure you. I just wondered if you would pop round and let Barry know that I arrived safely and check on the children for me.'

'For God's sake, woman. Can't you give over worryin' for one bleedin' night?' Chris said in her own blunt way. 'You're comin' home tomorrow. Why, Barry an' the kids will hardly have had time to miss you.'

112

'Even so, I would be grateful if you'd just pop round for me and let them all know I'm thinking of them.'

'Aw, I suppose you'll never let me live it down if I don't.' Chris sighed dramatically. 'Consider it done. But take a word of advice. Make the most of every minute, gel. Life's too short, an' no offence but your Barry is hardly a laugh a minute, is he? Blimey, I tell you now, if it were me there with that good-lookin' bugger he wouldn't know what had hit him.'

Grace chuckled, although inside, her heart twisted. First Philip and now Chris had questioned her marriage to Barry tonight and it was unnerving to say the least. When she placed the phone down she crossed to the window and stared out into the night. The lights below her were still twinkling brightly but somehow they had lost their charm now and suddenly she wished with all her being that she had never agreed to come. Once again she found herself being drawn to Philip as she compared his dark good looks to her husband. Just being near him could arouse feelings in her that she had never felt for Barry and it was frightening to say the very least. To her Barry represented everything that was solid and stable, whereas Philip could make her feel beautiful and special.

Angry with herself for allowing such thoughts, she began to fling her clothes off. As she crossed to the wardrobe to collect her night-dress she caught sight of herself in a long mahogany cheval mirror. She paused and stared. Her aunt had always taught her that it was dirty to look at one's naked body, but now she found that she could not help herself. A young woman with long slender legs looked solemnly back at her as she continued to stare. Her hair hung down her back in long silky ringlets, teased into curls by the wind outside. Her breasts stood high and pert, their nipples erect and proud, and between her legs a dark triangle rose temptingly to a smooth taut stomach. Suddenly deeply embarrassed she found herself wondering what it would feel like to have Philip's hands roving across her smooth skin. But she had no time to ponder, for just then the door suddenly opened and there he was. Colour flooded her cheeks as he stared at her hungrily, and yet she found she was rooted to the spot and could make no attempt to cover herself. He crossed to her slowly, drinking in the sight of her, and then he was an arm's length away and she could only stare at him as if mesmerised.

'Oh Grace. You're so beautiful. You must know that I love you. I think I have since the very first minute I met you.'

As he reached out and tentatively stroked her breast, a million fire-works exploded in her brain and she was helpless to stop him. Very

113

slowly he removed his jacket, allowing it to fall on the floor beside him, then his shirt and the rest of his clothes followed until he was standing before her naked. She stared up into his eyes, drowning in their depths, until very gently, his lips came down on hers and she knew that there was no going back. Perhaps deep down she had always known that this moment was inevitable since the second she saw him, so why fight it? A picture of Barry flashed before her eyes, but she pushed all thoughts of him impatiently away. This was the moment she had longed for, dreamed of, and she gave herself up to the pleasure of feeling Philip's strong arms about her, and breathing in the raw masculine smell of him. Very gently he led her to the bed and peeled back the covers. Almost before she knew it they were lying side by side, their arms entwined. For the first time in her life, Grace felt truly alive.

'Oh Philip, I think I'm falling in love with you,' she whispered, as his lips left a trail of fire on her breasts, and slowly their passion mounted until he could control himself no longer and he rolled his weight onto her. She gave herself willingly, whole-heartedly as joy coursed through her. So this then was love? Whatever it was she savoured every second, every sensation until finally it was over and she lay contented in his strong arms. Never ever had lovemaking been anything like this with Barry. Only then did guilt kick in as she stared at him from beneath her long dark lashes.

'What have we done?' she whispered fretfully, but he silenced her with a kiss.

'Shush, love. Don't have regrets now. We were meant to be. You and Barry were never suited. You must see that.'

She nodded numbly, finally accepting the truth of what he said. 'I think I married him because he was the first person to ever show me any real affection. And yes, he was a way of getting free from my aunt. But he's such a *good* person. If he ever found out what had just happened he would be devastated.'

Philip shrugged. 'These things happen. It's unfortunate, but you can't spend the rest of your life with a man you don't love just because of one mistake.'

'But what about the children?' Grace was glad of the darkness that hid the tears that were sliding down her cheeks.

'Don't think about that now. We'll just take one step at a time and see how we go from here.'

She nestled further into his arms, relishing the regular beat of his heart against her naked breast. After a time she nudged him gently. 'You should go back to your own room now.'

He laughed softly, but obediently swung his legs out of the warm bed. Padding across to his jacket, which he had so hastily discarded on the floor he took a packet of Park Drive from the pocket and after lighting one, he crossed to the window and stared out. She lay silent, watching him as he smoked his cigarette and the enormity of what she had just done slowly sank in. Eventually he turned and slowly dressed, then crossing to the bed, where she lay with the covers tucked up to her chin he kissed her softly full on the lips.

'Goodnight, sweetheart. I'll see you in the morning bright and early. We have to be at the ballroom for ten so we'll have time to have a nice leisurely breakfast, then we'll go and show them how it should be done.'

There was a trace of possessiveness in his voice, which she had never heard before that set her heart thumping. Already she was deeply regretting what had happened, but she was so drained emotionally that all she longed for was solitude and the chance to try and put her thoughts back into some form of order. She nodded numbly and lay until the door closed gently behind him.

Once she was alone she dragged herself from the bed and began to pace the room as tears coursed down her cheeks. She found herself thinking of her aunt – of all the times Emily had told her that she was bad, just as she had declared her mother had been before her. Perhaps she had been right after all? Barry was a good man, a kind man, and now whether she liked it or not she was an adulteress, and he didn't deserve it. But it was too late for regrets now; what was done was done. What she had to decide now was what was going to happen next.

Grace thought of Wendy and Simon and the small house that up until now had been her palace, and she knew then that nothing could ever come of her relationship with Philip. It had been a pleasant interlude in her otherwise humdrum life, and that was what it must remain. He had shown her briefly what it was to have money and to live another way of life. He had also shown her what lovemaking could be like. But now it must end; it was time to come back to reality. Tomorrow she would dance with him, but then she would tell him that they must never see each other again.

With her mind made up, she crept back into bed, trying to ignore the scent of him that still lingered, and there she lay, tossing and turning until the early hours when at last she fell into a restless sleep.

Chapter Twelve

Grace woke to the sound of rain lashing against the window. Her eyes felt heavy from lack of sleep. As she thought back to the previous night she wished again with all her heart that she had never agreed to come. But still, in a few hours they would be setting off for home, and then she determined that she would put the whole unfortunate incident behind her and become the sort of model wife that she knew Barry deserved.

She dressed casually for breakfast and was almost ready to go down to the dining room when there was a tap at her door. Guessing that it would be Philip, she snatched up her bag. She had no wish to be alone with him, for despite her resolutions she couldn't trust herself, so instead she slipped into the corridor to join him. He instantly sensed her coolness towards him, but ever the perfect gentleman, he said nothing; he simply followed her at a discreet distance to the lift, and she respected him for his tactfulness.

Breakfast was a silent affair. Grace merely picked at her food; the light-hearted mood of the previous evening was gone. It was a relief when it was time to go to their rooms and change for the competition. Philip seemed distracted, and as they were taking the lift, he asked, 'Do you mind me asking what you are thinking of wearing, Grace?'

She tensed as a picture of her homemade dress floated before her eyes. 'I shall be wearing my usual dress – the one I made myself. I hope you won't be ashamed of me. It's well-made, even if I do say so myself.' The proud jut of her chin made him admire her all the more.

'I could never be ashamed of you,' he hastened to assure her. 'But before you get changed I have something for you. Would you mind if I brought it along to your room?'

Every instinct she had told her to refuse, but politeness dictated otherwise. 'Of course you may,' she told him quietly. As they neared his room he nodded solemnly and disappeared through the door.

Minutes later, as she sat at her dressing-table doing her hair, there was a tap at her door and Philip appeared carrying an enormous cardboard box. She raised her eyebrows as he placed it down on the bed.

'Now please don't be angry with me. I had to guess at the size.' He looked almost embarrassed as curiosity got the better of her and she crossed to stand beside him.

'Go on, please,' he urged. 'Take a look and tell me what you think.'

Slowly she wrestled with the lid of the box and when it finally fell away she gasped at its contents. Nestling amongst a bed of tissue paper was the most beautiful ballgown she had ever seen. Speechless, she gently withdrew it and held it against her. The top was strapless, the bodice totally encrusted with pearls and sequins that caught and reflected the light all around the room. A full skirt that consisted of layer upon layer of stiff net petticoats topped off by a shiny silk over-skirt in a soft cream colour fell from the bodice. The colour, just as he had hoped, set off her dark hair and creamy skin to perfection.

'Oh Philip,' she whispered eventually, as she held it against her and twirled in front of the cheval mirror. 'It must have cost an absolute fortune. I . . . I can't accept this.'

'I sincerely hope you can,' he said. 'I'm afraid it wouldn't look right on me.'

Dragging her eyes away from the dress, she stared at him in disbelief. 'It's the most beautiful gown I've ever seen,' she breathed.

He sighed with relief. 'Thank goodness for that. But there's just one more thing you need to set it off.' Fishing in his jacket pocket he withdrew a long slim leather case and handed it to her. She placed the dress reverently across the bed before taking the box from him with some trepidation. When she sprang the lid she gasped again as a wonderful sapphire necklace winked up at her.

'Oh, this really *is* too much.' Her eyes were full of tears at his generosity, but he was in no mood to listen to her objections. Hooking the necklace from its velvet bed he fastened it around her neck and turned her to look in the mirror as he peeped across her shoulder.

'There, look – it might have been made for you. The sapphires exactly match the colour of your eyes, just as I knew they would. I have a feeling that you are going to be the belle of the ball, madam. And now, if you will excuse me, I must go and get ready myself. When I come back for you I shall expect to find you looking absolutely gorgeous – not that you don't already, of course.'

He slipped away before she could begin to voice the objections that he could see were hovering on her lips, and once alone again she stared at his presents open-mouthed. Never in her wildest dreams had she ever thought to own a dress or jewellery of this worth. The necklace alone must have cost more than Barry and she could earn in a month combined, and yet Philip had given them as if they were mere trifles. She chewed on her lip, knowing that she shouldn't accept them, but then her eyes fell on the homemade dress hanging on the wardrobe door, that she had so painstakingly stitched, and she was persuaded to give in to temptation. If she did, she knew that things would become even more complicated than they already were, for if she wore the dress, how could she tell Philip that she never intended to see him, let alone dance with him, again?

She fingered the folds of the dress. Never in her whole life had she owned anything so beautiful. Even on her wedding day she had opted to buy a suit that could be worn again, and now here she was confronted with a dress that would have done justice to a princess.

'I'll just try it on to see how it looks,' she muttered to the empty room, and within minutes she was staring at herself in the mirror. It was almost as if another person were looking back at her, for she hardly recognised herself. Just as Philip had said, the dress might have been made for her, for it fitted like a glove. The low-cut bodice clung to her, revealing a deep cleavage that made her blush, and as the skirt flared, the tiny sequins that were sewn here and there on it caught and reflected the dull light that poured through the window. She had swept her long dark hair into a chic French pleat on the back of her head and she looked sophisticated and glamorous. But it was the way she *felt* that was the biggest surprise to her, for suddenly she knew a confidence that she had never experienced before.

So lost in thought was she that Grace failed to hear the door open behind her, and when Philip came in, she started.

His eyes were devouring her, turning her blood to water as he kissed the smooth skin on her bare shoulder. 'You look absolutely breathtaking,' he whispered huskily, and she was caught up in the excitement of it all as her earlier resolve wavered. After all, she reasoned, what was the harm in enjoying herself? That was what she had come for, wasn't it?

She turned to him and flashed him a dazzling smile as she snatched up her coat. 'I'm ready if you are,' she grinned, and she meant it; she had never felt so alive.

The first glimpse of the Tower Ballroom had her momentarily speechless again. High above them, an enormous silver ball rotated, casting flickering lights across the dance-floor, and everywhere she looked, women in beautiful dresses stood talking with their partners. Others were warming up on the dance-floor, like multi-coloured butterflies, oblivious to the crowds around them, and there and then Grace determined that she would do Philip justice, even if this were to be the last time they would ever dance together. She shrugged out of her coat, acutely aware of the admiring glances she was attracting, and Philip hurried away to hang it up for her, allowing her a little while to gather her thoughts.

By the time he came back, with drinks in his hand, despite the fact that it was still morning she was composed and smiling and beginning to enjoy herself. The Babycham she drank calmed her even more and by the time the huge Wurlitzer organ rose from the side of the stage like Neptune from the sea, she felt she could have conquered anything. Philip had entered their names for the dances that they wanted to participate in, and now all she had to do was stand by and enjoy it and wait for their names to be called. When they were finally summoned to the floor, he took her arm calmly and she followed him without hesitation, and then she was in his arms and they were twirling around the floor as one, in perfect time to the music. As the morning wore on, they danced a foxtrot, a tango, a rumba and many more, and Grace felt as if she were in heaven. When a break was announced for lunch she was almost disappointed, for she felt that she could have danced for ever.

'When do we start again?' she asked eagerly, as Philip escorted her to a chair.

He chuckled, delighted to see her so happy. 'In about an hour. There are two more dances to go and then it's back to the hotel to pack, I'm afraid. That is, unless I can tempt you to stay for another night?' His eyes were twinkling with undisguised lust and she blushed furiously.

'You know I can't do that,' she whispered and he smiled, mindful of a note of regret in her voice.

'Ah well, I suppose all good things must come to an end, but never mind. For us this is only the beginning.'

She opened her mouth to tell him that this *wasn't* the beginning – it was the end – but then thought better of it. This was neither the time nor the place. There would be an opportunity to talk to him on the way home, and at the moment she was enjoying herself so much that she didn't want to spoil it.

The rest of the day passed in a blur and at the end of the competition when their names were announced as the winners of the Latin-American section, Grace beamed with pride. They went up to the stage to collect the modest cup and shake hands with the judges, and it was as they were on their way down from the stage that a portly middle-aged gentleman with an old-fashioned handlebar moustache and an extremely shiny bald head approached them.

'Have you ever thought of joining a formation team?' he boomed, in a voice that echoed around the ballroom. When Philip nodded enthusiastically, he led him towards a table and they were soon deep in conversation as Grace stood looking around her, clutching the cup with pride.

'I see my husband has collared yours,' a lady with a kindly face said in Grace's ear. 'Always on the look-out for new talent, he is, and I must say your display today was most impressive. You looked and danced like an angel. You were very worthy winners, my dear. In fact, you put the other couples on the floor to shame, including some of our own team.'

'Why thank you,' Grace began. 'But I should just point out that Philip isn't actually my . . .'

'No doubt Ronnie will be trying to persuade your man to join our team,' the woman butted in before Grace had had time to explain that Philip wasn't her husband. 'My name is Barbara, by the way, and my husband and I run the Irving School of Dancing in Hinckley, in Leicestershire. It's only up the road from you, as the crow flies. Our practice nights are Tuesdays and Fridays. I'm sure you'd enjoy it if you join us. We are only semi-professionals, of course, but we have a fair few successes under our belt even if I do say so myself, and we're always off here or there – all over the country we go and—' On and on she droned, giving Grace no chance to so much as get a word in edgeways until at last Philip rose from his seat and came to join her.

'Right then, we'd best get on.'

Grace smiled at him gratefully, glad of an excuse to escape the woman's constant chatter.

'Goodbye, my dear, so nice to talk to you,' she shouted. 'I do hope we shall meet again.'

'I hope so too,' Grace said politely as Philip steered her away, and soon they were on the steps of Blackpool Tower. Grace was still trembling with excitement and her face when she looked at Philip was elated.

'I can't believe we did it,' she whispered incredulously.

He chuckled. 'I don't know why not. The trouble with you, Grace, is that you underestimate yourself. With your looks and charm you could be or do anything. All you need is the right man behind you.'

She studiously avoided replying to his comment and the short taxi-ride to the hotel was made in silence as Grace proudly clutched the cup to her.

Once back in the privacy of her room she carefully removed the beautiful dress, and as she did so, the feeling of elation slipped away and sadness settled over her like a cloud. This was it, then; the magical interlude was almost over and now it was time to return to reality. But how would she ever face Barry after what she had done? Her stomach churned with shame at the very thought of it as she slowly began to pack her case.

It was dark by the time Philip had settled their bill and loaded the luggage into the back of his car. Grace leaned forward in her seat as he cruised along the sea-front, trying to lock every last glimpse of it into her memory, and then they were heading inland and a feeling of dread settled on her. She could feel him watching her from the corner of her eye and tried to pluck up the courage to say what had to be said.

'Philip, I . . .' She gulped deep in her throat. 'I want you to know that I've loved every minute of the weekend, but I . . . Well, the truth is, it has to end here. What we did last night was unforgivable. Please don't think I'm blaming you – far from it, in fact. It was all my fault. I think I just got carried away and I'm sorry. But it must *never* happen again. My children, and my husband for that matter, are the most important things in the world to me and I could never live with myself if I ever hurt them. You do understand, don't you?'

'Of course I do, Grace. But do you really think it will be that easy to stop what has started?' His voice held a trace of bitterness and she sighed.

'We have to be strong enough to stop it. I'll admit that I'm attracted to you, I'd be a liar if I said that I wasn't, but that isn't a good enough reason to destroy so many lives. You of all people should know that, seeing as you're going through a marriage break-up yourself.'

His hands clenched on the steering-wheel. 'I love you, Grace. How do I stop that? And what about our dancing?'

'I can't answer the first question, but I can answer the second. We must never meet again. That is the only way from where I'm standing.'

He looked so appalled that she hung her head in shame.

'Look, Grace, if you really mean what you say then I promise I will never step out of line again. But *please*, don't stop dancing with me. It's all I have to look forward to now.'

She chewed on her lip as she stared ahead into the darkness, her soft heart going out to him. She had no wish to cause him further pain and yet she knew that to continue seeing him would be simply asking for trouble.

'Why don't you give me a few days to think about it?' she asked, and he nodded miserably.

121

By the time they pulled into the outskirts of Nuneaton Grace's eyes were gritty with lack of sleep. Already the short stay in Blackpool had taken on an air of unreality and she longed for her home and all that was safe and familiar. He steered the car through the town centre and she drank in the sights of her hometown. And then he was turning into Marlborough Road and they were pulling up outside her little terraced house and her heart was heavy with guilt. The curtains were drawn tight across the windows and it looked cosy and inviting as she sat next to Philip not quite knowing what to say.

'Back to the real world,' she said eventually and he nodded, his face a mask of sadness. Without a word he climbed from the car and lifted her luggage from the boot to the pavement.

'Would you like me to carry it in for you?' he asked.

She shook her head quickly. 'No really, I'll be fine. You get off now.'

'Grace, I . . .' He took a step towards her, but she recoiled as if she had been stung and the look of pain on his face intensified, cutting her to the very core.

'*Please*, Philip. Don't say any more. I'll phone you at work in the week and let you know what I've decided to do about our dancing. Thank you again for a wonderful time. I'll never forget it.'

'Neither will I,' he said sincerely. 'In fact, right at this moment I'm wishing with all my heart that I could.' Without another word he turned and got back into the car and she stood on the pavement and watched as he drove away, then slowly she bent and lifted her case and carried it to the front door.

Barry had allowed the children to wait up for her, and the second she was through the door they hurled themselves at her as if they hadn't seen her for a month.

'Ooh, Mammy, we missed you,' they chorused as Grace knelt and covered their clean shiny little faces with kisses.

'I missed you too,' Grace laughed, and then her eyes locked with Barry's and her heart began to beat faster. 'Has everything been all right?' she asked.

He nodded. 'Just about as all right as it could be without you,' he said softly. Barry had never been a great one with words and she knew that this was the nearest he could come to telling her he had missed her. Guilt flooded through her again and she was relieved when he suddenly turned and headed for the kitchen. 'I'll go an' put the kettle on, eh? No doubt you'll be gaspin' for a cup o' tea. Then when you've tucked these little monsters in you can perhaps tell me all about it.'

Nodding, she ushered the protesting youngsters towards the stairs door.

'Oh Mammy, can't we stay up a bit longer? Didn't you bring us a present?' Wendy whined, but Grace just laughed and tapped her bottom.

'In answer to your first question, madam, no, you can't stay up any longer, it's way past your bedtime already. And in answer to your second question, yes, I did bring you both a present and you'll get them in the morning if you're very good, so come on now, no more arguing.'

Wendy and Simon sighed but did as they were told and soon she had tucked them into bed and was on her way downstairs to Barry again. He was sitting in his usual position in the chair at the side of the fire and he nodded towards the mug of tea he had made her, his eyes gentle.

'So, how did it go then?'

She looked away from him as she answered, 'Very well, actually.' She proceeded to tell him about the cup they had won and he listened intently until she had finished her tale, and then with a twinkle in his eye he nodded towards the stairs door.

'How about you come up an' tell me the rest in bed, eh?'

Swallowing hard, she avoided his eyes as she rose and started to switch the lights off. Barry was already in bed when she eventually got upstairs, and after checking on the children, she slowly undressed in the dark, folding her clothes carefully over the back of a small chair. When she slid into bed beside him his hands instantly closed across her breasts and she had the sensation of falling into a comfortable easy chair. There was no passion with Barry, not as there had been with Philip. Barry was gentle and considerate in his lovemaking, whereas Philip had been almost aggressive in his urge to please her. Barry was predictable and safe, Philip was exciting and had shown her a way of life she had never known, a way of life she now realised she had dreamed of since she was a small child. She lay back and closed her eyes and tried to relive the wonderful stolen night they had shared. And in that moment she knew that it couldn't be over . . . not yet. After all, what harm could it do if she carried on dancing with him?

Chapter Thirteen

'Grace off out tonight again, is she, love?' Daisy asked innocently.

She knew that she was treading on dangerous ground by asking, but to her surprise instead of getting angry with her, Barry nodded miserably.

'Yes, she is.' His voice held a wealth of sadness. 'I didn't mind fer a start, Mam, as yer know. But lately she seems to have changed.'

'What do you mean . . . changed?'

He shrugged. 'I don't know, it's nothing I can put me finger on exactly, an' o' course, I realise that now they're doin' so well on the dancin' circuit they need to practise more, but she's . . .' He gazed dejectedly into the fire and Daisy's heart missed a beat. There was something wrong here – she could feel it.

'How many nights a week do they practise now?' she enquired.

'Two or three.'

'Are you copin' wi' the kids all right?'

'Oh yes, Grace always makes sure that everythin's done before she goes out. It's just . . .'

When he became silent again Daisy suggested, 'Perhaps it's time yer put yer foot down, lad?' When he opened his mouth to object, she held her hand up. 'I know you think its none o' my business, son, and we've been down this road before. But I feel there's things as need sayin' for the sake of you an' the kids. So hear me out, please.'

Barry sighed and lowered his head, knowing that when his mother had something she wanted to say, it would take nothing less than a bolt of lightning to silence her.

Sure that she had his undivided attention she went on, 'The thing is, you better than anybody should know that I think the world o' Grace an' allus have. I reckon she had a right raw deal when she got left to the mercy o' that aunt of hers. Trouble is, she's seen very little of life, and a bloke like this here Philip could turn a girl's head. Every time she sets foot in here, it's Philip this, an' Philip that, an' I smell somethin' fishy. If you don't put your foot down an' stop her seeing him soon, I've got a nasty feeling you'll be making a rod for your own back. You just see if I ain't proved right!'

Barry pondered on her words. He too felt unhappy about Grace's relationship with Philip. She was still the perfect wife and mother she had always been – and yet, he sensed her distancing herself from him. Their sex life, which he had always known she endured for his sake, was even less frequent than it had been, and sometimes when he kissed her he felt her tense, although she never pushed him away. And then there was the way she dressed. She seemed to have matured somehow, become more sophisticated, making him feel even further below her than he already did. Even so, the thought of laying the law down and forbidding her to go out was unthinkable. If that was what made her happy, then so be it. He loved Grace more than life itself and there was nothing in the world that he would not have done for her.

'Look, Mam, I know you mean well an' happen me an' Grace are going through a bit of a sticky patch at the minute. Life can't always be roses round the door. But that's all par for the course in marriage, ain't it? We'll come out of it the other side, you'll see.'

'I just hope you're right, lad,' Daisy said quietly, but as she poured his tea she had her doubts.

'You look lovely, darlin'.'

Grace started – she hadn't heard Barry come into the room behind her as she put the finishing touches to her hair.

'Thank you.' She watched him in the mirror as he paced the room behind her, pausing to stare at the string of pearls about her throat.

'They new, are they?'

'What, these?' She fingered them self-consciously. 'Oh, they're just cheap ones that I got off a stall in the market.' She could hardly tell him that they were her latest present from Philip and had probably cost more than Barry could earn in a week.

He accepted her explanation without question, which made her feel even worse about lying to him. Tonight he seemed restless and ill at ease. He was usually fast asleep in the chair downstairs by now and she watched cautiously as he continued to pace, up and down, up and down.

'Goin' somewhere nice, are you?' he asked eventually.

Grace shrugged. 'Not particularly. We're going to practise with Ronnie and Barbara and the rest of the formation team in Hinckley, that's all. We have a competition coming up in a couple of weeks so we're trying to get in as much practise as we can.'

'I see.' He suddenly stopped his pacing and came to stand behind her. Placing his hands on her shoulders he bent and kissed the smooth skin of her neck. 'Don't suppose there's any chance o' gettin' you to change your mind and stay in' and keep your old man company, is there?'

Grace shrugged him off gently. 'Barry, you know I can't just let them down on a whim. There have to be at least six couples to make up a formation team, and one of the couples has had to pull out because the woman is pregnant. If Philip and I don't turn up, they will have to cancel the practice.'

'Well, in that case, why don't I get me glad rags on and come along with you then? Chris would come an' babysit the kids like a shot if I asked her.'

Totally flustered at the strange turn of events, Grace stared at him incredulously. 'Barry, you *hate* dancing, you know you do. We're only going to practise, you'd be bored sick.'

'Suppose you're right,' he muttered reluctantly. 'I just wanted you to see as I were takin' an interest, that's all.'

'I appreciate that,' Grace smiled placatingly. 'But it's a filthy night. You'd be far better to stay in and put your feet up by the fire. You've been working almost every hour God sent and you must be tired.'

Without so much as another word Barry turned and left the room. His shoulders were slumped and Grace sighed. She hated deceiving him and yet, it was almost as if she were on a roller-coaster that she couldn't get off with Philip. He was like a drug to her. She had promised herself when they got back from Blackpool that from then on, their relationship would be purely a dancing one. But when she was with him she felt like a different woman, young and beautiful and alive, and in no time at all they had become lovers again.

Sometimes the strain of their relationship was almost unbearable and she promised herself that she would end it, but then she would take one look at Philip's handsome face and all her good intentions would fly right out of the window. In fairness to him, he had never so much as once suggested that she should leave her family – probably, she reasoned, because he knew how much her children meant to her. Even so, the tension of leading a double life was beginning to tell on her and lately she had lost weight and was not sleeping well – a fact that Barry had picked up on. She knew he had sensed that something was wrong and lately he was trying to please her in any way that he could. But it wasn't enough. It only served to increase her feelings of guilt, and nothing he did could compare to Philip. She found herself living for the few stolen hours they could snatch together each week, and although her one night out had turned into two and sometimes three, still it wasn't enough.

126

Chris had noticed that something was wrong too, and now Grace avoided her like the plague, sure that her friend would be able to read her like a book and guess what was going on. Just then Wendy came bounding into the bedroom and flung her arms around her.

'Ooh, Mammy, you look lovely. Can I have some lipstick on?'

Grace laughed as her heart flooded with love. Wendy was in her little pyjamas and with her hair all freshly washed she looked absolutely adorable. 'I suppose so.' She unscrewed the lid of her lipstick as Wendy comically pouted her lips. 'There.' She grinned, as Wendy admired herself in the mirror. 'Now you are beautiful too. But come on. Let me finish getting ready or Philip will be here.'

'Don't *like* Philip,' Wendy suddenly declared petulantly.

Grace frowned at her. 'Why ever not?'

'Philip ain't got smiley eyes.' The child sniffed. 'Not like my daddy's.'

Grace's heart lurched as unbidden, she recalled a favourite saying of Daisy's. 'Out of the mouths of babes'!

'That was very rude, Wendy!' she snapped, then could have bitten her tongue off as the child's lip began to tremble at the uncharacteristically harsh tone of her mother's voice.

'Wendy, I'm sorry. I didn't mean to—' The apology came too late and her only answer was the sound of the bedroom door banging to as Wendy fled with tears streaming from her eyes. Grace jumped up from her dressing-table and ran out on to the landing, just in time to hear Wendy's bedroom door slamming resoundingly behind her.

She stood for some seconds, uncertain of what to do, and then with heavy heart she turned and went back into her own room. Best to leave it till later, she decided, until Wendy had had time to calm down. Suddenly the pleasure had gone from the night, before she had even so much as set foot out of the door. She was sorely tempted to phone Philip and tell him that tonight she couldn't make it. But one glance at the alarm clock on the bedside table told her that he would already be on his way, and so slowly she collected her coat from the wardrobe and went downstairs to wait for him.

He knew the instant she climbed into the car that something was wrong. As he pulled away from the kerb, he asked, 'What's wrong, then? You don't look your normal cheerful self.'

Shrugging despondently, she felt unable to tell him the true reason for her dejected mood. 'I just snapped at Wendy for no good reason,' she said instead.

'Huh! Is that all? I thought the end of the world was nigh. Trouble is, love, you're too soft on those children of yours. They've got you wrapped round their little fingers. I've no doubt that if you snapped

127

at her she deserved it – so don't go whipping yourself. Children are much sturdier than you think. No doubt she'll have forgotten all about it by tomorrow morning.'

'She may well do, but I won't,' Grace said, and turning slightly in her seat to look at him, she went on: 'I don't think I can keep this up much longer, Philip. All this creeping about, I mean. It's beginning to get me down and play on my nerves. I'm almost jumping at my own shadow. I don't think I'm cut out to have an affair.'

'So what you're saying then is that you want to end it, is that it?'

Tears trembled on her long lashes. 'I don't know what I want any more, to tell the truth.'

He pulled the car into the side of the road and would have taken her in his arms there and then, but she panicked and pushed him away as she dabbed at her eyes. 'Not here, Philip, please, someone might see us.'

'Oh Grace, darling, you're getting paranoid. No one has the faintest idea of what's going on, even the rest of the people in the formation team. We've been the souls of discretion. What we have between us is something very special, and as long as we're not hurting anyone, what harm are we doing?'

'I don't know,' she said wretchedly.

Obviously more than a little annoyed, he restarted the car. 'Look, I'll tell you what, we'll give the practice a miss tonight, eh? I'll take you for a nice drive out into the country and we'll find a quiet pub where we can sit and have a drink in peace. What do you say?' He turned the car towards Tuttle Hill. 'We'll head for Sibson and stop at the Cock Inn. We could get a meal if you like.'

By now, Grace was too depressed to much care where they went.

Just as Philip had said, the pub was quiet and he found them a table in the corner away from the regulars' prying eyes. Normally Grace loved to come here, for the Cock Inn was steeped in history and had an olde-worlde charm about it. It was reputed to be the oldest inn in England, and had once been the hideout of Dick Turpin, the legendary highwayman. But tonight even the old beams and the shining leaded windows did nothing to lighten her mood.

After one drink Philip took her elbow and led her back to the car. 'I'm going to take you to my garage in Meridan,' he informed her as he opened the passenger door for her. 'I think we need some time alone to talk things through. We can go into my office at the back.'

She climbed into the car unresisting, and Philip began to drive through the country lanes. Normally Grace loved the rolling Warwickshire countryside, even at night, but tonight it held no joy

128

for her and she stared unseeingly out of the window as he steered the car expertly around the winding twisty lanes. She was so lost in thought that it was almost a shock when he turned onto a garage forecourt some time later and turned off the engine.

The garage was not at all as she had pictured it to be. Even though it was a big, imposing building, it had a rundown, ramshackle appearance that was oddly at variance with the one beautiful car that she could see faintly shining through what appeared to be a small showroom window. The whole place looked neglected, as though it could do with a lick of paint and new management.

'Here we are then, this is my garage.' After fumbling in his pocket, Philip removed an enormous bunch of keys before unlocking the dirty glass doors and beckoning her to follow him. Once inside he saw her staring around the almost empty showroom.

'Place is a bit empty at the minute,' he explained hastily. 'I sold most of my stock over the last couple of weeks and haven't had a chance to replace it yet. I'm just about to have the whole place refurbished, so please excuse the mess.'

Seeing that he looked slightly embarrassed, she passed no comment but followed his broad back as he strode across the room until they came to another door at the back of the showroom. He clicked on the bare light-bulb and drew her inside. She looked around his office curiously. A large mahogany desk that must have been very impressive at one time stood in the centre of the room with an old but comfortable-looking leather chair pulled up to it. The wall behind it was taken up with three large filing cabinets from which the paint was peeling, and against the opposite wall was a very large threadbare settee, covered in old car magazines and paperwork. On the floor all around the edges of the room were tins of paint of every colour. She found herself wrinkling her nose at the musty smell of the place; grease and engine oil and paint all rolled into one.

Oblivious to her discomfort he crossed to one of the filing cabinets and withdrew a bottle of whisky and two glasses. He smiled when she raised her eyebrows and motioned her to the settee as he poured two generous measures of the amber liquid.

'Now don't go getting all prudish on me. This is purely for medicinal purposes, I assure you. You look like you could do with something to perk you up a bit. Here – try it. You might even find you like it.'

Handing Grace a glass, he laughed as she shuddered when she sipped it. 'There you are. A couple of those and you won't have a care in the world.'

Swiping the papers and magazines from the settee in a single stroke, he sat down and joined her, and slung his arm carelessly round her shoulders. She took another sip of her drink and shuddered again as it burned its way down into her stomach. In truth, she was not that keen on the taste, but what she did like was the effect it had on her when it had gone down – a nice warm glowing feeling inside. By the time she had almost finished the first glass she was beginning to relax. When he offered a refill she handed him her glass willingly.

'Feeling better now?'

She nodded. 'Yes, I am, but what are we going to do, Philip? We can't go on like this.'

He took her glass and placed it gently on the floor beside her before reaching into his pocket and extracting a small leather box.

'This is for you.' He pressed it into her hand and when she somewhat reluctantly opened it she gasped at the sight of a beautiful gold bracelet.

'Oh, Philip. You *must* stop spoiling me. Barry is starting to wonder where all this jewellery is coming from. I had to lie to him tonight and tell him that I'd bought these pearls from the market.'

'I enjoy spoiling you,' he said softly, and as she looked into his eyes she saw the longing there and was lost. He took her face in his hands and kissed her tenderly, but then his passion mounted and she felt herself responding. Philip was like no other man she had ever met. He was charming and suave and sophisticated and she was like putty in his hands. Wendy and Barry and her home were suddenly forgotten as he removed her clothes and she gave herself up to the joy of the moment. 'I'll end it tomorrow,' she promised herself as her passion grew to match his, but underneath she wondered if tomorrow would ever come.

Some time later when she had struggled back into her clothes and was trying to tidy her hair, she asked, 'Could I go and tidy up in the toilet, Philip?' He was still draped across the settee with a satisfied smile on his face that stretched from ear to ear.

'Of course. It's the door in the corner next to the filing cabinets.' When he thumbed towards the corner she lifted her handbag and hurried in the direction he was pointing. There were actually two doors side-by-side, so opening the first one she came to, she clicked on the light switch. Her eyes popped open in amazement. Rather than a toilet she found herself in a huge workshop. There were at least half a dozen cars all seemingly stripped down or in various stages of having resprays. Car number-plates and spray cans littered the floor. Realising that she had opened the wrong door, she began to

130

back out of the room only to collide with Philip who was right behind her, buttoning his flies and looking none too pleased.

'The toilet is *that* door there. I told you the one in the corner.'

'Sorry.' Grace sniffed indignantly as she brushed her hair in the mirror above the sink. She had obviously upset Philip – but why? What had she done, apart from going into the wrong room? Her face creased into a frown as she thought of all the cars in the workshop. Earlier, Philip had said that he had sold most of his stock. She shrugged. The cars in the workshop were probably just there for repairs and resprays. Pushing the matter from her mind she hurried back to Philip, suddenly very keen to get home and end the evening.

Barry was lying awake waiting for her when she crept into the bedroom much later that night, having cleaned her teeth twice over to get rid of the whisky smell.

'Had a good night, have you, love?'

Grace's heart sank as his voice came to her from the darkness. 'Not bad,' she muttered, as she started to slither out of her clothes. She had hoped that he would be asleep, for then she wouldn't have to lie. Lifting the bedclothes, she slipped in beside him.

Quick as a flash, his arms enfolded her. 'By God, you're froze, love. Come on – snuggle up to me, I'll soon get you warm.'

He sensed the tension in her and when she turned her back to him he began to gently massage it. 'There, how's that, eh? You're a bit tense, ain't you? Are you sure as there's nothin' on yer mind?' As he spoke, his hand found its way to her soft breast and unable to help herself, she shuddered and knocked his hand away.

'Look, Barry, I'm sorry but I've got a throbbing headache. Would you mind very much if I just went to sleep?'

He became completely still for a second and then untangling his arms from her, he moved to his own side of the bed.

She held her breath, waiting for him to remark on her rejection of him, but he said nothing; he just lay staring into the darkness as a cold hand closed around his heart.

'Long time no see, eh?' Chris grinned at Grace as she drew abreast of her in the street a month or so later. She had the distinct feeling that Grace had been avoiding her for some time now, but here was the perfect opportunity to catch up on the gossip.

'What you doin' about at this time o' day then?' Chris went on. 'I thought you were at work in the mornings?'

'I should be,' Grace admitted, 'but I felt so ill I decided to come home early.'

'Mm, come to speak of it you do look a bit peaky,' Chris replied, surveying her solemnly. 'I'll tell you what. It won't do you no good hanging around here on the street. Come on in an' I'll make you a good strong brew.'

'I won't if you don't mind,' Grace said quietly as another wave of nausea swept over her. 'To be honest, I just want to get home, but you're welcome to come to me for a cup if you like.'

Never one to miss the chance of a chat, Chris fell into step with her as they continued on to Grace's. Once inside, Chris flung her coat over the back of the settee and kicked off her fur-lined panda boots before dropping into a chair and holding her feet out to the fire. Picking up the newspaper she remarked. 'Brave bloke, ain't he?' When Grace didn't immediately reply she frowned and looked across at her.

As Grace caught her eye she seemed to come out of a trance. 'Sorry, Chris. What were you saying? I was off in a world of my own then.'

'I were sayin', Donald Campbell is going to try for a new record in the *Bluebird*. My Dick says as he is the best. But never mind about that for now.' All the while her eyes were following Grace around the kitchen. She sensed that something was wrong. Grace really did look awfully pale.

'So what's up?' she asked in her own abrupt way. 'Got one o' these here bugs that's flyin' around, 'ave you?'

Grace bit her lip as she carefully measured two spoons of tea into the teapot. She longed to talk to someone – in fact, she felt that if she didn't confide in someone soon, she would burst. But could she trust Chris? Could she trust anyone, come to that?

After pouring the boiling water into the pot she popped the tea cosy on while it mashed before joining Chris at the side of the fire.

'Chris, if I tell you something,' she began hesitantly, 'would you *promise* not to tell anyone else?'

Sensing that this was something serious, Chris nodded solemnly. She was well-known in the street for having a big mouth, but she also had a big heart to go with it and was loyal to her friends. 'Mum's the word,' she agreed.

Grace tried to think how to explain to her friend what was on her mind.

'The thing is . . .' she began, then faltered, and suddenly tears were streaming down her cheeks.

'Here, give over, gel. Nothin' can be *that* bad,' Chris said soothingly as she hurried across to her and draped her arm around her shoulder.

Fumbling in her pocket she produced a rather grubby handkerchief and pressed it into Grace's hand.

'Come on now, have a good blow while I pour the tea an' then you can tell me all about it.'

She placed a mug into Grace's trembling hand. 'There now, take a good gulp o' that an' tell me what's up. Me mam allus used to say, a trouble shared is a trouble halved, so come on – out with it.'

'Everything's such a mess,' Grace sobbed as she broke into a fresh torrent of tears. Chris scratched her head, for once completely at a loss as to what she should do. She stroked Grace's hair gently as she waited for her to regain control of herself. When she had quietened, she sat beside her on the settee and took her hand.

'That's better. Now, do you want to talk about it?'

Grace sniffed loudly. 'The thing is, Chris, I think I . . . I might be pregnant.'

'Lord above, is that *all*? Why, you daft ha'porth, I thought you were goin' to tell me sommat terrible.' Chris sighed in relief. That's nothin' to get in a state about. Your Barry will be pleased as punch when you tell him.'

'Oh no, he won't.' Grace's face was drawn as she stared at her friend. 'You see, Chris, the thing is . . . the baby might not be Barry's.'

The colour drained from Chris's face as she stared at her friend aghast. 'What, you mean . . . you've had . . .'

'Yes, I've been having an affair,' Grace admitted miserably.

Chris was so shocked that for some time she was speechless. Eventually she asked, 'Were it Philip?' When Grace nodded she whistled through her teeth. 'Well, I don't mind admittin' you've fair took the wind out o' me sails, gel. I never thought you had it in you. But the question is, what are you goin' to do now? Yer in a right pickle from where I'm standin'.'

'I don't know what I'm going to do,' Grace said shakily as tea slopped over her hand and onto the tiled hearth and the rug. 'What do *you* think I should do?'

The other woman inhaled deeply and stared into the fire as she pondered on her friend's dilemma. 'Are you quite sure as yer pregnant?'

'I haven't been to the doctor's or had it confirmed,' Grace said, 'but I know I am. I haven't felt like this since I was having Simon, and I've missed a couple of periods. Normally I'm as regular as clockwork.'

Chris nodded sympathetically. 'Well, I suppose a lot of it depends on what you want to happen next. Does Philip know about it yet?'

When Grace shook her head, Chris then asked. 'Did you have any plans to go away together?'

'Of course we didn't!' Grace said tearfully. 'You should know me better than that, Chris. I would never leave my family.'

'Mm, in that case there's only one option open to you. You'll have to finish it with Philip, let Barry think that the baby is his an' get on with it.'

'What . . . you mean *lie* to him?' Grace cried incredulously.

Chris nodded. 'That's exactly what I mean. I don't see as you've exactly got much choice have you, pet – an' you'll have to do it soon an' all, before you start to show. I mean, look at it this way: if you tell Philip, no doubt he'll want you to go off with him if he thinks yer might be carryin' his child. But if you're sayin' you want to stay with Barry, then you can hardly tell him you've been having an affair, can you? Barry is a placid bloke, admitted, but how would he feel if he knew his missus might be carryin' another man's child an' he were goin' to be left to bring it up? To accept that, he'd have to be a bleedin' saint.'

Grace hung her head as she saw the sense of what her friend was saying. But how could she lie to him over something like this and live with herself? And then there was Philip. What would he say if he were to find out? They had never so much as spoken of living together, let alone having a child. And what would the effect be on Wendy and Simon, if she were to take them away from their father whom they adored? The more she thought of it, the worse of a mess it became and she longed to turn the clock back, but knew that she couldn't. What was done was done, and now she would have to find a way out of this whole sorry mess.

'Look,' Chris squeezed her hand reassuringly, 'the only two people that know about this in the whole world are you an' me at present – an' as far as I'm concerned, it can stay that way. Not a word of what you just told me will ever pass me lips till me dyin' day, if that's the way you want it. Think on what I've said, Grace. You've been daft an' you've made a mistake, but you'd be a fool to give everything up. I know I've teased you about him bein' a bit boring, but Barry is a good bloke. Far better he live in happy ignorance than lose you. It would kill him, I'm sure it would. Anyone can see he absolutely worships the very ground you walk on, so don't destroy him, eh? After all, chances are it's his baby anyway.'

Grace nodded slowly. What Chris said made perfect sense. But would she be able to carry it through? If she did, it would mean living a lie every single day for the rest of her life and she wasn't at all sure that she could do it. One thing *was* for sure, though – if she hoped to keep her family she was going to have to try.

134

Chapter Fourteen

Philip closed his office door and advanced on her with open arms, but instead of falling into them as she usually did, Grace stayed where she was.

'Philip, please. You must listen to me, it's important.' Grace was chalk-white and shaking like a leaf.

'Oh, all right, if it's so important, hurry up and say it. We can perhaps get down to having some fun then,' he replied churlishly, unused to his attentions being spurned.

Grace took a deep breath as, avoiding his eyes, she began tremulously, 'I'm afraid I'm not going to be able to see you again, Philip. It's over.'

A hint of amusement showed in his face as he tried to remain solemn. 'Oh darling, how many times have you said that? You know you don't mean it.'

'I do, Philip. This time I really do.' Her chin had a determined thrust to it and he began to realise that she was deadly serious.

'It has to end right here and now,' she went on. 'I only came tonight because I didn't think it was right to tell you over the phone.'

Leaning heavily against his desk, he folded his arms and stared at her. 'But why? We're good together. You know we are.'

Nervously wringing her hands, she repeated, 'It has to end, that's all there is to it. So now if you don't mind, I'd like you to take me home.'

'But Grace, I love you, you know I do – and I think you love me too.' When he held his arms out to her again it was all she could do to stop herself from running into them. He could always have that effect on her, but suddenly she found herself questioning if what she felt for him was worth giving up her family for.

'Please, this isn't easy for me either but there is no other way.' Turning on her heel she strode from the room. Seconds later he snatched up his car keys and followed her with a face like thunder. The return journey was made in silence. When he pulled up outside her house he tried one last-ditch effort to keep her.

'Look, Grace, if it's the deceit you can't live with then we'll go away together. There would be no more lies – we could be together all the time.'

'And what about my children?' Her voice was dull and listless as he ran his hand distractedly through his thick dark hair.

'We'll take them with us if it's what you want,' he said, but she knew deep down that he didn't want them.

'And what about their father? How would I explain to them why I was taking them away from Barry?'

He hung his head as she gently squeezed his hand.

'Goodbye, Philip. I will never forget you.' Without another word she slipped from the car and scurried away to the darkness of the entry that divided the two houses, and there she cried as if her heart would break. After a while she heard him start the car and drive away and she felt as if a part of her had gone with him. Philip had shown her another way of life, but lately she had begun to question if what she felt for him was love or infatuation, for whilst he could still make her pulse race she had recently glimpsed a selfish side to him. And now she might be carrying his child. She could only pray that she would be able to live with herself.

Barry looked up in surprise when she walked in. 'Hello, love. I weren't expectin' you back so soon.'

'I wasn't feeling so good,' she muttered as she made to pass him, but he caught her arm and looked at her in concern.

'Come to think of it, you ain't looked too chipper for a couple o' weeks or so. Why don't you have the mornin' off tomorrow an' get yourself off down to the doctor's?'

'Oh, there'll be no need for that,' she assured him quickly. 'I'm probably just coming down with a touch of flu or something. An early night and I'll be as right as rain in the morning.'

'Fair enough then. You go on up an' get tucked in an' I'll bring you up a hot-water bottle an' a nice strong cup o' tea.'

When he climbed the stairs some minutes later he found Grace huddled beneath the blankets, seemingly fast asleep. He stood for some seconds looking down on her, then quietly placed the mug of tea on the bedside table and crept from the room.

Once downstairs again, he sank into a chair and buried his face in his hands. There was something more to this than met the eyes, he was sure of it, but what could he do unless Grace was prepared to talk to him about it? She had been crying, he'd known it the second she walked through the door. A wave of helplessness washed over him. He loved her more than life itself but all he could do was pray

136

that whatever it was that was troubling her would resolve itself. Sighing, he crossed to the window and drew back the curtain. The snow that had been threatening for weeks was just beginning to fall in great white flakes, making the small yard that they shared with the neighbouring house look clean and bright in the light that spilled from the window. Wendy and Simon will be pleased when they see this in the morning, he thought to himself, and then methodically he began to turn off the lights before retiring to bed, where he lay at Grace's side staring off into the darkness, his thoughts troubled.

'So did you tell Philip you wouldn't be seeing him again then?' Chris looked at her friend's pale face over the rim of her mug.

Grace nodded unhappily. 'Yes, I told him, but I'm still not sure that I'm doing the right thing. After all, if it *is* Philip's child, he has a right to know about it.'

'You can't be sure as it is his,' Chris pointed out sensibly. 'It could well be Barry's – an' if you get yourself into believin' that, you could put all this behind you with an easy conscience.'

'I wish it were that easy,' Grace muttered as she stared into the fire.

'It *is* that easy, and you've done the right thing, if you ask me. I don't mind tellin' you now it's over, there were things about that Philip as I didn't like, once I got to know him. It's nothin' that I can quite put me finger on. It were just . . . Oh, I don't know – perhaps he were too good to be true. Or was he? I've seen him talkin' to blokes that I didn't like the look of – shady types that don't quite fit in with his goody-goody image. If you ask me, you've had a lucky escape. I've never told you this before, but one night when we were all down at the Saint George's Hall I come across him slippin' this bloke a wad o' cash as made me eyes bulge. He nearly jumped out of his skin when he saw me behind him, which got me to thinkin' he were up to no good.' Chris frowned as she remembered back to the incident. 'Now what you have to do is pick yourself up an' put all this behind you. Not just for your sake but for Barry an' the kids. Have you told Barry about the baby yet?'

When Grace shook her head, Chris nodded. 'Perhaps it's just as well. Take one step at a time. Give it a couple o' weeks for things to settle down an' then tell him. There's no rush – you won't even be showin' for a while yet.'

Grace stared gratefully at her friend. She had no idea what she would have done without her; she was feeling totally out of her depth and miserable to the core. The thought of never seeing Philip again was heartbreaking and yet she knew that she had no alternative. She had to consider Barry and the children. Everything that Chris had said made sense. Now all she had to do was try and see it through; she had a sinking feeling that this might prove to be easier said than done.

Grace left work and hurried to the school to collect Wendy before rushing back to Daisy's to fetch Simon. He was due to start school soon, and she could hardly wait, for now the rushing from one place to another was beginning to tell on her with the pregnancy making her feel so tired. It was now early in December, with Christmas only weeks away, but she still had not as yet plucked up the courage to tell Barry about the baby, although she knew that she would have to soon. Already her breasts were swollen and tender, and she wouldn't be able to hide the truth from him for much longer.

The snow was thick on the ground and still falling with no sign of ceasing, which made the journey all the more difficult, so by the time Grace and Wendy reached Daisy's, she was breathless and worn out. Daisy took one look at her and ushered her into the fireside chair.

'Get yourself sat down, gel. You look fit to drop,' she ordered kindly as she bustled away to put the kettle on.

Grace smiled wryly. Daisy had the firm belief that a good strong cup of tea could cure all ills, and she wished with all her heart that things could be that simple. The atmosphere was still strained at home, although if truth be told that was down to her, not Barry. The last month had been sheer hell, but up until now Barry had made no mention of the fact that she had suddenly stopped going dancing – although he must have found it strange, to say the very least. Still, as she had discovered over the years, that was Barry, thoughtful to a fault. Every single day without Philip was so painful that sometimes she had to fight the urge to ring him, but slowly she was coming to accept that their affair was well and truly over. He had never tried to get in touch or pester her in any way, for which she admired him. Philip was a perfect gentleman, as she had discovered some long time ago, and he would never make her do anything that she didn't want to do.

She had become so lost in thought that when Daisy suddenly reappeared with her tea she almost jumped out of her skin. 'Oh sorry, I was miles away,' she said.

Daisy took a seat opposite her. 'Still feelin' under the weather then, are you?' She eyed her daughter-in-law thoughtfully.

Grace gulped. 'I suppose I am a bit.' She swirled the tea around in her mug as she avoided Daisy's searching eyes.

'Ah well, happen the first three to four months are allus the worst. Once you get the sickness out o' the way you'll start to feel better.'

Grace's head snapped up as she stared at Daisy incredulously. 'But . . . but how did . . . ?'

Daisy chuckled. 'I could have told you weeks ago but I were waitin' for you to tell me, gel. You don't have to be the Brain o' Britain to figure it out, you know. It were as plain as the nose on your face. There ain't much as slips past me. What I am curious about though is why you ain't mentioned it.'

Grace screwed her eyes tight shut. 'I suppose I was just waiting until I was sure,' she lied, feeling as if Daisy had the power to see into her very soul.

'Mm – an' have you told Barry yet?'

When Grace could find no answer, the older woman frowned and sat tapping her fingers on the arm of the chair. There was something far from right here, if she was any judge.

'Don't you think Barry will be pleased then?' she asked eventually.

Again Grace sat nervously twisting her hands in her lap as she stared into the fire. 'I'm not sure,' she whispered eventually. 'We were just beginning to get on our feet so I don't know how he'll feel about it.'

'Huh! Well, if that's all you're worryin' about, you should have your head looked at,' Daisy scoffed with relief. 'If I know our Barry he'll be as proud as Punch, so stop frettin' an' tell him.'

'I will,' Grace promised, but she seemed no happier, and as Daisy looked at her, the bad feeling she had deep in the pit of her stomach persisted.

The children were tucked up in bed and Grace and Barry were sitting either side of a roaring fire. Outside, the snow was still falling in a thick white sheet, but inside all was warm and cosy.

'Ah, this is the life,' Barry muttered contentedly as he propped his feet on the shining brass fender. Grace glanced at him nervously. All evening she had been waiting for the right moment to tell him, but somehow the right moment never seemed to come along. She knew now that she must tell him tonight, before Daisy did, but she quaked at the thought.

'I'll make us a cup o' cocoa, eh?' he asked eventually, and she nodded absently as she tried to prepare herself for the ordeal ahead. Tears stung at the back of her eyes as she heard him pottering about in the kitchen, and she remembered back to the time when she had told him she was going to have Simon. He had been so thrilled, and so was she. But how would he feel if she were to tell him the child that she was carrying now might not be his? She shuddered at the thought and knew then without a shadow of a doubt that she must try to convince him it was his baby, for all their sakes. By the time he came back she was sitting upright in the chair and had managed to compose herself.

'Barry . . . there's something I need to tell you.' She saw the fear flash briefly in his eyes and her heart twisted. Barry was such a good man and she hated herself for what she was about to do to him.

'What's that then?' He sipped at his cocoa and watched her guardedly over the rim of his mug. He was well aware that she had not been happy for some time, so what she eventually told him had his eyes starting from his head in amazement.

'I'm . . . er . . . I'm going to have a baby.' There, it was said, and now all she could do was wait for his reaction as he reeled from the shock. When it eventually came it only served to heighten her sense of guilt as his face lit up with delight.

'What? You mean you're . . . I mean, are you quite sure?'

She nodded. 'Yes, I'm quite sure. I'm nearly four months' so the baby should be born early in May next year.'

'Well, I'll be . . .' He scratched his head in bewilderment, hardly able to take it in. After the birth of Simon they had made a conscious decision not to have any more children for financial reasons, but now that she had told him there was another on the way, he was thrilled at the prospect.

'Oh, Grace.' He dropped to his knees in front of her and gathered her hands into his. 'This is *wonderful* news, though I must admit you could knock me down with a feather I'm so surprised. You are pleased about it, ain't you?'

He watched the doubt flicker in her eyes, but her voice when she answered was calm. 'I suppose I'm just a bit worried about how we'll manage,' she said lamely. 'It will mean I'll have to pack in work again for a time.'

He threw his head back and laughed. 'Aw, Grace. Ever the practical one, eh? We'll manage somehow an' the kids will be thrilled to bits when we tell them they're goin' to have a new brother or sister.'

She nodded, hating herself more in that moment than she had ever hated herself in her whole life. Now she knew that everything her aunt had ever told her was true: she *was* bad – wicked, even – and wondered how she would ever manage to live with herself and the terrible thing she was doing to her family.

* * *

For days Barry walked around with a huge grin on his face until her nerves were stretched to the limit. She told Chris as much one afternoon when she called in for coffee.

'I don't think I can keep this up,' she sobbed, as Chris listened sympathetically.

'Oh yes, you can. You ain't got no choice,' Chris declared sensibly. 'The worst bit is over now. Philip's off the scene an' none the wiser. Barry is happy as a sand boy – now all you've got to do is get on with it.' She looked across at her friend and was shocked to see how ill she looked. She was losing weight instead of gaining it, and her face was as white as the snow on the ground. Added to that, she was so nervy that she jumped at her own shadow, causing Chris to be deeply concerned for her.

'You've got to try an' pull yourself together, gel,' she urged, but her advice only served to bring forth a torrent of fresh tears.

'I don't know if I can.' Grace wrung her hands as she paced up and down the kitchen. 'You can't even *begin* to imagine how hard it is, hearing Barry making plans and thinking of names, when all the time I keep thinking deep down that the baby may not even be his.'

'Huh! From where I'm standin' there's a sight more chance of it bein' his than Philip's. An' if he's happy about it, that's all the more reason why he shouldn't find out what went on, ain't it? Don't think for a minute that him knowin' the truth would make things better. It would destroy him. You're actually doin' him a kindness by keepin' him in the dark, so don't you forget it.'

Grace paused in her restless pacing – she knew that what Chris said was true, and prayed once more for the strength to carry this terrible deception through.

The marketplace was almost empty as Grace made her way through the stalls. The snow had given way to needle-sharp lashing rain and the cold wind sliced through her, making her mood as miserable as the weather. Normally the town centre would be heaving with people on market day, but today the few shoppers who had ventured out had already scuttled away to the warmth of their firesides, and the marketplace was almost deserted. The traders huddled under their stalls, stamping their feet and blowing into their cold hands. She had only ventured out on this late Saturday afternoon to get the cabbage and cauliflower to go with the pork they were having for Sunday dinner, leaving Barry to keep his eye on the children, but already she was regretting it. The terrible nausea that she had endured since the beginning of her pregnancy showed no signs of abating as yet, and all she wanted to do was get her shopping done and get home as quickly as possible.

She had stopped at a fruit and veg stall and was eyeing the drenched display when someone tapped her gently on the arm. When she turned, she had the sensation of her blood turning to water as she found herself looking into Philip's remarkable blue eyes. He was wearing a light-coloured raincoat with the collar turned up against the rain, and his thick dark hair was plastered to his head, but even so he still looked incredibly handsome. Composing herself with an enormous effort, she resisted the urge to fling herself into his arms.

'What brings you here?' she asked politely.

He thumbed back over his shoulder. 'I had some business to discuss with a client, so we had lunch in the George Eliot Hotel.'

'I see.' It had been only a matter of weeks since she had finished their affair and yet to her it felt like a lifetime. Her heart was pounding as, without thinking, her hand fell to her stomach where the child was growing even as they spoke. What would he say if she told him? The urge was on her to do just that, but she knew that she wouldn't – couldn't, not ever.

'I miss you so much, Grace.'

She dragged her eyes away from his, unable to look at the longing in them. She had the sensation of choking and everything was beginning to swim about alarmingly. Surely there could only be one of him, so why was she suddenly seeing two?

'Philip, I'm so sorry. You'll have to excuse me, I'm not feeling too . . .' There was no time to say more for suddenly the ground was coming up to meet her and she escaped into a comforting darkness.

The next time Grace opened her eyes she found herself sitting at the traffic lights in Queens Road in Philip's car.

'Wh . . . what happened?' She felt as if she was floating as the red light turned to amber and then green and he pulled smoothly away.

'Don't worry. You fainted. Lucky I was there. I'll have you home straight away, just lie back and rest.'

She felt so disorientated that she could do nothing else. Her mind was in turmoil; she wanted to ask him to carry on driving so that she could enjoy his nearness, but she knew that she couldn't. In no time at all he drew the car to a halt in front of her little terraced house in Marlborough Road. After switching off the engine he turned to look at her. Struggling to sit up in her seat, she smiled at him weakly as her legs turned to jelly.

'I'm sorry about that. I don't think I've ever fainted in my life before. It's a good job you were there.'

'I'd better get you inside.' Climbing from the car he came around to the side to open the door for her. Her legs seemed not to want to do what she told them and she was glad of his strong arm around her as he helped her up the short path to the front door. When she pushed it open and walked unsteadily into the front room with his arm still about her waist, Barry, who was reading to the children, looked up quickly. At the sight of Philip his lips set in a grim line.

'Go into the other room, kids.' His harsh tone brooked no argument and sensing that something was wrong, Wendy and Simon scuttled away.

He waited until the door had closed behind them and then turned his attention back to his wife, who was as white as a sheet. 'So – what's goin' on then?'

Barry was usually a very polite man and Grace flushed at his rudeness. 'I'm afraid I passed out in the marketplace. Luckily Philip was there and kindly gave me a lift home. Thank goodness he was, otherwise the poor stall-holder wouldn't have known what to do with me.'

'Mm, very convenient.' Barry glared at Philip, who immediately bristled.

'Look here,' he said defensively. 'My bumping into Grace was pure coincidence, I assure you. I'd just had lunch with a client and it was as I was walking back through the marketplace that I happened to spot her.'

Barry sneered, clearly not believing him, and now it was Philip's turn to be annoyed as he turned an angry red.

'I would have thought under the circumstances that you would be more concerned about your wife's health than the fact that I accompanied her home. Aren't you even concerned that she fainted clean away?'

'Of course I'm concerned,' Barry snapped. 'Though I believe it ain't uncommon for a pregnant woman to pass out.'

Grace paled even further as shock registered on Philip's face. He stared at her wide-eyed as she lowered her gaze, unable to bear the question she saw there. Suddenly she knew that she could not go on with this pretence for much longer and tears began to stream down her cheeks.

'Barry, let Philip leave now, *please*. I'm sure he has things to do.' She was desperate to try and defuse the situation before it got out of hand, but Barry was on his high horse and nothing could stop him. He had waited a long time to tell Philip just what he thought of him and now he was determined not to waste the opportunity.

'Sounds good to me, an' as far as I'm concerned, he needn't waste his time comin' back. Things are just beginnin' to get back to normal round here since he stopped pokin' his nose in, an' what I say is good riddance to bad rubbish. Let him go an' try to turn the head of some other poor bloke's wife an' leave mine well alone.'

Grace gasped with shock. She'd never realised that Barry felt so strongly about the time she had spent with Philip, but now his feelings were gushing out of him like water from a dam. Philip eyed him coldly, then turning his attention back to Grace he asked the question she had been dreading.

'How far gone are you, Grace?'

She stared back at him, too terrified to answer, and then Barry waded in again as he came to place a possessive arm about her.

'What bloody business is it o' yours? Get out, go on – you ain't wanted around here!'

Philip's eyes locked tight with hers and no matter how hard she tried, she was unable to drag hers away from them. It had gone too far; she could continue with this charade no longer. She was not being fair to either Barry or Philip and she knew now that it was time for the truth.

'I'm about four months.'

His eyes were asking another question and slowly she opened her mouth to utter the words that she knew would change all of their lives for ever.

'I think the baby might be yours, Philip.'

A shocked silence settled on the room, and for long seconds all of them might have been set in stone. It was hard to say who looked the more stunned of the two men, but it was Barry who finally spoke first and the words he uttered struck terror into her heart.

'Get out!'

She stared at him appalled, knowing that she should have expected nothing less, and yet unable to believe he meant it.

'Now look here—' Philip was still reeling from the shock of her disclosure but Barry's temper was such that he wouldn't allow him to get a word in.

'And *you* get out an' all, and take your fancy bit with you. I must have been mad to close me eyes to what were goin' on for so long. Oh, I ain't daft, you know. I knew sommat were goin' off but you know the old sayin' – there's none so blind as them as don't want to see. Perhaps I hoped it would all blow over, but I ain't prepared to bring up a bastard. So, don't stand there tryin' to rub salt into the wound. You've got what you wanted, now take her an go.'

'Barry, no!' Panic gripped her and Grace hung onto his arm, but he shook her off. This was a side of Barry that she had never seen before and it broke her heart to realise that she deserved everything he was about to dish out. She was painfully aware of the fact that

the children were in the next room and prayed that they wouldn't hear what was going on.

'*Please*, Barry, at least let me try and explain—'

He pushed her roughly towards the door, causing her to lose her balance and almost topple into Philip's arms. Philip's face was a mask of horror and she had the impression that he would have liked to turn tail and flee and leave her to it. As she regained her balance she realised that there was no point in trying to talk to Barry until he'd had time to calm down, so she started to walk unsteadily towards the middle door.

'Where do you think you're goin'?' Barry's voice sliced into the silence that had descended as she paused to stare at him.

'I . . . I'm just going to get the children, and then perhaps I can come back and talk to you tomorrow when you're a little calmer.'

Barry laughed; a low ugly sound that grated on her nerves. 'Over my dead body on both counts. You don't think I'd let you take *my* kids to live with a scum like that, do you? An' as for comin' back to talk – don't bother tryin' if you know what's good for you. The only time I ever want to see you again is when you come back to collect your stuff, which will be on the step waitin' for you tomorrow.'

'Barry, *please*,' Grace was babbling almost incoherently. 'You can't stop me taking the children, that's cruel.'

'So is what you've done to me, you bitch. You just worry about the bastard growin' inside you, 'cos I'll tell you now, you'll never set eyes on the other two again for as long as there's a breath left in me body. An' don't think of takin' it to court either, 'cos there's no court in the land would hand them over to you when I've finished tellin' them what an unfit mother you are. Now get out, the pair o' you, whilst you still can, else I won't be responsible for me actions.'

Philip grasped her arm and, grim-faced, led her towards the door. The whole situation had taken on an air of unreality and Grace felt as if she were living a nightmare. She cast one last imploring glance at Barry as Philip shepherded her through the door, but he simply stood, his fists clenched at his side with a look of such pure hurt and hatred on his face that it tore at her heart.

Once outside, Philip pushed her unceremoniously into the car and pulled away from the kerb at breakneck speed as she sobbed uncontrollably at his side. He drove through the town, and after passing under the Coton Arches he drew into the Pingle Fields and stopped the car. Then he rounded on her furiously.

'Just *what* the hell is going on? Why in God's name didn't you tell me you were pregnant? And how could you be so stupid as to get pregnant in the first place!'

145

She stared at him incredulously. She had wondered how he would react if he ever found out about the baby, but she had never expected this in her wildest dreams. 'I've seen the Durex in your wallet and I thought you were taking care of that side of things. And how *could* I tell you?' she gasped. 'I wasn't sure that you'd be pleased, and judging by the way you're acting now, I wasn't far wrong, was I?'

'Huh! Well, you have to admit it was hardly the best way to find out, was it? Why didn't you just keep your mouth shut and stay with your husband? It would have been easier all round. We're in a fine mess now and no mistake.'

The tears stopped abruptly as she gazed at him in horror. 'But Philip, I . . . thought you loved me?'

'Oh, I do – of course I do,' he said a little too quickly. 'The question now is where do we go from here? Have you anyone you could go and stay with?'

'N . . . no,' Grace faltered.

Tapping his fingers on the steering-wheel he stared out of the window as he searched for a way out of the dilemma he found himself in. True, he was very fond of Grace – had been besotted with her at one time if he were to be honest with himself – but he had never envisaged her leaving her husband, let alone getting pregnant.

'Look,' he said eventually, seeing no alternative. 'I'll find you a B and B somewhere just for tonight and tomorrow, with luck, maybe Barry will have calmed down.'

'But I want to be with *you*.' Despite the fact that her heart was breaking at the loss of her children, she knew now that this might be for the best. After all, Philip had shown her a way of life she had never known existed before, so *surely* they could work something out together? During the weeks they had been apart she had slowly felt herself growing closer to Barry once more, but now after seeing Philip again, she realised how much she had missed him.

He started the car and drove slowly out of the dark field. 'I'm afraid that's impossible tonight. James and Gregory, my children, are waiting at home for me. Let's just wait and see what tomorrow brings before we do anything rash,' he said through gritted teeth, and with that, for now she had to be content.

She opened her mouth again to protest, but then clamped it shut and settled miserably back into her seat. Perhaps he was right – a night's rest to get their heads round the latest turn of events would do them both good. Tomorrow would be soon enough to begin their new life together.

Chapter Fifteen

They were almost halfway down Edward Street when Grace suddenly said, 'I've just thought of somewhere I may be able to stay.'

Philp slammed on his brakes and steered the car into the kerb.

'It's . . . it's just a little further down the road,' she said. 'Hetty Brambles. I used to work with her daughter Norma, before I was married, and if I remember rightly she used to take in lodgers from time to time.'

Nodding, he restarted the car and cruised slowly along until Grace pointed at a B&B sign hanging in the window of one of the large Victorian terraced houses. 'There's the sign in the window – look.'

He drew the car to a halt, grim-faced. 'That should do you for tonight then. I'll be back as soon as I can in the morning and then we'll see what's to be done.' His voice was so abrupt that fresh tears stung her eyes.

'Philip, I don't have anything other than the clothes I'm stood up in. I can't just go and knock on a door and expect her to take me in.'

Seeing the sense in what she said he nodded, and coming round to her side of the car, he courteously opened the door for her. Even with her eyes red-rimmed from crying she looked remarkably pretty in the light from the street-lamp and he began to think that perhaps what had happened wasn't such a bad thing after all. He might even rent them a house somewhere if her husband still refused to take her back, but that was something he would think about tomorrow.

Her eyes raked the front of the huge terraced house. The sign in the window was crudely handwritten and the house wasn't particularly salubrious, to put it kindly, if she remembered correctly. But then, she knew that she was in no position to be choosy, not for now at least, and after all it was just for one night. She followed Philip through a rusty creaking gate and up the short pathway to stand silently at his side as he rang the doorbell. For a second she thought that no one was in, for the house appeared to be completely in darkness, but then a light clicked on in the hallway and she heard someone shout.

'All right, all right. Keep yer bloody hair on. I'm comin', ain't I?'

147

The next second, an old woman opened the door a crack and peered out at them. 'Yes, what can I do for yer then?'

Philip drew Grace from where she was standing behind him as the old woman stared at her curiously.

'We were wondering, Mrs er . . .'

'Brambles, Hetty Brambles.' The old woman continued to stare at Grace, and she felt herself flushing, but then as recognition dawned on the old woman's face her mouth gaped open.

Philip was charm personified. 'We were wondering, Mrs Brambles, if you might have a bed for the night for my . . . err . . . friend here?'

'What – not for the pair o' you?' Hetty's eyebrows rose, seeming to almost disappear into the metal curlers that were placed haphazardly all across her grey head. There was something fishy going on here, she surmised almost instantly, but then she didn't want to turn away business. Money was hard come by. From what she remembered of Grace she was respectable enough, and if it were only for the one night it was hardly worth bothering about.

'Terms are three shillin's a night, money up front an' breakfast thrown in,' she sniffed, holding the door ajar so that they could step into the hallway.

Philip produced his wallet and pressed a ten-shilling note into her hand. 'I'm not sure what time I shall be able to get back in the morning, so I trust that will cover the room until I arrive.'

Snatching the money she pressed it greedily into her dressing-gown pocket. 'I might even rustle her up a bit o' supper for that an' she can stay all day as far as I'm concerned. Take your time.' She flashed Grace a toothless smile and then sighed. 'Sorry I look a bit of a sight, love. Me teeth have already gone into the glass at the side o' the bed an' I were goin' to get meself a nice early night. But seein' as you're here now, we can watch a bit o' telly, eh?'

Grace nodded timidly before turning to Philip as he backed towards the door. Her eyes were pleading, and for the first time she caught a glimpse of the man she had fallen in love with as he smiled at her kindly.

'Try to get a good night's sleep, love. I'll be back as soon as I can tomorrow, I promise. And don't worry too much, eh? Things will work out, you'll see.'

And then he was gone and Hetty was slamming the door loudly behind him.

'Right then, love, come this way an' I'll make you a nice cup o' tea. If you don't mind me sayin', you look as if you need it. Come on, follow me.'

Grace trotted behind her as the old woman led her to a door at the end of the hallway. She glanced around her as she went, taking in the faded wallpaper and the equally faded linoleum that covered the floor, which was exactly as she remembered it. The house was obviously poor but, she had to admit, spotlessly clean from what she could see, which was something at least. When Hetty pushed the door open, the warmth of the room rushed to meet her and as she stepped inside she found herself in a cosy sitting room. On a low table in a far corner stood an artificial Christmas tree strewn with tinsel and strung with fairy-lights that cast a rainbow of colours onto the faded wallpaper. A middle-aged man was sitting in a chair at the side of the fire with his shirtsleeves rolled up to his elbows and his braces dangling. As Grace entered he flushed and jumped to his feet.

'It's all right, our Will,' Hetty soothed. 'We've got a guest for the night. Do yer remember her? She used to be a friend of our Norma's. You've no need to disturb yourself. Sit yourself back down an' I'll go an' mash us all a nice strong cuppa.'

He sank back into the chair, keeping his eyes on Grace all the time as Hetty disappeared into yet another room that led off this one. Grace stood self-consciously plucking at the buttons on her blouse until the old woman returned some minutes later bearing a laden tray.

'Eeh, sorry, love. I completely forgot me manners. Take yourself a seat an' make yourself at home. You don't have to stand on ceremony here as yer should remember.'

Grace sidled onto a chair placed next to a remarkably nice oak table with barley-twist legs; the old woman deposited the tray on it.

'There, then.' She patted her curlers and ran her gnarled hands down the sides of her threadbare candlewick dressing-gown as she started to lay out some cups and saucers on the table.

'Do yer 'ave sugar, love?'

Grace nodded absently. 'Two, please.'

'Huh! Never would have thought it, lookin' at yer. You ain't as far through as a line-prop, but then if I remember right, you always were a skinny little thing.' Hetty good-naturedly spooned the sugar into the cup and then proceeded to pour the tea through a strainer before adding a liberal amount of milk. It was all Grace could do to stop herself from heaving as she stared at the milk-white liquid, but she sipped at it politely all the same when Hetty passed it to her.

'Well, I'd best introduce you properly seein' as you're goin' to be stayin' here. This is me son, William – I always call him Will though. Can yer remember him?'

149

When Grace shook her head, Hetty smiled and asked curiously, 'Are you still livin' round here?'

Grace lowered her eyes. 'Yes, I am actually.'

'Thought as much. I reckon I've seen you out an' about round the marketplace. Got a couple o' nippers now, ain't you, if me memory serves me right?' Hetty laughed at the look of surprise that flitted across Grace's face. 'I thought as much. There ain't much as gets past old Hetty Brambles, an' I ain't likely to forget anyone as pretty as you.'

When there was no answering smile on Grace's face, Hetty frowned. If she was not very much mistaken, this young woman was in grave trouble, though what sort as yet she had no idea. She didn't seem to have any luggage whatsoever, not even an overnight bag. And if she lived hereabouts and had two children, what was her husband doing, dropping her off here all alone? But then – what had the man called Grace? *My friend*, wasn't it?

Hetty was an astute judge of character, and decided that the young woman would open up in her own time if she had a mind to. In the meantime, she had no wish to pry. She waited for Grace to finish her tea before asking, 'Now, what about a nice corned-beef sandwich wi' a drop of HP sauce, love? Or I've got a nice bit of Edam cheese, and some of me home-made chutney to go wi' it.'

'I'm not very hungry, thanks.' In fact, all Grace wanted to do was to hide herself away and lick her self-inflicted wounds. She could not wait to be alone, but politeness forbade her from saying so. When Hetty suggested showing her to her room, Grace was relieved. She nodded at Will as she stood to follow her and, blushing deeply again, he nodded back.

'He's a bit shy, is my Will,' Hetty confided as she hobbled painfully towards the stairs. 'Even so, he's the salt o' the earth. Do anythin' for anyone, he would. Misses our Norma somethin' terrible, he does. Still, yer can't stop yer kids from growin' up an' flyin' the nest, can yer? She wanted me to join her and her family fer Christmas but I told her, there ain't no way you'd get me on a bloody plane, not in a month o' Sundays. Why she had to go an' marry an Army bloke an' go an' live abroad I'll never know, but there yer are.' There was pride in her voice as she spoke of her son and daughter, and Grace felt herself warming to the woman all over again, just as she had so many years ago when she had occasionally visited the house in her lunch-hours with Norma.

The room that she was shown to was surprisingly pretty and comfortable, and she glanced around appreciatively. The middle of the floor was covered in a large threadbare but still-colourful carpet, and around the edge of it was some of the same linoleum that she had seen in the hall. The bed was covered in a patchwork quilt all the colours of the rainbow, and hanging at the long, narrow sashcord window were pretty pink curtains. A huge wooden wardrobe took up almost all of one wall, and next to it was a chest of drawers in a different wood. On them was a vase of plastic daffodils, which Grace was amused to see were the ones that had been given free with packets of Daz soap powder. She knew about them because Daisy had an identical bunch, and had been buying washing powder as if it was going out of fashion for weeks, just so that she could get the free flowers.

Thoughts of Daisy brought her mind back to her family, and the old woman watched as her eyes suddenly flooded with tears again.

'Is there anythin' I can do for yer, love?' Her voice was kindly.

'N . . . no, thank you. I . . . I'm so sorry.' Grace fumbled in her coat pocket and taking out a handkerchief, she blew her nose noisily.

Sensing that Grace needed to be alone, Hetty bustled towards the door. 'The bathroom is second door on the right. Should be plenty o' fresh towels in there. If yer need anythin' else just give me a shout, eh?'

Grace nodded. 'Thank you.' And then Hetty was gone and at last she was alone. Crossing to the window, she drew back the curtain. Through the glass, a sea of rooftops stretched away into the distance. One of those rooftops was hers, and beneath that roof her husband would be putting her children to bed. There would be no goodnight story from her tonight; no goodnight story from her ever again if Barry had his way. But then, she reasoned, there was time for him to calm down and change his mind, for although what she had done to him was unforgivable, she had never been a bad mother – had she?

Dropping the curtain, Grace began to pace the room as she tried to put her thoughts into some sort of order. Whatever had made her blurt out the truth like that? She had no answer, and yet strangely she was relieved that she had; the strain of living a lie had been intolerable. At least now everything was out in the open and things might start to sort themselves out. She would get her children back and Barry would surely find someone else – someone who was worthy of him – then she and Philip and the children could all live happily ever after. Even as she hoped for such an outcome she knew that it was highly unlikely; it sounded too much like a fairy story and she of all people knew that fairy stories never came true.

*　　*　　*

151

Chris glanced at the clock. Grace had promised to come round for a coffee this evening but she was almost an hour late already and her neighbour was beginning to worry. She glanced at the clock again – almost eight o'clock. She'd boiled the kettle so many times that it had almost boiled dry and now she crossed to turn it off and refill it. Jenny was upstairs, probably fast asleep by now, and Dick had gone down to the Nags Head for a game of darts.

She chewed on her lip indecisively. Every instinct she had told her that something was wrong. Grace was one of the most reliable people she knew, and would not have let her down without good reason. Either she was ill or, God forbid, something worse. Chris's stomach rebelled at the thoughts that were chasing through her mind. Grace wouldn't be silly enough to break down and tell Barry about the baby, would she? The way her nerves had been the last few days it was a distinct possibility and Chris shuddered to think what might have happened if she had.

There was only one way to find out and that was to pop round there. There could be some perfectly simple explanation for Grace being late. One of the children might be ill, or Barry might have had to go out somewhere. Whatever the reason, she knew that she wouldn't rest now until she was sure that all was well, so she crossed to the deep cupboard under the stairs and took her coat from a hook, then after listening at the stairs door for a moment to ensure that Jenny was quiet she slipped out into the damp dark night.

It took only a matter of minutes to reach Grace's neat little home and she slipped into the shadowy entry, glad to escape from the cuttingly cold wind. Tapping at the back door, she hopped impatiently from foot to foot as she willed Grace to open it. She knocked again, louder this time, but still there was no answer, although the chink of light that shone from the gap in the drawn curtains told her that someone was in.

Cursing softly to herself, she retraced her steps down the entry to try her luck at the front door. Barry's motorbike and sidecar were parked neatly at the kerb, which meant he must be in, so why was no one answering? By now she was shivering, and deciding that no one was going to come, she had just turned to leave when the front door suddenly opened a crack and Barry peered out at her. Shock made her stop in her tracks for he seemed to have aged ten years and was ghastly pale.

'Barry, whatever's the matter? You look as if you've seen a bloody ghost!'

He turned and shuffled away, leaving the door to flap in the wind.

Cautiously she followed him inside, closing it firmly behind her. Everything was neat and tidy just as it always was, although she was quick to notice that the fire had burned dangerously low and the television was switched off. That in itself was strange, for there was nothing Barry liked better in the evenings than to settle down by a roaring fire in front of the television set.

'Where's Grace an' the kids?' She hardly dared to ask, but knew that she must.

Dropping heavily into a chair he thumbed towards the ceiling. 'I've put the kids to bed an' Grace is . . . Well, if you must know, Grace is gone.'

As she stared into his blank, empty eyes a cold hand gripped her heart.

'What do you mean, she's *gone*? Gone where?'

'Wi' her fancy man. Don't suppose there's much point in tryin' to keep it quiet. It'll probably have gone round the street like wildfire in no time. This sort o' gossip usually does.'

For one of the very rare occasions in her life Chris was speechless as she sank down beside him. He glanced at her shocked face and laughed bitterly.

'Life's a funny thing, you know, Chris. Here were me sittin' back all smug thinkin' I had it all when in actual fact, I never had nothin'.'

'That's not true, Barry, an' well you know it. Grace is a good wife an' I'm sure whatever's happened will sort itself out. Now come on. Tell me what's gone on.'

He sighed as he ran his hand distractedly through his hair. 'Ain't that much to tell.' He shrugged. 'Grace went out this afternoon to do a bit o' shoppin' an' turned back up wi' that Philip in tow. Then she tells me that the baby she's carryin' might be his and not mine. Funny, ain't it? I think I always knew deep down, but I shut me eyes to it. I always felt that there was somethin' between 'em. I suppose I just kept hopin' as whatever it was would fizzle out. There were all the trinkets that kept croppin' up. Grace kept tellin' me she'd bought 'em off the market but I ain't completely thick. I know quality when I see it an' Grace were never one to go spendin' money on herself anyway. An' then there was the way she suddenly seemed to start holdin' me at arm's length. But then, let's face it, he were much more Grace's sort than me, weren't he? Rich, handsome – the gift o' the gab. Huh! He could show her a way o' life that I *never* could, not in a million years, so in fairness to her, it's no wonder she had her head turned, is it?'

Guilt flooded through Chris. She had known about the affair before he did, and had encouraged Grace to keep quiet about it to spare his feelings, but obviously her advice had fallen on deaf ears and now Barry appeared to be a broken man.

'Oh Barry, I'm so sorry. What are you going to do?'

Again he shrugged. 'To be quite honest, right at this minute I ain't got the foggiest. I don't think it's sunk in yet.'

Chris draped her arms gently about his shoulders. 'She'll come back, you'll see,' she promised, but his head snapped up as he glared at her.

'Over my dead body she will – not wi' some other man's bastard growin' inside her. I don't think you quite understood. When I said she'd gone, what I should have said was – I kicked her out. I might not have a lot but I do have me pride. I would have laid down me life for her if need be, Chris. I worshipped her, but if I am to be honest, I don't think she ever loved me. Do you know somethin'? In all the years we've been together she never told me she loved me – not once. I think she only married me to get away from that witch of an aunt of hers, but I could stand that. She was a good wife an' I loved her enough for the both of us. I kept thinkin', Things will change – but they never did an' now they never will. She's gone and that's an end to it.'

'But what about the children? Why didn't she take them?' Chris asked tremulously.

''Cos I wouldn't let her, that's why. And I'll tell you somethin' else an' all. If I have my way she'll never so much as set eyes on them again.' There was so much hurt and bitterness in his voice that she was horrified.

'You can't mean that, Barry. Grace adores the kids – you know she does. It will kill her if you keep her away from them. Anyway, how would yer manage on your own wi' your job an' everything?'

'I'll find a way.'

Realising that now was not a good time to talk sense to him she said, 'All right then, I'll tell you what – drop 'em off to me in the morning on your way to work an' I'll make sure as Wendy gets to school. Then we'll take it from there, eh? See how yer feel when you've had time to calm down a bit.'

He bowed his head and nodded, and quietly she let herself out, aware that he needed some time alone to try and come to terms with what had happened.

A tap at the door made Grace pause in her restless pacing, and the next second it opened just a crack and Hetty's head peeped round.

'It's only me, love. I heard yer walkin' about an' wondered if

154

there were anythin' I could get yer afore I locked up an' come to bed.'

Grace smiled. 'No, Mrs Brambles – I mean, yes, there is actually. I can't get off to sleep so perhaps you could let me have a key? I think a walk might clear my head a bit.'

'No problem, love. Though I can't really say as I approve of a young woman wanderin' the streets at night. Not wi' all these bloody mods an' rockers rampagin' about causin' mischief. Still, you're old enough to please yourself. You'll find the key in the lock downstairs, an' don't call me Mrs Brambles – the name is Hetty.'

'All right . . . Hetty – thank you. I'll see you tomorrow morning. Don't worry, I won't disturb you when I come back in.'

Hetty chuckled. 'You'd have a job. Sleep like the dead I do, once I drop off. It would take an earthquake to wake me, but remember what I said, you just be careful now.'

'I will,' Grace promised, and as Hetty softly closed the door she slipped into her coat, which she had hung neatly in the great monstrosity of a wardrobe. Soon she was out in the street. She breathed deeply. Now that she was out she had no idea at all where she was going, so she headed for the town centre. It was deserted save for the odd few who were rushing from one pub to another so that they wouldn't miss last orders being called.

A thick fog was forming now that it had stopped raining and in places she could barely see her hand in front of her, but all the same it was a relief to be out and about. She came to Bond Gate and of habit her feet started walking in the direction of her aunt's house. It had been a long time since she had walked that way but tonight the urge was on her to see something and somewhere familiar.

On the Leicester Road bridge she paused to look down on Trent Valley railway station that ran beneath it. The platforms were deserted, except for one solitary guard who was huddled deep into a thick coat as he waited for a train to arrive, and after a time she walked on and turned into Oaston Road. It was strange walking this way after such a long time and when she came to her aunt's house she stopped to stare at it. It was as if time had stood still, for everything was exactly as she remembered it. The curtains were the same. The front step was still painted the same deep red colour, and the same identical doormat still lay at the front door. Most of the other houses in the street had brightly coloured Christmas trees sparkling in the windows, but the windows of her aunt's house were unadorned.

A feeling of sadness washed over her. Until she had met Barry her aunt had been her whole world, and although the way she had treated her had left a lot to be desired, still she wished that things could have been different. Aunt Emily was the one person in the world who could have told her what her parents had been like, but for some reason known only to herself, she never would. Grace had always yearned to know more about them. As a child she would lie in bed and dream about them, creating in her mind imaginary characters who closely resembled a handsome prince and a beautiful princess, who would one day come to save her from her wicked aunt. But they never had come and as the years wore on she'd come to accept that they never would. This was real life.

She sighed, glad of the thick fog that would hide her should her aunt happen to look out of the window. After some minutes she moved on to the gates of the cemetery. Tonight it held no fear for her. Once, what seemed a lifetime ago, she had shivered with terror when her aunt locked her in the cellar because of the close proximity to the graveyard, but now she found herself envying the souls that lay beneath the cold marble gravestones. For them the anguish of living was over. Her hand settled on her stomach and she began to cry as she wandered amongst the tombstones like a spectre in the night. She hated herself for feeling this way, but she hated this unborn child even more. This child would be the cause of her losing her other children and her husband, and at the moment she didn't know how she would cope with it. Had she been able to, she would gladly have torn the alien thing that was growing inside her from her body, but unless Nature took its course and caused her to miscarry then she was stuck with it.

Pausing, she rested against a gravestone that was leaning drunkenly in the mist and began to think of Philip. His reaction when he first heard the news about the baby had not been what she might have hoped for, but then in fairness, the way it had come about must have been something of a shock to say the least, so she supposed she should forgive him. She moved on, heading for the entrance again, but then steered towards the chapel instead. It loomed out of the mist and she slipped quietly inside, enjoying the peaceful atmosphere of the place.

Moving slowly to the altar she knelt and began to pray.

'Dear Lord,
Give me strength to face the days ahead.
Give me strength to be a better person.
Forgive me for my sins, and please keep Wendy and Simon and Barry safe.
Amen.'

She waited for a sign that she had been heard, but there was nothing but a ghostly silence, and in that moment she felt more alone than she had ever felt in her whole life.

Chapter Sixteen

'So, how did yer sleep then, love?' Hetty asked kindly as Grace walked into the kitchen. She was standing at the cooker frying a large panful of bacon. The mere smell of it made Grace start to feel nauseous.

'Not too badly, thank you.' She nodded at Will as she took a seat and he immediately blushed a deep red and hastily stared down at his plate. Hetty grinned, but tactfully made no comment before prattling on again.

'Aw well, it's to be expected. The first night in a strange bed is always the worst. Happen you'll be back in your own bed tonight, eh? Nice plateful o' bacon an' eggs be all right for yer, love?'

Grace's stomach revolted at the very thought. 'No thanks, Hetty, just a cup of tea will be fine.'

'Huh! That's hardly a good start to a day,' Hetty grumbled as she ladled the bacon onto a plate and carried it across to Will. 'I always reckon breakfast is the most important meal o' the day. My Will has a good fry-up every mornin', don't yer, son? Sets him up for a good day's work, so it does.' She beamed at him with pride before addressing Grace again.

'My Will works in the gardening department at Riversley Park. Got green fingers, he has, even if I do say so meself. He's very highly thought of, he is.'

If possible, Will blushed an even deeper shade and began to cram his food into his mouth as if he couldn't get away from the table quickly enough.

Grace looked across at him. He was actually a very nice-looking man. He had plenty of curly fair hair, and he was tall and muscular, which made Grace wonder why some woman had never snapped him up. Was it because he was so painfully shy? As yet, she had not heard him utter so much as a single word. But then it was hardly any of her business. The feeling of nausea was getting worse, and when Hetty suddenly started to pile two fried eggs onto his already laden plate she could bear it no longer and jumped up from the table, almost overturning her chair in the process.

'I'm so sorry, would you please excuse me?' Clamping her hand firmly across her mouth she shot from the room as Hetty watched her go with a deep frown on her face.

So, she was pregnant an' all then, was she? She had suspected as much, but this morning's little episode had confirmed it as far as she was concerned. Mm, there was definitely somethin' amiss here. Badly amiss, if the way Grace was behaving was anything to go by.

When Grace returned to the kitchen some minutes later, looking very pale, she found Hetty with her arms immersed up to the elbows in hot soapy water as she washed the pots at the deep stone sink. There was no sign of Will and she rightly guessed that he had left for work.

'Ah, so here yer are then. Feelin' better are yer, love?'

Grace nodded as she perched uncomfortably on the edge of a kitchen chair, but Hetty's next words almost caused her to slip off it.

'So when's the babby due then?' Keeping a watchful eye on her, Hetty dried her hands on a rough piece of towelling.

'May.' Grace kept her eyes downcast as Hetty crossed to the table and took the tea cosy from the big brown teapot. Without a word she poured them both a cup and slid one across the table to Grace. Grace thanked her and sipped at her tea. She could feel Hetty's eyes boring into her and had the strangest feeling that she could see right into her soul.

Today the old woman was dressed in thick woollen stockings that bagged unbecomingly around her ankles and a bright wraparound pinny, tied at the waist over a faded jumper. The curlers were still in her hair but today they were covered in a head square that she had wrapped around her head in turban fashion so that only one metal curler was visible on her forehead. Her face was so wrinkled that Grace found it impossible to gauge how old she might be, but her eyes were still bright and the most striking shade of blue that Grace had ever seen.

'Yer havin' a bad time of it at present, ain't yer, love?' Hetty whispered eventually. Grace nodded tearfully, fighting the urge to pour her heart out to the kindly old woman.

'Well, every cloud has a silver lining,' Hetty told her, reaching across the table to squeeze her hand. 'I'll tell yer what. After you've finished your tea I'll read your tea-leaves. I've got the gift, yer know? Just as me gran had before me. I go off to the Spiritualist Chapel in Queens Road at least twice a week an' you'd be surprised how it can help if you're feelin' troubled. You ought to come along some time.'

Grace was not at all sure that she wanted her tea-leaves read – not even sure that she believed in such things, if it came to that – but she

159

drained her cup anyway and passed it across to Hetty who swirled the cup around before tipping it upside down on the saucer.

After staring at the leaves for some seconds, she frowned. 'Mm . . . see a lot of heartache at the minute.'

Grace was not impressed. After all, hadn't she just admitted that she was going through a bad time? Even so she sat patiently as Hetty continued to stare.

'You're at a crossroads in your life an' yer have to decide which way to take. You've had a lot o' heartache right from when yer was just a nipper, from what I can see. But the heartache ain't over yet, I'm afraid. Things ain't always what they seem at first glance. I can see . . .' She stopped abruptly and pushed the saucer away from her. Grace noticed that the colour had drained from her face and she suddenly seemed nervous.

'Ah, what do I know anyway?' she gabbled. 'Here I am sittin' here like the pot's on, when I've got a list o' jobs as long as your arm waitin' to be done. Take no notice o' me, love. I'm just a silly old woman.'

She rose from the table and hastily changing the subject, she asked, 'What time is your . . . er . . . friend comin' round for yer then?'

'I'm not sure,' Grace said, feeling ridiculously unnerved by the episode that had just taken place. 'I'm not in the way, am I?'

'O' course you ain't. In fact, I shall be sorry to see yer go. It's nice to have a bit o' company in the day. I get lonely when Will's gone off to work, specially in the summer. He works really long hours then.' Hetty carried the rest of the pots to the sink, ushering Grace back into her chair when she offered to help.

'My Will's a nice lad, yer know, but he's a bit, what shall I say – slow, like – as you've probably noticed. I always hoped some nice girl would snap him up, for he's got a heart as big as a bucket, but some people ain't very good at lookin' at the person within, are they? They just go on face value, more's the pity. That's somethin' to beware of. All that glitters ain't always gold, as I discovered to me cost many years ago. Still, that's another story an' I don't suppose yer want to listen to the ramblin's of a silly old woman.'

Grace rose from the table. 'I don't think you're a silly old woman at all, Hetty. I think you're very kind.'

'It's nice of yer to say so. But now, go on, get yourself away an' get ready for your friend to come. Yer can wait for him in the front room if yer like. There's some nice bits o' furniture in there. Best room in the house, it is – only gets used on high days an' holidays. You'll be able to watch for him out o' the front window.'

'Thanks, Hetty.' Grace walked towards the door and as soon as she had disappeared through it, Hetty sank back into her chair and lifted her saucer again. She studied the tea-leaves intently for some minutes and then shuddered. My God, perhaps it was as well the poor girl didn't know what was in front of her, for if she did, she might have decided to end it all there and then. Hetty was aware that not everyone was as strong as she was, or at least as strong as she'd had to learn to become over the years. Shuddering again, she crossed to the sink and tossed the saucer into the hot soapy water.

When Grace entered the front room she paused to stare around in astonishment. The rest of the house, or at least what she had seen of it, was modest to say the least, but this room was so luxuriously furnished that it almost took her breath away. A huge Indian rug covered the floor and the furniture that was spaced around the walls would have done justice to a high-class antique shop. Grace had always loved old furniture and guessed that the contents of the room must have been worth a small fortune at least. Here and there, fine bone-china ornaments were placed on small occasional tables; they were also arranged along the length of the mantelpiece, and on closer inspection she saw that they were all Royal Doulton. She moved from piece to piece, fingering them in awe, admiring the craftsmanship that had gone into making them. Never in her wildest dreams would she have imagined Hetty owning anything so valuable, but then as Hetty had pointed out, people were not always what they seemed. Perhaps she had once been married to an antique dealer or somebody very rich? There was no way of knowing, and Grace knew that it was none of her business anyway, so stifling her curiosity she settled herself by the front window to wait.

It was almost two o'clock when Philip's sleek car pulled into the kerb outside Hetty's huge Victorian terraced house. Grace, who was watching from the window, sighed with relief and hurried outside to meet him. He smiled and draped his arm around her shoulders before following her back into the house.

'Are you all ready to go?' he asked.

She flashed him a wry smile. 'Of course. I hardly have anything to pack, have I?'

He tutted at his thoughtlessness. 'Sorry, I wasn't thinking. But we can soon put that right. Are you ready to go and face the music?'

'If you mean, am I ready to go and speak to Barry, he won't be home from work yet.'

161

'Right, then in the meantime we'd better go and have a look at this.' He handed her a leaflet with a picture of a lovely house on the front of it. 'I just popped into the estate agent's,' he explained, 'to look at properties to let. This was the one that caught my eye. We could be in for Christmas, apparently. It's out at Fenny Drayton – what do you think?'

Grace studied the photograph. 'It looks like the ideal place to bring up children,' she said quietly.

Seeing the tears that were shining on her long dark eyelashes he pulled her into an embrace. 'Look, Grace. I've had time to get my head round all this now. Things are going to be all right, I promise. Now that he's had a chance to calm down we'll go and see Barry tonight, and if he *still* won't let you have the children then we'll fight him through the courts if need be. I know that we made a mistake, but that doesn't make you an unfit mother. I promise you, we'll get the children back – do you hear me? It might take a little time so you'll have to try and be patient. In the meantime if we rent somewhere like this it will go in your favour when it does go to court. You can show them that you have somewhere nice to take the children to. And this will be only the start. Later on we can buy somewhere.'

'Oh Philip.' Hope shone in her eyes for the first time since this whole sorry mess had started. 'Do you really mean it?'

'Of course I do. The only trouble is, it might mean you staying here for another couple of nights at least until we can move in. Do you think you could manage that?'

She nodded. 'Yes, I could. Hetty is really nice actually, and so is her son.'

'Oh, is he now?' Philip teased. 'I can see I shall have to keep my eye on you, young lady, or I shall be getting jealous. Where is the old dear anyway?'

'She's through here. Follow me and we'll just go and check that it's all right with her.'

Grace led him along the hallway and as they entered the kitchen Hetty looked up from the newspaper she was reading. Removing the glasses that were perched on the end of her nose she stared at Philip solemnly before saying, 'You've come for her then?'

Philip nodded and flashed her a dazzling smile as he turned on the charm. Normally it had women falling at his feet but it left Hetty cold and straight-faced as she continued to stare at him.

'I was wondering,' he continued, unabashed, 'if it might be possible for Grace to stay for a few more nights?'

'Grace is welcome to stay here for as long as she likes,' Hetty told him shortly. 'How many nights were yer thinkin' of?'

'I'm not quite sure yet, to be honest,' he admitted. 'But I should be able to tell you when we return later this evening.'

'Fair enough.' Hetty replaced her glasses and without another word went back to reading the newspaper.

'I thought you said she was nice,' Philip hissed as he took Grace's elbow and led her from the room.

She grinned. 'She is to me,' she said with a hint of amusement. 'It seems that she hasn't taken to you though.'

'That's the understatement of the year,' Philip muttered as he opened the front door and then side-by-side they made their way to the car.

The second she heard the door close behind them, Hetty scuttled along the hallway with an agility that would have done justice to a woman half her age to watch them leave from the front window. The wrinkles on her forehead deepened.

'Smooth-talkin' smarmy git,' she muttered to the empty room as she watched him hold the car door open for Grace. When they had gone she turned slowly and her eyes roamed around the room.

Once, the possessions in this room had meant the world to her. At one time there had been even more than there was now, but some things had found their way into the pawnshop over the years for a mere fraction of their worth, and had never been reclaimed, as Hetty struggled to bring up her son and daughter. Time had taught her that possessions were not important. It was people that mattered, and she had a sinking feeling that Grace was about to discover the same thing – the hard way, as she had. Still, the only way to learn was by making your own mistakes, and hard as it was to stand by and watch, there was nothing she could do. Sadly she pottered away, closing the door carefully behind her.

Philip glanced at his passenger as he stopped at the junction at the bottom of Edward Street.

'Would you like me to take you home first so that you can collect a few of your things?' he said.

Grace shook her head. 'There wouldn't be any point. I haven't got my key.'

'Never mind.' Hearing the despair in her voice he tried to turn her attention to other things. 'It looks a nice house, doesn't it? The estate agent has let me have the keys for a couple of hours.' He flashed Grace a dazzling smile.

Sighing, she nodded and settled back into the deep leather seat. It would soon be time for Wendy to come out of school – that is, if she had gone today – and she wondered who Barry had arranged to fetch her. She was missing the children already, and was sorely tempted to go to meet Wendy herself, but she realised that this would only upset Barry all the more, so she dismissed the idea almost immediately. She wondered if Daisy would be looking after Simon, but again, she was too ashamed of what she'd done to even consider facing her, so at the moment she had to accept that there was no chance of seeing either of the children. Still, Philip had promised that somehow he would get them back and with that for now she had to be content.

The car glided smoothly along and soon they were leaving Nuneaton behind as they headed for the countryside. The small village of Fenny Drayton was situated between Weddington and Sibson. Grace had often passed through it, most recently when she and Barry had taken the children on a rare outing to Twycross Zoo on the motorbike and sidecar. But never in her wildest dreams had she anticipated living anywhere so idyllic, let alone being driven there in an expensive car. In other circumstances she supposed that she would have been happy – ecstatic, in fact – but at the moment all she could think about was the deep hurt she had caused Barry and the longing to see her children. If Philip noticed her pensive mood he was tactful enough to refrain from mentioning it and soon they were pulling onto the drive of a house that made Grace's eyes stretch wide. It was detached, with gardens on all sides. Beyond the gardens, for as far as her eye could see, was rolling countryside. There was no entry here, no shared yard, just a sense of peace and tranquillity. She followed Philip to the front door and waited as he fumbled for the right key. At last he located it, and after following him inside, she found herself in a hallway that was as big as her small front room back at home.

'It's all fully furnished,' he informed her cheerfully, 'so we won't need to rush out and buy anything. That is, if you like it, of course.'

He pushed open the first door they came to and Grace was confronted by a lounge that might have come straight out of a magazine. There was a deep-pile carpet on the floor that reached all the way to the skirting boards, and an expensive-looking three-piece suite in the latest leather-look fashion that was becoming so popular. At the back of the house was a large kitchen with a twin-tub washing machine and an expensive-looking cooker with an eye-level grill.

'The owners have gone abroad for nine months,' Philip explained to her. 'They certainly believed in all the mod cons, didn't they?'

164

She nodded, too overawed to speak, and so the inspection continued as they went from one tastefully furnished room to another. There were three beautiful bedrooms and a bathroom that took Grace's breath away, as well as a dining room decorated in cream and gold. It was so lovely that Grace wondered if she would ever dare let the children eat in there.

Lastly, they went into the back garden through French doors that led off from the lounge. It was there that Philip asked, 'So – what do you think then? Does it pass muster?'

'Oh, Philip.' Grace stared at him from moist eyes. 'It has to be the most beautiful house I've ever seen. But it must be *awfully* expensive. Are you quite sure that you can afford it?'

He laughed. 'Of course I can. We wouldn't be looking at it otherwise, would we? I've already told the estate agent that if you like it we'll take it on a six-month lease for a start. By then you'll have had the baby and we'll be able to start looking around for a place of our own.'

When they had reached the bottom of the garden, Grace turned to look back at the house. The air was alive with the sound of birdsong and she felt sure that she must be dreaming as she stood beneath the leafless branches of a huge copper beech tree. It was idyllic – and suddenly she knew that things must work out. How could they not, in such surroundings with a man like Philip to look after her? She slipped her hand into his; even now in December when the garden was far from its best she loved it. It was the sort of house that she and Barry had always joked about buying if they ever won the Pools – and now here it was, hers for the taking.

'It's just perfect,' she sighed.

Satisfied, he led her back up the winding garden path. 'Right then, we'll pop back into Nuneaton and get all the papers signed. By then Barry should be home from work and we'll be able to pick your clothes up.'

'And the children, of course,' she said quickly.

He frowned. 'Look, Grace, I wouldn't bank on getting them back. Not today at least. Obviously you know Barry a lot better than I do, but I'd say he needs a bit longer to get his head round all this.'

When she glanced at him fearfully he added, 'Don't look like that. He'll come round, you'll see. He just needs time to come to terms with things. I could be totally wrong, of course. You might find that he has their bags packed ready and waiting. I just don't want you to build your hopes up, that's all. He'll soon see that he can't manage the children on his own, and when he does, he'll be glad to hand them over to you.'

She wished that she could be as confident as him, but the niggling doubt in her stomach was beginning to make her feel sick again. It was then that she felt it. Her hands flew to her stomach and a look of wonder washed over her face.

'Grace – what is it? Are you ill?'

She looked at him from shining eyes. 'Philip, it moved. I just felt the baby move.'

He coughed uncomfortably. 'Isn't it . . . er – a little bit early for that?'

'Not for a third baby,' she grinned, and suddenly the animosity she had felt towards this unborn child fled. Suddenly it was real, a tiny little person in its own right, and no matter what the future held she knew that she would love it, just as she loved her other children.

'Come on,' she said with a new confidence. 'Let's go and do what needs to be done.'

It was almost six o'clock when they pulled up outside her house. As Philip made to climb from the car she placed her hand on his arm and stopped him. 'It might be best if I went in alone,' she said sensibly.

Sucking in his lips, he nodded. 'I suppose you're right. But if you need me, just stick your head out of the door and give me a shout.'

She smiled sadly. 'Barry might be many things, Philip, but he's not a violent man. I'll be fine, honestly. You just wait here and I'll be back before you know it, hopefully with the children.' With a confidence she was far from feeling she swung her long slender legs from the car and strode up the short path to the front door.

Barry inched the door open, and glared at her. He was unshaven and she was shocked to see that his eyes looked wild and were red from lack of sleep.

'Wait there!' he barked, and to her horror he slammed the door in her face. Within seconds he flung it open again and tossed a suitcase onto the wet ground at her feet.

'There, now take your stuff an' go.'

'But Barry . . . the children. Won't you even let me see them?' Her tortured voice cut deep but he stood his ground.

'They ain't *your* kids any more,' he stated coldly. 'You gave up all claims to them when you decided to get yourself a fancy man. As far as I'm concerned, you'll see them over my dead body, so sling your hook.' His eyes moved past her to the car parked at the kerb, and her heart ached as she saw the look of utter despair that flitted across his face. But in an instant it was gone, replaced by a look of bitterness.

'Just go, Grace. What you tryin' to do, rub salt into the wound?'

'Barry, *please*, just listen to me. I never set out to hurt you – I swear it as God is my witness. What I've done is wrong, I know that, but please, *please* don't take my children away from me. It will be Christmas in no time, and I need them with me.' She was openly sobbing now, but he stared at her coldly and started to shut the door.

'Happen you should have thought of that before, eh? Why should I lose them for what you've done wrong? They're my kids an' all, you know, and they'll be spending Christmas here wi' me where they belong, in the comfort of their own home. Now just go, Grace. Ain't you done enough damage?'

'Barry, *please*. Look, this is where I'm staying.' With desperation lacing her voice she grabbed the piece of paper with Hetty's address written on it from her coat pocket and pressed it into his hand. 'If you should have a change of heart you can find me here. I'm staying with Norma's mother in Edward Street.'

The door closed quietly as she stood with tears streaming down her cheeks, mingling with the needle-sharp rain that had begun to fall. Suddenly she could stand it no more and she threw herself at the door and began to hammer on it with her fists.

'Barry, I want my children. Do you hear me? Please, I'll beg if that's what you want.'

In a second Philip was out of the car and at her side. 'Grace, come away,' he urged, but she fought him as he started to drag her down the short pathway.

'Get off me. Don't you understand? I need my children!' But her strength was no match for his and in seconds he had bundled her unceremoniously into the car before he dashed back to grab her case and throw it into the back seat behind her.

She huddled into a ball as tears flooded from her eyes. Sensing that there was nothing he could say to comfort her, he started the car and drove away. By the time they got back to Hetty's her grief had quietened to dull hiccupping sobs and he sat at her side in silence in the light from the street-lamp.

'Look,' he said eventually, when it seemed that the uncomfortable silence that had sprung up between them would go on for ever, 'I hate to leave you like this but I'm afraid I've made arrangements for this evening. Let's get you inside, eh? I'm sure you'll feel better in the morning after a good night's sleep. And don't forget what I said. If Barry doesn't have a change of heart we'll fight him through the courts once we've moved into the house.'

Sniffing loudly, she blew her nose on a huge white handkerchief that he handed her. 'Couldn't you cancel your arrangements for tonight?' she pleaded.

Unable to meet her eyes he looked away. 'I'm afraid I can't. I have to see a very important client who puts a lot of business my way. But I'll be back as soon as I can tomorrow – I promise.' He leaned across her and opened the door, and she almost fell into the road before coming to stand on the pavement to look at him from huge frightened eyes.

'Things will be all right, won't they, Philip? I mean – I *will* get the children back soon, won't I?'

He looked away from the pleading in her eyes.

'Of course you will,' he muttered uncomfortably. 'Now go on, get yourself in out of this rain or you'll catch your death of cold. I'll see you sometime in the morning if I can get away from the garage.'

With a final smile he pulled away from the kerb and she stood and watched until the tail-lights of the car had disappeared from sight. Then slowly she turned around and made her way into Hetty's, which for now at least was the only home she had. And all the time a vision of Barry's haunted eyes swam before her and she felt as if her heart was about to break.

Chapter Seventeen

'So, where's *he* off to tonight then?'

Grace had just stepped through the front door and, detecting the hint of sarcasm in Hetty's voice, she flushed. 'Philip does have a business to attend to. I don't expect him to be with me twenty-four hours a day, holding my hand.' Realising that she'd snapped, she was instantly contrite. 'I'm sorry, Hetty. I didn't mean to bite your head off. I'm just a bit touchy at the minute, that's all.'

Philip had just dropped her off, just as he had every single evening since she had left home, and unwittingly Hetty had touched a raw nerve. Grace had been staying at Hetty's for three nights now, and although Philip had seen her for a few hours every day whenever he could fit her into his hectic timetable, he hadn't as yet spent one single night with her. Still, she tried to console herself, things would be different when they moved into the house.

Hetty smiled at her good-naturedly. 'Don't worry about it, love. I asked for it, pokin' an' pryin' into other people's business when it ain't nowt to do wi' me. Come on through to the kitchen an' I'll mash us a cup o' tea, eh? I dare say Will might be ready for one an' all now. I was just ploughin' through the ironin'. And then perhaps I could show yer the latest photos I had from our Norma of her new babby.'

'That would be nice.' Grace mustered up a smile. 'I had a letter from her not so long back, but I haven't had any photos.'

When she followed Hetty into the kitchen, Will, who was engrossed in a programme on the television, glanced up at her and smiled shyly. He was beginning to be a little more relaxed in her company now and Grace really liked him. He was such a kind gentle man it would have been hard not to. Hetty bustled across to the sink to fill the kettle and while she was waiting for it to boil she moved across to an enormous wooden ironing board. Lifting the heavy iron she attacked a crisp white sheet with a vengeance.

'Done anythin' nice today have yer, love?' the elderly woman asked, then wished she could take the words back. 'Forget I asked that. I'm off again, ain't I? Stickin' me big nose in where it's not wanted.'

'It's all right, Hetty. I know you mean well.'

As Grace sank onto a hard-backed kitchen chair, Hetty was concerned to see how pale she looked. The poor girl seemed to be a bundle of nerves, although in the circumstances Hetty supposed it was fairly understandable. Of course, Grace had never whispered so much as a word about why she was staying there, but Hetty was an astute woman and had managed to work it out for herself. She would have bet an arm and a leg that Grace had left her husband and Philip was her fancy man. Normally she would have condemned most women for that, yet from what she knew of Grace from the past, and from what she could see of her now, Hetty guessed that there was much more to this little scenario than met the eye. Perhaps her husband had been a wife batterer – or an alcoholic, perhaps? Whatever he was, Grace was obviously deeply unhappy, probably because she'd had to leave her children. And then there was the one she was carrying, of course. Was it Philip's? Hetty had no sure way of knowing, but what she *did* know was that she had not taken to Philip, not at all. There was something about him that made her flesh crawl, although Grace seemed to be completely under his spell. Still, it was early days yet and Hetty hoped that the girl would see through him, just as she had. Folding the sheet she had just ironed she placed it on a neat pile on the table then went to lift the kettle that was singing merrily and mashed the tea.

'You'll likely be leavin' us soon then, eh?' she remarked, as she stirred the pot.

Grace nodded. 'Yes, I will, Hetty. The day after tomorrow actually, if all goes to plan.' In a way she would be sad to leave, for although she had only known Hetty properly for a few short days she liked her a great deal and knew that she would miss her – Will as well, if it came to that. Half of her was longing for the time when she and Philip would have their own place and start their new life together, but the other half of her was dreading going without the children. Here at least she was close to them, even if she wasn't allowed to see them. But once she moved to Fenny Drayton they would be miles apart, and the thought was daunting to say the least. She had pushed the Fenny Drayton address through Barry's door two days ago, hoping that he would have a change of heart and at least let her spend some time with them in the future, or perhaps get in touch here at Hetty's, but up until now he had ignored her. Deep down she couldn't blame him.

An idea suddenly occurred to her and as she sipped at her tea it began to grow. She felt that if she didn't confide in someone soon she would burst, so when she saw that Will had fallen into a doze she looked anxiously across at Hetty. Somehow she sensed that she could trust her and so, hesitantly, she asked, 'Would you mind if I talked to you, Hetty?'

'Course I wouldn't,' Hetty chuckled as she dragged a chair up to the table to join her. 'Talkin' comes free.' She scratched her head, sending one of her metal curlers off on a curious slant. 'What's on your mind, love?'

'I'm not sure where to start.' Grace fiddled nervously with the fringes on the tablecloth. 'I've been a bit of a fool, I suppose. In fact, I've been an idiot. Philip isn't my husband, as you've probably gathered. I met Barry when I worked with Norma and we eventually got married, six years ago. We bought a little house in Marlborough Road. I thought I was happy, or at least as happy as I'd ever been . . . but then I met Philip. We share a love of ballroom dancing and when he asked me to be his dancing partner I was thrilled. You see, Barry has never been one for going out much. He prefers his own fireside. For a while everything was fine – the arrangement suited us both, but then . . . I started to feel more for Philip than I should and things just sort of got out of hand. I can't blame anyone but myself.'

It was a story Hetty had heard many times before. 'Was your husband bad to yer?' she asked softly.

Grace shook her head without a second's hesitation. 'Far from it. Barry is a thoroughly good man, although I'm not so sure that I ever loved him. Philip is just so different somehow – so alive and exciting. But it's not Barry I'm so concerned about. It's Wendy and Simon, our children. I broke down and told him about me and Philip and the baby, and he threw me out. I don't blame him, of course, but it's tearing me apart, being kept away from them. Do you think it would do any good if I went round and tried to speak to him?'

'Mm . . . now there's a question.' Hetty stroked her chin thoughtfully and after a time peered at Grace. 'Do yer really want to know what I think yer should do?'

Grace nodded solemnly, and Hetty went on cautiously, 'I'm only sayin' 'cos you're askin', so don't get takin' no offence, but I reckon yer should go to your husband an' throw yourself on his mercy. *Beg* him to take yer back, if need be.'

Grace stared at her incredulously. 'But I don't want to go back, Hetty. I just want my children with me. I love Philip.' The uncertainty in her voice belied her words and Hetty frowned.

'You might think yer do now, love, but there's all sorts o' love, believe me. There's the mind-blowin' sort as you're experiencin' right

171

now with your new man, an' then there's the safe comfortable sort as yer had with your husband. Now the first is by far the more excitin' of the two, admittedly. Trouble is, it rarely lasts. Once yer start to live together yer see each other for what you are – warts an' all. The second sort goes on for ever. An' as for your children . . . well, what can I say? Trouble is, yer can't have your cake *and* eat it. Looking at it from your husband's point o' view, he's probably feelin' like his whole world has fallen apart at the moment, and he won't want to lose his kids an' all, will he? Sayin' that, I think yer should go and see him, and think on what I said on your way round there. This Philip might be a decent bloke, or he might not. Either way . . . will it last? You have another little 'un comin' along soon, and yer have to think o' that one too, don't you, pet?'

Grace stared at the table. She hadn't wanted to hear that, but all the same there was some sense in what Hetty had said – only as regards to the children though. The rest of it was rubbish, for she knew that once she had got the children back, she and Philip would live together happily ever after. She loved him, and he loved her. Believing that, was the only thing keeping her sane at the moment.

'Thanks for the chat, Hetty,' she mumbled, reaching across to squeeze her hand. 'I'm sorry to unburden all my troubles on you.'

'Think nothin' of it, love,' Hetty replied. 'That's what friends are for. An' I don't think you're a bad girl, Grace. You've just bin led astray, that's all. We can all have us heads turned, but things have a way o' comin' right in the end. Now go on, get yourself round there while you're in the mood. There's no time like the present. Go an' see that husband o' yours.'

'I think I will.' Grace rose from the table and smiled at Hetty grate-fully. 'Thanks for listening,' she said softly. 'If I hadn't confided in someone soon I would have gone mad. I feel a bit selfish now after what you must have gone through when you lost your husband. My troubles are self-inflicted, but it must have been much worse for you when you were widowed, especially when you had two young chil-dren to bring up.'

Hetty opened her mouth to speak, but then she thought better of it and clamped it shut. She watched Grace walk from the room and as her eyes settled on Will her heart was heavy. Grace had obviously chosen the path she was going to take and nothing she or anyone else said would change it now. She could only pray for Grace's sake and the child she was carrying that things *would* come right in the end. As for the comment Grace had just passed about her own situ-ation – huh! Hetty could have enlightened her, but pride had prevented

172

her from doing so. The past was the past, and nothing she said now could change it, so best leave things as they were and let Grace believe what she would.

Barry's eyebrows almost disappeared into his hairline when he saw his wife standing at the door. He glanced behind her, expecting to see Philip's car at the kerb, but when he saw that Grace was alone, he opened the door and reluctantly allowed her in. The children's toys were scattered across the floor and her heart ached at the sight of them. An awkward silence stretched between them. Barry had aged, and there was a stoop to his shoulders that Grace had never noticed before. His eyes, which she had always considered to be one of his best features, were sunk deep into his head, making him appear ill, and he was ghostly pale. When he saw her looking at the toys he shrugged.

'The kids ain't here, if that's what you've come for. They're stoppin' with me mam for a few days. It's difficult in the mornings, with me bein' at work.' All the aggression had burned itself out and shame washed over her as she saw what she had done to him. He was merely a shadow of the man he had been, and in that moment the enormity of the step she had taken came home to her and she hated herself.

'Couldn't we come to some arrangement, Barry? With the children, I mean. Why don't I have them in the week and you have them at the weekends? It can't be easy for your mother. She isn't getting any younger, is she? That way we could all be happy.'

He stared at her as if she had taken leave of her senses. 'HAPPY! HAPPY! Huh! Is that supposed to be some sort o' cruel joke or what? How can I *ever* be happy again – or the kids, for that matter? Don't you realise what you've done, Grace? You've destroyed all that we worked so hard to build up over the years, just for the sake of some smooth-talkin' bastard who'll drop you the minute he's had enough of you. And where will you be then, eh? There'll be another mouth to feed an' all by then.'

Grace lowered her head and wrung her hands. 'I didn't come here to argue, Barry. I came here to try and sort out something for the children. None of this is their fault, so why should they be punished for what *I've* done? I'm really sorry for what's happened. If I could turn the clock back I would, but I can't change it now, you know that.'

He began to pace up and down the floor like a caged animal as he ran his hand distractedly through his hair in the manner that she had always found so endearing. Suddenly he stopped abruptly and turned to face her. '*Why* did you have to tell me, Grace? I was happy, so were the kids. If you'd kept your mouth shut I'd never have been none the wiser an' I would have loved the baby, you know I would.'

Although she had promised herself that she wouldn't, she began to cry softly. Deep down she still cared about him a great deal, as she always had, but this feeling was nothing compared to what she felt for Philip.

'I had no choice, I couldn't live with myself.' The words sounded ineffectual even to her own ears, but it was all she could think of to say.

He stared at her. 'Well, if that's all you came for, happen it's time you were leavin'. There ain't any more to be said, is there? I loved you, Grace, more than I've ever loved anybody in me whole life, but I always knew as you never loved me. I suppose, lookin' back, I should have realised that some day you'd meet somebody who you *would* love. In fact, I lived in fear of it. Well, now you have, so go an' be happy. Funny, ain't it? Now I've got over the first shock of it, I find I can't hate you. I'd like to, 'cos it would make things easier for me, but I can't. I suppose it's the way I'm made. I will say this though. Wendy and Simon are mine, and if need be I'll fight you tooth and nail through every court in the land to keep them, so be warned. I don't intend to lose them as well.'

She shuddered at the sincerity of his words and in that moment she realised that if she were ever to see her children again, she would have a battle on her hands.

'So be it then. I came here hoping that we could come to some arrangement that we could all be happy with.' Her chin jutted with determination and her wonderful eyes flashed as she stared back at him. 'If you want a battle then you've got it, Barry. But be prepared, Philip is willing to hire the best solicitor there is, if need be.'

'Huh! Money again, eh? There are some things in life that are more important, you know?' His eyes were flashing as dangerously as hers by now, and realising that this was fast developing into an argument that would get them nowhere, she began to back towards the door.

'I think you were right. It *is* time I was going.'

As the fight went out of him his shoulders sagged. There was so much he wanted to say, but what was the point? Grace had made her choice and he did have *some* pride. He watched her storm from the room, slamming the door so hard behind her that it danced on its hinges. Silence settled around him like a cloak, and dropping his head into his hands, he sobbed.

Chapter Eighteen

'Do come in,' Emily smiled as she held the door wide for her friend to enter, and it was all Miss Mountjoy could do to contain the news she had to come to impart as she followed her along the hallway. Despite the fact that she professed to being riddled with arthritis, she had almost run the distance from her own home to Emily's and now she was bursting to tell her.

Once she was seated sedately at the table with her hands folded primly in her lap, she waited until Emily had made the customary cup of tea before beginning.

'I think I should tell you, dear, before anyone else does, that I have heard some rather disturbing news about Grace.'

Instantly, she had Emily's undivided attention. In the years since Grace had left home, Miss Mountjoy had followed her every move, for she lived only doors away from Barry's mother, so got to hear via the neighbours all that went on.

'Well?' Emily demanded as Miss Mountjoy sipped at her tea, enjoying herself immensely.

'Well, first of all I just need to say that I'm not one for gossip as you know, dear, so what I have to tell you gives me no joy whatsoever . . . But the thing is, word has it that Grace has left her husband for another man.'

Emily almost choked on her tea as her eyes started from her head.

'It's true, I assure you,' Miss Mountjoy piped up. 'Apparently she started to go dancing with this gentleman and before you know it, she's run away with him! Left her husband and children without a by your leave, by all accounts. But then it's hardly surprising, is it, when you think back to how she treated you. Sadly, that isn't the worst of it though . . .'

When she paused to sip at her drink again it was all Emily could do to stop herself from throttling her there and then.

'*Well?* Get on with it then!' she barked.

Miss Mountjoy sighed dramatically for effect. 'The thing is, it's rumoured she's carrying her fancy man's child, which is why her husband slung her out.'

Emily couldn't hide the smirk of satisfaction that played on her lips. 'So . . . just as I predicted, no good came of her passion for dancing then. Didn't I warn her a million times right from when she was a child that it would be her downfall?'

'You did, dear. And how right you were. But I don't want you worrying about it. You did all you possibly could for her, now it's time for the ungrateful young woman to get her comeuppance.'

Emily bit into a ginger biscuit as she basked in what Miss Mountjoy had just told her. Oh, revenge was *so* sweet!

'Goodbye then, love. You take good care o' yourself now, do you hear me? An' if ever you're by this way, pop in and see me. You'll always be welcome.'

'Thanks, Hetty, I'll do that.' As Grace stepped away from the old woman with tears in her eyes, she saw Philip glance at his expensive wristwatch. He swung her suitcase up effortlessly, and without so much as a glance in Hetty's direction, strode out to the waiting car.

Grace followed him silently and within seconds the car was pulling away from the kerb as she raised her hand in a final wave to Hetty. She peeped at Philip but he was intent on the road ahead so she settled back in her seat and said nothing as he headed for the outskirts of the town. Soon they were in the countryside. A feeling of panic engulfed her; everything was happening so fast, but still she sat silent until at last they pulled up outside the house that was to become her home in Fenny Drayton.

'Here we are then.' Philip bounded out of the car and lugged her suitcase from the back seat. Grace followed him into the house; it was just as beautiful as she remembered it, but strangely it brought her no joy. When Philip disappeared up the stairs with her case she slowly made her way through to the kitchen. When he came back down he pointed to some brown paper carrier bags on the kitchen table.

'I did a bit of food shopping before I came to pick you up. I think you'll find there's everything you need to keep you going in there for a couple of days at least.'

The feeling of panic intensified as she stared at him. 'What do you mean, keep me going? Don't you mean *us*?'

'Ah well . . . bit of a problem there, I'm afraid. Unfortunately, I shan't be able to move in properly for another couple of days. Business – I'm going to be out of town. But don't worry – you'll be fine. I'll be back for the weekend at the latest, and by then you'll have had time to settle in.'

When he saw the look of horror on her face, the smile slid from his lips and an expression of irritation flitted across his features.

'But Philip, what about the children? You said we'd get a solicitor.' Tears spilled down her pale cheeks as he gathered her into his arms.

'We *will* get a solicitor, but nothing's going to happen overnight, is it? Next week will be plenty soon enough to start looking into that, and by then Barry might have calmed down enough to be reasonable.'

Swallowing the lump that had formed in her throat she raised a smile. 'I suppose you're right,' she admitted reluctantly.

Stepping away from her, he inched towards the door. 'Right, I'd best be off.'

She watched as he hurried away, and minutes later his car roared off the drive and she was alone as a deafening silence settled all around her. She moved around mechanically, opening cupboards and looking into one silent room after another. Come on Grace, she told herself firmly. Pull yourself together. If the children are going to be coming soon you have to get the place ready for them.

She located the airing cupboard in a corner of the huge bathroom and after selecting some brightly coloured bedding she quickly made up the two single beds in the room next to the bedroom that would be hers and Philip's. Next she hurried back downstairs and put away the shopping that Philip had done. Then she went upstairs again and slowly unpacked her case. By now the light was fast fading from the afternoon and as she approached the French windows in the dining room that led out onto the garden she saw that a misty drizzle had begun to fall. Everywhere looked deserted and suddenly loneliness engulfed her. The children would be home from school now; she wondered what they would be doing. Normally they would be chatting away to her about what they had done during the day while she rushed around organising the dinner. Barry was a terrible cook, Daisy had always joked that he could burn water, and Grace hoped that they would be getting a decent meal. Still, she tried to cheer herself, they would soon be with her and then they could all start to get on with their lives again.

She made herself a cheese sandwich – there seemed little point in cooking just for herself. But it tasted like sawdust and lodged in her throat so eventually she threw it in the bin and made do with two very strong cups of tea instead, before dragging herself off to bed for an early night.

The first night in her new home was not at all as she had envisaged it would be. The strange noises of the countryside made her toss and turn restlessly. She had imagined lying in Philip's muscular arms as they planned their future, but once again she was alone. Even more alone than when she had lived with her aunt. She found herself thinking of her now as the tears that had been threatening slowly streamed down her cheeks to dampen the pillow. Could it be that her aunt had been right all along? Was she really evil? She tried to push the thoughts away. No, of course she wasn't. She had only married Barry to escape her aunt and now that she had found someone she really *did* love she deserved to be happy. Everyone did. Soon the children would join her and they would all live happily ever after. As she tried to convince herself she finally fell into an uneasy doze.

Philip phoned her twice over the next few days and finally reappeared late on Friday night, brandishing a bottle of wine and a small suitcase, and looking more than a little sheepish.

'Sorry, love. I couldn't get away before.' His eyes swept the lounge appreciatively. There was a fire burning in the grate and Grace had polished the furniture until he could see his face in it. 'Someone's been busy,' he commented, and Grace flushed at the praise, so pleased to see him that she would have forgiven him anything.

'Well, I didn't have much else to do, did I?' she said. 'Come and see what I've done upstairs. I've got the bedroom all ready for Wendy and Simon.'

She dragged him towards the stairs, but when they reached the top his arm slid around her waist and he led her straight to their room. 'Show me later.' His voice was husky with desire and for the next hour she gave herself up to the sheer joy of having him all to herself. Much later she got up to make them something to eat and he followed her back down the stairs.

'Where are the rest of your things?' She nodded towards his case, which was lying where he had left it at the side of the front door. He shrugged as he pulled her back into his arms.

'I won't be needing any more than that for now, not for the time being at least.' His lips were leaving little trails of fire all around her neck. 'If we're going to be moving again when the baby comes I may as well leave the rest of my stuff at home.'

'Home? I thought this was going to be our home.' When she pulled away from him he saw the panic in her eyes.

'Of course it is.' His voice was placating. 'But you have to accept that I'll still be staying at my old home now and again. Just when my children are there.'

'And your wife . . .'

He shrugged. 'She's still there too,' he admitted grudgingly. 'But you know that there's nothing between us. Hasn't been for ages. She moved into another bedroom months ago. I just want to try and keep it civilised for the sake of the boys, that's all.'

As he was about to take on her own two Grace felt that it would have been unreasonable under the circumstances to complain so she settled back into his arms and sighed. 'Everything seems a bit of a mess at the minute, doesn't it?'

'Not really. We just need a settling-down period, that's all.' His hand found its way beneath her thin cotton dressing-gown, and suddenly all thoughts of the children fled as she once again lost herself in the magic of being with him. This was love as she had always dreamed it would be, and for now there was no one in the world but them.

Their first weekend together was idyllic. They went for walks in the fields that bordered the house, and when darkness fell Grace built huge fires that roared up the chimney as they curled up in front of it together with a bottle of wine. Yet still there was an ache for the children she had left behind and Philip saw the yearning in her eyes whenever she spoke of them. On Monday morning she stood on the doorstep straightening his tie as she looked up into his eyes.

'I thought I might catch the bus into Nuneaton today and see if Barry might let me see the children. Unless you've made an appointment to see a solicitor, of course.'

He saw the hope in her face and shuffled from foot to foot uncomfortably. 'Look, Grace, you know what it was like last week. I hardly had time to breathe, what with getting you settled in here and work and one thing and another. I'll phone a solicitor sometime this week. That is, if Barry's in a better frame of mind. I wouldn't count on it though. I have a feeling he isn't going to give in gracefully and I think you ought to resign yourself to the fact that we may have a battle on our hands to get the children back. It could take some time. And anyway, Wendy might be at school, then you'll have gone all that way for nothing.'

As he voiced her worst fears, a look of misery settled on her face and she wondered who would be looking after Simon. 'I think I'll go and see just the same. If I go late afternoon and they're not at home with Barry, Daisy will probably be looking after them. Will you be back this evening?'

He shook his head. 'Afraid not, love. James, my oldest, is home from university today so I ought to make the effort to see him. I'll be back tomorrow though, and you have some money, don't you? If you need me for anything else, phone me at the garage.'

'I will,' she promised, and seconds later he was gone and the silence of the house once again wrapped itself around her.

It was almost four o'clock in the afternoon before the bus pulled into the station in Nuneaton. Grace looked around at the familiar places and realised that she had missed them. It seemed very noisy after the days she had spent in the countryside. Everywhere she looked, people were rushing around trying to finish their Christmas shopping, but she was keen to see the children now so she set off through the marketplace. It was bitterly cold and shoppers with their heads bent against the biting wind hurried past her as if she was invisible. By the time she paused in front of the small terraced house that she had used to call home, her cheeks were glowing and she was breathless. Hesitantly she tapped at the door, and as she heard the sounds of her children playing inside she felt as if her heart was breaking. The door inched open and Daisy stared at her open-mouthed. 'Good God above! *Grace* . . . what are you doin' here?'

Grace felt colour flood her cheeks as she looked away from the woman she had come to love. 'I . . . I . . . Well, I've come to see Barry – and the children.'

Daisy glanced nervously across her shoulder. Grace could hear the children and it was all she could do to stop herself from elbowing Daisy aside.

'Barry's at work.' Daisy's eyes were cold as she looked back at Grace. 'It might be best if you came back when he's in.' She would have pushed the door to, but Grace put out her arm and stayed her.

'*Please*, Daisy. Let me just see them for a moment or two. I know you must be angry with me, but I *need* to see them. I can't bear it. This is tearing me apart.'

Daisy sadly shook her head. 'I ain't angry with you. Disappointed, yes. An' you know what? The worst of it is, I saw it coming – probably before you did, if truth be told. Still, what's done is done, an' if you don't want to cause even more heartache than you already have, then my advice to you is to go away an' leave us all in peace. It would just upset the little ones to see you, and then for you to clear off again. I reckon you've already done enough damage, don't you?'

Daisy held up a cautionary hand as a light of desperation flickered in Grace's eyes. She could sense that her daughter-in-law was about to push her way in and knew that she mustn't allow it at any cost. Barry and the children had been through enough.

'Pull yourself together, Grace, and ger yourself away home. You can only make things worse by coming here.'

Grace was openly sobbing now, and despite the fact that Daisy had tried to harden her heart against her, she found herself softening. 'Have you come to ask Barry to take you back?' she whispered. When Grace shook her head, Daisy's eyes filled with tears. Glancing back to where the two children were engrossed in a jigsaw on the hearthrug, she battled with her conscience. After a few minutes she admitted miserably, 'I'd let you see them if it were up to me, but at the end o' the day blood's thicker than water, an' if Barry says you're not to see them, then I have to stand by me own. I'm sorry, Grace, but you'll have to leave. It seems you've made your choice, so there's no more to be said. One thing I *will* tell you though: for all our Barry's as soft as clouts, you've broken his heart, and if it's left to him, I doubt he'll ever let you so much as clap eyes on these two again.'

Without another word she began to close the door, and Grace heard Simon say, 'Who's that, Gran?'

'It's nobody, pet.' The door closed in her face and Grace wished with all her heart that she could die there and then.

She staggered blindly back along the pavement as tears gushed from her eyes, then she ran as if the hounds of hell were at her feet, almost as if she were trying to leave the heartbreak behind. By the time she reached the end of the street it had started to rain heavily, cold stinging drops that mingled with her tears and ran down her frozen cheeks.

Somehow she made it back to the bus station where she huddled miserably in a bus shelter whilst she waited for the bus to Fenny Drayton. The buses to the village ran infrequently and it was nearly two hours later before she staggered off the bus in the village and dragged herself back to the house. Once inside she dropped heavily into the nearest chair, pulling her sodden coat around her. She was shivering and yet she felt hot, almost as if she was on fire, but she sat on in the silence as darkness settled around her, and there she remained until the first light bathed the sky the next morning.

When Philip returned the next day he found her subdued and running a dangerously high temperature. Her hair was unwashed and her eyes were dull and glazed. He felt her forehead and frowned. 'You should be in bed,' he told her, then swinging her into his arms as if she weighed no more than a feather, he carried her upstairs. She lay staring at the ceiling as he bit on his lip wondering what he should do. 'Do you want me to call a doctor?' he asked eventually.

She shook her head. 'No, I'll be fine. I've just caught a chill, that's all.'

181

Nodding, he backed out of the room and left her until the next morning. She came downstairs while he was getting ready for work and he was relieved to see that she looked slightly better.

'Ah, you're up and about again then, that's good.' He had never been very good with invalids and was glad that he would not have to miss going in to work.

'I'm fine,' she said quietly. She filled the kettle at the sink and began to prepare his breakfast as he watched her with a frown on his face.

'What's wrong, Grace?' he asked, when he could bear the silence no longer. 'I know you're not well but there's something else, isn't there?'

'I went to see the children yesterday.' Her voice was so full of abject misery that he scowled. He had guessed that it would be something to do with those blasted brats, but had not dared to broach the subject.

'And?'

She shrugged. 'Daisy was looking after them till Barry got home from work and she made it more than plain that I wasn't welcome. She wouldn't even let me see them. I wasn't even allowed into my own home.'

'But it's *not* your home any more,' Philip pointed out.

Her chin sank to her chest as the tears that were never very far from the surface rose to her eyes.

'*This* is your home now, Grace – here with me, and the sooner you learn to let go of your past the easier it will be. We have a child of our own to look forward to now.'

Although she knew that he was speaking the truth, the truth was so painful. She had never once envisaged having to leave the two children she already had, and the thought of never getting them back was terrifying. She had known so little love in her life until she met Barry and gave birth to Wendy and Simon, and only now that she had been forced to leave them behind did she fully realise how much they had meant to her.

'Look, will you try to be patient for a while – for me?' Philip asked. As his arms went around her she leaned heavily against his shoulder and stared up at him from empty eyes. When she nodded tearfully he smiled with satisfaction.

'That's the girl. You have to give these things time. Barry is bound to be feeling hurt at the minute, what man wouldn't? But he'll come round, you'll see. Ask yourself, how long can he cope as he is? Once the initial shock has worn off he'll see it's for the best if you take the children. You're only going to make him more determined to keep them if you keep bothering him right now – it's a bit like rubbing salt into the wound. Do you understand what I'm saying?'

Again she nodded. There was sense in what he said, but all the same the thought of having to sit back and not see them for a while was almost unbearable. But then – what other option was there?

For the next few days, Grace followed Philip's advice and kept away from her hometown, apart from one time when she paid Hetty a brief visit. Philip came and went and she set herself to the task of preparing the house for the children. After all, the way she saw it, Christmas would be upon them before they knew it and the children would be bound to have joined her by then. She scrubbed the house from top to bottom and polished every stick of furniture until it shone. When Philip was at home she cooked him meals that made his mouth water. She wished that they didn't have to spend nights apart, but then supposed that it would be unreasonable to expect him to give his own family up completely. After all, he *was* prepared to take her children when the time was right, and his own children were older. Village life was much quieter than she had expected it to be, and some days she found herself searching for something to do. She went for long solitary walks in the countryside and started to knit little cardigans in readiness for the new arrival as well as brightly coloured sweaters for Wendy and Simon. The child inside her grew steadily and the waistbands on her skirts became increasingly tighter. She kept promising herself that soon she would go shopping for some new clothes, but somehow the thought of travelling into Nuneaton without going to see the children was unbearable so she kept postponing the outing.

It was one evening when they were getting ready to go out that Philip started to tease her. 'You weren't thinking of going out in *that*, were you? You look like a hippie that's been thrown out of the commune, all flowery.' He grinned as he nodded towards the skirt that was stretched across her stomach.

She frowned. 'Well, what am I supposed to wear? I *am* pregnant, you know. This is about the only thing I have left that still goes around me and it is quite usual for pregnant women to gain weight.'

The smile slid from his face as he adjusted his tie in the mirror, studiously avoiding her eyes. 'I am well aware of that fact, Grace. But you know . . . Well, if you don't mind me saying so, old girl, you've hardly looked your best for the last couple of weeks.'

Bright colour flooded her cheeks. 'Do you know something, Philip? It's actually quite hard to look your best when you spend half your entire life heaving your guts up, and the other half worrying yourself sick about your children.'

This was the nearest they had ever come to having a row and he snatched his jacket from the back of a chair as he stormed towards the door. 'Pardon me for having an opinion, I'm sure. I'll tell you what – I'll sleep at home tonight and perhaps you'll be in a better frame of mind when I come back tomorrow.'

'But I thought we—' The sound of the door banging behind him silenced her and slowly she sank down onto a chair. What had brought that about? Now that she came to think about it, he had been on edge ever since he came in that evening.

She heard the car start and after crossing to the bedroom window, was just in time to see him reverse off the drive at breakneck speed and go haring off down the road. The irritation she had felt only moments before at his thoughtlessness gave way to tears as she turned to stare about the empty room. Perhaps she had been a little sharp with him? After all, as her reflection in the mirror told her, she *had* let herself go just lately. She sat down on the dressing-table stool and stared at herself. A woman who seemed to have aged years in just a few short weeks stared back at her. She was ghastly pale and her hair, which had always been one of her best features, looked lank and life-less. Apart from her stomach she had lost weight, making the mound that was her unborn child appear even more prominent. On top of that, Philip did have a point – the skirt she was wearing was hardly flattering.

She had never felt as ill as she did now when she was having Wendy and Simon, but then she reasoned, she had not been under pressure and worrying herself half to death. Every hour away from them was like a week and sometimes she would lie awake long into the night sobbing into her pillow as she thought of them. She was now living in a house that she had only ever before dreamed of living in, and yet she found herself missing the cosy little terraced house that she and Barry had made their own. She even found herself missing Barry and his quiet gentle ways, but it was too late for regrets now, what was done was done and somehow she would have to make the best of it.

The feeling of guilt intensified as she made her way slowly down-stairs where she paced restlessly up and down the lounge. Philip had said that he was going to spend the night at his house in Meridan and she hovered by the phone as she tried to decide if she should phone him. He had asked her never to contact him there except in dire emergencies, but surely this *was* an emergency? She had to tell him that she was sorry – and what harm could it do anyway? He had told her that his soon-to-be ex-wife was hardly ever in anyway – she

184

was always off gallivanting with her fancy man, as Philip called him.

Taking a deep breath, she dialled the number before her courage could fail her. The phone seemed to ring for ever, but just when Grace was beginning to think that no one was going to answer it, a woman's voice came to her down the line.

'Hello? Cheryl Golding speaking.'

It was a gentle, refined voice and for a moment Grace was so shocked that she was rendered totally speechless. Eventually she gasped, 'H . . . hello – is Philip there, please?'

'Oh, I'm so sorry, my husband is away on business until the day after tomorrow. Could I leave a message for you?'

'No . . . no, it's quite all right, thank you. I'll . . . er . . . I'm sorry to have troubled you.'

Grace slammed the phone down as if it had bitten her. 'My husband is away,' the woman had said, but then as commonsense replaced the shock, Grace began to calm down. Of course Philip was still her husband, for the time being at least, so naturally she would still refer to him as such, particularly if she thought that a caller was a client of Philip's. Yes, that's what it was, she tried to convince herself. Wearily she dragged herself back up the stairs to take off the offending skirt that had started all the trouble in the first place. He'll be back tomorrow, she told herself, and he was, armed with the most enormous bunch of roses that she had ever seen, a bagful of very tasteful maternity clothes, and a beautiful emerald bracelet that made her gasp. In no time at all, all was forgiven and she knew that she had made the right choice.

Chapter Nineteen

'What's up then, old gel? You look like you just lost a bob an' found a tanner. You ain't frettin' about our Barry again, are you?' Stan's voice was kind as he glanced at his wife's troubled face.

She shrugged. 'I'm worryin about all of 'em, if you want the truth. Barry, the children – an' Grace an' all.' Her initial anger at her daughter-in-law's betrayal had long since been replaced by concern and it showed now as she fidgeted nervously. 'The thing is, Stan – how is Barry goin' to cope over Christmas with the children all on his own? I've asked him to come here, but you know what he's like. Too bloody independent for his own good if you ask me. He just said as he'd manage, but it ain't goin' to be much of a Christmas for them kids, is it? Not without their mam, an' he's still sayin' as she can't even see them. Our Wendy ain't hardly stopped cryin' since the day Grace left, poor little sod. It ain't quite so hard for Simon 'cos he's that much younger an' don't understand so much what's goin' on.'

'I know the kids have taken it hard, love,' Stan sympathised, 'but it has to be our Barry's decision. He's hurtin', so I suppose it's fairly understandable. He has to come to terms with what's happened in his own time, and until then there ain't much as we can do except give him our backing.'

'I just wish now as there was somethin' I could have done,' Daisy lamented. 'I knew no good would come of her associatin' with that bloody bloke. I saw this comin' an' I said as much to our Barry. In a way though, I blame meself. After all, it were me as encouraged Grace to go dancin' in the first place. She missed out on so much as a child, livin' with that bloody old harridan of an aunt of hers, an' I thought she deserved a bit o' fun. Little was I to know it would lead to this though, eh?'

'What's done is done an' there ain't no point in cryin' over spilt milk now. There ain't no point in blamin' yourself neither,' Stan said philosophically. 'Grace was old enough to make up her own mind. But you know, I still don't think she's a bad girl at heart. Just had her head turned, that's all. Barry is a grown man an' things have a habit o' comin' right in the end. Meantime you've got to stand back an' let him deal with this as he sees fit.'

Daisy nodded, and dragging herself out of the comfortable old chair she shuffled away to put the kettle on.

Grace sat back on her heels and viewed the small pile of gaily wrapped presents with satisfaction. Philip was more than generous with the weekly allowance he gave her and this had enabled her to shop for presents for Wendy and Simon. Now that they were wrapped she wondered how she would get them to the kids. She had written numerous letters to Barry but they'd all come back unopened so she knew that there was little chance of him allowing her to see them. As she pondered on her dilemma, it came to her – Daisy could deliver the gifts for her. Glancing at the clock she saw that it was not yet lunch-time – and there was no time like the present. A bus was due in the village in less than an hour and if she hurried she would be in time to catch it. With her mind made up, she bustled away.

She was just buttoning her coat when a rap came on the front door. Frowning, she looked towards it, wondering who it could be. As far as she was aware, only Philip and Barry knew where she was living. Deciding that it was probably a canvasser she hurried across to open it and found herself confronted by two youths who looked slightly unsavoury to say the very least. Something about them was vaguely familiar, but try as she might she couldn't think where she had seen them before.

'Yes?' With her head held high and her hand nervously gripping the door handle she stared back at them. 'Can I help you?'

'Yeah,' the taller of the two replied, as he glanced back nervously across his shoulder. 'Yer can tell us where the gaffer is.'

'The gaffer?' Puzzled, Grace stared back at him, and then as realisation dawned she smiled and relaxed a little. Now she remembered where she had seen them before. They were employed in the workshop at the back of Philip's garage, which would explain their dirty paint-spattered clothes. She had seen them once when Philip had called into the garage to pick something up. 'If you mean Philip, I'm afraid he's away on business at the moment,' she told them.

The smaller of the two, who looked as if he hadn't washed for a month, stared at his friend in agitation. 'So *now* what do we bleedin' do?' he spat.

Digging the lad viciously in the ribs with his elbow, the other replied, 'Watch yer lip.' Turning his attention back to Grace, he asked, 'When do yer expect him back, missus?'

'Probably tomorrow,' Grace said. 'Is there anything I can help you with?'

187

Ignoring her question, the taller one grabbed his friend's elbow and began to haul him unceremoniously down the sweeping drive. Grace sniffed. Ignorant little devil, she thought indignantly. It wouldn't have hurt him to answer a civil question. I was only trying to help. She watched as the two youths climbed into a gleaming BMW before roaring away. I shall have to ask Philip to teach his staff a few manners, she promised herself, and then pushing the incident from her mind, she hurried back inside to finish getting ready.

There was a hint of snow in the air as the bus drew into the station in Nuneaton and it was bitterly cold as Grace alighted, clutching the precious presents. She had all the time in the world, as Philip was not coming home tonight. In fact, he had spent very little time with her since they had moved into the house. But then she accepted it gracefully. He did have another family to see, after all, as well as a business to run, and once she had her own children back with her, which he assured her constantly she eventually would, then she wouldn't be so lonely.

Strangely, it felt nice to be back amongst the hustle and bustle of her home town again. Country life was proving to be very solitary and not at all what she had expected it to be. The villagers were a close-knit community and did not welcome strangers easily. In a way this suited her, for she had no wish for them to discover that she and Philip were living in sin. Instead she tried to busy herself as best she could, living for the times when Philip was with her.

Picking her way through the shoppers who thronged the market-place, she clutched the bag of presents. She had barely taken a dozen steps when suddenly she came face to face with Miss Mountjoy. The woman's eyes dropped to Grace's swollen stomach and a flicker of distaste flitted across her features.

'Hello, my dear. I heard of your . . . er . . . predicament.'

Grace bristled defensively. 'If you are referring to this,' she glanced down, 'it is not a predicament, it's a child.'

'Mmm, well . . . whatever. I was actually referring to the fact that you and your husband have separated.'

Grace felt her cheeks flame and for a moment was at a loss as to what to say. As they stood there, the snow that had been threatening for days began to fall in great white flakes that settled on Miss Mountjoy's severe black hat.

'Well,' seeing Grace's obvious discomfort the older woman made to step round her, 'I shall have to be off. You know what it's like, never enough hours in the day to do the Good Lord's work. Shall I remember you to your aunt?'

Grace flushed an even deeper shade of red. 'Yes . . . yes, please do. How is she?'

Miss Mountjoy's lips puckered. 'Not well. Not well at all, my dear. But then, you wouldn't know that, of course, not having seen her in such a long time.'

Grace looked away from the cold condemnation in the woman's eyes. 'That was not my choice, Miss Mountjoy. It was my aunt who chose not to see me, not the other way around, I assure you.'

'I'm quite sure she had her reasons, but then that is nothing to do with me, of course. And now as I said, I really must be on my way. Goodbye, Grace. Merry Christmas.'

'Goodbye.' Grace inclined her head and watched as the straight-backed woman disappeared into the crowds. A wave of desolation swept through her. She had lost her aunt – she had lost Barry and the children, but then she tried to console herself, she still had Philip and a brand new baby to look forward to. Even as she was thinking it the child suddenly fluttered inside her. Her hand flew to her stomach. Compared to Wendy and Simon this baby scarcely moved at all, almost as if it sensed that its mother regretted its conception. The feeling of guilt intensified.

People were beginning to stare at her and she moved on quickly through the snow that was falling faster by the minute. All at once the need to see her children was more than she could bear. A glance at the large clock in the marketplace told her that it was approaching the end of their lunch-hour and without even realising that she was doing it, her steps moved in the direction of Wendy's school. This might be the only chance she got to see her before Christmas, for she was aware that she would be breaking up for the holidays that very afternoon. She hurried along Coton Road and turned into Edward Street, and soon the palings that ran around the school came into view.

By now the snow was settling like a thick white blanket and she moved cautiously into the shelter of some trees that surrounded the playground. From here she could see the children laughing and playing. Her eyes swept over them and then suddenly there she was, Wendy happily scraping up the snow and making tiny snowballs. She was throwing them at anyone who passed, totally oblivious to her presence. She frowned when she saw that she wasn't wearing her hat or mittens. Her father must have forgotten to put them on when he dressed her this morning, and she worried that she would catch cold.

189

Her own hands, which were gripping tight to the cold metal railings, had turned blue, but the pain in her fingers was as nothing compared to the pain in her heart. She longed to call to her, to see the look on her face when she caught sight of her. But it was more than she dared do. She had given up all rights to her for now, until Barry had a change of heart, and she could only watch from afar as her heart twisted painfully in her chest.

The unborn baby suddenly fluttered again, and one of her frozen hands dropped from the railings to stroke her swollen abdomen as if comforting the child within. Only yards away was the child's sister, and for the first time she allowed herself to accept that this unborn child might never know her, or her brother for that matter. Tears spurted from her eyes, melting the snow that had settled on her pale cheeks, but still she stood as if rooted to the spot until the school bell sounded, heralding the end of the lunch-hour. She watched her daughter file into line before being led back into school by an harassed-looking grey-haired teacher. Suddenly there was silence all around her. If only . . . She stopped her thoughts from going any further. The time for if onlys was long past and now she must live with the consequences of her actions.

With one last glance at the deserted playground she stepped away from the shelter of the trees and started to pick her way through the heavily falling snow. There was an urge on her to go back to the little terraced house that she had made her home with Barry. To tell him that she was sorry. But she could never go there again. From now on, her home must be with Philip and the unborn child inside her; at that moment the realisation brought her no joy.

She was so lost in thought and so distraught that when a hand settled on her arm as she made her way down Edward Street, she started. Looking up fearfully, she stared straight into Hetty Brambles's kindly face.

'Why, love, whatever's the matter? I thought it were you from back there but till I got a bit closer I couldn't be sure wi' the snow comin' down as it is.' Hetty took her arm and led her towards the front door. 'I've been wondering how yer were getting on, an' now seeing as you're on the doorstep yer may as well come in an' have a cuppa wi' me. Yer look frozen through – it'll warm yer up a bit.'

Without argument Grace followed her and soon they were in the comforting warmth of Hetty's homely kitchen. The old lady pushed Grace into a chair and stabbed at the fire with a poker before crossing to the deep sink to fill the kettle. Once she had put it on to boil she turned her attention back to Grace.

'So, is it something you want to talk about – whatever it is that's upset you, I mean.'

Grace blew her nose loudly on a large white handkerchief that Hetty took from the ironing basket and handed to her.

'It's nothing really,' she said quietly, as she tried to compose herself, but then the pain was too great and she burst into a fresh torrent of sobs. Hetty took her in her arms and gently stroked her hair.

'That's it. You let it all go. Better out than in, I always say.' Gradually the sobs subsided to dull hiccupping whimpers, and only then did Hetty release her to bustle away and mash the tea. By the time she returned Grace looked totally spent and was staring into the fire, her thoughts back at the school with her daughter. She took the tea and sipped at it and after a time she confided, 'I just went round to the school to see Wendy. I made sure she didn't see me, of course. That would only make things worse with Barry. But he still hasn't let me see them, Hetty. It will be Christmas in a few days and it's tearing me apart.'

Hetty nodded in understanding. 'I can see that. But then you knew it wasn't going to be easy, love. Time is a great healer an' happen things will work out in the end. Barry won't always feel as hurt as he does right now, an' when he's had time to come to terms wi' what's happened no doubt he'll have a change of heart. That's only my thoughts, o' course. You know him better than me.'

'I thought I did.' Grace sighed. 'But I never thought he'd react like this. Barry is such a gentle man. I've never heard him say a wrong word about anybody, apart from my aunt. But then that's another story.'

Hetty nodded down at Grace's stomach. 'An' how is this little 'un coming along?' She tried to keep the feeling of dread that settled on her every time she so much as thought of the unborn child from her voice.

Grace smiled sadly. 'Everything seems to be all right, but you know, Hetty, sometimes I find myself hating this baby. What I mean is, how can I ever love it, knowing that he or she is the means of keeping me from my other children?'

'You'll love it all right,' Hetty reassured her. 'After all, the poor little mite didn't ask to be born, did it? And it might just be that this child will need your love even more than the other two do.'

When Grace stared at her curiously, Hetty flushed. 'Oh, hark at me, rattling off at the mouth again. How is that bloke o' yours treatin' yer anyway?'

Grace stared down into her drink. 'Philip treats me very well –

191

when he's with me, that is. He still has to spend a lot of time with the children from his marriage so we actually only get to spend about three or four days a week at the most together at the minute. That will change when the baby comes, of course. At the moment we're just renting a house, as you know. But when the baby is born we're going to buy one and then Philip will move in with me properly.'

'Mmm.' Hetty stared into the fire as she avoided Grace's eyes. 'An' how do yer like livin' out in a village?'

'It's a lot quieter than I'm used to,' Grace admitted eventually.

Again Hetty nodded. 'Not quite what yer thought then?'

'Not really, but then I led such a hectic life before, what with working and the children and the house to look after. I suppose once this one comes it will be a totally different kettle of fish altogether. I haven't forgotten what hard work babies are. And hopefully by then I'll have the other two back as well, so I'll be run off my feet and I won't have time to get bored.'

Hetty pursed her lips but made no comment and the two women sat on in silence for some time until eventually Grace rose from her seat and smiled at Hetty gratefully. 'Thanks for lending me a shoulder to cry on. I don't deserve it really. After all, I have no one but myself to blame for the situation I find myself in. I can hardly blame Barry for feeling as he does, can I? I mean, how many men would accept the fact that their wife is carrying another man's baby?'

'What makes you so sure that you are?'

Grace was so taken aback at Hetty's question that for a moment she was speechless. The fact that the baby might be Barry's was something that she hadn't allowed herself to contemplate since Chris had said the very same thing, but then she shrugged resignedly. 'Well, I suppose there *is* a chance that the baby could be Barry's, but what does that matter now? He's hardly going to want me back after all that's happened, is he? He obviously hates me.'

'I shouldn't be too sure about that if I were you,' Hetty remarked. 'Why do yer think he's actin' as he is? It's because he's hurtin', that's why. Why, although I've never met the lad it's plain he thought the world o' yer, an' love like that don't die overnight, you just mark my words. There's a very thin line between love an' hate; it can swing either way when things ain't goin' as they should. The question is – would yer want to go back if he were willin' to take yer?'

'No, I wouldn't . . . Only for the sake of the children.' Grace's voice was hesitant and her colour rose as confusion swamped her.

Seeing her reaction, Hetty shrugged. 'There's only you as can know that. But I have to say, from where I'm standin', yer don't seem a hundred per cent sure.'

'Of course I am! I love Philip and he . . . he loves me.' Grace was indignant now as Hetty patted her arm.

'Whatever yer decide I wish yer well, love. An' don't forget – if ever yer need me, I'm right here. Now yer just take care, eh?'

'I will, Hetty, and thanks.' Grace impulsively leaned across and kissed Hetty's wrinkled cheek then snatching up the bag that contained the presents she made her way along the cold hallway.

When Hetty opened the front door she gasped. 'Lord love us, would yer just take a look at that? Why, if it carries on comin' down at this rate we'll all be snowed in for mornin'. Yer just make sure as yer don't get goin' your length now, the pavements must be right slippery. Hurry up an' do whatever it is yer have to an' then get yourself away home, do yer hear me?'

'I hear you.' Grace grinned as she stepped out into the fast-falling snow. Once she had reached the pavement she paused to wave before hurrying on her way.

By the time she turned off the main road to take a short cut across Fife Street rec she could barely see a hand in front of her and was shivering with cold, but she was determined that nothing would stop her from delivering the children's presents. So she hurried on as best she could with the bag she was carrying becoming heavier by the minute.

At last she was standing on Daisy's doorstep, breathless and more than a little nervous about the reception she might receive. It took every ounce of courage she had to knock at the door, and when she heard someone shuffling towards it she shivered with anticipation. It was Daisy who opened the door and her mouth gaped with surprise when she saw Grace standing on the doorstep. For a moment she was speechless but then she stood aside and ushered Grace into the house.

'You'd better come in.' Her voice was short as she struggled with her emotions. The maternal side of her wanted to berate Grace for the hurt she had caused her son, but the other side of her realised in that moment that she still loved the young woman. In the time that Grace had been married to Barry, Daisy had come to look on her as the daughter she had never had and it was hard to hate her now, looking so cold and poorly.

Once inside, Grace slowly lowered the heavy bag to the floor. 'I'm sorry to trouble you, Daisy, but I have some Christmas presents here for the children and I wondered if you would be kind enough to pass

193

them on for me? You'll find a little present in there for you and Stan as well, and one for Barry too. I . . . er . . . got him one of those Rael Brook shirts he likes.'

'Oh, Grace.' Daisy lowered her head as tears flooded her eyes. 'A right Christmas this is goin' to be, ain't it, wi' the family all torn apart as it is?'

Could she have known it Grace was struggling with her emotions too as she wrung her hands and looked on the woman whom she had come to regard over the last few years as the mother she had never known.

'I'm so sorry, Daisy.' The words sounded inadequate even to her ears, but they were all she could think of to say. 'I swear I never set out to hurt anyone. Things just sort of happened. If I could turn the clock back I would. As it is, I'm not even going to be there to see Simon on his first day at school. Please try to forgive me. I miss you *so* much.'

'I miss you an' all, love,' Daisy admitted brokenly, and then somehow they were in each other's arms crying their eyes out.

'Will you stay for a cup o' tea?' Daisy asked eventually.

Grace shook her head as she pulled away from the comforting shelter of her mother-in-law's arms. There was no point in delaying and she wanted to be away, especially now she saw that Simon wasn't there.

'No, I won't, Daisy, thanks all the same. I've done what I came to do and now I ought to be off.' As she turned to the door, the older woman watched her helplessly.

'Happy Christmas, Daisy.' Grace suddenly paused to look back at her imploringly. 'Will you do just *one* more thing for me?'

'If I can.' Daisy felt as if her heart were breaking and the pain intensified as Grace whispered, 'Will you wish Wendy and Simon a Happy Christmas too, and . . . and tell them that I love them?'

Daisy was too choked with emotion to speak, so instead she simply nodded as Grace slipped away, quietly closing the door behind her.

The buses were running late due to the atrocious weather conditions and by the time Grace got back to Fenny Drayton it was well after tea-time and pitch dark. She staggered drunkenly up the road that led to the house Philip had rented for them, to be welcomed by empty black windows and a silence that weighed heavy on her. After letting herself in, she stood trying to get her breath back in the freezing hallway. The fire had burned out and the trip to the coalhouse outside seemed miles away, but she knew that she needed to get warm so she set herself to the task, putting the kettle on in between. She had just settled in front of a fire that had barely flickered into life when the phone rang and she rushed into the hall to answer it. It was Philip and her heart lifted at the sound of his voice.

'Hello, darling. Are you coming home tonight after all?' She desperately needed company, but his answer had her soul plunging to the depths of despair.

'Sorry, love, I'm afraid no can do. In fact, I'm ringing to tell you that I won't be able to get back tomorrow either. Something's come up with one of the children and I need to be here to deal with it.'

Desperately trying to keep the disappointment from her voice she said lightly, although she longed to tell him that she needed him too, 'All right then, I understand. Shall I expect you the day after tomorrow?'

'Yes, I hope so.'

She could hear people talking in the background behind him and sensed that he was in a hurry, so she said quietly, 'I love you, Philip.'

'Hmm . . . yes, you too.'

The phone went dead in her hand and once again the all-enveloping silence closed around her as the words of her aunt's prophecy rang loudly in her ears.

Chapter Twenty

'As I was saying, dear, I have no wish to distress you, but I have to say that Grace was looking quite poorly. Why she ever left you in the first place I shall never understand, after all the sacrifices you made for her. Still, young people nowadays seem to have no thought for anyone but themselves, unfortunately.' Miss Mountjoy, who had almost broken her neck in her haste to get to Emily's and relate her meeting with Grace, sipped at her tea as Emily looked suitably concerned.

'Well, at least I have the satisfaction of knowing that she was well cared for whilst she was living with me,' Emily simpered as she dabbed at her eyes with a handkerchief. 'The problem was, she was always a wilful child, just as her dear departed mother was before her. But – what happens to her now is no concern of mine. If the rumours you have told me are true, then the girl has brought disgrace on our family name. I always knew the obsession she had with ball-room dancing would lead to no good and I tried to tell her so on countless occasions. It's her husband and her poor children I feel sorry for, not to mention the child of sin she will be shortly bringing into the world.'

'Quite!' Miss Mountjoy, who had already been there for over an hour, drained her cup and rose as she adjusted her hat and patted a wayward strand of hair back under its brim.

'Well, as much as I have enjoyed our little tête-à-tête I shall have to be going now, Emily dear. Shall I see you at church on Sunday?'

'Of course, and thank you so much for calling.' Emily accompanied her to the door, and once the front gate had closed behind her she returned to the kitchen where she crossed to the bureau and opened the drawer. A smile of satisfaction played around her lips as she stared at the solicitor's letter in her hand. Another nice cheque to put in the bank, and still Grace was none the wiser, nor would she ever be, as long as Emily had her way. As for the other matter – so what if her sister Sarah was still trying to find her? The solicitor had strict instructions to reveal her whereabouts to no one – and it would be more than his reputation was worth, were he to do so.

Admittedly, it had been a body blow when Grace had first left her, but now – well, things were working out very nicely, thank you very much. In Emily's opinion, it was Grace's love of dancing that had led her to the position she was now in. But one day, hopefully, it would be she who was dancing on Grace's grave. Only then would her revenge be complete.

'Did you get the tree, darling?' The question burst from Grace's lips the second Philip walked through the door. It was the day before Christmas Eve and he had promised faithfully that he would pick one up on the way home, but if his empty hands and guilty expression were anything to go by, he had forgotten.

'Sorry, love. I've been so rushed off my feet I completely forgot all about it.' He watched the smile slip from her face and followed her into the kitchen as she hurried away to put the kettle on. There was a large pan of beef stew and dumplings simmering on the top of the oven and the smell of it made his stomach rumble in anticipation.

'Not to worry, there's always tomorrow, though the best ones will be gone if you don't get down to the market early.' Grace tried to hide her disappointment as she fixed a smile on her face. Christmas without a tree took her back to her childhood with her aunt, and she tried not to think of the times she had spent trimming the tree at home with Wendy and Simon, their little faces all aglow with excitement. Philip shuffled from foot to foot, looking decidedly uncomfortable as the false smile again slipped from Grace's face.

'Is there something wrong, Philip?'

Hearing the concern in her voice he sat down heavily at the kitchen table. 'Not *wrong* exactly, but there is something I need to talk to you about, yes. But not until after dinner, eh? That stew smells delicious, so let's eat first.'

Grace served the meal with a sense of foreboding hanging over her, and it wasn't until they had finished eating and had settled themselves on the sofa in front of the fire before she dared to ask, 'Well?'

'Ah, before I forget – I've got something for you.' Fumbling in his jacket pocket, he produced a tiny leather box and placed it in her hand. 'Happy Christmas, darling.'

Grace snapped open the lid and a pair of perfectly matched diamond earrings winked up at her. 'Oh Philip, they're *beautiful* – but why are you giving them to me now? It isn't Christmas Day yet.'

'Well, that's what I wanted to talk to you about.' The guilty look was back on his face as he stared into the fire for some seconds before plucking up the courage to go on. 'The thing is, the wife's gone off on one of her walkabouts again. She's probably gone to spend Christmas with one of her fancy men and so . . . Well, I hate to do this to you, Grace, but I'll have to spend Christmas with the children.'

Instead of looking annoyed, as he had expected, Grace looked relieved. 'Oh, is that all? Of course you should be with your children. They can come here to us. It's about time I met them anyway. We have to get to know each other sooner or later.'

'No, darling. I appreciate the offer but I don't think that would be a good idea. Not just yet anyway. The boys still haven't come to terms with the fact that their mother and I are splitting up, and I want to take one step at a time.'

'So what you're saying is, you want to spend Christmas at your other house with them?' Grace looked so despondent that he squirmed uncomfortably in his seat.

'Of course that's not what I *want*. I want to spend Christmas quietly here with you. But what choice do I have? I can hardly leave them to fend for themselves with the daily help, now can I? I'm so sorry, Grace. I was really looking forward to our first Christmas together, but then we have every Christmas for the rest of our lives to look forward to, don't we? Just think, by this time next year the new baby will be here and we'll have Wendy and Simon, not to mention my two. We'll be run off our feet looking after them all, so please try to forgive me for this one last time alone with them. I'll be back the day after Boxing Day, I promise, and then we'll celebrate it late. Just you and me, what do you say?'

'There isn't much I can say, is there?' She looked into the fire so that he wouldn't see the tears in her eyes and after a time she stood and nodded towards the kitchen. 'I'd better go and clear the table.' Her heart was breaking as she thought of the lonely Christmas ahead, but in a second he was at her side and pulling her into his arms.

'Leave the damn pots until morning and come to bed.' His lips left trails of fire around her neck and she felt herself melting, just as she always did whenever he touched her, so without so much as another word she followed him to the stairs and by the end of the night she had forgiven him, and even given him her blessing to spend Christmas with his children. After all, as she told herself, what choice did he have? His children, and her own, were the innocent victims of their affair – and as he had quite rightly pointed out, this would be their last Christmas apart, after all.

*   *   *

It was the morning of Christmas Eve and for the first time in almost two weeks it had finally stopped snowing for a while. Grace had covered the turkey in greaseproof paper and put it on the coldest part of the thrall in the pantry; it seemed pointless to cook it just for herself. She had cleaned the house from top to bottom and now the rest of the day stretched endlessly in front of her. Apart from the vase of holly that stood on the mantelshelf no one would have known on entering that it was Christmas at all, for there was not even a tree to mark the occasion. Her mood was sombre, bordering on deep depression as she tried to force herself not to think of Wendy and Simon.

She had moved into the kitchen to make herself a cup of tea, more for something to do than because she really wanted one, and it was whilst she was filling the kettle at the sink that a movement in the garden caught her eye. Turning off the tap she leaned closer to the window, and there it was again. Someone was running through the deep snow beneath the leafless trees, crouched low as if he was afraid to be seen. She stepped out into the garden and her breath hung on the air as she shouted, '*Oy!* You – what do you think you're doing?'

The youth stopped and cast a terrified glance across his shoulder. 'S . . . sorry, missus. I weren't doin' no harm, really I weren't. Me ball came over the hedge an' I was just goin' to get it back. I . . . I didn't think you was in.'

The voice was childlike and Grace was shocked to see that the boy had paled to the colour of the snow beneath his feet. Now that she looked at him more closely she saw that he wasn't as old as she had first thought him to be. Perhaps thirteen or fourteen at the very most, although his voice and the way he was acting, almost as if he had committed a criminal offence, suggested a much younger child.

Her face softened as she smiled at him. 'Oh, in that case then, get your ball. I'm sorry I shouted at you. You startled me, that's all.'

He nodded and almost fell his length in his haste to reach a ball that she now saw resting on the thick blanket of snow. Once he had retrieved it, he turned as if to scuttle away, but Grace's voice stayed him again when she called, 'Do you live in the village?'

He gulped deep in his throat before nodding and she was shocked to see that he was close to tears. 'Aye I do, down Witherley Lane there wi' me mam an' dad. But you ain't goin' to tell me dad that I came in your garden, are you? He'd wail me backside.'

Grace had the urge to grin and bit down on her lip before replying, 'No, I'm not going to tell your dad. What's your name, by the way?'

He gulped again. 'It's Billy, missus. Billy Bamford.'

'Well, Billy, how would you like to come in and have a cup of tea with me? I was just about to make one for myself and it would be nice to have a bit of company.'

He scratched his head and then shook it regretfully. 'I can't, missus. I've got me dog, Sophie – over there, look.'

Grace's eyes followed his pointing finger and sure enough, there under the shelter of one of the trees was one of the strangest-looking mongrels she had ever seen. One of her ears pointed to the heavens, whilst the other lay flat against her head. Her shaggy coat was a mixture of black, tan, and so many other colours that she looked as if someone had thrown pots of paint across her.

'She's a very unusual dog,' she said eventually, for want of something to say.

Instantly, Billy beamed. 'She is, ain't she?' he said proudly. 'An' I would have liked to have a cup o' tea wi' you, missus.'

'Then in that case you shall, and so can Sophie. Come in out of the cold, both of you.'

He let out a whistle and instantly the little dog leaped through the snow until she was at his side, then cautiously the boy approached her. Once he drew level, Grace ushered him past her into the kitchen where he took off his cap and twisted it nervously in his hands. The dog flopped down on the carpet as nodding towards the kitchen table Grace told Billy, 'Sit yourself down, the tea won't be long. We might even find some biscuits in the tin if we're lucky.'

Now Billy was really smiling. 'I like biscuits, missus, an' Sophie does too. Jammie Dodgers is me favourites. Me mam always says I'd live on 'em if I could – but that wouldn't be good for you, would it? Me mam says as you have to have fruit an' vegetables to be healthy. Me dad grows lots o' veg in the garden. Not in the winter though, 'cos they won't grow in the snow, will they?'

Grace smiled back at him as she put the kettle on to boil and prepared the teapot. There was a lump forming in her throat for the child, who now that he was close she saw was obviously backwards. 'So, how old are you then, Billy?'

'I'm twelve, nearly thirteen,' he informed her proudly, and as he spoke his eyes travelled around the spotless kitchen. 'You ain't a dirty whore at all. Not like they was sayin' in the village shop. Your house is really clean.'

Grace's hand trembled and she kept her eyes fixed on the cups as he went on to ask innocently, 'What's a whore?'

Her cheeks felt as if they were aflame with shame and humiliation, but thankfully she was saved from having to reply for just then the kettle began to sing and she turned away to mash the tea. By the time she had poured it and presented him with a plateful of mince pies and biscuits that made his mouth water he had thankfully forgotten all about his question and he flashed her a brilliant smile as she struggled to compose herself.

'So, Billy, have you lived here for long?'

Shaking his head he swallowed a mouthful of mince pie, sending crumbs flying everywhere. 'Naw. We used to live in Nuneaton, but the other kids picked on me 'cos I was different, so me mam an' dad bought the cottage an' we moved out here. I don't mind bein' different though, 'cos me mam says as I'm *special*.'

'I think your mam is right,' Grace smiled, warming to the child in front of her. 'I bet she's very proud of you.'

'She is,' he informed her, puffing out his chest. 'An' when I leave school I'm goin' to work wi' me dad on his coal lorry deliverin' the coal. I'm very strong, you know.'

'I'm sure you are.' Grace passed a biscuit under the table to Sophie, who had wormed her way across to them on her belly. As the dog looked up at her, Grace saw why Billy loved her so much, for she had the most wonderful deep brown soulful eyes. By now he was eyeing the plate greedily again and Grace pushed it across to him. 'Go on,' she encouraged. 'Eat as many as you like. I'm here on my own over Christmas and it would be a shame for them to go to waste.'

'Why are you on your own?' he asked, as he happily helped himself to another pie.

Grace flushed. 'Well, it's a long story,' she muttered, but thankfully Billy was so intent on the plateful of pies in front of him that he didn't press the point. Soon he had cleared the plate and after wiping the back of his hand across his mouth he leaned back in his chair and flashed her a smile that lit up his whole face. 'You're really kind, you are,' he stated.

Grace beamed with pleasure. 'Why, thank you, Billy. That's a nice thing to say. You're very nice too.'

As his hand dropped to stroke Sophie's head he looked at Grace's swollen stomach. 'Do you have a baby in there?'

Grace nodded. 'Yes, I do, but it isn't due to be born for another few months yet.'

'Mm . . . will you be living here for a long time?'

'No. After the baby is born we'll be moving back to Nuneaton because . . .' Grace coughed. This young man seemed to be full of questions that were proving to be very difficult to answer – yet they were asked with such innocence that it was hard to take offence. She

201

decided to divert him by asking a few questions of her own. 'Do you go to school in the village, Billy?'

'Naw, I go to a school for special children on the way to Tamworth. I can do me ABC an' me sums now, an' my teacher says I'm doin' really well. I go on a big bus that picks me up outside the Royal Red Gate every mornin'. It brings me back after school an' all, every single day. That's good, ain't it?'

'It certainly is,' Grace agreed admiringly.

Suddenly he leaned towards her and asked. 'Would you like to go for a walk? We could cut across the fields to Upton.'

'Well . . .' Grace looked uncertainly at the snow-covered landscape through the window. 'It's hardly the weather for going out walking, is it?'

'Course it is,' he laughed. 'Me mam always says as a good walk never hurt nobody an' if it's cold then you wrap up warm. Me mam says as fresh air puts roses in your cheeks.'

'I think your mam sounds like a very wise woman.' Grace smiled. 'And do you know what, Billy? I think a walk might be just what the doctor ordered to blow the cobwebs away.'

Billy frowned and looked slightly confused by her comments, but he said nothing as she struggled into her boots and a warm woollen coat that she fetched from the coat hook in the hall. Soon she was well wrapped up and ready to go at the back door. 'Right then, let's be off, young man. I've barely been further than the end of the back garden so it will be nice to have a guided tour. I can't go too far, mind. I tend to get tired carrying this around.' She patted her tummy as he followed her out into the snow with Sophie close at his heels.

They tramped through the village until they came to the main road that led to Sibson, and then they fell into step as they strolled along side-by-side. Billy kept up a constant stream of cheerful chatter and Grace found she was actually enjoying herself, although it was quite difficult to walk through the deep snow.

Soon she was panting. 'I think that's about it for today,' she puffed after they had gone about a mile. When Billy's face fell with disappointment, she patted his hand. 'I'll tell you what. How about we do it again another day? That is, if you have the time, of course.'

He nodded eagerly. 'I'd like that. Come on, I'll take you back through the haunted wood.'

When Grace raised her eyebrows he giggled. 'Sometimes when I can't get to sleep me mam tells me stories about the haunted wood. I ain't never seen a ghost in there though.'

It was almost an hour later before they arrived back at the house and by then Grace was so tired that she felt as if she could have slept right through Christmas. She had enjoyed herself more than she cared to admit, being in the company of a child again, although it had emphasised how much she was missing her own children. When she held her hand out to Billy he flushed with pleasure, feeling very grown up as he solemnly shook it.

'Thank you so much, Billy. I really enjoyed our little outing. I've seen more of the surrounding area this afternoon than I have in the whole of the time I've been living here.'

'There's lots more places to see yet,' he informed her enthusiastically. 'There's Ratcliffe Culey, an' Shackerston . . . there's a steam engine there, but it's too far to walk in the snow. Another time though, eh? What's your name anyway?'

Grace told him and he rolled the word around on his tongue. 'That's a nice name,' he said eventually, as if he had given it his personal seal of approval. 'Will you be my friend, Grace?'

'I would be very honoured to be your friend, Billy,' Grace replied solemnly and again he beamed with pleasure as he backed away from her.

'I'll come an' see you again then, shall I?'

She nodded and he skipped happily away with Sophie bounding through the deep snow beside him. Grace watched until he turned a bend and was lost to sight, then reluctantly she turned and entered her empty house. She felt a measure of pity and sympathy for the child she had just befriended, for as the day had worn on it had become even more apparent that Billy had the mind of a child only half his age. And yet, he seemed happy with his lot and obviously had a loving family who adored him just as he was. 'Special' . . . that's what he said his mother called him, and the more Grace thought of it, the more she realised that this was just what he was. Other children would age and grow cynical, including her own children, but Billy would always remain unspoiled and childlike. Perhaps it was just as well that not everyone was the same. On this sobering thought she went into the kitchen to make herself a solitary meal.

The snow started to fall again on the evening of Christmas Eve. On Christmas morning Grace awoke to deep drifts that seemed to have completely obliterated the landscape. It had drifted against the back door and she had to fight her way through it to the coalhouse. She passed the morning quietly with a book in front of the fire, and it was almost two o'clock in the afternoon when she was toasting some

203

bread on a long brass toasting fork in front of the fire that a knock came on the door.

On opening it, she found Billy and Sophie standing on the doorstep. It was all she could do to stop herself from laughing aloud, for they were both white over. 'Come in quickly,' she urged, as the draught from the open door made the fire flicker and spit. 'You'll freeze where you stand if you stay out there much longer.'

Smiling broadly, Billy inched past her into the warm kitchen with Sophie close at his heels and almost instantly the snow on his clothes began to melt and steam in the warm atmosphere.

'Here, let me take your coat and cap,' Grace offered. When he did as he was told she hung them to dry across a large wooden clothes-horse that stood in one corner of the kitchen.

'I didn't expect to see you on Christmas Day,' she remarked as he followed her into the sitting room.

Swiping a lock of his unruly ginger hair from his forehead he explained, 'Me mam an' dad are settlin' down in front o' the fire to watch the Queen's speech an' let their dinners go down. An' then they're goin' to watch *The Wizard of Oz* but I've seen that, so bein' as you'd said you were goin' to be on yer own, me an' Sophie thought we'd come an' see as you were all right. Me mam doesn't mind if I go out as she knows as I'll be all right with Sophie.'

'That was very thoughtful of you.' Grace lifted the bread on the toasting fork and once again held it out to the fire.

Billy frowned. 'What you doin' that for?'

'This is my Christmas dinner,' she answered. 'There didn't seem much point cooking for one, so I thought I'd make do with a bit of toast.'

Billy's expressive face crinkled into a look of horror. 'Crikey. That ain't much of a dinner. We had turkey an' Christmas puddin' an every-thin, an' I found the sixpence in the puddin' an' all – look.' He proudly held out a shiny silver sixpence as Grace looked suitably impressed.

'That was lucky. What are you going to spend it on?'

'Gobstoppers, they're me favourites,' he said without hesitation. 'When the village shop opens again, that is. It shuts for Christmas, you know?'

'Yes, I imagine it would.' Grace carried the toast that was now a golden brown back into the kitchen, and after taking the butter dish from the pantry she started to spread it across her meagre Christmas fare. Billy meantime had spotted the untouched Christmas cake that stood next to the pressed glass milk jug and sugar bowl on the table. His mouth watered as he said, 'Me mam has made us a cake for tea.

I wanted some after me puddin' but she said as I was to wait for tea-time. Me mam says she reckons I've got hollow legs an' I'm a bottom-less pit 'cos she can't seem to fill me up. But me dad says it's normal to be hungry all the time 'cos I'm a growin' lad.'

'Well, how about if you try a bit of mine to keep you going then?' Grace suggested. 'Do you think you could find room for a slice without it spoiling your tea?'

Billy's eyes sparkled. 'Oh, it wouldn't spoil me tea,' he assured her quickly, so pulling the plate towards her she cut him a huge slice and ushered him back into the sitting room. He tucked into the cake as if he hadn't eaten in a month while Grace looked on in amusement, and when he was done he rubbed his stomach contentedly. 'That were grand, that were. Nearly as good as me mam's.'

Grace took this as a huge compliment, for it seemed in Billy's eyes that no one was quite as good as his mam – and this was just as it should be. In actual fact, she was more than a little pleased to see him because she had begun to feel very lonely and isolated. She had been expecting Philip to ring her all day, but as yet she hadn't heard from him. Still, she tried to console herself, he was no doubt taken up with trying to cope with the children on his own, and it wouldn't be easy for them, for this would be their first Christmas without their mother, just as it was for Wendy and Simon. Her appetite suddenly fled and she dropped the toast back onto her plate.

'Don't you want that?' Billy nodded at her plate.

'Not really,' Grace said. 'It seems that I'm not as hungry as I thought I was.'

'In that case then, pass it over here. Me an' Sophie will polish it off. Me mam allus says waste not want not.'

Grace passed him the plate and watched in amazement as the toast too disappeared in record time. 'Do you know, Billy? I think your mam was right. I think you must have hollow legs.'

Wiping a smear of butter from his chin with the back of his hand he smiled broadly, and then they sat in companionable silence for some time in the warm glow of the fire. It was almost four o'clock by the time Billy left, and when Grace showed him to the door she was horrified to see that the snow was coming down faster than ever, so thickly in fact, that you could barely see a hand in front of you. 'Are you sure that you'll get home all right?' Her voice was worried as she stared out into the blizzard.

He chuckled. 'I know me way round here like the back o' me hand. I could get home wi' me eyes shut.'

'Even so, perhaps I ought to wrap up and come back with you?'

205

Billy flapped his hand at her. 'Naw, really – there's no need fer that. I'll be home by the time you've got yer warm clothes on. Shall I come back an' see you again another day?'

'I should be most disappointed if you didn't,' Grace assured him.

He flushed with pleasure. 'Right then, I'll be off. Thanks for the cake an' everythin'.' He started to back away with Sophie having to leap through the snow beside him, and within seconds the darkness had swallowed him up.

Grace shuddered and shut the door; it was then that a wave of utter despair washed over her. It was Christmas Day and for the first time in her entire life she was completely and totally alone. Even more so than she had been in the years she had lived with her aunt. She wondered if Wendy and Simon were all right – if they were missing her, whether Barry was coping, and slowly tears washed over her face. But then she tried to look ahead, for this time next year she would have her children back, just as Philip had promised, and they would be a real family again. First though, she must get through this feeling of utter loneliness.

Taking the only photo of the children she had from her handbag she stared at their precious faces then, curling up in a ball on the settee, she held it to her heart as she drifted off into a sleep that was instantly filled with dreams of other photos that she would rather not have remembered.

'No, Aunt, please. I didn't mean to pry and look at your photos. I'll never do it again, I swear.' Her screams seemed to fill the room, enraging her aunt all the more as she dragged her towards the door that led to the cellar.

'You always promise never to be bad again, but you can't help it, can you? It's inbred in you. But I'll knock it out of you, don't you doubt it.'

'I only wanted to know who the pretty lady standing next to my mother was in the photo. The name written underneath her was Sarah,' the child whimpered, but her aunt was unmoved.

'All you need to know is that she is as dead as your parents. I'm all that you have left in the world, and if it weren't for me you'd be stuck in a children's home somewhere.'

Starting awake, it took Grace some moments to realise where she was and to shake off the feeling of panic that had wrapped itself around her. Her eyes dropped to the smiling faces of her children again and she curled up once more and let fresh tears pour down her face.

Chapter Twenty-One

'I'm so sorry, darling. You know if I could get there I would. But the roads are so awful there's no way I'd get through,' Philip explained in a voice as sweet as syrup.

'But, Philip, you *promised* you'd be home today! You said we'd have a belated Christmas together. The turkey's in the oven and everything's ready for you.' Grace was close to tears.

'I can hardly be held responsible for the weather, now can I?' he asked reasonably. 'Just look out of the window, for God's sake. I'd need a tractor to get through those drifts and according to the forecast there's no sign of it ceasing just yet.'

'Well, when *will* you be home then?'

Ignoring the note of desperation in her voice he told her calmly, 'As soon as I possibly can, of course. You don't think I want to stay here on my own, do you, when I could be with you? The children have left and I can assure you, it's as dead as the grave here.'

Guilt washed over her as she realised that she was being unreasonable. The only person she had seen all over Christmas was Billy, not that she would have wished to see any of the other villagers. Whenever their paths crossed, the local housewives tended to pass her by as if there was a dirty smell under their noses. Still, just a few more months and she would be gone from here to start a new life with Philip.

'I'm sorry,' she muttered meekly. 'Of course it isn't your fault. But you will come as soon as you can, won't you?'

'That goes without saying. I love you, Grace.'

She melted at the soft tone of his voice. 'All right then, darling. I'll look forward to seeing you in the next couple of days. Goodbye.'

After replacing the phone she looked around the cold hallway and then with nothing better to do, returned to the kitchen to check on the dinner. Her first instinct was to switch it off, but commonsense told her that it would be silly to waste good food, and anyway, if Billy came round he would help her eat it. Sighing, she savagely stabbed the potatoes in the pan with a fork before picking up her book again. Her life with Philip, and even village life if it came to that, was not turning out to be what she had expected at all.

Grace shifted uncomfortably in the chair as she watched Philip adjust his tie in the mirror. He was looking remarkably handsome in a dark suit and a pale blue shirt that she had just ironed for him, and a little stab of envy swept through her as she gazed down at her bump, on which the daily newspaper rested. She had just read of the Government's decision to stop the provision of free school milk to schools and heartily disagreed with it, but right now her attention was fixed on Philip.

Outside, the cold February rain was flinging itself against the window. Thankfully the snow had finally thawed late in January, but since then rain had taken its place with a vengeance and everywhere was flooded and waterlogged. She had barely set foot out of the house for weeks and the thought of an evening out was appealing.

'I could always get ready and come with you?' she suggested hopefully.

'Now, why would you want to do that?' he asked. 'Look at you – you're as big as a house. Not only that, you'd be bored sick within an hour. These business dinners can be very tedious affairs, I assure you. No, you stay here and rest and I'll be back before you know it.'

Grace pouted resentfully. Philip always had an excuse lately when she suggested they go out together and she was beginning to wonder if he was ashamed of her. Oh, the flowers and the expensive presents still came as regularly as clockwork, but it had been absolute ages since they went out together. Laughing, he crossed to her and tipping her chin up he kissed her gently on the lips. 'Don't frown like that, sweetheart. It really doesn't become you.'

She felt like a small child, being reprimanded. 'Sorry, I just get a bit fed up shut away here all the time, that's all.'

'Well, it won't be for much longer,' Philip promised. 'The baby will be here soon, and then you won't have time to get bored.' As a thought occurred to him, he asked irritably, 'Will that boy be coming round again tonight?'

'If you mean, Billy, I have no idea – though I hope he does, because apart from you he's about the only person I ever get to talk to these days.' Again her voice was sulky, and it became more so as she saw him shudder involuntarily.

'I don't know why you don't like Billy,' she snapped.

He scowled. 'I would have thought that was fairly obvious. I mean, he's not exactly . . . Well, he's a bit slow, to put it kindly, isn't he?'

'So? It wouldn't do if we were all the same, would it? Billy might be a bit slow, as you put it, but he has a heart as big as a bucket and his parents adore him.'

'That's just as well then, because no one else is going to, are they?'

Grace stormed from the room. What had begun as a pleasant conversation was fast developing into an argument and so she decided that the best thing she could do would be to keep out of Philip's way until he left. Minutes later she heard the door slam behind him. She went back into the sitting room and slowly sank into the fireside chair. They seemed to be having more and more arguments just lately, but then, if truth be told, at least half of them were instigated by her. It wasn't that she *meant* to upset him; it was just that she got so lonely, and he always seemed reluctant to be seen out with her lately. That, added to the fact that he still hadn't contacted a solicitor about getting the children back from Barry, was playing heavily on her nerves. It looked like she was doomed to yet another night of listening to the Rolling Stones' LP that Billy had had for Christmas, and which he absolutely adored. She quite liked the Rolling Stones, but there was only so much of it she could take, and tonight she was in no mood for it.

As she sat strumming her fingers on the arm of the chair her eyes fell on a ledger Philip had left on the side table. She could have sworn he'd said he needed to take it with him to his business dinner, but now that he had left so hurriedly she had no way of letting him know that he'd gone without it.

A thought suddenly occurred to her. She could vaguely remember him saying that he was going to have to call into his house in Meridan to pick up some more paperwork on the way, and if she was lucky she might just catch him there. Apparently, the house was now empty and up for sale, so if she just kept ringing she was sure to catch him. Heaving herself up out of the chair she waddled into the hall and dialled his number. Almost instantly, someone picked up the phone.

'Hello?' A woman's voice came to her down the line and for a moment Grace was so shocked that she was rendered temporarily speechless.

'Hello?' the voice persisted pleasantly.

Pulling herself together with an effort, Grace asked, 'Who am I speaking to, please?'

'Cheryl Golding. May I help you?'

Grace slammed the phone down as if it had bitten her. What was Philip's wife doing there? Philip had told her she had left before Christmas. A thousand possibilities flitted through Grace's mind and she had to stop herself from bursting into tears there and then. There must be some logical explanation, she told herself, but by the time Philip returned at almost midnight she had worked herself into a towering rage. She confronted him the second he put foot inside the door. 'You went without your ledger,' she flung at him accusingly.

Shrugging, he looked slightly guilty. 'I know I did, but the mood you were in I thought I'd manage without it. I have a copy ledger at home anyway, so I picked that up on the way.'

'Your *wife* had it ready for you, did she?' Her eyes were flashing as she stood hands on hips confronting him, and for the briefest of seconds he looked slightly nonplussed.

'Just what is that supposed to mean?'

'It means that I rang your house when I realised you'd left it behind – and who should answer the phone but your wife.' Grace was red with rage now but his next words brought her down to earth with a bump.

'Well, that hardly surprises me, being as she had called in to pick up the rest of her things. I rang her last week and asked her to fetch them at her earliest convenience. I can hardly sell the house with her clothes still hanging in the wardrobe, now can I?'

Grace felt colour seep into her cheeks and for a moment she was speechless. He stood staring at her until eventually she asked in a very meek voice, 'Why didn't you tell me then?'

'Huh! After the way you just jumped to conclusions I should think that's fairly obvious. I knew how you'd react so I thought it best if I just got it over and done with once and for all.'

'Oh Philip, I'm so sorry. It was just such a shock hearing her voice, that's all.' She hung her head as crossing the distance between them he drew her into his arms.

'It's all right, darling. I should have told you I'd been in touch, I suppose. I just want all this side of it to be over so that we can get on with our lives. But you have to trust me, Grace. There's no future for us if you don't.'

'I know,' she whispered brokenly as she nestled against his chest. 'I think everything's getting to me at the minute and so I put two and two together and came up with five without waiting for you to explain. It won't happen again, I promise.'

'There will be no reason for it to happen again. My wife has gone for good now. All that remains is for me to see a solicitor and start divorce proceedings. And while I'm at it I'll get him to start a custody case for Wendy and Simon. How does that sound?'

Grace's face lit up in a radiant smile and her heart lifted. 'It sounds wonderful,' she whispered, and for the first time in weeks, months even, the future looked bright again.

Grace poured some more milk into Billy's glass and he slurped at it noisily. The kitchen was full of the smell of a steak and kidney pie she had baking in the oven for when Philip got home from work. She had cleaned the house from top to bottom and now as Billy saw her glance at the clock he asked, 'Will Mister be home soon?'

When she nodded he slid off his seat. 'Me an' Sophie had best be off then.'

'There's no need for you to rush off, Billy,' Grace said.

He shook his head as he inched towards the door. 'S'all right. Me mam will have me tea ready anyway, an' I don't think Mister likes me and Sophie very much.'

'Don't be silly, of course he does,' Grace lied, amazed at how astute the child could be, but Billy was wiser than he seemed and had no intention of staying.

'I'll come again tomorrer, an' I'll do you a nice picture at school.' He had just reached the open back door. Spring sunshine was flooding into the room when a shadow fell across him and he almost jumped out of his skin. Seeing that it was a woman, he sighed with relief and with a final smile he was gone, leaving Grace to stare at her visitor curiously.

She was a woman of medium height with a shapely figure and a stunningly pretty face. Dressed in a smart two-piece suit in a lovely shade of blue that perfectly matched the colour of her eyes, her shining brown hair was drawn back into a becoming chignon on the back of her head.

'May I help you?' Grace asked.

The woman looked her up and down, her eyes resting for long seconds in horrified fascination on Grace's extended stomach. 'Actually, I think it's *me* who may be able to help *you*.' The visitor stared at her coolly as Grace stepped aside for her to enter the kitchen. Once inside, the woman's eyes travelled around the spotlessly clean room before coming to rest on Grace again.

'You must be wondering who I am.'

When Grace nodded, the woman continued, 'I am Philip's wife – Mrs Cheryl Golding. I think it's about time you and I had a little chat, don't you?'

Grace gasped, and seeing her distress, the woman drew out a chair from the kitchen table and ushered her onto it as she eyed her stomach with distaste.

211

'If you've . . . come to see Philip about the divorce, I'm afraid he isn't in from work yet,' Grace stuttered, and her eyes grew wide with surprise as the woman threw back her head and laughed.

'What divorce would that be then?' she asked. Her voice softened somewhat as she saw the genuine distress on Grace's face and suddenly she sighed. 'May I sit down?'

When Grace nodded, the woman joined her at the table before placing her hands in her lap and looking up at Grace.

'Are you under the impression that Philip and I have separated?' When Grace nodded again she pursed her lips. Cheryl Golding had come here determined to do battle with this young woman but she was finding it increasingly difficult. 'Then I'm afraid he has misled you.'

When Grace opened her mouth to protest the woman held up her hand. 'Don't say anything, my dear. Believe me, you are not the first and if I know my husband, you certainly won't be the last – although I have to admit he's never gotten anyone into . . . er . . . trouble before.'

Before Grace could say anything she continued, 'But then we'll cross that bridge when we come to it. Of course, he will have to provide for the baby when it comes, but for now – how much do you want to end the affair?' As she spoke she was rummaging in her handbag and when she withdrew a bundle of notes Grace gasped.

'Are you . . . *seriously* offering to pay me to keep away from Philip?'

'Well, of course I am. You must know that it can't go on?'

Trembling uncontrollably, Grace stood up, and after stretching to her full height she pointed towards the door. 'I think you had better leave right now. You have it all wrong. Philip and I *love* each other. We are going to get my other two children back and move away to be a real family when the baby is born.'

The woman laughed – a cold, bitter laugh that turned Grace's blood to water. 'I find that highly unlikely, my dear. Philip never had time for our own children, even when they were young, let alone someone else's. And as for you living happily ever after . . . All I can say is that that's improbable too. Philip always comes back to me in the end, when these affairs have run their course.'

'So if he's as you say, why do you stay with him then?' Grace flung at her, and suddenly the woman's shoulders stooped.

'I suppose I put up with it because I love him.' Her eyes were sad as she stared at Grace. 'And because I know that underneath, he loves me too – but Philip is a very egotistical man. He needs his little bits on the side to feed his ego. I'm just sorry you've had to be hurt, that's all, because I don't mind admitting, you're a cut above the sort of woman he usually mixes with. I . . .'

Her voice trailed away and suddenly she asked, 'Do you think I might have a glass of water, please? This is most distressing and I'm feeling a little . . .'

Without hesitation Grace quickly crossed to the sink and filled a glass with water. Hurrying back to the table she placed it in front of Philip's wife, who lifted it to her lips and sipped at it daintily.

When she had once again composed herself, the woman stood and slowly made her way to the door before turning to look at Grace for one last time, asking, 'Where do you think Philip is on the nights that he doesn't spend with you?'

Grace squared her shoulders defensively. 'With his children or working away.'

The woman shook her head sadly, and Grace was shocked to see that there were tears sparkling on her long dark lashes. 'On those nights he is with me,' she whispered, and then she turned and left, closing the door quietly behind her as Grace struggled to come to terms with what she had said. She sank down heavily onto the nearest chair and was still there almost an hour later when Philip breezed into the kitchen as if he hadn't a care in the world.

'Phew, what's that smell?' he laughed, grabbing a tea-towel and opening the oven door. Black smoke flew into the kitchen as he took the burned pie from the oven and tossed it onto the wooden draining board. 'Blimey, Grace. I reckon you overdid it.' But then the smile slid from his lips as he noted her chalk-white face staring blankly off into space. 'Is something wrong?'

She turned to stare at him and the man she saw before her was suddenly a stranger. 'I had a visitor this afternoon,' she stated flatly.

Frowning, he took a seat opposite her. 'Oh, let me guess. Was it that oddball, Billy, again? Don't tell me he brought that damn Stones' LP around again.' There was a hint of amusement in his voice but there was no answering amusement in hers as she told him quietly, 'No . . . actually it was your wife.'

She had the satisfaction of seeing the colour drain from his face as he stared at her in disbelief. 'If this is your idea of some sort of sick joke, Grace, then I have to tell you I find it in very poor taste.'

'It's no joke, I can assure you. And neither, for that matter, were the things she told me.'

Unable to look her in the face a second longer he stood and began to pace up and down the length of the kitchen like a trapped animal.

'Just what the hell was she doing here?'

213

Grace laughed mirthlessly. 'Oh, she just came to pay me off, that's all, as apparently she has paid off all your other little bits on the side in the past. Trouble was, she hadn't allowed for *this*.'

She stabbed a finger into her distended stomach as he walked to the table and pressed his hands so hard on the edge of it that his knuckles showed white. 'Exactly what the hell has the evil bitch been telling you?' he spat.

Grace stared back at him for some seconds before answering, taking in every feature of his handsome face. 'She told me that I'm not the first woman you've had and that you have no intention of ever divorcing her. And do you know what, Philip? She wasn't at all like the picture you had painted of her. In fact, under other circumstances I might have quite liked her.'

'I . . . don't know what to say.' Dropping heavily down into the chair again his mouth worked convulsively although no words came out. After a time he looked at her beseechingly. 'I think it's about time I came clean with you, don't you?'

When she nodded, he took a ragged breath and went on. 'The thing is, Grace, I'm ashamed to admit it, but I haven't been entirely honest with you. When I first met you . . . Well, I suppose I never intended it to get serious. But then . . . I came to realise that I loved you and when you told me that you were going to have a baby I knew that my path was planned. I *have* had other light-hearted affairs over the years, I admit, but never *anything* like what is between you and me – and they only came about because of the lack of affection I got at home. Oh, no doubt you thought my wife was lovely. She *is* on the outside, but inside she's as cold as ice. She only came here today to try and spoil what's between us because she's jealous and I told her that I want a divorce. You *have* to believe me, Grace. You do, don't you?'

He leaned across the table and took Grace's hand in his but she snatched it away as she stood up and stared down at him coldly. 'I really don't have much choice, do I, Philip? This is your child I'm carrying so I suppose we're both at your mercy. My husband is hardly going to want me back, is he?'

She walked from the kitchen and climbed the stairs slowly as the baby inside her kicked lustily. Perhaps the child is feeling as betrayed as I am, she thought, and then she made her way to the bedroom she shared with the man for whom she had given up her family, before turning the key in the lock. Perhaps tomorrow she would feel differently, but for tonight she couldn't bear to have him near her.

Chapter Twenty-Two

'How would you like a trip into Nuneaton, Billy?' Grace asked the lad one sunny but chilly afternoon in February. 'I desperately need to do some shopping for some things for the baby, and then if we have time we might even fit in a trip to De-Di-Mascios ice-cream parlour.'

Billy's eyes sparkled with anticipation at the very thought of it. 'I shall have to run home an' check as it's all right wi' me mam.'

'Of course you must, but don't rush. The bus doesn't come for over an hour yet so there's plenty of time,' Grace assured him as he backed towards the door, and then he was gone with his lanky legs flying in all directions. She laughed affectionately and wandered down the garden as she waited for him to return.

It had been a funny few weeks, all in all. Philip had been almost lavish in his affections and they had settled back into some sort of normality following his wife's visit. Grace had forgiven him, although the things Mrs Golding had said still played heavily on her mind – or they would have done if she had allowed herself to dwell on them. For the majority of the time she was able to keep her fears at bay, it was easier that way. But deep down, something precious was lost for ever and sometimes she had the choking premonition that their relationship was doomed to failure, just as his wife had prophesied. The ache to see her children grew as the child inside her continued to grow, but she had refrained from even mentioning them to Philip, hoping that any day he would come in and tell her that a solicitor had begun the fight to get them back.

There were less than two months to go until the birth of the baby now, which had prompted her into the proposed shopping trip. She had considered turning one of the spare bedrooms into a nursery, but rejected the idea almost as soon as it occurred to her. After all, there was little point in going to all that trouble if they were intending to move shortly after the birth. Unlike Barry, Philip was totally useless at jobs about the house; he could barely change a fuse, and so as Grace was in no fit state to decorate at present, it would have meant paying a professional decorator to come in.

Grace considered that the money would be better spent on things for the baby, which was the reason for the shopping trip today.

Drawing in a deep breath of air she looked about the garden, which was beginning to burst into life. Primroses and crocuses were displaying their colours to the spring sunshine; cattle were grazing in the field that bordered the end of the garden and she could hear birdsong all around. Yet strangely, Grace felt no joy in her surroundings any more, nor had she for some time. The village, and even the house, had become somewhat of a prison, and more and more she found herself missing the terraced home in Marlborough Road. Back there, in a short while Barry would be filling the little pots in the back yard with Busy Lizzies and geraniums that would assure them of a blaze of colour throughout the summer, and the children would be arguing over whose turn it was to water them . . .

Grace's eyes filled with tears at the thought but just then Billy came hurtling breathlessly round the corner and she pulled herself together with an effort. Billy had become her constant companion over the last few weeks and sometimes she wondered what she would have done without him, for he had the ability to make her smile, and he always saw the best in everyone.

'Me mam says as I can come. An' she says as yer to clip me ear if I ain't on me best behaviour,' he reported earnestly.

She laughed as she walked back down the garden towards him. His mother had obviously made a valiant attempt to tidy him up. His hands and face were clean, which was a rarity, and she had even attempted to tame his mop of unruly hair with a dab of his father's Brylcreem, but even as Grace smiled at him, it was springing back into an untidy mass of ginger curls.

'I'm very pleased to hear it,' she told him. 'I shall need someone strong to carry the bags for me.'

Puffing out his chest, he flexed the muscles in his arms to show his strength. 'I'll carry *all* the bags,' he informed her solemnly and then followed her into the kitchen to wait while she put on her coat and collected her bag.

The bus was exactly on time and Billy kept up a constant stream of cheerful chatter as they drove into the town. 'That there is Caldecote Hall behind the trees. It's a boardin' school for kids that come from overseas, and me mam says as you have to be rich to go there.'

Grace looked suitably impressed.

'There's a kennels up there fer stray dogs an' all. That's where me dad got Sophie from. It was hard to choose, I don't mind tellin' you.

I wanted to bring *all* the dogs home, but me dad said as I could only have one so I chose Sophie.'

'Well, I think you chose very well,' Grace told him and he nodded in agreement as the bus moved on into Weddington.

'I miss *Children's Hour* on the radio,' he prattled on. Me dad likes to have the telly on now instead. He likes to watch the racin' drivers. Jim Clark is his favourite. He's got a Lotus,' he told Grace, sure that women wouldn't know about things like that. 'Me dad reckons Jim Clark is the best.' His voice droned on as Grace stared from the window. When the bus finally pulled into the bus station Billy helped her down the steps and then as they approached the cattle-market his eyes grew round as he stared at all the animals. Billy, as Grace had long since discovered, was a gentle-hearted lad and it broke his heart to see the sheep and cows in the pens.

'It ain't fair for 'em to be caged up like that,' he complained as Grace dragged him past. She felt very much the same if truth be told, so it was a relief when they left the cattle-market behind and came to the brightly coloured stalls beneath the clock in the Market Square. Billy instantly brightened as he gazed around at all the new sights. There seemed to be hundreds of stalls to his mind, and thousands of tantalising smells hanging on the air.

Grace smiled as she saw him lick his lips at the sight of the pie stall. 'Come on, young man,' she said briskly. 'I have no intention of feeding you until you're carrying at least half a dozen bags, so let's get shopping.'

In Abbey Street they found a stall that sold baby clothes and Grace bought a dozen Zorbit terry-towelling nappies, along with some tiny nightgowns and vests. Next stop was Boots the Chemists where she added some glass feeding bottles and teats to their collection. She would need them to give the baby a drink of boiled water. And so it went on until Billy was positively laden down with shopping bags.

By now, the lad was sweating from his exertions and so, taking pity on him, Grace led him towards De-Di-Mascios for his promised treat. The marketplace was absolutely heaving with shoppers, and they had to pick their way through them as they moved slowly along Queens Road. The ice-cream parlour had just come into sight when suddenly Grace stopped dead in her tracks and the colour drained from her face, causing Billy, who was close on her heels, to almost career into the back of her.

'What's wrong, Grace? You look like you've seen a ghost.' Following her eyes he saw that she was watching a fair-haired man with two young children and a pretty young woman walking along on the other side of the road. 'Do you know them?' he asked, but Grace was so shocked that she didn't even hear him. She felt as if her heart was breaking.

It was Barry and the children, and the shock of seeing them so unexpectedly was almost more than she could bear. She wanted to run across to them and tell them how much she loved and missed them, but instead she stood as if she had become rooted to the spot. Barry was saying something to the young woman, who laughed in reply as Simon tugged on her hand and pointed at a water pistol on the toy stall. Wendy was holding Barry's hand and it suddenly struck Grace what a lovely family they made. A family that no longer included her, for Barry had obviously found himself someone else.

The realisation struck her full force and she was shocked at how painful it was. He was slightly thinner, but it suited him, and she had forgotten how lovely and thick his blond hair was. He still had the stray lock that would flop across his forehead, the one that she used to brush away. But, of course, she would never be able to do that again. She had forsaken that right months ago. Dragging her eyes away from him she concentrated on the children. Under a warm jacket, Wendy was wearing one of the pretty smocked dresses that Grace had made for her the summer before, and she saw with a start that it now barely reached her knees. She seemed to have shot up in just a few short months and Grace was stunned. Simon too had grown and the urge to run across and take them all in her arms was overwhelming.

Suddenly, a million emotions that she had never known she was capable of feeling sprang to life inside her. Jealousy, hatred almost, and a pain that cut so deep it left her feeling breathless and empty. A tug on her sleeve made her look down at Billy, who was staring up at her with fear in his eyes.

'It's all right, Billy,' she managed to say, and then she took his arm and tugged him along behind her until at last they turned the corner into Dugdale Street where she leaned heavily against the wall.

'We could go home if you ain't feelin' so good,' he whispered, and knowing how much he had been looking forward to his trip to the ice-cream parlour made her feel even worse.

'I think that might be a good idea, love. I'll make it up to you another time, I promise. But just give me a minute first to pull myself together, would you?'

He nodded numbly, his eyes huge in his worried face, until at last she took a deep breath and began to retrace her steps, with Billy following closely behind. The bus journey back to the village was

218

silent as Grace stared blankly from the window, going over and over in her mind the sight of her family with the young woman. When they reached the house, Billy dropped the bags into a pile at the side of the kitchen door and then slowly backed away. 'I'll perhaps see you tomorrow then, eh?'

'What?' Grace tried to concentrate on what he was saying as he shuffled from foot to foot.

'I said, I'll perhaps see you tomorrow.'

'Oh, yes . . . yes, of course – and thanks, Billy.'

He turned and fled, and Grace was left alone with her thoughts.

Much later that evening, Philip watched with concern as Grace pushed her food around her plate. 'What's wrong, darling? Had a bad day?'

Her eyes were still red-rimmed from crying earlier. 'Not bad really,' she shrugged and then, unable to keep it to herself any longer, she blurted out, 'I saw Barry in Nuneaton today while I was shopping for things for the baby with Billy.'

'Oh, I see.' Philip loosened his tie and looked mildly uncomfortable. 'What did he have to say?'

'Nothing. He didn't see me. He was with the children and . . . and a woman.'

Philip coughed to clear his throat. 'Well, I suppose it was inevitable that he would find himself someone else eventually. You couldn't expect him to break his heart over you for ever, could you? I would have thought it would make you feel better. I mean – knowing that he's getting on with his life.'

Grace kept her eyes downcast so that he wouldn't see the heartache there. 'I suppose there is that in it,' she said meekly, and the rest of the meal passed in silence.

As the gentle-faced woman across the desk from him looked at him hopefully, the solicitor shifted uneasily in his seat. He had had absolutely no idea who she was when she made the appointment with him, but now that he *did* know, he found himself in a very difficult position indeed. Fancy her being Emily Westwood's sister! He would never have guessed it, even if he had been aware that Emily had a sister, for they were as different as chalk from cheese. Emily had always struck him as being a cold fish of a woman, whilst this one was attractive and had a kindly way about her.

'You must understand, Mrs Bishop, that to do what you are asking would be quite unethical. Although I do sympathise with your predicament.' The solicitor coughed and tugged at his starched white collar as he looked at the woman sitting opposite him. If he were to be honest, he had never cared for Emily, but then she had been a valuable client over the years and professionalism forbade him from disobeying her instructions now, although he would have liked to. Oh yes, he would have loved to, for from what he had seen, the young woman, Grace, whom Emily had brought up, had never had much of a life. She would probably have been far better off with the other sister sitting in front of him now, but still, that was none of his business. He rose from his chair, and Sarah, taking that as the sign that their meeting was over, rose with him.

'I'm sorry to have troubled you, Mr Bullen, and I thank you for your time. I do understand your dilemma, believe me. But before I leave, would you just answer one question for me?'

He hesitated for a moment before slowly nodding his head. 'If I can.'

'Is Grace aware of me?'

Relief showed in his face. Thankfully this was a question that he could answer quite truthfully. 'I really have no idea, dear lady – and I can say that with my hand on my heart. Now will *you* answer a question – strictly off the record, of course – for me?' When she inclined her head he went on, 'Why is it so important that you contact Grace after all these years?'

She chewed on her lip for a second before raising her head and staring him straight in the face with eyes that were still a startling shade of blue despite her advancing years. 'Let's just say I need to ease my conscience. I don't need to tell you, Mr Bullen, that Emily is not the gentlest of women, and over the years I have regretted leaving Grace to her tender mercy. Not that I had much say in the matter at the time. I was considerably younger than Emily when Grace was deprived of her family, and she, as the eldest, was the automatic choice of the courts to take Grace on. Even so, it was a terrible shock when she just vanished with the child. I did try to find her initially but then my own children came along and I don't need to tell you that life was hard in the postwar years. It wasn't until they had grown up and I was widowed that I started to worry again, and I have been looking for Grace on and off ever since. Still, at least I know now that she's somewhere in Nuneaton, and if it takes me until my dying breath I shall find her, I promise you.'

Mr Bullen extended his hand and when she took it he shook it warmly. 'Then I wish you well with your search and the best of luck. I am only sorry that I haven't been able to be of more help to you.'

'Thank you.' She walked from the office, and as the door closed softly behind her he sighed. Sometimes life could be cruel.

Outside in the street, Sarah stood for a time, gazing up and down it thoughtfully. For all she knew, Grace could have walked straight by her, and neither of them would have known who the other was. Her niece would be a young woman now, possibly even married with a family of her own . . . So why, she asked herself, is it so important that I find her? The answer came back in a single word. *Emily!* She shuddered at the memory of the older sister whom she had always feared. Cold, bitter and twisted. Admittedly, she had suffered enough to make her become like that. But then again, the suffering had been self-inflicted in a way. Then Sarah stopped her thoughts from going any further. Time was a great healer. It might just be that Emily would have mellowed with age. She could only hope so, for Grace's sake.

Chapter Twenty-Three

'I was in town today,' Grace told Philip, as he shrugged his arms into a freshly ironed shirt. 'I happened to go by the Co-op pram shop and they had the most wonderful pram in the window. A Marmet – coach-built too, it was.' She watched him closely for a reaction and when none was forthcoming, she went on, 'So, should I go and put a deposit on it?' Up until now he had been more than happy to leave the buying of the baby's things entirely up to her, but she felt on such an expensive item that he ought to have a say at least.

He shrugged. 'Look, if I were you I'd hold fire on a pram for a bit longer at least. I mean, it's obvious you've fallen in love with it, but is there really any point in having a large pram, living out here in the sticks as we do? I would have thought a smaller affair, something that would fold up and fit on the bus, would be more useful.'

Her face fell with disappointment. Philip was generous to a fault with her. In fact, she now had more jewellery than she felt she could ever possibly wear – yet when it came to anything for the baby he seemed totally uninterested. Worse still was the fact that she knew he was probably right on this one. Still, it had been a lovely pram. She could just see herself pushing it along with a beautiful bouncing baby inside. She didn't argue the point for now though. Instead she asked, 'So, where are you going tonight?'

A slight frown creased his forehead as he looked at her. 'Do I have to account for myself every single time I want to step out of the door, Grace?' His tone softened as he saw her lip tremble and turning, he wrapped his arms around her ever-expanding waistline. 'Sorry, darling. I've had a lousy day at work. I'm only going up to the Golf Club to see a prospective client. I should be back in no time. Meanwhile, why don't you curl up in front of the television or read a good book?'

She had the urge to yell at him that she was sick of curling up in front of the television, and that her eyes were almost crossed with so much reading. She couldn't remember the last time he had taken her out, and she was beginning to feel like a prisoner. Oh, a prisoner in a gilded cage, admittedly – but a prisoner all the same. Instead she disentangled herself from his arms and crossed to the window. The garden seemed to have burst into life after the long winter, just as the child inside her would shortly. But still the thought of it brought her no joy, and the need to see her son and daughter grew stronger, if possible, by the day. Coming to stand beside her he planted a hasty kiss on the back of her neck.

'Right, I'll be off. Have a good evening, darling.'

She heard the door close behind him, followed by the sound of the car engine starting on the drive. And then the silence closed in on her again as slowly she turned and made her way downstairs.

Billy called round to see her later – when he noticed that Philip's car wasn't there – and her face lit up at the sight of him. He seemed to be the only friend she had in the world at present, except for Philip and Hetty, of course. Sophie was close at his heels as usual, and Grace bent with difficulty to stroke her as she trotted towards her.

'Had a good day, have you?' Grace asked the lad.

Billy sniffed loudly as he kicked at a stone. 'Not particularly. I went to the shop fer me teacher in me lunch-hour an' some lads from the school up the road from mine started pickin' on me. They said as I was from the thick school an' started pokin' fun at me. I never said nothin' to them, so why did they have to be so horrible, Grace? I don't go to a thick school, do I? It's a *special* school, ain't it?'

He looked so miserable that Grace's heart went out to him and a surge of anger started in the pit of her stomach. As it rose, it threatened to choke her.

'No, you *don't* go to a thick school, Billy. It's a special school, just as your mam told you. Those boys are just jealous because they're not special and they can't go there. They are very ignorant and the best thing you could do would be to ignore them.'

'That's what me mam said,' he informed her, and then, perking up slightly, he asked, 'What you doin' here all on your own? Has Mister gone out again?'

Grace replied, 'You make it sound like he's always going out, Billy.'

'Well, he is, ain't he? Don't he like to take you out any more?'

What was it they said? 'Out of the mouths of babes'? 'To be honest, now I have to lug this around I don't feel much like going out any more. I tend to get tired.' Grace patted her stomach and Billy nodded.

'You're goin' to have a bastard, ain't you? I heard 'em sayin' so in the village shop. Why couldn't you just have a boy or a girl? An' what is a bastard, Grace?'

She was so shocked that for a moment she was speechless, but then, hoping to distract him, she said, 'Come on, let's have a drink. I'm dry as a bone. I might find you a bit of chocolate too.'

223

Long after he had gone, Grace paced restlessly up and down the living room, going over and over in her mind what he had so innocently repeated. No wonder the village women ignored her, the dirty whore now bringing forth a bastard.

She took in the deep-pile carpet and the expensive furniture, and for the first time she allowed herself to ask, *Was it worth it?* Philip still had the power to turn her legs to jelly, admittedly. But now that the initial novelty of living together had worn off he seemed to have cooled towards her. *No, of course he hasn't,* she denied immediately. *It's just that now I'm so big with the child, things are bound to slow down. Once the baby is born, we'll move away to a new home, get the children back and we'll all live happily ever after.* She desperately wanted to believe it, but deep down inside, where she couldn't lie to herself, a niggling doubt remained.

It was the last week in April when Grace suddenly had the urge to scrub the already spotless house from top to bottom. The urge was so strong that she could barely wait to get Philip off to work so that she could begin. As soon as he'd left she started at the top and began to systematically work her way through the bedrooms. The child inside her was unnaturally quiet, and she intended to take full advantage of the fact. When every bed was stripped and remade, she carried the huge bundle of washing down to the kitchen, and after filling the twin tub she washed it all and hung the items out to dry on the line, where they flapped in the warm breeze. Next she tackled the bathroom with a large box of Ajax, scrubbing and scouring until everything gleamed and her hands were red raw. She worked her way into the hallway, polishing everything that stood still, and was shocked, when she glanced at the clock, to see that it was already eleven-thirty. She made herself a pot of tea and after a hasty snack, the activities resumed.

By mid-afternoon the house was gleaming and Grace was feeling smugly satisfied with herself. Philip rang at four to say that something had cropped up and he wouldn't be home that night, but instead of slipping into a depression as she normally did, she just quietly assured him that this was fine, and put the phone down with a smile on her face before hurrying into the garden to bring in the washing. She ironed every single thing in the pile, folding it neatly across a huge wooden clotheshorse that stood in a far corner of the kitchen to air. Then she manhandled the heavy wooden ironing board back into the cupboard under the stairs before standing with hands on hips to admire all her hard work. At last she allowed herself to take

224

another break. The kettle was just coming to the boil when Billy appeared at the kitchen door.

'Ah, you must have smelled the teapot,' she teased, and never needing a second offer, Billy skipped across the shining quarry tiles to take his place at the kitchen table. She rubbed her back as she prepared the cups.

Frowning, Billy asked, 'Is everythin' all right, Grace?'

'Of course it is. I've just got a touch of backache, that's all. I've probably overdone it a bit today. But never mind, I've finished so I can put my feet up now.' She pushed the biscuit tin across the table to him and he immediately took out a Garibaldi for himself and a Rich Tea finger biscuit which he passed under the table to Sophie. Looking around the kitchen approvingly, he said, 'Looks like you've been doin' a spot o' spring-cleaning.'

'That's the understatement of the year.' Grace poured milk into two cups. 'It's a good job you weren't here earlier,' she joked, 'because everything that stood still got polished or washed. Ouch!'

A searing pain pierced through her lower back and instantly Billy was at her side, his face a mask of concern.

'What's wrong?'

Grace gripped the edge of the sink until the pain had subsided and then assured him feebly, 'It's nothing to worry about, really. I probably pulled something today. I'm fine now.'

Billy began to shuffle from foot to foot – a sign that Grace had come to recognise as him being highly agitated. 'Look, Billy, sit back down, will you?' she said in an effort to calm him. 'If I don't get this tea poured soon it will be stone cold.'

Billy reluctantly did as he was told, although he kept his eyes fixed firmly on her as she handed him a delicate china cup and saucer. The next pain came as she was raising her own cup to her lips, and it was so unexpected that her tea splashed all across the freshly scrubbed table. The severity of it made her gasp, and this time Billy really panicked.

'Grace, somethin' *is* wrong. It ain't the baby comin', is it? When will the Mister be home? Shall I run an' fetch me mam?'

Flapping her hand at him she clutched at her stomach and waited for the pain to pass. 'No, Billy, don't do that. It's going off again now.' She had gone as white as chalk and alarm bells began to ring in her head. It couldn't be the baby coming – it was far too early. She still had a month to go. She tried to remain calm as she looked across at Billy. 'Why don't you get yourself off home? I think I might just go and put my feet up for an hour.'

He shook his head vehemently. 'I ain't goin' nowhere just yet, not till I know as you're all right. You could go an' lie down though. Me an' Sophie will be down here if you need anythin' then.'

Grace looked at his troubled face, and in that moment she came to realise just how much he had come to mean to her in the few short months she had known him. He had the body of a young man and the mind of a child, but he also had more compassion in his little finger than anyone else she had ever known, almost as if someone Higher Up had granted him feelings to make up for the other things he lacked. She saw by the look on his face that it would be pointless to argue so instead she smiled at him gratefully.

'I'll just go up and have half an hour then, if you're sure, but if you get bored, take yourself away home. I'll be fine.'

She had almost reached the door that separated the kitchen from the sitting room when suddenly she felt a rush of warmth between her legs. Gasping with horror she looked down to see that she was standing in a puddle of water. Her waters had broken, but she had no time to dwell on the fact before the next pain tore through her. She began to panic. What should she do? Philip had said that he would be away for two days, so would it even be worth phoning the garage, or would he have already left? Deciding that she really had little choice but to try, she staggered into the hall and snatched up the phone with shaking fingers. Even if he had left, surely someone would be able to get word to him? She needed him now. The phone seemed to ring for ever but then at last someone lifted it, and Grace instantly recognised the voice of Philip's wife.

'It's Grace. Could I speak to Philip, *please*?'

There was silence for a few seconds and then at last the woman said frostily, 'I'm sorry, Philip isn't in right now. Could I take a message?'

'I . . . I think I'm having the baby. Would you get word to him?' She could only imagine how the woman on the other end of the phone must be feeling, but what choice did she have? This was Philip's child as well as hers, or at least she had always thought it was. Again the terrible silence and then at last the woman said, 'I'll see what I can do.' Then the phone went dead in her hand.

'Billy?'

He approached her with a look of stark terror on his face as she tried to smile at him reassuringly. 'Can you tell the time, Billy?'

His head wagged from side to side.

'All right then, no matter. Can you help me into the lounge where I can see the clock? I need to time how far apart the pains are.'

226

Instantly, he helped her to her feet from where she had sunk onto the stairs, and as she leaned heavily on his arm he helped her back into the lounge. Twenty minutes later she stared at him from eyes that seemed to have sunk deep into her head. The pains were coming regularly now, every five minutes, and she knew that she couldn't wait for Philip any longer.

'Billy, I want you to be a big boy now. I want you to dial 999 and ask for an ambulance. Tell them my address and ask them to get here as quickly as they can. Do you think you could manage that?'

He nodded vigorously before haring away into the hall, but he was shaking so much that it took a few attempts before she finally heard him talking to someone. At last he appeared back in the doorway, his face as white as her own.

'Ambulance is on its way, an' they said I'm to stay wi' you till they get here.'

'Good boy.' She took his hand and clung to it as if it were a lifeline, and all the time her heart was crying, *It's too soon – it's too soon.* Now she could admit to herself that she had never really wanted this baby, for it had been the cause of tearing two families apart. But then, the child had never asked to be born and now it might even lose its life before it had begun because of her selfishness. Just as her aunt had told her on countless occasions, she was truly wicked. She began to cry, and by the time the ambulance arrived, with its bells piercing the quiet of the village, she was sobbing uncontrollably.

'I'm not even eight months yet,' she told the ambulanceman with terror in her eyes.

He patted her hand in comforting fashion. 'Not to worry, love, we'll have you at the George Eliot before you can blink your eye. Now just do as we tell you an' everythin' will be fine.'

Billy kept hold of her hand as they loaded her onto a stretcher and carried her out to the waiting ambulance. Just before they lifted her in, he bent to kiss her softly and it tore at her heart to see that he was openly crying.

'Don't worry, Billy,' she panted. 'I'll be home soon. You be a good boy for your mam while I'm gone, eh?'

He nodded and then the doors clanged shut and she was lost in a world of pain as the ambulance sped towards Nuneaton. When they arrived at the hospital, a nurse was waiting for them and they wheeled her straight into a delivery room. A straight-faced doctor examined her and then gravely shook his head. 'I'm afraid there's no stopping it now, Mrs Swan. You've gone too far, but try not to worry. Lots of new babies survive at seven or eight months nowadays. We have an incubator all ready and waiting.'

All the while he was talking, two nurses were peeling her clothes from her as a midwife donned some gloves and approached the bed. The pain was coming in continuous waves and somewhere behind the doctor's shoulder was a huge black hole that seemed to be getting closer and closer by the minute. Blind panic engulfed her – she mustn't fall into the hole. If she did, she might never climb out, and suddenly she was a child herself again, and her screams echoed around the sterile delivery room as she began to slip in and out of consciousness.

Where was Barry? Why wasn't he here with her?

And there were two children with the faces of angels holding their arms out to her.

There was a gown. The sort of gown she had always dreamed of, and she was floating around the dance-floor in the arms of a handsome man, to the soft strains of a waltz.

But where was Barry? He and the children seemed to be fading away and she couldn't hold on to them although she screamed for them to stay . . .

'Please, Mrs Swan. You *must* push when I tell you. You're almost there now.'

The voice dragged her back to the present. It was coming from a long way away and now she was back in the light. A harsh fluorescent light that made her blink and turn her head. But where was she? And where was Barry? Who *were* all these strange faces leaning across her, and what alien being was inside her, trying to force its way out of her?

'Barry! Barry, where are you?'

The doctor and the midwife exchanged a worried glance.

'Is her husband here?' The doctor bent to Grace as the midwife shook her head.

'I've no idea. She came in by ambulance, as an emergency. I don't even know if her husband is aware that she's here.'

'Well. No time to worry about it now. Pass me the knife, I'm going to have to do an episiotomy. And the forceps. If we don't get this baby out soon we're in danger of losing both of them.'

'Yes, Doctor.' Without question the midwife lifted a wickedly sharp knife from a dish at the side of the bed and Grace saw it glint in the harsh light. She was beyond caring. If the knife could end her suffering,

228

then so be it. Let it happen sooner rather than later. The black hole was inching closer again, but now she welcomed it as she slipped into its inky depths.

'Mrs Swan – Grace – can you hear me?'

Grace frowned and kept her eyes tight closed. It had been nice in the darkness, but now someone was trying to bring her back again. Back to the pain, for although she kept her eyes shut, still she was aware that she ached everywhere. There was a needle in the back of her hand, and as she slowly blinked she saw that it was attached to a drip at the side of the bed. As her eyes began to focus she saw a number of people standing around the bed looking down on her.

One of them, a grey-haired man with gold-framed glasses perched on the end of his nose, leaned closer and smiled at her kindly.

'Welcome back to the land of the living, Grace. You had us worried there for a time.'

She was in a hospital. Slowly, it all began to come back to her. The baby – she had come here to have a baby. But where was it? As if he could read her thoughts, the man smiled at her again.

'You had a daughter, Grace – a little girl. She's in intensive care and holding her own. She's very tiny, of course, and she has . . . er . . . Well – there are a few other problems. But for now all you need to know is that she's doing well. You have a good sleep now, and when you're feeling a little stronger, Doctor Lane, the pediatrician here, will come and talk to you about her.'

Grace wanted to know now. What problems did her daughter have? But she was tired. So tired that her eyes were closing of their own volition and soon she was fast asleep again.

She next woke to the sound of a tea trolley rumbling up the middle of the row of beds. A glance at the window told her that it must be very early in the morning, for the light was struggling to find its way through a gap in the thin curtains. Even as she watched, a nurse in a starched white apron and bonnet swept them open before coming to stand at the foot of her bed and lifting some charts that were attached to it.

'Good morning, Mrs Swan, and how are we feeling today?'

Grace tried to ignore the pain as she pulled herself up onto her pillows. 'Better, I think. But how is my baby? Did I dream it, or did someone tell me I'd had a little girl?'

'They certainly did, and as far as I know she's doing as well as can be expected. When you're feeling up to it, we'll wheel you down to Intensive Care to take a look at her. But for now, we need to build

229

your strength back up. You lost a lot of blood during the delivery, which is why we gave you a transfusion. Now, are you going to eat some breakfast for me?'

The very thought of food made Grace's stomach revolt, but she nodded meekly as the nurse swept away to fetch her a tray of food.

She saw that she was in a ward full of women, and as she drowsily looked about her, the woman in the next bed smiled and said, 'Hello, dearie. Out for the count yer were last night when they fetched yer up to the ward. Feelin' a bit better this mornin', are yer?'

'Yes, thanks.'

'Just as well then. Soon as the nurses have seen to us lot, they'll be bringin' the babbies in for us to feed.'

'I doubt they'll be bringing mine,' Grace told her sadly. 'Mine is in the Intensive Care Unit. I haven't even seen her yet.'

'Ah, that's too bad, that is.' The woman folded her arms beneath her swollen breasts and hoisted them up comically. 'So what's wrong wi' the poor little mite then?'

Grace was saved from having to answer by the Sister approaching up the ward like a battleship in full sail. She stopped at the bottom of the neighbouring bed and frowned on the unfortunate woman. 'Now, now, Mrs Bright, Mrs Swan is still recovering from a very difficult birth and she needs her rest.' As she spoke she was plumping up the woman's pillows, and when she was quite satisfied, she ran her hands down her spotlessly clean apron and walked away.

The woman raised her eyebrows and hissed at Grace, 'Old battleaxe, she is. The nurses stand to attention when she's on the warpath. I reckon she'd have been better suited as a Sergeant Major than a Sister.'

Just then the double doors at the end of the ward swung open and Mrs Bright lost all interest in Grace as she saw a nurse wheeling a small cot on wheels towards her. It stopped at the foot of her bed and the young nurse lifted out a tiny baby wrapped in a blue blanket and placed it in her arms. 'There we are then. There's certainly nothing wrong with this young man's lungs – he's been screaming his head off in the nursery. I think you're going to have a job to fill the little chap up.'

As the baby nestled into his mother's arms, Grace felt a lump form in her throat and turning on her side she snuggled down beneath the blanket. She felt as if she had been beaten with a sledgehammer, but worse than that was the fear that was growing inside her. How was her baby today? What was wrong with her? And where was Philip? Surely someone must have got word to him by now? She thought back to the birth of Wendy and Simon. It had been all the nurses

230

could do back then, to stop Barry from seeing her immediately after the birth. In fact, he had flatly refused to go home until he *had* seen her. And oh, how thrilled he had been! Tears filled her eyes, and in that moment she might have been the only person in the world, for never before in the whole of her life had she ever felt so totally and utterly alone.

Chapter Twenty-Four

The morning seemed to go on for ever. The nurses came and went with startling efficiency, delivering the newborn babies to their mothers every three hours on the dot, and then wheeling them away back to the nursery again after they had been fed. Grace was asked to express some milk into a jug, which was then rushed away to the Intensive Care Unit. But no one offered to take her to see her baby.

Grace's mind had been working overtime, and as it drew near to lunch-time she'd convinced herself that she had given birth to a monster at least.

When a grey-haired gentleman in a white coat eventually stopped at the end of her bed and smiled at her, she frowned. He seemed vaguely familiar, but she couldn't think where she had seen him before.

'Good morning, Mrs Swan. I'm Doctor Lane. I was present during your daughter's delivery last night. Do you remember me?'

Grace nodded. Now she remembered: he was the pediatrician who had spoken to her the night before.

Fear showed in her eyes as she stared back at him. 'The baby's dead, isn't she?'

'Oh, goodness me, no.' After closing the curtains around the bed, he pulled up a chair. 'In actual fact, the baby is doing far better than we dared hope, everything taken into consideration. She weighs a little under five pounds, which is not a bad weight at all, considering she was some weeks premature.'

'But?' Grace kept her eyes fixed on his face and looking down at his hands, which were folded in his lap, he sighed.

'There *is* a but, Mrs Swan. I would be a liar if I said there wasn't. We have been doing various tests on her throughout the morning, so until we have completed them and got the results back, as you will appreciate, I cannot tell you definitely what is wrong with her. But . . . well, to be honest she does show all the signs of having Downs syndrome.'

'Oh my God!' Grace's hand flew to her mouth as a look of horror settled on her face. 'You mean – I've given birth to a mongol?'

'Now, Mrs Swan, please don't distress yourself. You have given birth to a beautiful baby girl, and that is how you must think of her. All the signs up to now indicate that she is fairly healthy. We *have* detected a heart defect, which unfortunately is common in these children. But of course, we shall monitor her closely as she grows and there is no reason at all why she shouldn't lead a normal life. If you feel well enough after dinner we could wheel you down to the Intensive Care Unit to see her.'

Grace shook her head as panic engulfed her. She *had* given birth to a monster, just as she had feared. What would Philip say? Suddenly she wanted to run as far away, from here as was possible.

The doctor patted her trembling hand and smiled at her sympathetically. 'I know it must have come as a shock to you, my dear, but once you have seen her, you'll realise that things are not as bad as you think they are. She really is a lovely little girl. The nurses down in Intensive Care are almost fighting over who gets to look after her. For now, though, I am going to leave you to get used to the idea. I shall come back this afternoon and if you feel up to it I shall take you personally to meet her.'

When Grace merely turned her head away he rose quietly and slipped through the curtains, leaving Grace to sob as if her heart would break. What was it her aunt had used to say? *The sins of the fathers shall be visited upon the children.* Well, how right she had been. Because of her own wickedness, an abnormal child had been brought into the world. A child who, for all Grace knew, might not even survive. Perhaps it would be just as well if she didn't. After all, how would she ever cope with caring for a monster? The tears came faster still and within an hour her pillow was soaked and her eyes redrimmed.

It was mid-afternoon before the kindly doctor reappeared. By then Grace had settled into a dull sort of lethargy and she stared at him blankly as he smiled at her.

'Are you ready to go and meet your baby now, Mrs Swan?'

She nodded. What choice did she have? She would have to see it sooner or later so she might as well get it over with, although she shuddered at the thought. The doctor nodded to a pretty young nurse who was hovering at his side, and instantly she shot away to return, seconds later, with a wheelchair.

It took both of them to get Grace into it, and she was shocked at how weak she was. Her legs seemed to have developed a mind of their own, and had it not been for their hands supporting her, she would have fallen her length.

233

The woman in the next bed smiled at her as they wheeled her past. Her baby was nestling on her chest, greedily feeding from her full breasts, and there was a look of utter contentment on the woman's face.

'Off to meet yer little 'un are yer, love?'

Grace ignored her as the nurse, who closely resembled Twiggy, the model who was much in the news at present, hurriedly wheeled her past. The doctor and the nurse exchanged a worried glance, but then they were slamming through the double doors and heading for the tiny lift that would take them down to the ground floor and the ICU. They pushed Grace through a labyrinth of corridors that were all painted a dull cream, before coming to a halt in front of some doors that had gaily coloured Disney characters painted on them. The doctor rang a bell and within seconds a nurse, who was dressed in a long gown that covered her uniform, opened the door. On her head was a cap that completely covered her hair, and she wore a mask across her mouth.

'Ah, Doctor Lane. Brought Mrs Swan to meet the baby, have you? Come in, we've been expecting you.'

They wheeled her inside and the nurse pointed apologetically to some hooks where a selection of gowns and masks were hanging. 'I'm afraid I shall have to ask you all to put one of these on. As you might appreciate, Mrs Swan, we have to be very careful about infection in here.'

They helped her into a gown, and then whilst the painfully thin nurse who had accompanied her returned to the ward, the doctor and the nurse who had just greeted her pushed her into a small ward. It was full of incubators, most of them occupied, and Grace tried not to look inside them as they wheeled her past. When they stopped in front of one, she had the urge to turn and run.

'Here she is then, Mrs Swan. Try not to be too frightened of all the equipment. It's mainly to monitor her progress, and not nearly as scary as it looks, I assure you. She's a little beauty if you don't mind me saying so, and she's *so* good. She has the temperament of an angel. She's taking all her feeds, little by little, and she never cries, not even when she's hungry.'

Grace stared at her hands, which were hanging slackly in her lap as the doctor looked at the nurse.

'Why don't you and I go and get the kettle on, Nurse? I'm sure Mrs Swan doesn't need us present while she says hello to her daughter.' Before Grace could protest, he pushed her as close to the incubator as he could, and without another word, took the nurse's elbow and

234

walked away. 'We'll be back shortly,' he called to Grace when he was almost halfway down the room, and then the door closed behind them and Grace was alone, save for the sleeping infants in the incubators all around her.

She sat for what seemed a long time, with her head bowed, but then the temptation to peep at the child became too much, and fearfully she raised her head. Wheeling herself a little closer with considerable difficulty, she steeled herself to look into the plastic cot. The child was fast asleep. There seemed to be wires and tubes hooked up to every part of her, and Grace felt a pang of pity. The baby didn't look at all as she had expected her to, except for her eyes, which were slightly slanted, giving her a somewhat Oriental look. She was remarkably pretty – not at all like the little monster she had imagined. She had a shock of fair hair, and as Grace watched her, she suddenly stretched and opened her eyes. They were a startling shade of blue, and un-expectedly Grace felt a surge of emotion. This was *her* baby. How could she ever have thought that she wouldn't love her or want her? She was beautiful – so tiny and vulnerable. Special – just as Billy was.

Tentatively she pressed her hand through a hole in the side of the incubator, and as the baby's tiny hand closed around her finger, Grace's heart opened wide: love flooded through her and the bond was made.

Through the glass in the top of the door further down the room, the doctor smiled with satisfaction. 'That's the first hurdle crossed,' he informed the nurse. 'If I'm any judge, we'll have problems keeping Mum away from here now.' It was a situation he had been forced to witness far more times than he cared to remember in his career, but this time it looked as though things would work out just fine. Relieved, he went off to enjoy a well-earned cup of tea, content to leave mother and daughter to become acquainted.

The baby was now two days old, and Grace was spending as much time as the nurses would allow down in the Intensive Care Unit with her. If the women in the neighbouring beds, and the nursing staff, had detected a definite lack of a father's presence, they had tactfully refrained from mentioning it, but now Grace was becoming deeply concerned. Where *was* Philip?

All the other women had lockers that were sagging beneath the weight of fruit, flowers and cards, but as yet she had not had so much as a single visitor and visiting times were becoming occasions to be dreaded. Tonight looked set to be no different, but then suddenly the doors swung open and Philip appeared, clutching a huge bunch of flowers and wearing a very sheepish expression.

235

'Hello, Grace.' He stood at the end of the bed looking so handsome that every woman in the ward was openly staring at him, and suddenly Grace forgave him and her heart fluttered just as it always did at the sight of him.

'I would have come sooner, but I was working away when they got word to me. Are you all right, darling?'

'Yes, I'm fine now, Philip. I had the baby. It's a little girl.'

'Oh.' He shuffled from foot to foot, looking so uncomfortable that Grace couldn't help but smile.

'Why don't you come and sit down,' she offered, pointing to a chair at the side of the bed. He did as he was told as her eyes searched his face. 'Don't you want to know how the baby is?'

'Of course I do. I . . . er . . . suppose I'm just more concerned about you at the minute.' He pushed the flowers at her and she smiled. Philip looked totally out of place as a hospital visitor. He was much more at ease on a dance-floor or sitting in some fancy restaurant. Not that they would have much time for that sort of thing in the next few months. He would have to become accustomed all over again to bottles and night feeds and nappies hanging everywhere. The thought was amusing and she found herself smiling again. The smile was wiped from her face though, when he asked, 'So when do I get to see the baby?'

She knew that this was the ideal opportunity to tell him of the child's special needs, but somehow she could only stare at him mutely as she sought for the right words. If she told him the truth, he might react as she had done, but if he could only go and see her, then how could he fail to fall in love with her, as Grace had done?

'She's down in the Intensive Care Unit at present,' she managed to say eventually. 'All premature babies have to go there as a matter of course. But she's doing very well. I know you'll love her, Philip. She's so beautiful and so tiny – like a little doll. Even the nurses down there have fallen in love with her.' As she spoke, Grace beckoned to a nurse who was walking down the centre of the ward, and after a hurried discussion with her she turned back to Philip with a smile on her face.

'She's going to go and fetch me a wheelchair, and then you can wheel me down to Intensive Care.'

He nodded, and soon he had her tucked into the chair that the nurse had provided and they were trundling along the corridors that smelled faintly of stale disinfectant on their way to see the baby.

'Don't be afraid of all the tubes and drips that are attached to her,' Grace warned him. 'They do look a bit daunting, I admit, but tomorrow, all being well, they should be able to come off, and then as soon as she starts to gain a little weight we'll be able to take her home.'

Philip said nothing; he just nodded, looking more and more uncomfortable by the minute, until at last they reached the doors of the ICU. All the nurses there knew Grace by now, and they smiled at her as Philip wheeled her down the ward, all of them eyeing him appreciatively.

Dr Lane was leaning across the baby's crib as Grace approached and he flashed her a warm smile.

'Ah, just in time to hear the good news, my dear. This little madam is doing so well that if she carries on as she is, we'll be able to take her out of the incubator in another few days and put her into a normal cot. You'll be able to have that cuddle you've been longing for then.' His eyes moved to Philip and he extended his hand. 'And you must be Barry, Grace's husband. She was calling for you on the night of the delivery.'

Grace felt colour flame in her cheeks. Quickly she tried to explain. 'No, this is Philip, my . . . er . . . the baby's father. You must have misheard me, Doctor Lane.'

Sensing her distress and seeing the stony look on Philip's face, the kindly doctor quickly tried to right the situation. 'I'm so sorry. I've probably got you mixed up with another mum that delivered that night. Do forgive me for my mistake. But whatever your name is, you're here at long last, and that's all that matters. I'll leave you to it, whilst Grace introduces you to your daughter. And by the way – congratulations. You have a lovely baby there. You're a very lucky man.'

Philip solemnly shook the extended hand and the doctor hurried away. His wife was forever telling him that he could win a gold star for putting his foot in it, and it seemed that this was one of the occasions when she had proved to be right.

Meanwhile, Grace wheeled herself as close to the crib as she could, beckoning Philip to follow her, then she watched him closely as he took his first look at his daughter.

He frowned, as if something was puzzling him as he stared down at the sleeping child. Looking back at Grace, he asked quietly, 'What's wrong with her eyes?'

This was it; Grace knew then that she could postpone the moment no longer. 'Our daughter has Down's syndrome, Philip.'

She watched as shock and disbelief registered on his face. Without a word he sank heavily into a chair that was placed at the side of the crib. Gently she took his hand and shook it up and down.

'I know it must have come as a shock to you, darling. I admit it was to me. But look at her – she's beautiful. And it's not nearly so bad as you think. She does have a heart defect, and she'll probably be a little behind in her development. But we'll cope, you'll see.'

He shook his head from side to side and his hand flew to his mouth as he tried to digest what she had just told him.

'What you're saying is – the child is a *mongol*?'

Grace swallowed the lump in her throat. His words were cutting into her like a knife. But then, in fairness, had her reaction not been exactly the same? He just needed time to get used to the idea that was all – as she had.

'I don't think I can handle this, Grace,' he went on in a rush. 'I'm not very good with people who are not normal, as you know.'

'You will,' Grace assured him with a confidence that she was far from feeling. 'Now, come on. Let's go back upstairs and give you a chance to come to terms with it.'

He rose immediately, only too glad of an excuse to escape. Gripping the handle of the wheelchair he paused to take one last look at the tiny infant. 'She doesn't look anything like me, does she?' he commented.

'Oh, all new babies tend to look pretty much the same,' Grace replied.

'Mm.' He wheeled her back to the ward with a speed that had her clutching the arms of the chair. He seemed impatient to be gone now, and sensing that he needed some time alone to get used to the idea of having a handicapped child, she didn't pressure him to stay.

Once the nurse had helped her back into bed, she asked him, 'Would you mind bringing a bag in with some clothes for me and the baby to come home in?'

'Of course, I'll drop them in tomorrow. But I'd better be off now. Things to do, you know?'

'Of course.' When Grace offered her cheek he bent and pecked it politely before rushing away as if the very Hounds of Hell were at his feet. He'll be fine tomorrow, she tried to reassure herself – but somehow a niggling doubt remained.

Grace remained in hospital for another two weeks. During that time Philip came to see her very briefly twice more, and on each visit made up some excuse not to go and see the baby again. He didn't show any desire to discuss names, and when Grace ask him if he'd had time to register the baby he shook his head. Grace was not unduly worried. She was sure that once she was home, he would come to love the child as she did, and was prepared to give him time to accept that their child was, in some ways, slightly less than perfect. Grace herself spent as much time as she could down in the ICU. As the nurses had forecast, the baby was slow at taking her feeds, but Grace had endless patience with her, so that slowly but surely, she started to gain a little weight. It was only a few ounces, but Grace saw it as a major step forward and loved her more with every day that passed.

When Dr Lane informed her that he felt the child was well enough to leave hospital the next day, Grace cried with joy and relief. She was still very weak, but getting about slowly without the aid of a wheelchair now, so immediately the doctor had left her bedside she took some pennies from her purse and walked as fast as she could from the ward to find the payphone and let Philip know the good news. She rang him at the garage, guessing that was where he would be, and thankfully he answered almost immediately.

'Philip, wonderful news. The doctor has just said that the baby and I can come home tomorrow. Will you be able to fetch us?'

'Well, I, um . . . I suppose so. What time are they going to discharge you?'

He didn't sound particularly pleased to hear from her, but then she excused him, just as she always did. After all, she knew that he must be run off his feet or he would have taken the trouble to come and see her more often in the hospital. 'About ten o'clock in the morning, if that's all right?'

'Very well. I'll see you then. Goodbye, Grace.' As the phone went dead in her hand she chewed on her lip. Still, just one more night and then they would all be together again, and they could begin the life they had planned as a family. The thought cheered her as she made her way back to the ward, much more slowly this time.

Grace was in a happy frame of mind when she woke the next morning. The day was bright and clear as if it was trying to match her mood. She dressed the baby carefully in the tiny baby clothes that she had asked Philip to bring in for her, billing and cooing at her all the time. By nine-thirty she was ready, and she carried the baby into the small waiting room that was attached to the ward to wait for him. She had a list of instructions a mile long on how to care for the child, but she didn't find it daunting in the least. To Grace the baby was the same as any other, apart from the fact that she was special, as Billy was. She could hardly wait to see him, and his reaction to the child, and every few minutes she glanced from the window, looking for a sight of Philip's car.

Ten o'clock came and went. She told herself that he must have been unavoidably detained and tried to quell her impatience, but as the minutes ticked away she began to grow agitated. Where could he be, and why hadn't he got word to her that he was going to be late?

Eventually she took some pennies from her pocket and made her way to the payphone with the baby safely tucked in one arm. She dialled the number of the garage, but no one answered, and after a few attempts she slowly went back to the waiting room, telling herself that he must be on his way.

It was almost eleven-thirty when the Sister stuck her head round the door. 'Still here, Mrs Swan? I thought you would have left some time ago.'

'I should have,' Grace admitted with a trace of annoyance in her voice. 'My . . . er . . . Philip hasn't shown up and there was no answer when I rang him. He must have been held up.'

'Mm.' The Sister sniffed her disapproval, as she smoothed an imaginary crease in her snow-white apron. 'In that case then, perhaps I should arrange for an ambulance to run you home. Baby will be due for a feed soon and we don't want her to be put out of her routine, now do we? Wait there, I'll be back shortly.'

Grace nodded meekly; no one argued with Sister, as she had discovered in her time on the ward. Twenty minutes later she was loaded into the back of an ambulance and they were going home at last.

It was strange, she thought, as they pulled into the village some time later. Everything looked exactly the same as when she had left it, and yet so much had happened since then.

She noted immediately that Philip's car wasn't on the drive, and after thanking the kindly ambulancemen profusely she tottered up the drive with the baby in one arm and her bag in the other. Negotiating the key into the lock was tricky as she balanced the baby in her arms, but at last she managed it and she was home.

She laid the sleeping child gently on the settee and tucked some cushions around her. Everything was exactly as she had left it in the house, and yet some deep instinct told her that it was different somehow.

Shrugging her shoulders, she crept into the kitchen, intent on making herself a cup of tea before the baby woke up for her feed. A decent cup of tea was the one thing she had craved in the hospital, and after the stewed affairs she'd become accustomed to, she felt as if she could drink a whole potful to herself. She checked the fridge and was glad to see a couple of bottles of milk in there. It was as she was filling the kettle at the sink that her eyes fell on a sheet of paper propped up against the sugar bowl on the table. Settling onto the nearest chair she began to read it.

Dear Grace,

There is no easy way to tell you this so I am just going to say it. As you must be aware, things have not been right between us for some time. I have grave doubts as to whether the child you have just given birth to is mine. In fact, I feel in my heart that it isn't, and I know that I could never have feelings for it. I can see no future ahead for us and so I have become reconciled with my wife. I hope that you and your husband may be able to put this unfortunate affair behind you too. The rent on the house is paid until the end of next month. You will also find some money in an envelope to tide you over on the chest of drawers in the bedroom. I am deeply sorry that things have had to end as they have and I wish you luck in the future.

Philip

The letter fluttered from her hand as shock registered on her chalk-white face. It must be some sort of joke. Philip would never do this to her. *Would he?* Suddenly she was running across the kitchen and was taking the stairs two at a time. She hovered in the doorway to their bedroom then crossing to the wardrobe, she flung the door wide. Empty coat-hangers stared back at her, and on the chest of drawers was an envelope just as he had promised. She opened it with shaking hands. There was a small bundle of pound notes inside. After counting them she found that there was thirty pounds there. *Thirty pounds!* And no home to go to after the end of next month. A baby to care for – and all she had in the world was thirty pounds. That was all that Philip had thought she was worth.

Burying her head in her hands she began to sob, and yet strangely she found that she wasn't crying about the fact that Philip had left her. Now she could see him for the shallow man that he was, but then hadn't she felt so for some time? Deep, deep down she knew that she had, but she had wanted so much to hold on to the dream, to the perfect, fairytale, happy-ever-after ending – all her life she seemed to have been chasing it. Once she had thought that she would find it with Barry. But then Philip had come along, with his charm and his dashing good looks, offering a way of life that she had imagined would be better than the one she had with her husband, and so she had sacrificed everything for him. Only now, when it was too late, did she admit that she had had her happy ending staring her right in the face all along, with her husband and her family. Their house, modest as it was compared to the one she was in now, had been filled with love and laughter, built on solid foundations of kindness and

241

affection. Barry had never been boring, as she had once thought him. He had been gentle and caring and kind. But it was too late now. Barry had someone else, someone who no doubt returned the love he gave, as she never had – someone who deserved him.

She had no way of knowing for sure who the baby's father was. But there was one thing she *was* sure of – and that was that she was her mother.

Downstairs was a child who had no one else in the world apart from her, and from now on it would be up to Grace to give this little girl the best life that she could, for she was the innocent victim in this whole sorry mess.

Chapter Twenty-Five

Sarah stood aside for the congregation to file past her out of the church. Every Sunday morning for weeks she had steadfastly visited different churches in Nuneaton for the morning service, hoping to catch a sight of Emily, but up to now she had been sorely disappointed. Today she was standing outside the parish church of Chilvers Coton, waiting to have a word with the vicar when he left. Eventually her patience was rewarded and as he stepped from the now-deserted church, pulling the great doors to firmly behind him, she hurried forward.

'Hello.' Holding out her hand she flashed him a warm smile. 'May I say how very much I enjoyed the sermon?'

He immediately smiled back at her and shook the proffered hand. 'Why, thank you, my dear. Is it your first visit to Coton?'

'Yes – yes, it is.' Sarah tried hard to keep the note of desperation from her voice. 'Actually,' she hurried on, 'I was wondering if you might be able to help me? You see, I'm looking for someone – my sister. We were estranged many years ago and now I'm trying to find her. Her name is Emily Westwood. Would you happen to know if she ever attends this church? She might bring a young woman called Grace with her.'

She waited hopefully as he stared off into space for some seconds, his wispy grey hair blowing in the breeze as he searched his memory, but when he eventually looked back at her, he shook his head sadly.

'I'm sorry, my dear, I'm afraid the name doesn't ring a bell at all. I know most of my parishioners but I can honestly say that isn't a name that's familiar.'

'Oh!' Sarah was unable to hide her disappointment and now his kindly face registered concern.

'I'm so sorry. Was there some reason that made you think your sister might attend *this* particular church?'

'No, none at all,' Sarah admitted. 'To be quite honest with you, I might be on a wild-goose chase. When my sister was younger she was highly religious and attended church every Sunday. That was when she lived in Coventry before she moved to Nuneaton. I can only hope that she still does, so I've been systematically visiting different churches in Nuneaton, hoping for a glimpse of her. The trouble is, there are so many churches . . .'

'Quite,' he said gently. 'But don't you have any idea which area she might live in?'

'No, that's the trouble – but anyway, I've taken up enough of your time. Thank you.' Sarah had just turned and started to walk away when the vicar's voice slowed her steps.

'You might try Nuneaton parish church. It's just outside of the town centre, and if your sister lives anywhere near the town, that's probably the church she would attend.'

Sarah smiled back at him. 'Thank you, I haven't tried there yet. Perhaps next week . . .'

He nodded and watched as she walked away with her shoulders stooped. Then offering up a silent prayer that the poor woman's efforts to be reunited with her sister might be realised, visions of roast beef and crisp Yorkshire puddings suddenly danced in front of his eyes and he sped away towards the vicarage as fast as his short stubby legs would carry him.

'Hello, Grace, I heard you was home.'

Grace beamed when she opened the door to find Billy waiting on the doorstep with a short ginger-haired woman standing behind him.

Billy thumbed across his shoulder at her. 'Me mam were wonderin' if you'd mind us havin' a look at the baby?'

'Of course I wouldn't mind,' Grace quickly assured him. 'I can't wait for you to meet her, as a matter of fact. And it's high time you introduced me to your mum. Do come in.'

They stepped past her into the hallway but Billy was so keen to see the baby that he scooted away to the lounge, leaving the two women to introduce themselves.

'I'm May.' With her twinkling blue eyes, Grace took to Billy's mother immediately.

'It's so nice to meet you at last,' Grace told her sincerely as they warmly shook hands. 'I really don't know what I would have done without your Billy on the day I went into labour.'

May's eyes shone with pride. 'He's a good lad, is my Billy. He's got a heart made of gold, though I have a lot to thank you for as well. For the kindness you've shown to Billy, I mean. Not all the villagers are as accepting of him as you are. He tends to get shunned because he's a bit . . .'

'Special?'

The woman smiled at her gratefully as Grace took her elbow and led her towards the lounge door, which Billy had left swinging open in his haste to see the baby. They found him hanging over the crib.

'Cor, Grace. She's a really lovely baby, ain't she?' As Billy stared at the baby in awe, Grace felt a lump rise in her throat. Billy wasn't looking at the child as other people would. He was looking at her as Grace did, as the beautiful child that she was – with or without a handicap.

She came to stand beside him and gently draped her arms around his shoulders. 'Yes, she is lovely, Billy. But I don't have a name for her yet. Perhaps you could help me choose one?'

Billy's eyes sparkled with sheer pleasure. 'What? You *really* mean it?'

'I certainly do. I can't just keep calling her "Baby" for ever, can I?'

'Mm . . .' He pursed his lips. 'I ain't rightly good at choosin' names, if I'm honest. When me dad fetched Sophie from the kennels it was me mam as chose her name, weren't it, Mam? But I'll certainly think on it.'

Just then, the baby stirred and Billy started to hop from foot to foot in his excitement. 'Do you reckon as I could hold her, Grace, while you go an' get her bottle ready? I'll be real careful, I promise.'

'I can't think of anyone I would sooner trust her with,' Grace said kindly, and he puffed out his chest with pride as he hopped onto the settee and held out his arms. Grace lifted the baby from the crib; she was just beginning to make a little mewling sound as she realised it was dinner-time. But the second Grace placed her into Billy's outstretched arms she stopped and stared up at him from wide blue eyes. Billy was holding her as if she was the most delicate piece of china in the world, and satisfied that he could be trusted, Grace nodded at his mother and hurried away to prepare her milk. Sadly, breast feeding had not been too successful and she had been forced to resort to bottle feeding. As she was doing so, her eyes fell on the ledger she'd placed on the kitchen table. It was the only thing that Philip had forgotten, and she knew that sooner or later he would have to come for it. She had very mixed feelings about seeing him.

One side of her, the proud side, never wanted to set eyes on him again. The other side, the lonely side, was curious to see how she would react to him when she did. But the worst feeling of all was the bitterness she felt towards him; it bordered on hatred and it frightened her, for never in her life had she experienced such feelings before, although she felt he deserved it. After all, the way she saw it, she had sacrificed everything for him, and he had just discarded her when he

245

tired of her. Over and over she would think of the time his wife had visited her to warn her of his fecklessness. Perhaps if she had listened to Cheryl Golding, things might be different now – but then again, had it not been too late already?

She stared out across the fields from the kitchen window. It was funny, but the house held no charm for her now. Oh, it was a beautiful house, admittedly. But now she thought back over the time she had lived here, it had never been home. Perhaps the old saying was right – home is where the heart is – and now Grace knew without a shadow of a doubt that her heart was back in a house only half the size of this one, with Barry and her children. Time and time again she had considered going to him and begging him to take her back, but commonsense told her that there were too many things against her. Firstly, how could she expect Barry to bring up another man's child – a handicapped child at that? Secondly, she was penniless – or almost – and he would be bound to think that she was running back just for somewhere to go. And thirdly, and worst of all, Barry had someone else now. The thought of him with another woman made tears spring to her eyes, but there was no point in dwelling on the fact; she deserved everything she had got. What was done was done, and now she had to figure out some way of earning a living for herself and the baby.

She was startled when May suddenly appeared at her elbow, and seeing her distress the older woman patted her hand. 'Don't upset yourself, love. I'm a firm believer that everything happens for a reason. You've got a beautiful little girl in there and I just pray that she'll bring you the same joy as Billy has brought to us. She's special, just like my Billy. Oh, I know you've got a lot of other stuff goin' on in your life to cope with too, right now. You can't keep secrets in a little village like this. It's like living in a goldfish bowl. Everybody seems to know your business. But never forget that you've been blessed with that little one in there.'

Grace nodded tearfully, feeling somehow that in this gentle woman she had found a friend.

She walked slowly back into the sitting room with May close on her heels and the glass bottle full of milk for the baby, and Billy sat on the edge of his seat and stared in rapt fascination as Grace fed her.

'If she were a boy it would be easy to choose a name for her,' he said thoughtfully. 'Me best friend at school is called George, but you can't call a girl George, can you?'

Grace rolled the name around on her tongue. 'Well, I suppose we

246

could – if we called her Georgina. We could shorten it to Georgie. What do you think, Billy? Georgina Swan has a nice ring to it, doesn't it?'

Billy's face lit up. 'I think it's a grand name. It sort of suits her somehow, don't it, Mam?'

Grace and May both chuckled.

'Do you know, Billy?' Grace laughed. 'I think you're right – it does. So are we all decided then? We shall call her Georgina Swan?'

May and Billy nodded in unison and so it was that from that moment on, the child was called Georgina. Officially so from the very next day, when Billy's father kindly drove Grace to the Register Office in Nuneaton to register her birth.

Over the next few days, Billy and his mother were constant visitors and Grace began to wonder how she would ever have coped without them. Billy would sit for hours with Georgie, as she was affectionately named, on his lap, never tiring of just staring at her with a look of wonder on his face, or he would do little jobs about the house, or run errands to the shop.

Grace quickly discovered that May was nothing at all like the other women in the village, who tended to keep themselves very much to themselves. She felt more and more that in May Bamford she had found a friend. She was slowly but surely regaining her strength, and the baby seemed to be thriving, although feeding times tended to be lengthy affairs, as the staff at the hospital had warned her.

'Me mam says that if you ever need anyone to mind her, she'd be happy to give you a break any time.' Billy's eyes never once left the baby's face as he spoke and Grace was deeply touched.

'Well, thank your mam very much indeed, Billy. I might just take her up on the offer sometime in the next few days. There are some things that I need for Georgie that I can't get in the village shop, and seeing as how I never got round to getting a pram, I doubt I'd be up to carrying her all the way round town just yet.'

Billy lit up with excitement at the prospect. 'That's sorted then. Just say when you want to go, an' me mam will come an' fetch her.' His expression suddenly darkened. 'Grace,' he muttered tentatively, 'ain't the Mister still not come home yet?'

Billy was astute enough to realise that things were not as they should be, and now that he had asked, Grace saw no point in lying.

'The Mister won't be coming home again, Billy,' she told him quietly. 'You're bound to find out sooner or later so I may as well tell you. He's left me, and the way I feel at the minute, all I can say is "Good riddance to bad rubbish".'

Billy's mouth gaped as he stared at her in horror. 'What? You mean he ain't *never* comin' back? But what will happen to you an' Georgie? Don't you want him to come back?'

'No, I definitely do not!' Grace's colour rose with the tone of her voice. 'If you must know, Billy – I just wish to God I'd never set eyes on him.'

Billy was speechless; never once in the time he had known Grace, apart from when she had called to him that time in her snowy garden, had he ever so much as heard her raise her voice or say so much as one bad word about anybody. But worse was yet to come, for just as if speaking about him had conjured the man from thin air, they both heard a car pull onto the drive. She knew instantly that it could only be Philip.

'Here, Billy.' She thrust Georgie unceremoniously into his arms. 'You stay in here with her and look after her for me. I'll talk to Philip in the kitchen.' She straightened her skirt and patted her hair, very aware of the fact that she was far from looking her best, and then straight-backed, she strode into the kitchen, as if she were going to do battle.

She heard Philip's key in the lock and the sound of his footsteps along the hallway. Then he was at the door of the sitting room, where he glared at Billy, and stared at Georgie as if there was a dirty smell under his nose.

'Where's Grace?' he demanded shortly.

Terrified, Billy nodded towards the kitchen. 'She's in there, Mister.'

Without another word he stormed across the spacious room and then he was in front of Grace as she stared at him coldly.

'I should imagine that is what you've come for.' Her voice was as cold as her stare as she nodded towards his ledger, and suddenly he felt the familiar stirrings she could always evoke in him, and flashed her the smile that had always turned her to putty in his hands.

'Oh, Grace. *Please* don't be like that. I'm so sorry for what happened. I know it sounds feeble, but I've never been very good with handicapped people, as you well know. And when I saw the baby, well—'

'Don't insult me by going any further,' she spat. 'After all, as you quite rightly pointed out, there is a *very* strong possibility that Georgie isn't yours anyway. So you can walk away with a clear conscience. Her name is Georgina *Swan*.'

'But I don't want to walk away. I thought I did, admittedly – but then, when I saw you just now, I realised that I still have feelings for you.'

248

'And your *wife*? Will she have a say in your decision, and give us her blessing?' Grace's eyes were flashing. He had never seen her so angry before, and it excited him.

'She needn't know.' When he took a step towards her, she stepped back and glared at him. 'We could carry on as before, but no deceit this time. What I mean is, she'll think I'm working away for a few nights a week, but I could be here with you. I'd make sure that you never wanted for anything. It could be a whole new start for us.'

As she looked back at him her spirits lifted for the first time in days; there were no feelings, nothing. Now she could see him for what he really was, and in a strange sort of way she almost felt sorry for him.

'So what you're suggesting is, you carry on living with your wife and keep me here, as your bit on the side?'

'Grace, really. Vulgarity doesn't become you. What's gotten into you, for God's sake?'

'I'll tell you what's gotten into me if you really want to know,' she said. 'I've finally come to my senses and can see you for the fickle ladies' man you really are. And do you know what, Philip? I pity your wife. She's welcome to you – I wouldn't have you back if you were the last man on earth. In fact, I'll go so far as to say, I rue the day I ever set eyes on you.'

'Now there's no need to be like that.' He held out his hand but she slapped it away.

'No? So I should welcome you back with open arms, should I? Not likely, Philip. I don't think I've ever hated anyone in my whole life before, but I'll tell you now, *I hate you*. In fact, I could *kill you* for what you've done to me. Now take your ledger and *get out* – and if I never set eyes on you again in this lifetime or the next it will be a day too soon.'

Seeing that she meant every word she said, he slowly picked up the ledger. 'What are you going to do?'

'That's no concern of yours. And here, take this with you as well.' Storming across to a jar that stood on the kitchen worktop she withdrew the thirty pounds he had left her on the day she came home from the hospital. 'Take your filthy money too. It's quite an insult really. Is that all I was worth, a measly thirty pounds? I should imagine even lowly prostitutes get more than that. Now get out before I do something I might live to regret, because I'll tell you now, if you stay much longer I won't be responsible for my actions.'

He stared at her in disbelief. This was not the pliable woman he had known; in fact, he would never have dreamed that Grace could

249

talk as she was doing now. She had always been so gentle, so eager to please. That was perhaps what had begun to bore him. But now . . . Well! His eyes moved up and down her hungrily. The stress and strain of the last few days had taken their toll on her and the weight had dropped off her as if by magic. No one would have believed that she had only very recently given birth to a child. She was back to her usual slim figure, and although she looked frail, standing there with her cheeks flushed with anger and her eyes sparkling, she also looked incredibly pretty.

He took another step towards her and now she really did explode as his hand settled on her arm. Snatching up the ledger, she flung it at him with all her might, and when it struck him full in the face, it would have been hard to tell who was the more shocked of the two of them. Blood spurted from his nose, but Grace's anger was not spent yet. Grabbing the heavy book from the floor where it had fallen she thrust it at him again, with such force that he almost over-balanced.

'Now, *get out*.' Her eyes moved around the kitchen and came to rest on a knife that was on the wooden draining board. She snatched it up and advanced on him menacingly. 'If you know what's good for you, you'll go now while you can. And if you ever come back, I swear – *I'll kill you*.'

He hoisted the ledger under one arm, as with his other hand he tried to stem the bleeding from his nose. All the same she was grat-ified to see that he was inching towards the door.

'You've taken leave of your senses, woman!' Now his anger matched her own, although he had no intention of staying to find out if she would carry out her threat. He paused just once in the sitting-room doorway to stare threateningly at her.

'You'll live to regret this day, you just mark my words.'

Billy, who was sitting as still as a statue with the baby clutched in his arms, stared in horror as Philip's starched white shirt turned to red – and then he was gone and Billy started to cry and tremble uncontrollably.

When the sound of Philip's car roaring off down the drive reached them, a heavy silence settled on the room, broken suddenly by the baby who started to howl noisily. Grace pulled herself together with an effort and looking down at the knife in her hand she dropped it as if it had bitten her, as the realisation of what she had just done struck her full force. But then, what option had she had? Just the thought of Philip laying his hand on her now made her feel dirty, and although she felt guilty for upsetting Billy, still she felt that Philip had deserved no better. All her life she had bowed down to people, tried to please. But not any more! From now on she would please herself and nobody else.

She took the baby from Billy's arms, and when she had quietened her, she laid her on the settee before turning her attention to the boy. He was staring at her as if she was a stranger, and her heart twisted as she took his shaking hands in hers and rocked them up and down.

'I'm so sorry you had to see that, Billy. Just try and forget it, eh? I didn't know I had such a temper and I'm afraid it rather got the better of me. Still, if it keeps *him* away from us it won't be such a bad thing, will it?'

'Would you *really* have killed him, Grace?' Billy's eyes were huge as he stared up at her.

She searched her mind for an answer. 'Do you know, love – if I'm to be really honest I have to say I'm not sure *what* I might have been capable of it he'd pushed me. But thank goodness we didn't have to find out. Now stop looking so scared. You must know I would never hurt *you*. In fact, I don't think I've ever hurt anybody – well . . . not physically anyway. So . . . how about we have a good strong cup of tea and forget it ever happened?'

Billy nodded as she hurried away to put the kettle on, but deep inside he knew he would never forget the look on Grace's face as she had brandished the knife at Philip for as long as he lived.

'Now are you quite sure you have everything you need?' Grace asked for at least the tenth time.

Grinning broadly, May Bamford nodded as she hitched Georgie more tightly into her arms. 'I think if we take any more stuff, she might as well move in with us. What do you say, Billy?'

He giggled as he moved the heavy bag of baby things Grace had packed from one arm to the other.

'Anybody would think as Grace were goin' for a fortnight instead of just goin' off to do a bit o' shoppin' for a few hours, wouldn't they, Mam?'

It was two days after Philip's visit, and Grace had decided to take up Billy's mother's offer of babysitting while she popped into Nuneaton to do some shopping with the cash she had left. She had slept badly for the last two nights, as the bags under her eyes testified, and May felt that the break would do her good.

'Now you just take yourself off for a bit an' don't fret about this one here. She'll be right as rain, I promise you. We're lookin' forward to havin' her all to ourselves for a while, ain't we, Billy?'

251

Grace smiled at her gratefully. 'Right then, I'll leave her in your capable hands while I get myself ready. And thank you again, May.'

'No need to thank me, love. Like I said, it will be nice to have a baby in the house again.'

As Grace watched them walk away, it was all she could do to stop herself from running after them and snatching the baby back. This would be the very first time she had left Georgie since she had given birth. But then, soon she would have to get used to leaving her with someone while she went out to work to feed them both. Meantime, she intended to pawn the jewellery that Philip had bought her. She had no wish to keep it now, and the money it raised would come in very handy. But leaving Georgie was a depressing thought and she closed the door quietly.

Half an hour later she was at the bus stop on the main Sibson road. Two other women from the village were waiting before her, and when they saw her walking towards them they put their heads together and began to whisper, only to cease talking abruptly when she reached them. Grace felt tears of humiliation prick at the back of her eyes as they looked her up and down as if she were nothing more than a trollop, but all the same she held her head high until at last a Midland Red bus trundled to a stop in front of them.

She alighted after them, but the bus was almost empty and she could hear every word they said as they took a seat opposite her.

'It's utterly disgusting, if you ask me, the comings and goings there have been at that house since *she* moved in. No shame. No shame at all, that's *her* trouble.' The older of the two women sniffed. 'It's common knowledge she ran off and left a husband and two small children, then she goes and kicks this one out when she's had enough of him. Bleeding like a stuck pig he was, when he left the other night; she must have a temper like a banshee. And then there's the baby, of course. Is it any wonder it's as it is with a mother like her? Still, I suppose you can't blame the child. We ought to feel sorry for it. I mean, I ask you – what sort of a life is it going to have with a mother like that? It will probably end up in a home when she tires of it and a new chap comes on the scene.'

On and on it went until at last Grace could stand it no longer and she rounded on them.

'Have you ever heard the saying, "people who live in glass houses shouldn't throw stones", ladies? Well, perhaps you should live up to it, because in the time I've lived in the village I've heard things that would make your hair curl, believe me. Take your husband for a start.' She stabbed her finger at the woman nearest to her. 'Off he goes to play golf every Saturday without fail, doesn't he? Huh! Does he hell. Ask him about the little widow in Ratcliffe Culey. As for you,' she now stabbed her finger at the second woman, who was staring at her open-mouthed, 'your husband has bordered on being a nuisance to the woman next-door-but-one to me ever since the day I moved in. Always popping round to see if she needed anything doing – only when her husband wasn't in, of course. Until eventually she was so uncomfortable with it, I heard her tell him that if it continued, she would have to come and see *you*. That soon stopped his gallop. So, ladies – I suggest that in future you pay less attention to what everyone else is doing and concentrate more on what your *own* husbands are up to! I thought when I moved into a village that I would get away from gossiping women, but I was wrong, wasn't I? The only difference between the village and the terraced houses where I used to live is that back there, the women gossiped on the doorsteps. Here they gossip over the fences.'

At that moment the bus pulled up at a stop in Caldecote, and struggling to her feet Grace grabbed her bag and got off. As her temper started to ebb, she sighed and leaned heavily against a tree, watching the bus trundle away into the distance. Now here she was, stuck in the middle of nowhere, and it would be at least an hour before another bus came. For the second time in two days her temper, which she had never even known she had, had got the better of her and it was frightening, to say the least.

The hopelessness of her situation suddenly struck her full force, and the tears that had been building up inside her burst like a dam. She felt as if she were drowning in them, as they poured out of her eyes and her nose until she was breathless and faint. But at last they began to slow and she pulled herself together with an effort.

She thought briefly of going to see Hetty, with whom she had kept in contact over the last difficult months, but then she thought better of it. It must be at least a three-mile walk into Nuneaton, and she doubted if she would be strong enough to make it, whereas it couldn't be much more than a mile back home. One thing was for sure – there was no way that she felt like shopping now. Wearily she turned, and taking the short cut across the fields, she headed for home.

Philip paced his office as a picture of Grace floated before his eyes. Women had always flocked to him like bees to a honey pot, as he had discovered years ago, and Grace had been no exception. However, she was also the first woman who had ever rejected him. Strangely, he found this mildly exciting, almost a challenge. His nose was still

253

swollen and bruised from their argument two days before, but rather than hold this against her he found that she was never out of his thoughts. So much so that he knew he was going to have to go and see her again.

'Frank!' His voice echoed around the garage from his position in the doorway of his office. Almost immediately, a grey-haired man in stained overalls slithered from beneath a car that was up on ramps in the workroom.

'Yes, boss?'

'I want you to hold the fort – I've got to go out for a while. Do you think you could answer the phone and such till I get back? I shouldn't be more than a couple of hours at most.'

'No problem, boss.' Frank wiped his oily hands on an equally oily rag and flinched as Philip strode past him with a face like thunder. Now there was a man with something on his mind, if he wasn't very much mistaken. Still, he wasn't going to complain. While the cat was away the mouse would play, and anything had to be better than lying on your back under a greasy old engine. The arthritis in his hands was playing him up something terrible, and lately he had begun to question how much longer he could keep this job up. Philip was a hard taskmaster. All the more reason to take advantage of a couple of easy hours. Time for a fag and a look at the *Mirror*. As he hurried away to put the kettle on, Philip got in his car and accelerated off the forecourt.

Four hours later Frank frowned as he stared up at the clock in Philip's office. It was already after six, and the garage normally shut at five-thirty. He hadn't heard so much as a dickie-bird from the boss since the minute he had left, and if he didn't get home soon his old lady would have his guts for garters, especially if his dinner got spoiled. He started to hunt around in the drawer of Philip's desk. Ah, there they were – the garage keys. Best thing he could do would be to lock up and get himself away home. Philip was bound to have another set, and if he didn't, well . . . he knew where Frank lived. After all, he couldn't expect him to wait about all night. The boss was probably off with one of his fancy pieces somewhere and had lost all track of time.

Shaking his head at the thought, Frank began to methodically lock the doors, one after another. Some blokes just didn't know when they were well off, did they? Lovely lady, Mrs Golding was. Patience of a saint, she must have, to put up with his womanising all these years. And then there was that lot back there. His eyes moved to the other, larger workroom that backed on to his. He could still hear the youths

254

Philip employed banging and hammering away in there. Strange that he was never allowed in there, not that he really wanted to go in. They were a bad lot as far as he was concerned and to his mind up to no good. Still, he had learned long ago to keep his head down and ask no questions. The least he knew, the least he had to worry about. A job was a job at the end of the day, so after checking that everywhere was secure, he set off for home, pushing his hands deep into his oily overall pockets and whistling merrily.

A shadow suddenly blocked out the sunlight that was streaming through the window and Grace, who was stretched out on the settee, blinked. When she saw Philip standing over her she was instantly awake and would have been on her feet if he had not pushed her back against the cushions.

Rather than go straight to the Bamford's cottage for Georgie, she had decided to come home and put her feet up for an hour. But now she wished with all her heart that she hadn't, for there was a look on Philip's face that made her feel suddenly very vulnerable. His face was still swollen from the last time she had seen him, and she was aware that he might have come here to pay her back.

Putting on a brave front, she demanded, 'What do you want? I thought I made it quite clear I never wanted to see you again.'

'You didn't mean that. It was just temper talking. Besides, it didn't help with that halfwit being here.' His arrogance made her temper rise yet again.

'If you're referring to Billy, let me assure you that he is far from being a halfwit, as you so crudely put it. That child has more genuine feelings in his little finger than you have in the whole of your body!'

'Now, Grace.' Philip realised instantly that he had said the wrong thing and quickly changed tack as he took a seat at the side of her. 'I didn't mean it quite like it sounded. I suppose I'm just put out with him because I couldn't tell you what I had come to say in front of him.'

She inched away from him, suddenly finding the smell of his aftershave overpowering. Strange, that – she had always found it so appealing before, but that was before she had seen him for what he really was. As his hand groped towards her she hastily rose.

'Why don't you just tell me what you've come for, and stop wasting my time, Philip?'

He saw the repugnance on her face and slowly his own anger began to build.

'Why so high and mighty all of a sudden? Got your eye on a new bit, have you?'

'Huh! I would have thought that was more *your* department than mine. According to your wife when she paid me a visit, I wasn't the first and I've no doubt I won't be the last. I was just one in a long line, wasn't I, Philip? I wonder why you are suddenly interested in me again. Is it because I've seen through you, and I'm not dancing to your tune any more?'

Grabbing her wrist, he twisted it painfully and she gasped. Her fear excited him. Made him feel in control again.

'*Nobody* rejects me – just you remember that, Grace. This affair will be over when *I* say it is and not before. Do you understand me?'

Still with a tight grip on her wrist he pulled her down beside him, and a scream began to build in her throat as his other hand found her tender breast and kneaded it roughly.

The hopelessness of her situation washed over her. She was completely alone and at his mercy; even if she was to scream, there was no one to hear her. His lips were leaving trails of wet kisses all around her neck and she had to fight the nausea that rose in her throat. His fumblings became more urgent as his passion mounted and it was then that she suddenly leaned forward as far as she was able and sank her teeth into his hand. He let out a scream that would have done justice to a wounded animal, and for one blessed moment his hold on her relaxed. But then, before she could scramble away from him, he grasped her again and threw her against the back of the settee with a force that took her breath away.

His hands were clawing at her underclothes and she felt her nylon underskirt tear as he ripped it aside and began to claw at her knickers. And then suddenly they were on the floor and he was rolling on top of her, and the situation took on an air of unreality.

'Philip, *please*-no! I beg you! Don't do this.' She was screaming and sobbing, but her words fell on deaf ears, then he was thrusting inside her and she wanted to die, for never in her worst nightmares had she ever imagined anything so sordid or terrible as this. At last, after what seemed an eternity, it was over and he rolled off her to lie panting at her side. She lay staring at the ceiling, violated, bleeding and in agony, and when at last she turned to him, making no effort to cover herself with her torn clothing, the tone of her voice turned his blood to water.

'I wish you were *dead*. You will live to regret this day.'

He paled, and scrambling to his feet, pulled his clothes together hastily. There was something in her eyes that terrified him, for although they were dry now, they were brimming with raw hatred and this time, he knew without a doubt that she meant every single word she said.

'Look, I'm sorry,' he tried. 'I shouldn't have done that. But I wanted you so much, my feelings just got the better of me.'

When there was no reply, he backed towards the door. 'I . . . er . . . I'll go now and come back when you've had time to calm down, eh?'

There was blood all over his clothing. His from his bitten hand and hers from where he had raped her, but there was no time to worry about that now; he knew that he had to get away, and fast. There was no telling what she might do otherwise.

'I'll . . . er . . . Goodbye, Grace.'

The door slammed to behind him and silence settled around her like a cloak as she lay praying for death to claim her.

Much later in the afternoon, she pulled herself together with an effort. She had no wish to take advantage of May's kind nature and knew that it was time to fetch Georgie home.

After dragging herself off to the bathroom, she scrubbed herself within an inch of her life. At least, she thought with a shudder, she couldn't get pregnant again. Her poor tender insides had not recovered from the birth trauma yet. She ran a comb through her tangled hair. There was nothing she could do about her red-rimmed eyes so she just shrugged her arms into her coat. It hurt her to walk, and she was just limping towards the front door when someone suddenly rapped loudly on it. Grace almost jumped out of her skin as panic engulfed her.

What if it was Philip again? She dismissed the thought almost imme- diately. Philip had a key and would never knock. Approaching the door on legs that had turned to jelly, she asked, 'Who is it?'

'It's me. An' it's bloody freezin' out here so open the door an' let me in!'

Gasping with relief as she recognised Hetty's familiar voice, Grace flung the door open and almost tumbled into the old woman's arms as fresh sobs shook her body.

'God above. Whatever's the matter, gel?' Hetty cried as she rocked her to and fro.

Fumbling for her handkerchief, Grace blew her nose loudly and managed to raise a watery smile. 'Oh, take no notice of me, Hetty. It's just so nice to see you, that's all.'

'Bloody hell. I'll have to come more often, if it pleases yer that much,' Hetty chuckled, but underneath she was worried. Grace looked absolutely dreadful. The weight had dropped off her and if she wasn't very much mistaken, the poor girl had been crying. She was a complete bundle of nerves.

'So,' she said, hoping to calm Grace down a bit. 'Where's this lovely new babby o' yours then? I got your letter tellin' me all about her, but this is the first chance I've had to get out here. Christ, talk about the back o' beyond. Yer wouldn't get me livin' out here fer a flyin' pig.'

'Actually, I was just going to fetch Georgie when you knocked on the door,' Grace told her. 'May, that's Billy's mother, he's a little friend of mine, offered to have her while I went into town to do a bit of shopping.'

'Huh! If you've been into Nuneaton yer could have called round an' seen me an' saved me the trip then.'

'I didn't go in the end,' Grace admitted. 'I set out to, but . . . I didn't feel so good.' Her voice trailed away. She would have trusted Hetty with her life but was too ashamed to tell her about any of the awful events of the day.

'Right, we'll go an' fetch the babby then, an' when we get back yer can tell me how things are goin',' Hetty declared.

Hetty, Billy and May hit it off instantly and by the time Grace left with the baby fifteen minutes later, anyone might have thought they'd known each other for years.

Hetty was totally enthralled with Georgie and once they were back in Grace's home, Grace almost had to prise her off the woman in order to give her a bottle.

'She's a little sweetheart,' Hetty declared as she cooed over her. In truth she had only intended to stay for a few minutes, but Grace seemed so low that she was reluctant to leave her. When at last Georgie was fed and changed and tucked down in her crib, Grace made them both a cup of tea with some scones and jam. Following her into the kitchen, Hetty asked, 'What time is Philip due home then?'

When Grace's face crumpled, Hetty knew that her earlier suspicions were true.

'The lousy bugger has left yer, ain't he?'

Grace bowed her head and nodded.

Sighing, Hetty shook her head. Hadn't it been obvious all along that this relationship was doomed to failure? And hadn't she tactfully tried to tell Grace as much, a dozen times or more? Still, there was no point in kicking the poor soul when she was down by saying 'I told you so'. Instead she said, 'It ain't the end o' the world, gel. You'll get through this an' come out on the other side, you'll see. You'll get over him an' all, but what are yer plannin' on doin' now?'

Grace longed to pour her heart out and explain that she *was* over him already. That she never wanted to set on eyes on him again. But how could she, without telling Hetty what he had done to her that very afternoon? Instead she shrugged.

'I haven't really had time to think about it yet. This place is paid for until the end of the month then I'll have to find somewhere for Georgie and me to go. I'll need to get a job too 'cos we can't live on fresh air.'

'Well, it goes without sayin' that there's always a place fer yer both in my home,' Hetty told her immediately.

Touched by this dear woman's kindness, Grace totally broke down. 'Oh Hetty, I've been such a fool,' she sobbed. 'How could I ever have given my family up for such a weak and shallow man? Why didn't I see him for what he was?'

'Cos he had the gift o' the gab an' a fat wallet that turned yer head, that's why,' Hetty told her wisely. 'Try not to fret too much, though. It ain't the end o' the world. Things have a habit o' turnin' out right in the end, as I told yer once before.'

Composing herself as best she could, Grace held her hand, wanting to believe her with all her heart and yet knowing deep down that things would *never* be right again.

It was as Hetty was leaving some time later that Grace finally dared to ask, 'Have you heard how Barry and the children are?'

Hetty nodded. 'As a matter o' fact, I have. Not long after you moved out here I had a visit from yer mate, Chris. You'd told Barry you were stayin' wi' me an' he must have told her. Then, not a couple o' weeks since, I saw Chris again in town. O' course, me bein' the pushy sod that I am, I went over to have a word. She were with an' older woman an' two children who turned out to be Daisy, yer mother-in-law, an' your two little 'uns. When push come to shove I realised I half knew Daisy anyway, from seein' her at Bingo. Anyway, the kids looked fine, though Chris is a little hurt 'cos yer haven't stayed in touch.'

Grace bowed her head in shame. 'I suppose I was too embarrassed to write,' she whispered and Hetty nodded in understanding.

'Well, happen it's time yer paid her a visit. Good friends are few an' far between, an' when yer find one, yer should hang on to 'em.'

Seeing the truth in what she said, Grace nodded. 'I will go and see her, I promise. Just as soon as I'm feeling a bit better.'

'Right, well – just see as yer do then. An' remember, there's a home waitin' fer you an' the babby with me if yer want it.'

Grace clung to her for a moment then watched sadly as Hetty walked away before locking and bolting all the doors. The last thing she needed was another visit from Philip, but God help him if he did show his face again, for she knew that she wouldn't be responsible for her actions.

Chapter Twenty-Six

The voice of the congregation rose to the rafters, but Sarah barely heard it as she looked round at the pews. Then suddenly, her hands gripped the hymnbook she was holding as her eyes almost started from her head. Four rows in front of her was a woman in a grey hat that almost matched the colour of the hair that peeked from beneath it. There was something familiar in the rigid stance and the way she held her head high. Much to the annoyance of the people on either side of her, Sarah began to inch her way along the row of pews until she was almost at the end. From here she had a better view of the woman and she stared at the back of her head, oblivious to the tuts of the people she had disturbed.

Her heart began to thump so painfully loud that she was sure the person next to her must hear it. The singing suddenly stopped and the vicar's voice requested that the congregation be seated as he continued with his sermon. Sarah sank into her seat, her eyes never once leaving the woman in front of her. The service dragged on, and when at last it finally came to an end, Sarah let out a sigh of relief. And then the congregation were forming an orderly queue as they filed from the church to shake the vicar's hand at the door as they left.

Sarah's eyes stayed tight on the woman as she walked sedately up the aisle. Yes, it *was* Emily, she was sure of it now. Older, of course – but still recognisable. She waited until the woman had taken her leave of the vicar then slid from her seat and quickly followed her.

When she entered the bright sunshine she blinked and looked around in panic. What if she had lost her? But no – there she was, talking to another equally severe-looking woman. She stayed back within the shadow of the church walls until the two women began to follow the path through the churchyard, then with her own features party hidden by a headscarf, she discreetly began to follow them.

'Mrs Swan – Mrs Grace Swan?' The tall man in the dark suit looked at Grace enquiringly, and glancing over his shoulder, she was stunned to see a police car parked at the end of the drive.

'Y . . . yes?' Her voice betrayed her nervousness as she tried to think why they might be there.

The dark-haired man stared at his colleague, a short balding man with glasses, before looking back at Grace. Taking an identity card from the top pocket of his suit he flashed it at her, saying, 'DI Metcalfe. Could we come in and have a word, do you think?'

'Yes. Yes, of course.' Flustered, Grace stood aside as the two men filed silently past her. She ushered them into the lounge where they frowned when they saw Billy and his mother. May Bamford had Georgie on her lap, and was billing and cooing at her, but when she saw that Grace had visitors she immediately began to rise.

'No, don't go,' Grace implored her as a terrible sense of foreboding settled around her like a cloud. 'I'm sure that whatever these gentlemen have come to say can be said in front of you.' Lifting Georgie into her arms she cuddled her protectively.

DI Metcalfe shrugged. 'As you wish.'

Grace motioned towards some chairs but the man shook his head, looking slightly uncomfortable. He had had no idea that Grace was the mother of a small baby, and it was going to make what he had come to do that much more difficult.

'Mrs Swan, I have come to ask you to accompany us to the station to assist us with our enquiries.'

'What enquiries?' Grace's mouth gaped open as she stared back at the solemn-faced detective.

'Well, I . . . um . . . I think that might be better discussed in private,' he told her.

'But my baby – what am I supposed to do with her? How long will I be gone? And what am I supposed to have done anyway?'

'Don't fret about her,' May reassured her. 'You get off if you must. Me an' Billy will collect everythin' we need for Georgie an' she can come down to our house with us till you get back.'

Grace clung on to the baby as May frowned in dismay. The poor girl had been so on edge for the last few days that she seemed to be jumping at her own shadow.

'I will come with you if I must, but only if you tell me what this is all about. Something has happened to my children, hasn't it?' Grace asked tremulously.

Seeing her chalk-white face, the detective was quick to reassure her. 'There is absolutely nothing wrong with your children, Mrs Swan, I assure you.'

'Then what is it? *Please* tell me. I don't mind my friends hearing.'

He sighed. 'Very well. We need to talk to you about your whereabouts on Saturday.' He began to shuffle from foot to foot before continuing. 'I . . . er . . . that is, we believe that you were the partner of a certain Mr Philip Golding for a time.'

Grace nodded. 'Yes – yes, I was, but Philip and I parted not long ago.'

'Mrs Swan, I have to inform you that unfortunately, Mr Philip Golding was found dead in his car on a lay-by about half a mile away from here early this morning. It seems that he had been dead for some time, and seeing as we have reason to believe that you were a close friend of his, we need to eliminate you from our enquiries.'

Grace clutched at the arm of the chair as the floor rushed up to meet her, and Billy and his mother gasped in horror.

Philip dead! The shock of it made her speechless and she prayed that she was having a bad dream. Things like this didn't happen in real life, only on the television.

'He . . . *can't* be dead,' she stuttered as Billy's mother hastily snatched Georgie from her shaking arms. 'I only saw him recently and he was fine then. What happened to him?'

'Ah, now that I'm afraid I can't tell you just yet. Not until we're at the station. All I can say at this stage is that Mr Golding's death was definitely not accidental. So, please . . . if you would just come with us, we'll try to get this over with as quickly as possible for you.'

'Blimey, Grace. Did he come back? You know – after you made his nose bleed? You said you'd kill him if he did.' Billy's eyes were like saucers and he would have said more but one stern glance from his mother shut him up abruptly.

'Don't pay no heed to him,' she gabbled quickly. 'Our Billy's gob tends to run away wi' him. I'm allus tellin' him as it will get him hung one o' these days. Grace an' her chap just had a tiff, that's all. She ain't got it in her to kill a fly. It was just temper talking.'

'I see.' The detective stared at Grace thoughtfully, before looking back at Billy. 'It might be that we'll need to talk to you as well, young man. Could you give your name and address to my colleague, please?'

Billy was so terrified at the new turn of events that he wished he had never opened his mouth, and his mother had to give the policeman the details because he had been rendered temporarily speechless.

'You . . . you surely don't think *I* had anything to do with his death, do you?' Grace said incredulously.

'At this stage of the enquiries, Mrs Swan, everyone is a suspect,' DI Metcalfe told her. 'But as I said, we are not arresting you. We are merely asking you to accompany us so that you can make a statement – and then hopefully we will be able to eliminate you from our enquiries. Now – if you are quite ready?'

Grace's eyes were dry but so full of pain that May Bamford's heart went out to her. She had always thought of Grace as a nice young woman since the day she had befriended her Billy. Somewhat misguided certainly, in her choice of a partner. But for all that, she would have staked her life that she was no murderer.

'Go on, love. Don't you get frettin' about Georgie. She'll be fine wi' us an' you'll be back before you know it.' She squeezed her arm gently as Grace passed, flanked on each side by a policeman, and Grace flashed her a bewildered smile. And so began what was to become one of the longest days of her life.

'So, Mrs Swan – you are saying that on Saturday you were out shopping?'

'Yes, I was.' Grace sighed; she had already told him that at least a dozen times. As she stared back at the policeman across the desk he held her gaze.

'And this being the case then, you will be able to substantiate this with receipts for some of your purchases, I presume?'

'Well, I . . . No – not exactly. You see, what I should have said is, I *did* set off to go shopping but . . . something happened and I didn't get to town in the end.'

'Really? And what was this something that happened?' Grace looked from the policeman to the young WPC who was sitting at his side, furiously scribbling down everything she said. The first feelings of panic set in.

'Well, I'd . . . I'd rather not say. It's quite personal.' The words sounded tame even to her ears and her stomach sank.

DI Metcalfe's tone changed as he stared across at her coldly. 'So is murder, Mrs Swan. Look, I think it's time you started to be completely honest with us, don't you? You have already told us that your relationship with Mr Golding ended quite recently, and from things we have heard from other witnesses, it seems that you did not part on good terms. Would I be right in saying that? In fact, after the way he walked out on you, leaving you with a young baby to care for, you must have felt quite bitter towards him?'

'No, yes – well, I suppose I did.' Grace's head was beginning to throb as the questions went on and on. 'But I didn't kill him, I swear it.'

'You threatened to, though – at least, according to young Billy Bamford, you did. You even resorted to violence, did you not?'

264

'I *was* angry.' Grace felt as if he was digging her into a hole and the feeling of panic intensified. 'Philip had previously made it clear that our relationship was over and that he could never be a father to Georgie. Then one day he turned up to collect his ledger, and when he saw me, he . . . he changed his mind; he said that he wanted to continue with our relationship – to keep me as his mistress. At that I just lost my temper and said the first thing that came to mind to make him leave. But he wouldn't, so in the end I threw his ledger at him. I didn't mean to hurt him, though.'

Changing his tack, the detective came at her from another angle. 'So, you never got into Nuneaton on Saturday at all then?'

'No.'

'So where *did* you go?'

'I went back to the house.'

'Did anybody see you?'

'Not that I know of. I walked across the fields.'

'Why did you not go into Nuneaton?'

Realising that he would keep on until she told him the truth, Grace said, 'If you must know, some other women from the village were on the same bus as me. They were talking about me quite loudly so that I could hear them, and some of the things they were saying were very rude, to say the least. In the end I lost my temper and gave them a mouthful and then I stormed off the bus.'

'Yet another incident of you losing your temper, Mrs Swan. Can you name these women?'

Grace sighed. 'Yes, I can.' She quickly gave them the women's names and addresses and watched as the policewoman scribbled them down.

'And you are saying that you have not seen Mr Golding since the incident that young Billy witnessed?'

Grace gulped deep in her throat as her chalk-white face now flooded with colour. Noting her discomfort, the detective leaned forward in his seat.

'Mrs Swan, will you answer my question, please?'

Still it seemed that Grace had been struck dumb, and suddenly he nodded at another policeman who was standing behind her.

The officer stepped forward and handed the detective a plastic bag. A bloodstained knife clattered out of it onto the table and Grace stared at it in horrified disbelief.

'Do you recognise this knife, Grace?'

When she nodded, he repeated: 'Is this your knife?'

Again she nodded. 'Yes, it used to be my favourite. I used it for everything – and then some time ago it went missing. I . . . I thought I must have thrown it out with the potato peelings or something.'

The detective rose and after retiring to a far corner of the room he had a whispered conversation with his colleague before returning to the table.

'Mrs Grace Swan, I have to inform you that this is the knife that was used to stab Mr Philip Golding to death. You admit that the knife is yours and can give no satisfactory explanation as to where you were on Saturday. Also, there was a bite-mark on Mr Golding's hand that looked as if it had been done by a woman, so I am arresting you for the suspected murder of Mr Philip Golding. You do not at this stage have to say anything, until a solicitor who will be appointed for you is present. But I have to inform you that anything you do say may be taken down and used as evidence against you . . .'

His voice droned on and on, but thankfully it was lost on Grace, for she had retreated into a world where for now no sound could penetrate, only the wild beating of her heart.

'Good heavens above! Have yer seen this, our Will?'

Will, who had fallen into a doze in front of the fire, started awake and peered at Hetty curiously. His mother was sitting at the kitchen table, her glasses perched precariously on the end of her nose, with the *Tribune*, the local newspaper, spread out before her, and he saw at a glance that she had gone as white as a sheet.

'What's up then, Mam?'

She gulped deep in her throat before managing to answer him and he saw that she was deeply distressed.

'It says here as Grace has bin taken into custody fer the suspected murder of Philip Golding.'

'WHAT!' Will's mouth opened and shut for some time, giving him the appearance of a goldfish before he managed to respond. 'Yer must 'ave it wrong, Mam. Grace wouldn't hurt a fly.'

'Well, that ain't what it's sayin' here, lad. They arrested her this mornin', accordin' to this. *Surely* there must be some mistake.'

Hetty flung herself away from the table and began to pace agitatedly up and down the length of the kitchen. 'We've got to do somethin',' she commented, more to herself than Will. 'The poor girl must be beside herself – an' what about that poor babby she's just had? Who the hell is lookin' after young Georgie?'

'Calm down, Mam. There ain't nothin' to be gained from you gettin' all worked up about it,' Will told her gently. 'Come mornin'

266

I'll go down to the nick an' try to find out what's goin' on. Then we'll decide what's to be done from there.'

Hetty paused in her pacing to stare at him. There were times like now when her Will surprised her, for all that he was a bit slow. 'Thanks, lad,' she muttered and then she sank back into her chair. It would be a waste of time even bothering to go to bed; she knew that she would never sleep tonight.

Sarah Bishop stared up at the windows of the house before her. She had followed Emily home from church on more than one occasion and knew the way to Oaston Road off by heart now. Every window except one was in darkness, which told her that Emily was home. She shuddered and took a deep breath, then pushed the gate open, and before she could give herself time to change her mind, she hurried up the path and rapped firmly on the door. Her heart was hammering and she had the urge to turn and run, but before she had the chance to do so, she heard an inner door open and, through the glass in the door, saw someone walking along the hall towards her. Within seconds, the door swung open and she found herself face-to-face with the sister she had thought she would never see again.

'Hello, Emily.'

For a moment Emily simply stared at her, but then as recognition dawned on her face, she visibly paled. *'Sarah!'* For a moment she was speechless but then pulling herself together with an enormous effort she frowned. 'What do *you* want?'

'Charming,' Sarah commented dryly. 'I've spent years trying to find you, to make sure that you were all right – and this is the greeting I get.'

Emily drew herself up to her full height. 'Well, as you can see, I am perfectly all right, so . . .'

Sarah shook her head in despair. She had imagined this reunion in her mind a million times and had hoped that time would have softened Emily. But unfortunately, it seemed that her sister was just as bitter and twisted as she had been when she'd disappeared all those years ago, taking their niece, Grace, with her.

'I also want to see my niece. The one you took away all those years ago,' Sarah told her boldly. The nervousness was gone now, replaced by anger. 'Aren't you going to ask me in?' she demanded, and before Emily could answer, she strode past her into the house. Emily watched her march along the hall towards the only room that was lit before closing the door and following her. Once they were both in the kitchen they stared at each other for some seconds before Sarah looked away

267

to glance around the room. It was much like Emily, plain and spotlessly clean, without ornamentation of any kind apart from the desk that Sarah recognised as the family heirloom.

'So!' Sarah drew herself up to her full height; there seemed no point in beating about the bush so she asked what she had come to find out. 'Where is Grace?'

'*Grace?*' As Emily's cool veneer momentarily slipped she looked flustered. 'What do you mean – where is Grace? Grace is a grown woman now and left home long ago.'

Sarah frowned. 'Very well. Perhaps you could give me her address. I'd like to see her.'

'I'm afraid I can't do that,' Emily faltered. 'You see, Grace got herself into trouble with some young man. We . . . we didn't part on good terms. She was bad, evil like her mother and—'

Sarah stared at her incredulously. 'Don't talk such *rubbish*! Mary was the gentlest, kindest woman you could ever wish to meet. It was you who caused all the trouble.'

Emily's features distorted with hatred, a hatred that had simmered in her for many long lonely years. 'Oh yes, of course you would take *her* side, even though it was *me* that was wronged!'

The anger that Sarah had felt faded away as she stared into her sister's haunted face. 'Look, Emily, what happened was a long time ago now and I'm sure that neither Mary nor Richard meant it to happen. It was just one of those things.'

'Huh! That's easy for you to say,' Emily retorted. 'I just wonder how *you* would have felt if your sister had pinched your fiancé right from under your nose. Can you even *begin* to imagine how humiliating it was for me, to be jilted, right after the invitations to our engagement party had gone out? And then to have to stand by and watch her play the blushing bride and the doting mother when Grace came along.'

Sarah bit on her lip. 'It wasn't quite like that, Emily, and well you know it. Richard and yourself hadn't been right for a long time. You weren't good for each other, and if it hadn't been Mary it would have been—'

'SHUT UP!' Emily screeched as she covered her ears with her hands. 'You're wrong, I tell you. Richard loved *me* until that she-devil set her cap at him with her fluttering eyelashes and her sweet words.'

She looked as if she were on the verge of tears, and for a time Sarah stared at her helplessly as she struggled to find something to say. The silence seemed to stretch on for ever until eventually Emily pulled herself together enough to look back at her sister. The years had been kind to her, she noted. In fact, although she was now in her early fifties Sarah was still a very attractive woman, just as Mary had been. Again she felt the injustice of it all. Both Mary and Sarah had been blessed with good looks whilst she had always been plain. And yet for all their looks it had been *her* with whom Richard had fallen in love, until Mary had set out to steal him, that was. Even now, all these years on, his betrayal of her with her own sister still cut like a knife. Sighing, she suddenly sank onto a hard-backed chair at the side of the table.

'What exactly is it you want, Sarah?' she asked bluntly.

'As I already told you, I'd like to see Grace.' Sarah was determined to stand her ground until Emily told her where their niece was.

Emily strummed her fingertips on the table as she wrestled with her conscience, then slowly she rose and walked across to a wooden paper-rack that stood at the side of the empty fire-grate. Lifting a newspaper from it she brought it back to the table and flung it down in front of Sarah. 'Read that, and then perhaps you'll see what I meant when I told you that Grace was bad.'

Frowning, Sarah dragged the paper towards her and as she leaned across it the headlines seemed to jump off the page at her and the colour drained from her face. 'This must be a mistake!' she gasped. 'It says that Grace has been arrested for the suspected murder of her former lover.'

Emily shrugged. 'It's no mistake, believe me. I told you, she's bad through and through.'

Her words fell on deaf ears, however, for Sarah was frantically scanning the rest of the story. When she had finished reading she looked back at Emily.

'What are you doing to help her?' she asked.

Emily laughed mirthlessly. 'What *could* I do, even if I wanted to?'

'You could have got her a good lawyer, for a start, or has she done that herself? She would have taken control of her inheritance by now, so she could easily afford it.'

When Emily quickly diverted her eyes a worm of unease began to wriggle in Sarah's stomach. Once again she glanced uneasily around the room. It was plain, admittedly, but all the same it looked a good solid house and would have cost far more than Emily could afford.

'Did you buy this house with some of the money that Richard left for Grace?' she demanded suspiciously.

Now Emily's hands twisted together nervously. 'Well . . . yes, of course I did. I had to have *somewhere* to bring her up, didn't I? And I did right by her, believe me. She had the best education, she went to the grammar school and—'

269

'Never mind about the education,' Sarah said coldly. 'Rightfully, this is Grace's house, isn't it?'

When Emily did not reply, Sarah felt her anger rising again. 'Is Grace aware of that fact, Emily? Or of the trust fund that her father had set up for her? And furthermore – does she know that *I* and my family exist?'

Emily ignored her, and suddenly all Sarah's worst fears were confirmed. 'She doesn't know about me, does she? You only took her in for the money her father left in trust for her, didn't you? For the money and so that you could punish her for the wrong you felt her father had done you.' Springing forward, she gripped Emily's arm and spun her round to face her.

'Right – this stops *now*. Do you hear me? I'm not going to go anywhere until you tell me exactly what's gone on.'

For the first time that she could ever remember, Sarah saw tears start to flow from her sister's eyes. She suddenly looked very old and frail, but Sarah had hardened her heart against her and for now she could only think of Grace.

Falteringly, Emily began to tell her of Grace's meeting with Barry, of her love of ballroom dancing . . . and as she spoke, Sarah formed a picture in her mind of the loveless life Grace must have endured as a child at Emily's mercy, and she lowered her head and wept.

Shifting uncomfortably from foot to foot, Hetty stared at the door in front of her, before raising her arm and knocking on it. When it opened and she found herself staring into Barry Swan's face, she started to babble.

'Forgive me fer comin' round here, lad. I ain't usually one fer pokin' me nose into other folk's business but I don't know what else to do. I'm Hetty Brambles. My Norma used to work wi' Grace in Courtaulds some years back.'

As recognition dawned, Barry's first instinct was to shut the door in her face. This then was the woman who had harboured Grace when he had first kicked her out. However, seeing her distress he eventually stood aside and ushered her into the main room, where she stood wringing her hands.

When Hetty thrust the newspaper telling of Grace's arrest into his hands and breathlessly told him of the latest developments, he listened in stunned silence and paled.

Hetty had flown round to his house as if she had wings on her feet and now he was in a quandary. What could he do? He and Grace were still legally married, but they had been separated for some time

270

now and she might not welcome any interference from him. When he told Hetty as much her eyes flashed.

'Well, if you can't help her, then who will?' she demanded.

His shoulders sagged as he ran his hands through his hair in the old familiar gesture that Grace had used to love. 'I really don't know, Hetty,' he admitted, and in that moment she saw the pain still bright in his eyes.

'Yer still love her, don't yer, lad?' she asked softly.

He opened his mouth to deny it, but then shook his head. 'Even if I did, it's gone too far now, Hetty. What's done is done an' there's no goin' back. Grace has a child with Philip.'

'Quite certain o' that, are yer then?' she sniffed.

He narrowed his eyes. 'Just *what* is that supposed to mean?'

'Well, from where I'm standin' the babby could quite as easily be yours as it were his,' she pointed out. 'Yer were still married an' livin' together when she dropped fer the little 'un, so there's a fair chance it could be yourn. Let's face it, if Grace weren't the sort o' gel she were you'd never have had an inklin' that it weren't yours, would yer?'

He digested her words and after a few moments she turned towards the door. 'Happen I've done what I come to do, lad. I thought you had a right to know what were goin' on. I shall be off to the police tomorrer an' fetchin' the little mite to stay wi' me an' our Will while they sort this whole sorry mess out. An' have no doubt – they *will* sort it out. Grace might have bin daft an' had her head turned by that smooth-talkin' bastard she went off wi', but I'd stake me life she ain't no murderer. I'll tell yer somethin' else as well while I'm at it, fer what it's worth. If Grace were to tell the truth, I reckon she'd tell yer there ain't a day gone by when she ain't regretted leavin' you an' them little 'uns up there.'

She thumbed towards the ceiling as if to give emphasis to her words then with a final nod at Barry who was staring at her open-mouthed, she opened the door and slipped out into the cool night air.

Chapter Twenty-Seven

'Look, Mrs Swan, if you don't talk to me there's hardly any point in me being here. I can't help you unless you tell me exactly what you know.' The solicitor who had been instructed to represent Grace looked beyond her bowed head at the policeman who was standing silently witnessing the meeting. The officer shrugged, and after another few moments of silence the lawyer lifted his briefcase and snapped it shut.

'Very well. We will leave it for today,' he told Grace, and although the words were blunt they were said kindly. 'Luckily they have agreed to keep you here rather than transfer you to a prison until the case comes to court. Perhaps before then you could tell the police when you're ready to see me, eh?'

Again no response; Grace merely sat staring off into space as if she were not even aware of his presence. The solicitor sighed and followed the policeman to the door, and within seconds Grace was alone. Her eyes idly worked their way around the cell as the door clanged shut behind them. Apart from a tiny table and a chair and a bed that had a thin blanket folded neatly on the end of it, it was empty. Grace didn't care. She was beyond caring. Except for Georgie, of course. And Wendy and Simon, who were always in her thoughts night and day.

Once they reached the reception area the solicitor looked at the police officer in despair. 'I think you ought to get a doctor in to look at her,' he ventured. 'She looks as if she's on the verge of a break-down to me.'

'You could be right,' DI Metcalfe admitted. 'I don't mind telling you, I don't think she should be locked up. This case is going from bad to worse since we got the investigation under way.'

When the kindly solicitor's eyebrows rose into his hairline the policeman took his elbow and drew him into a corner of the room. The reception area was busy and he didn't want to be caught talking out of turn.

'The thing is, it turns out this Philip Golding wasn't quite what he appeared to be,' he whispered. 'Seems he had some sort of a racket going on with stolen cars. When our lads went to the garage to talk to the staff there, they caught some youths red-handed spraying up some top-of-the-range stolen motors. They were being pinched to order, it seems, then being resprayed and having their numberplates changed before being passed on.'

The solicitor whistled through his teeth. 'So if that's the case, Philip Golding could have made himself a few enemies then?'

'Absolutely,' the officer agreed. 'The youths squealed like stuck pigs once they knew they were cornered. We've got them all in for questioning even as we speak, and they are telling us that Philip Golding had quite a few people who were out for his blood.'

'I see.' The solicitor tapped his chin thoughtfully. 'This doesn't appear to be quite the cut and dried case we thought it was, and in view of what you've just told me, I think Mrs Swan should be released on bail whilst the enquiries continue. After all, we don't really have any evidence to say that she *did* commit the murder, do we? Apart from the fact that the murder weapon was one of her knives – and that doesn't prove anything.'

'You could be right, but you'd have to ask them higher up about that,' the policeman answered him. Just then their attention was drawn to a small woman at the desk who was obviously in a blazing temper.

'I'm tellin' yer, lad, I ain't goin' nowhere till yer let me see Grace. I know yer have her here, an' if you think fer a minute that she could commit murder then yer must have shit in yer eyes.' The old woman leaned menacingly across the counter as the young Constable behind the desk stared back at her, unsure of how to handle the situation. Striding across to her, DI Metcalfe asked, 'Is it Mrs Grace Swan you're talking about, madam?'

She rounded on him, her eyes flashing. 'Well, o' course it is! Just how many Graces do you have locked up here?'

'Perhaps we could continue this conversation somewhere a little more private,' he said coaxingly as he went to take her elbow.

Slightly placated now that someone was listening to her, Hetty drew herself up to her full height. Slapping his hand away, she sniffed, 'Right then, lead the way.'

DI Metcalfe lifted the flap on the counter and beckoned her to follow him, and with the solicitor close on her heels he led them along a corridor until they came to an empty room. After ushering her inside he turned to her and asked without preamble, 'So how are you connected to Mrs Swan?'

'I'm her friend, Mrs Hetty Brambles. An' at the minute, I'm about the only one she has, from the looks of it!'

273

'Very well, and why do you want to see her?' he asked politely.

Hetty let out a long drawn-out breath. 'Eeh, lad. Seein' as how you're a copper, yer seem to be a bit short in the brains department. The poor gel has not long since had a babby, an' I've come to see who's lookin' after it fer her. I can go an' fetch the poor little mite an' take care of it while yer sort this mess out.'

The solicitor looked at the policeman appealingly. 'I can't see anything wrong in that,' he said. 'In fact, I think in view of the circumstances you should allow Mrs . . . er . . .'

'Brambles. Hetty Brambles is the name.'

'I think you should allow Mrs Brambles a short visit.'

'Well . . .' DI Metcalfe looked from one to the other of them and then made a decision. 'Very well then, but it can only be a very short visit and I will have to have a Constable present.'

Hetty suddenly sagged like a balloon that had had the wind sucked out of it, and shortly afterwards she was led to the cells where Grace was being held. Her heart twisted as she walked into the bleak room. Grace was staring off into space and didn't even look up when the cell door slammed shut behind Hetty.

'Oh, Grace.' Dropping on to the bed beside her, Hetty gathered Grace's cold hands into her own and began to rub them. 'Whatever happened to bring it to this, gel?'

Grace slowly turned her head to look into Hetty's eyes and it was then that the tears she had held back for so long suddenly erupted.

'I *didn't* kill him, Hetty,' she sobbed.

Gathering the young woman into her arms, Hetty gently stroked her hair. 'Shush now, love. Yer don't need to tell me that. An' never you fear, they'll find the buggers as did. But in the meantime, what about little Georgie? Who's takin' care of her?'

'Billy's mother has her,' Grace managed to tell her.

'Right then, I'll be goin' to fetch her today an' she'll stay wi' me then till this whole sorry mess has bin sorted out.'

Grace stared at her incredulously. 'But why, Hetty? Why would you do that for me?'

'Why?' Hetty shrugged. 'Let's just say as once upon a time I were in a very similar situation to what you are now. Not bein' accused o' murder,' she hastened to say when Grace's eyebrows rose, 'but drawn to the wrong sort o' bloke just as you were.'

When Grace stared at her in confusion, Hetty cast a self-conscious glance at the young Constable who was standing discreetly by the door before continuing. 'I ain't Mrs Brambles. I'm a Miss,' she confessed. 'I bought this here wedding ring meself to save me kids

274

from embarrassment when they started school, an' I told everyone as I was a widow, but I weren't. Yer see, just like you I were in a stable relationship wi' a lad that had bin brought up in the same street as me. Engaged to be married we were, an' we would have bin. But then along comes this man wi' a flash car an' a bit o' money an' I had me head turned good an' proper. Promised me the earth, he did, an' strung me along fer years, till I got caught wi' our Will that is, an' then it turns out that he were married. He promised that he'd leave his wife an' he bought me the house in Edward Street. He were an antique dealer, which is why I've so many nice bits an' bobs about the place. Anyway – time moved on an' soon I found I'd fallen for our Norma. It were then I got to thinkin', what will they feel like when they know that their dad is married to someone else, what would they think o' me when they got old enough to realise? So I gave their dad an ultimatum. "It's either yer wife or me. I don't want to be yer bit on the side any longer," I told him. Needless to say, he chose to stay wi' his wife, which is when I decided to tell everyone I'd bin widowed. I found out the hard way that all that glitters ain't gold, just as you did. The difference is, I'd lost the bloke I should have had by then – but your Barry still loves you.'

'No, he doesn't,' Grace told her desolately. 'I saw him some time ago with the children and a young woman.'

'Well, yer could have fooled me,' Hetty muttered. 'When I spoke to him last night he were worried sick about yer.'

Grace dropped her eyes. 'Why have you told me all this, Hetty?' she asked dully.

The old woman shrugged. 'I just thought it would help yer to know that you ain't the only one who ever went off the rails. But still – that ain't why I come, so tell me, would yer be happy fer me to fetch the babby from Billy's mam an' take care of her?'

'Oh yes, Hetty, I would. I can't think of anyone else who I would trust more with her,' Grace told her gratefully.

'Right, that's settled then. She'll be wi'me by nightfall. An' in the meantime, let's hope as this lot get off their arses an' go an' find the *real* culprit.' Casting a withering glance at the young policeman she leaned across to kiss Grace goodbye, then without another word she followed the young man from the cell and left Grace to ponder on all that she had told her.

It was two days later when a policeman entered Grace's cell and told her that she had been granted bail. She was free to go for now, although she would have to report to the police station every day whilst the investigation into her former lover's death continued. Grace left the station in a daze. She was still deeply in shock after learning of Philip's death. But strangely, she felt nothing. The love she had once thought she had felt for him was as dead as he was now. Once outside on the pavement, she stared around her. Everywhere looked so big after her days in such confined quarters, but she didn't pause for long, for now she could hardly wait to see her baby again. She hurried through the town to Hetty's, where she received a rapturous welcome.

'Who put up my bail?' she questioned Hetty after lunch and a prolonged cuddle with Georgie, who had been spoiled shamelessly, first by May and Billy and then by Will and his mother in her absence.

'I don't know, but all I can say is, God bless 'em,' Hetty retorted and with that, for now, Grace had to be content.

She spent the night at Hetty's, and went to an appointment with her solicitor the following day. It was he who enlightened her. 'It was your aunt who put up the bail money,' he informed her, and Grace almost slipped off her chair with shock.

'You must be mistaken!'

He shook his head as he checked his files. 'No, I assure you, it's here in black and white. A Mrs Sarah Bishop.'

Grace stared back at him as a frown creased her brow. 'But I don't have an aunt called Sarah.'

'According to my files you do.'

'Is there an address for her?' she asked, bewildered.

After peering down at his notes he nodded, then pulling a sheet of paper towards him he scribbled down a Coventry address and a phone number. Grace left his office with the paper clutched in her hand as she tried to make some sense of it all. Aunt Emily had never told her of another aunt – and yet . . . some distant memory was trying to surface. *Sarah* – the name was vaguely familiar. The memory surfaced as she lay in bed that night with Georgie snoring softly in her crib beside her.

Suddenly she was a child again and Aunt Emily was angry with her because she had caught her looking at a photograph.

'Who is Sarah?' she had asked her aunt, and her inquisitiveness had cost her a spell in the cellar. The lady had been standing next to her mother in the photograph and now Grace could remember thinking how alike they had looked. But why would Aunt Emily have kept her from knowing this other aunt, who had suddenly turned up out of nowhere? At present she had no idea, but one thing she did know, she would make it her business to find out. First thing tomorrow she

276

would ring the number the solicitor had given her and then she would go and see her Aunt Emily and get to the bottom of it all. With her mind made up she fell into a fitful sleep.

The following morning Grace was giving Georgie her bottle, which was always a lengthy process, when a knock echoed down Hetty's hallway.

'Who could that be at this time o' the mornin'?' Hetty mumbled as she pulled the belt of her old candlewick dressing-gown more tightly around her, then without waiting for an answer she shuffled away.

Seconds later she reappeared looking slightly confused. 'There's a lady here wantin' to see yer, Grace. She says as she's yer auntie.'

Hetty ushered the woman who was standing behind her into the kitchen, and without being asked hastily crossed to Grace and scooped the baby from her arms as the two women confronted each other.

'Why don't yer take yer visitor into the front room, love?' she suggested tactfully, and when Grace hesitated she flashed her a smile. 'Go on,' she encouraged. 'I'll see to the little 'un. You two obviously have things as yer need to talk about.'

Grace rose from her seat hesitantly. 'Would you like to come this way?'

Without a word the woman, who was looking as ill-at-ease as Grace herself was feeling, nodded and followed her.

Once in the privacy of the front room they faced each other silently, neither of them quite knowing what to say. Somehow, Grace knew that this was the aunt the solicitor had told her about the day before, for there was a look of her mother about her. Aunt Emily had never allowed her to keep a photo of her mother or her father, but the glimpse she had once had of them had stayed etched in her mind. The woman facing her now was older, yet strangely familiar. She looked very smart in a two-piece suit in a soft dove-grey that was complemented by black shoes and a matching handbag. Grace was suddenly embarrassed as she realised that her own hair wasn't even brushed, and that there were milk stains on her cheap Crimplene skilt.

'You must be wondering who I am and why I'm here,' the visitor finally said.

Grace shook her head slowly. 'I think I know who you are. The solicitor told me about you yesterday. I think you might be my aunt.'

The woman smiled as her eyes welled with tears, for Grace was so like her late sister Mary that it was painful to look at her. But now was not the time to think of herself. Right now, Grace needed all the help she could get and Sarah was determined to give it to her.

'Yes, I am your aunt, Grace,' she admitted.

Grace suddenly felt anger so intense that she wanted to lash out. 'So where have you been all my life then? And why have you suddenly decided to crawl out of the woodwork now?'

Sarah bowed her head. 'Perhaps if I explained everything to you right from the beginning you might understand.'

The fight suddenly went out of Grace and she motioned Sarah to a chair as she sank into one herself. 'I suppose you could try,' she muttered dully.

Perched uncomfortably on the edge of one of Hetty's best chairs, Sarah fought the urge to rush across and take Grace into her arms. She had not set eyes on her since she was just a tiny girl, and she looked so vulnerable and alone that Sarah's heart went out to her.

Slowly she began. 'There were three of us – sisters, that is. Emily, Mary and myself. Mary, your mother, was a lovely girl, always laughing and full of fun. You look remarkably like her. In fact, when I first set eyes on you, it gave me quite a turn.' Her eyes misted as her thoughts travelled back to the sister she had loved and lost, but then she pulled herself back to the present with an effort. 'Anyway, when we were all in our late teens and early twenties, Emily met Richard Collins and we were all surprised when they began to go out together and then announced their engagement. Emily was . . .' she struggled to find the right words before going on. 'Emily was quite straight-laced, whilst Richard was funloving and easygoing. He was also from a very good family. When she first brought him home we were all quite surprised, but of course we wished them well and hoped that they'd make a go of it. They were an ill-matched couple to say the least, and after a time the cracks in their relationship began to show. By then Richard was a regular visitor to the house and it became obvious that he was attracted to Mary. His feelings were returned – although I have to say, neither of them did anything about it. Your mother loved Emily and would never have hurt her. Even so, Emily and Richard drifted further and further apart, and within a few weeks, he called off the engagement. Emily was devastated. You can imagine how she felt when, after a time, she found out that he had started to see your mother.'

Grace stared at her in disbelief. 'Are you telling me that my mother actually married Aunt Emily's ex-fiancé?' she gasped.

'Yes, love, I am. But try not to blame them. They were *so* in love and so right for each other that it was a pleasure to see them together.

278

And then after they were married and you came along they were as solid as a rock. By then I was engaged to be married myself. We had lost our parents some years before, and so for a long time there were just the three of us looking out for each other. Sadly, Emily never forgave Mary. In fact, somehow she convinced herself that she was the reason Richard had finished with her. And then . . . your parents were killed while he was on leave, during an air raid on Coventry.' She shuddered at the memories, but forced herself to go on. 'I had just left home to get married and you were little more than a baby. It turned out that your father had been very wealthy and had made a will to the effect that all he possessed should be put into a trust fund for when you were twenty-one, should anything happen to him and your mother. It was when this became known that Emily put herself forward to become your guardian. I remember having grave doubts about it, but I was pregnant with my first child, and obviously as the eldest, Emily was the natural choice to take care of you. Then suddenly you both seemed to disappear off the face of the earth. I went round to visit you one day, to find the house locked up and empty. I tried to trace you for a while, I swear it, but then I had my own baby to worry about and before I knew it, another one on the way. It's a poor excuse I know, and I don't expect you to forgive me, Grace, but things were hard after the war and I got so wrapped up in trying to care for my own family that I managed to convince myself that wherever you were you'd be all right. And then suddenly the children were grown up and making their own lives, and when I lost my husband I knew that I had to find you – to make sure that you were all right . . .'

When her chin suddenly sank to her chest, Grace felt a stab of pity for her. She wanted to hate her for leaving her at the mercy of her Aunt Emily all those years, and yet how could she? For could she honestly now say that she was perfect after what she had done to her own children and Barry?

'Don't cry, Aunt Sarah,' she whispered gently. 'We've found each other now and none of us are perfect. Me least of all.'

Suddenly they were both out of their seats and in each other's arms, and their tears mingled as they hugged each other.

'Please forgive me, Grace. I've been to see Emily and I realise the sort of life you must have had. She's so bitter and full of hatred. I'd hoped that time would have softened her, but that's no excuse, I should have looked for you years ago.'

'Never mind, you're here now.' Grace took her hand and together they sat on the settee as they studied each other. The next hour passed in a blur as Sarah told Grace all the things that she had always longed to know about her mother.

It was Hetty who finally interrupted them when she stuck her head round the door. 'I thought yer might both be ready fer a cuppa and a piece of me best gingerbread.' She smiled, placing a tray down on the ornately carved coffee-table in front of them.

'Thanks, Hetty.' Grace flashed her a grateful smile. 'Come and join us. This is my Aunt Sarah.'

'Well, I gathered as yer were related.' Hetty grinned. 'You're as alike as two peas in a pod.' She held her hand out to Sarah who shook it warmly. 'Yer very welcome, love. This 'un here needs all the support as she can get at the minute wi' all this lot goin' on, an' I gather it's you as we have to thank fer puttin' up her bail?'

'Well, no, it wasn't me actually,' Sarah explained. 'It was Emily who paid it – with Grace's money. You see, Grace is actually a very wealthy young woman. The house that Emily lives in belongs to Grace, bought with money that Grace's father left in Emily's trust until Grace was twenty-one. Grace should have had any remaining monies *and* the house transferred across to her then, but somehow my sister managed to wangle things so that she hung on to it.'

'Well, I'll be . . .' Hetty mumbled. 'The wicked old sod. So, what can we do to make sure as Grace gets what is rightfully hers now?'

Taking the cup of tea and slice of cake that Hetty held out to her, Sarah said, 'I think perhaps we ought to go and see Emily's solicitor first, and then we'll pay a visit on Emily and inform her that she has a certain time to vacate the premises.'

'But what will happen to her if we do that? Where will she go?' Grace asked.

Hetty shook her head in exasperation. 'See what I'm up against?' she told Sarah. 'Soft as a brush, this one here is. An' to think she's on a suspected murder charge. Huh! From where I'm standin', if she were goin' to kill anyone, it ought to have bin that there aunt o' hers fer the way she treated her. Still, it's never too late to put things right. You two get yerselves off an' do what needs to be done whenever you're ready. I'm too old to be chasin' around now so I'll stay here an' keep me ear out fer the little 'un.'

'Oh Hetty, I really don't know what I'd do without you,' Grace told her, and when Hetty looked back at her there was a wealth of love shining from her eyes, for she had come to love Grace as her own daughter.

'That's one thing as yer can rest easy on, fer you'll never have to, not while there's breath left in me body.' Hetty picked up a piece of gingerbread and took a hefty bite. Now go on the pair o' yer,' she said through the crumbs. 'Get yerselves away an' let's see if we can't make some sense of all this.'

After the meeting with Emily's solicitor, Grace and Sarah walked side-by-side through the town in silence. They were both deeply shocked to discover the lengths Emily had gone to, to keep Grace from knowing of her inheritance. It seemed she had woven a pack of lies and somehow managed to deceive him. He had obviously been under the impression that Grace knew the house in Oaston Road was rightfully hers. He had also produced a pile of forms, all falsely signed in Grace's name, to acknowledge her allowance each month from the age of twenty-one. He had apologised profusely and pointed out that what Emily had done was a criminal offence. He had also said that Grace would be quite within her rights to press charges against her aunt, but Grace had refused for now so that she could have time to think. Sarah was almost beside herself with rage when she thought of how her niece had been wronged. Her temper suddenly erupted in an outburst as they approached the gates of Riversley Park.

'How *could* she be so mean?' she spluttered, but Grace just shook her head and led her towards a bench outside the museum. So much was happening in her life that she was beginning to feel strangely detached from it all. In the space of mere weeks, she had given birth to a child with Downs syndrome, been accused of Philip's murder, had a long-lost aunt turn up out of the blue, and now discovered that in actual fact she was a very comfortably off young woman, when only hours before, she had thought she was penniless. Sinking onto a bench she stared into the slow-moving waters of the River Anker as she tried to take it all in.

'What do we do now then?' her aunt asked, feeling totally out of her depth. She was beginning to wonder what she had let herself in for, yet strangely she had no regrets, and was determined that now she had found Grace she would make it up to her for all the years she had been absent from her life.

'I suppose I'll have to go and see Aunt Emily,' Grace said quietly. 'And then we'll decide what's to be done.'

'There's no decide about it!' Sarah told her sharply. 'She's done you out of what's rightfully yours for long enough. You have a new baby to think of now, so you'll have to stand firm and give her notice to quit the house. At least then you'll have somewhere to take Georgie to live. And from what the solicitor's just told us, you won't have to worry about working either. If you manage your allowance properly you'll be comfortable, at least for a few years.'

Grace touched the key the solicitor had given her tucked deep in her coat pocket. He had also shown her the deeds to the house in her name, and yet she still couldn't take it in.

'I think I'll let the solicitor write to her and talk to her first before I do go and see her,' she said eventually. 'At least that way, it will give me time to calm down and take it all in. To be quite honest, I'm not sure that I *want* to live in that house again. It doesn't hold the happiest of memories, and I want Georgie to be brought up in a nice place where she'll be happy.'

'A house is just bricks and mortar, Grace. A home is what you make it,' Sarah pointed out.

Grace nodded. 'I know you're right, Aunt Sarah, but I just don't think I'm up to it at the minute. Perhaps tomorrow . . .'

Sensing that Grace was almost at breaking-point, the older woman squeezed her hand. 'You're right, love. It's been a big day for you one way and another, what with everything else that's going on. Come on, let's get you back to Hetty's and see if we can help her with the lunch.' So saying, she gently took Grace's arm and led her away.

Chapter Twenty-Eight

The letter in her hand slipped from her fingers and fluttered onto the table as shock pulsed through Emily. So – even now, after all these years, Mary was determined to humiliate her yet again, even from beyond the grave. Emily had no doubt that it *was* Mary behind this latest turn of events, or Grace, her daughter at least, which in her mind amounted to the same thing. Bitterness replaced the shock as Emily began to pace up and down the kitchen like a soul in torment. After a few moments she strode back to the table and snatching up the letter she reread it as though somehow this time it would read differently, but the words remained exactly the same. Her solicitor requested her to make an appointment to see him at her earliest convenience to discuss her niece's inheritance.

Sarah. Unbidden, the name sprang to mind. She would be a party to this, coming here after all these years sticking her nose in where it wasn't wanted. But then she should have expected no more, for hadn't she always taken Mary's side? Emily flung the letter down and her balled fists leaned so heavily on the solid oak tabletop that her knuckles turned white. Her mind was whirling as she tried to think what she should do. There was no way she would ever sign the house or the money Richard Collins had left her over to Grace, when it was Emily herself who was entitled to it, not that thankless child she had been forced to bring up. If Richard had married her as he would have had it not been for Mary, then it would have been hers anyway.

Emily stepped away from the table, her eyes still tight on the letter, and as the back of her knees connected with a chair she sank heavily onto it. In her mind's eye she suddenly had a vision of handing the keys to *her* home over to that chit Grace. She could see Grace walking from room to room, surveying what Emily had made into her domain. And the child – it was rumoured that Grace had given birth to a child that wasn't quite right, a halfwit no doubt, which was no more than Grace deserved, but she would die before she let the creature across *her* doorstep. She stood back up so quickly that the chair overturned and clattered onto the polished red quarry tiles, but Emily didn't even hear it.

The shame; how would she bear the shame if it were to become known that she had lived for years on what the solicitor obviously believed to be Grace's money? She could imagine the people at the church looking down their noses at her as the image she had so carefully built over the years crumbled around her. And where would she go if Grace *did* get the house? She would be homeless, penniless. Her hand pressed into her chest as she tried to imagine it, and she squeezed her eyes shut tight. Slowly now she crossed to the small desk in the corner. Fumbling for the key, which she still kept by habit in her pocket, she clumsily unlocked it, then as her shaking fingers pressed the tiny switch that would open the hidden compartment, it sprang open and her eyes rested on the photograph of Richard. As she lifted it to look at the features that were still as clearly engraved on her mind as they had been all those years ago, the tiny diamond engagement ring that he had once slipped on her finger winked up at her. Lifting it she placed it on the third finger of her left hand, then, with his photograph still clutched tightly between her fingers she crossed to the chair at the side of the empty fire-grate and slowly sat down.

It had been many, many years since Emily had cried, but now the tears flowed, hot scalding tears that found their way through the wrinkles of her embittered face. She knew in that moment what she must do. She would never hand the keys to her home over to a murderess, for that was what Grace was. Nor would she face the looks of condemnation on the faces of the church people. Her eyes moved around the familiar room, then she stood and quickly drew the curtains on the bright sunny morning. Calmly she crossed to the gas cooker that stood to one side of the room and turned on all the rings and the oven, wrinkling her nose as the smell of gas seeped into the kitchen. She tidied her hair in the only mirror in the house and straightened her tweed skirt across her thin hips, then sedately she seated herself back in the chair and after dabbing at her cheeks with a spotless white handkerchief she folded her hands neatly in her lap and closed her eyes, the very epitome of quiet elegance.

'Just what the hell is so urgent that I have to come straight away?'

Grace's solicitor looked none too pleased as he glared across the desk at the young Constable who was on desk duty. He was due in court in precisely one hour and had hoped to spend the time going over his notes. The young man lifted the flap on the counter and beckoned the solicitor to follow him, which he did, glancing at his watch irritably as he went.

'They've just sent a Panda car to fetch Mrs Swan an' all,' the young bobby threw across his shoulder and now the solicitor paused in his steps to frown at him.

'Why – has there been some new evidence come to light or something?' he asked.

The young officer positively beamed. 'You could say that, but it ain't what you think. Here we are, sir. The Sarge is waiting for you in here.'

Striding past him, Grace's solicitor found himself confronted by an harassed grey-haired Sergeant who immediately held his hand out.

'Ah, good of you to come so quickly,' he said pleasantly. 'I'm sorry to call you out at such short notice, but I'm sure when you hear what I have to tell you you'll forgive me.'

'That remains to be seen,' snapped the solicitor. 'So now, if you wouldn't mind telling me what's going on, I *do* have to be in court in less than an hour.'

'Of course.' The Sergeant motioned him to a seat and then quickly began to speak. He had almost finished his story when a tap came on the door and the same young Constable stuck his head round it.

'Mrs Swan's here, sir,' he informed his superior.

'Excellent.' The Sergeant looked at the solicitor enquiringly. 'I think we're about ready to tell her now, don't you?'

The solicitor, who now had a smile on his face that lit up the dingy little office, nodded. 'Absolutely!'

The policeman hurried away, leaving the door slightly ajar, and seconds later reappeared with Grace following white-faced behind him. Her eyes moved nervously from one to the other as she was shown into the office and offered a seat, and then as they began to relay the story, her mouth gaped in amazement.

'Mrs Swan, I have some news for you. This morning Mrs Golding arrived at the station and admitted to the murder of her husband, Philip. I have to say you would have thought she'd come in to report nothing more than a lost handbag, for she was as cool as a cucumber. But be that as it may, what it means is that, Mrs Swan,' the Sergeant told her, 'you are now free to go.'

Grace stood up on legs that suddenly felt as if they had developed a mind of their own. 'Is it . . . is it *really* over?' She'd heard everything they had told her and yet somehow her mind couldn't seem to take it in.

The Sergeant smiled at her kindly. 'For you – yes, it is over. For the murderer . . . well, it's only just beginning. Good luck, Mrs Swan. I hope things will start to improve for you from now on.'

*   *   *

When the same Panda car that had taken her to the station only a short time before delivered her back to Hetty's, Grace saw her standing in the front-room window nervously chewing her nails as she stared up and down the street.

The second that Grace set foot through the door Hetty grabbed her elbow and almost dragged her into the kitchen where she pressed her down onto the nearest chair.

'God love us!' she exclaimed. 'Whatever's happened now? You're as white as a sheet, love.'

'I've been cleared of Philip's murder,' Grace told her. 'It's all over, Hetty. I'm not under suspicion any more.'

'Eeh! Then we can thank the Lord fer that.' Hetty dropped onto the chair opposite her. 'So – have they got the buggers that did it? Them bloody scoundrels were it, who were into pinchin' an' sellin' on cars fer him?'

Grace shook her head from side to side. She could still hardly believe it herself, so it wasn't easy trying to explain to Hetty, but before she could go on, Georgie whimpered. She was lying in her crib at the side of the fireplace and without being asked, Hetty immediately rose and popped her dummy back in, then content that the baby was happy again she hurried back to Grace.

'Come on, then, don't keep me in suspense. Who were it?'

'It . . . it was Philip's wife.' Grace ran her hand across her eyes as Hetty gasped.

'*His wife!* Well, bugger me. But then when yer come to think of it she had good cause, didn't she? I mean, if he were a womaniser as she once told you he were.'

'It wasn't just that,' Grace told her. 'Apparently the garage originally belonged to her father and Philip only started to run it when her father died, although it then actually belonged to her. It seems her father never had time for Philip when he was alive. Anyway, somehow she got wind of what he was up to. You know – selling on stolen cars and what not, and then I suppose she just snapped when Philip and I . . .' Her voice trailed away as shame washed over her. To think that she had been partly the cause of a woman committing murder!

Seeing her deep distress, Hetty caught her hand and shook it up and down.

'Now don't let's be having none o' that,' she scolded. 'If it hadn't bin you it would've bin some other poor bugger he would have had under his spell. In fact, I never meant to tell yer this but I think yer should know now. I've seen him out wi' more than one woman in

286

his car when yer were livin' together, swannin' around the town when he'd told you he were workin' away. I don't want to rub salt into the wound, Grace, but I think yer should know you were just one o' many. And if yer don't want to take my word fer it, ask Chris, yer friend. She's seen him out an' about an' all, an' she asked me if she should tell yer.'

As Hetty's words sank in, strangely, Grace found that she wasn't surprised. In fact, if she had been honest with herself, she had had suspicions on more than one occasion, but she had given up so much for Philip and she had so wanted their relationship to work that she had turned a blind eye.

'Here, there is sommat as don't quite make sense,' Hetty suddenly mumbled as she tried to put the pieces all together in her mind. 'I thought it were supposed to be one o' *your* knives that killed him! How the hell did she get hold o' one o' them?'

'She told the police that she stole it on the day that she came to try and pay me to keep away from Philip,' Grace explained.

Hetty nodded. 'Ah! Well, there yer are then. She'd obviously had it in her mind to do it fer some time. Yer can't help but feel a bit sorry fer her and them poor lads, though, can yer? The life that rotten sod led her, I'm only surprised she didn't do it before. But what you have to remember in all this, is that you're in the clear. It's over, Grace. You an' Georgie can get on wi' yer lives now an' try to put all this behind yer.'

Grace suddenly began to sob as if her heart would break. 'Oh Hetty, I've made such a mess of everything.'

The old lady was round the table in a flash, gathering her into her arms. 'Now then, that's enough o' that,' she soothed. 'Philip Golding were as smooth as butter. He could've charmed the birds off the trees if he'd a mind to. It's no wonder you had yer head turned, so stop blamin' yerself. Yer can't turn the clock back – now you have to pick yerself up an' get on wi' things, but make no bones about it, things always happen fer a reason. Yer need to get that old witch that brought yer up out o' the house that's rightfully yours next, an' then you an' Georgie will have yer own place to stay. Not that you ain't welcome here, o' course. You an' the little 'un can stay here fer as long as yer like as far as I'm concerned. An' things will come right in the end, you'll see.'

Grace clung to her, wishing with all her heart that she could believe her, but somehow no matter how hard she tried, she could never see her life being right again.

*   *   *

287

'So, just how much longer is this bloody nonsense goin' to go on for then?' Hands on hips, Daisy Swan glared at her son.

'I don't know what you mean, Mam,' Barry muttered as he averted his eyes from her furious gaze.

'Don't you *dare* give me that, our Barry, you know very well what I mean. Ain't Grace suffered enough for her mistake? An' look at you – I can't remember the last time I saw you properly smile. An' what about the kids? I'm the first to admit that when Grace first took off with that fly-by-night I was bitter towards her, but you can't hold a grudge for ever, otherwise it eats away at you. You're not only punishing Grace by not allowing her to see Wendy and Simon, you're punishing them *too*!'

'In case you'd forgotten, Grace has got another little 'un to worry about now,' Barry retorted, and the hurt in his voice made her anger disperse as quickly as it had come.

'I won't argue with that, lad. But you know, the poor little mite didn't ask to be born and . . . Well, I promised meself I'd never say this, but it needs to be said: have you ever stopped to think that the child just *might* be yours? Think about it. You an' Grace lived together as man and wife until the day she admitted that she'd been seeing that Philip. She didn't *have* to tell you, but that's the sort o' girl Grace is, and so I say again, please consider at least letting her see the children. You don't need me to tell you how much the kids miss their mam, God bless 'em. There ain't a day goes by when Wendy don't ask when Mammy will be comin' home. Grace has gone to hell and back in the last months, what with being under suspicion of murder and giving birth to a handicapped child. Can you truthfully tell me, hand on heart, that you really don't love her any more?'

When Barry remained silent, Daisy sighed, 'Well, I've had me say. Now it's up to you.' So saying she quietly turned and walked away, leaving her son deep in thought.

Long after Daisy had returned to her own home he sat staring at the ceiling as the tears that still after all this time were never far from the surface pricked at the back of his eyes. His mother had left him with a lot to think about, and the thoughts were painful. What if she was right and the baby *was* his? If only Grace had never told him of her infidelity he would have gone on none the wiser and loved the child no matter what was wrong with it. And Wendy and Simon – *was* he doing them an injustice in keeping them away from their mother? His mam hadn't lied when she said how much they missed her. He knew that better than anyone, for he was the one who was forced to listen to them crying for her night after night when he had tucked them up in bed.

His thoughts whirled round in neverending circles. Deep down, despite all he had said, he still loved Grace, had never stopped loving her – although he doubted that she still cared anything for him. Perhaps she never had? Perhaps he had just been a means of her escaping her aunt? His eyes came to rest on one of Wendy's dolls that lay discarded on the floor at the side of the chair. It was dressed in a tiny frock that Grace had once knitted for Wendy as a surprise, and now the tears began to fall unchecked as he lifted it and held it to his chest. Perhaps it was time to soften a little? After all, as his mother had quite rightly said, Grace had more than paid for her mistake.

There and then, Barry decided that as soon as he felt able, he would go to meet her and tell her that she could see the children. It was probably far too late for them as husband and wife, but he could no longer condone keeping the children away from their mother. With his mind made up he methodically began to turn off all the lights before making his way to his lonely bed.

Hetty smiled at Sarah, who was cradling Georgie in her arms. They had just finished Sunday lunch and now as Grace helped Hetty to clear the dirty pots from the table, Sarah was taking advantage of a cuddle with her great-niece, whom she had obviously come to adore. Sarah's own children were all now grown and flown the nest and so she had been spending as much time as she could with Grace. This had been encouraged by Hetty, who felt that Grace needed all the support she could get, for she was still obviously in deep turmoil after all she had been through. It was no hardship for Hetty to allow Sarah access to her home; she liked the woman and a friendship had sprung up between them. She had just put the kettle on to boil so that they could wash their Sunday roast down with a good strong cup of tea when there was a knock on the front door.

'Get that, would yer, our Will? I bet it will be Billy and May. I've invited 'em round for tea.' Hetty asked as she spooned tea-leaves into the sturdy brown teapot, and Will immediately rose from the comfortable fireside chair and pottered away along the hall. When he returned seconds later, wringing his hands, Hetty frowned. His left eye was twitching, a sign that something was wrong. Will's eye always got a tic when he was nervous or upset.

'Well – who is it then?' she demanded, seeing no sign of the expected visitors. 'Don't stand there like the cat's got yer tongue. Spit it out, lad.'

Will's eyes flew to Grace. 'It's . . . it's the coppers – an' they want to see Grace,' he finally managed to tell them.

The colour drained out of Grace's face, but taking control of the situation, Hetty headed for the front door, elbowing Will unceremoniously out of the way as she went.

'Good God above, whatever can it be now?' she muttered to herself. When she opened the door to find herself confronted by a young policewoman and a slightly older man she glared at them.

'Now what's up?' she barked, making them both jump. 'What's she supposed to have done now? Ain't you lot got nothin' better to do than hound the poor gel?'

'I assure you, madam, we haven't come here to hound anyone, and Mrs Swan hasn't done anything,' the policeman assured her. 'However, I'm afraid we have some rather bad news and we would like to see Mrs Swan.'

With her lips pursed into a tight thin line, Hetty allowed them to step past her into the hall, then with a toss of her head she nodded towards the kitchen. 'Yer'd better come this way then,' she muttered ungraciously.

When the two police officers entered the kitchen they found Grace shaking like a leaf as she stared at them from frightened eyes. 'What's happened now?' she asked tremulously and her heart was screaming, *Oh please God, don't let anything have happened to Barry or the children.*

The older officer, who had been designated to tell her the bad news, gulped deep in his throat before asking hesitantly, 'Are you the niece of Miss Emily Westwood?'

Grace's head bobbed up and down.

'Then I'm sorry to have to tell you that Miss Westwood was found dead in her house a short time ago. It seems that a friend of hers, a Miss Mountjoy, was concerned when your aunt didn't attend church, so following the service she called round to the house to see if she was unwell. Apparently the curtains were drawn and when Miss Mountjoy could get no response to her knocks she contacted us. Eventually we broke the door down and unfortunately we found . . . Well, we found your aunt dead. It seems that she had been so for some time. I'm so sorry, Mrs Swan. I'm going to have to ask you to accompany me to formally identify your aunt's body.'

Grace felt as if she were floating as she tried to digest what the policeman had told her. A hushed silence had fallen on the kitchen, but eventually it was Grace who broke it when she asked, 'Did . . . did my aunt die of natural causes? Was it her heart?'

The man shuffled from foot to foot uncomfortably, but then after glancing at his colleague he shook his head. 'No, Mrs Swan, it doesn't appear to have been her heart, although there will be a post mortem, of course. I'm afraid it appears that your aunt gassed herself.'

290

'*Suicide!*' Sarah's shocked voice echoed around the silent room as Grace felt the floor rush up to meet her. The next thing she was aware of was Hetty holding tightly to the back of her neck as she thrust her into a seat and pushed her head between her knees.

'That's it, there's a good gel, now yer just take nice deep breaths.'

Hetty's voice seemed to be coming from a long, long way away, but gradually a strange sort of calm settled on Grace and she slowly raised her head.

'I'll come with you now,' she said as she looked at the two officers.

'Surely to God this could be done tomorrer?' Hetty demanded. 'The poor girl's in shock, anyone can see that, an' it's hardly suprisin' wi' what she's gone through one way or another in the last few months.'

'It's all right, Hetty. I . . . I'd rather get it over and done with – really,' Grace reassured her. 'Will you keep an eye on Georgie for me while I'm gone?'

'That goes wi'out sayin', but I still ain't sure as yer should be doin' this alone.' Hetty could not keep the concern from her voice as she stared at Grace anxiously and once again Grace wondered what she would ever have done without the help of this kind woman.

'I'll come with you,' Sarah offered. She was almost as pale as Grace, but Grace shook her head.

'No, it's all right, thanks. I'd rather do this alone.'

She walked unsteadily towards the two police officers and then with a final smile at Will, who was still standing nervously wringing his hands, she followed them outside to the waiting police car.

'Where is my aunt?' she asked as the car pulled smoothly away from the kerb.

'She's in the morgue at the George Eliot Hospital at present,' the young policewoman told her and then they fell silent as they made the short journey.

'There's no hurry,' the solemn-faced mortuary attendant told her. 'Just go in when you feel ready.'

Sarah stared blankly through the glass window at a white sheet that was presumably covering her aunt's body on a slab in a small sterile-looking room. She wanted to go in and get it over with, yet somehow although she told her feet to go, they seemed rooted to the spot.

The police officers and the attendant stood back, and Grace forced herself to move forward. There – her feet were doing as they were told now, her hand was on the door-handle: she only had to push it and she would be in the room. She heard the door close behind her and then she was there, right next to the table. She only had to draw the sheet back and she would see her aunt, but now it was her hands that wouldn't do as they were told, for although she wanted to look they simply hung limply at her sides.

Her mind seemed to be playing tricks on her; the mound that the sheet covered looked so small. Surely her aunt had been larger than that? And the sheet, it was so white, so white that it almost hurt her eyes and she found herself wishing that she could get Georgie's nappies that clean. She had to stifle the urge to laugh. What was she doing standing here thinking about laundry when she had come to identify the body of her aunt? But was it her aunt? Of course it wasn't, Grace was convinced of it. When she did pull the sheet back it would be someone else lying there, not her Aunt Emily.

Glancing up, she saw the sympathetic eyes of the WPC boring into her, and it was then that her hand suddenly shot out and grasped the sheet. With a quick flip she pulled it aside and found herself staring down into the face of her aunt.

She gasped, for although it *was* her aunt, it was Emily as she had never seen her before. She looked as if she was fast asleep, and as the idea occurred to Grace she took a step back, for the fear of the woman was still there, as strong as it had always been. Her hands were crossed neatly across her chest and Grace's eyes were drawn to a diamond ring that sparkled on the third finger of her left hand in the harsh fluorescent light. For the first time Grace's eyes filled with tears. Was this poor wizened-up old woman really the one who had been able to strike terror into her very soul? She looked so frail and tiny lying there that it was hard to imagine she could ever have scared anyone. Slowly the bitterness and the anger she had felt towards her seeped away, to be replaced by pity and compassion. In life, Emily had been her own worst enemy, for Grace had always wanted to love her. Instead, Emily had chosen to lock herself away in a world of bitterness and now she had died all alone with no one to care.

Over the last months, Grace had cried so many tears that she was convinced she had no more left to cry, but now they suddenly spurted from her with such force that she had the sensation of drowning. They seemed to be coming from every opening, and it was hard to breathe; in fact, she didn't even know if she wanted to breathe any more. She was tired; so tired that the thought of just going to sleep and never having to wake up again was welcome. And then the laughter bubbled up inside her and she was shaking so much that her legs could no longer hold her. The laughter echoed from the cold white walls but she was beyond caring now. She was vaguely aware of the door being pushed open and people rushing towards her, but still the tears and the laughter took her breath away as someone put strong arms around her. And then it came; the welcoming, comforting darkness and she closed her eyes and let it take her where it would.

'How is she today then?' Sarah asked as she slipped off her coat.

Hetty shrugged and taking it from her, she flung the coat carelessly across the banister at the bottom of the steep staircase. 'About the same,' she sighed. 'The solicitor called in earlier an' she signed some papers, but I ain't too sure that she knew what she were signing. She's asked him to put the house up for sale, but he persuaded her to wait a while to be sure that's what she wants. Personally I reckon it would be fer the best, especially after all the money it cost fer the funeral. After the way Emily treated the gel, yer wouldn't think Grace would have insisted on the best of everythin' fer her, would yer?'

Sarah made no comment as the two women entered the kitchen side-by-side. After checking on Georgie, who was curled up in her crib looking for all the world like a little angel, Sarah asked, 'Have you seen anything else of Barry?'

Hetty shook her head. 'Not fer a couple o' days. Yer know, it makes me so mad! It's as plain as the nose on yer face that he still loves her, an' between you an' me I think she still loves him. I told him he could go up an' see her if he wanted to, but he just shook his head an' said no, but to tell her that as soon as she were feelin' more herself she could see the kids.'

'Have you told her this?' Relief spasmed across Sarah's troubled face, but Hetty shook her head. 'Perhaps you should,' she suggested thoughtfully. 'This might be just the thing to bring her back from wherever she's gone to. She certainly isn't here with us, is she? It's almost as if her mind has switched off so that nothing else can hurt her.'

'Yer don't need to be tellin' *me* that,' Hetty sniffed indignantly. 'In case yer'd forgotten, it's *me* as is seein' to her *an'* the babby. The doctor reckons as there's nothin' wrong with her physically, it's up here as needs to mend.' When she tapped at her head, Sarah was instantly repentant.

'Oh Hetty, I'm so sorry. I didn't mean to offend you. I know that you're doing all you can. But if it's getting too much for you I could always have them to stay with me.'

Hetty's good humour returned as she crossed to the kettle. 'I ain't offended, love. A bit tired perhaps, that's all – not to mention frustrated.

I feel so useless. I mean, I'm seein' to all her physical needs yet I can't seem to get through to her.'

'Then it's time something was done,' Sarah said, and the words had barely left her mouth when she was up and striding towards the door again with an air of determination.

'Here, where you off to? I was about to make yer a cup o' tea,' Hetty shouted to her retreating back.

'I shan't be long,' Sarah assured her. 'But I think it's time I went to see Barry again. If anything can bring her out of this I reckon it's a visit from him and those children, and so I'm going to arrange it – even if I have to drag him here kicking and screaming.'

Hetty's wrinkled face broke into a smile of admiration. 'You go fer it then, gel. An' the very best o' luck to yer.'

'Oh, for God's sake, Hetty! Will you *please* sit down? You're making me nervous with all this pacing.'

Hetty grinned at Sarah across her shoulder. It was now three days since Sarah had paid Barry a visit and soon, if he kept his promise, he would be arriving with the children to visit Grace.

'Do yer reckon he'll come?' she asked yet again.

Sarah smiled at her reassuringly. 'He'll come,' she said confidently. 'Barry doesn't seem like the sort of man to break a promise.'

Almost before the words had left her mouth, there was a knock at the door and Hetty almost jumped out of her skin.

'That'll be him,' she stated nervously as her eyes flew around the room checking that all was as it should be. Everywhere was spick and span and on the table was an assortment of cakes that she had spent the whole morning baking for Grace's children.

'Shall I let them in?' Sarah offered.

Hetty shook her head and moved purposefully towards the door. 'No, love, I'll do it. You go an' put the kettle on, eh?' She found Barry straight-faced with the children either side of him hopping from foot to foot in their excitement. Hetty opened her mouth to speak but before she had the chance, Wendy asked, 'Is our mammy here?'

Hetty had to swallow the huge lump that rose in her throat before she could reply. 'Yes, darlin', she is, but get yourselves inside an' then I'll just have a little chat to you all before yer go up to see her, eh?'

Once inside, the children stared at her expectantly as bending painfully to their level she told them, 'Your mammy might not be quite as yer remember her fer a start, loves. Yer see – she's bin quite poorly recently but I reckon seein' you all will do her more good than any medicine the doctor could prescribe.'

'She's not goin' to die or . . . or go away again, is she?' Simon asked fretfully.

'No, no, not at all. But now come on, I reckon you've waited long enough. Let's go up to her, shall we?' Hetty began to herd them in front of her up the steep staircase, and when they got to the top she led them to a door at the end of a long, dimly lit landing.

'Here we are then, this is yer mammy's room. I told her yer was comin' so I've no doubt she'll be waitin' fer yer.'

She pushed the door open to see Grace sitting at a chair by the window, her face alight with hope, but before she could say a word the children saw her too, and leaping away from Barry they flew across the room to be wrapped in her arms as tears streamed down her face.

'Oh, my darlings, how you've grown!' The words were choked but her eyes were alive for the first time in months. With the children still tightly clutched to her she looked over their heads and her eyes found Barry's.

'Thank you,' she said softly, and deeply embarrassed Barry nodded and lowered his eyes.

Hetty slowly shut the door then quietly crept away to join Sarah and Georgie in the kitchen downstairs.

Some time later, the two women heard the sound of footsteps on the stairs. Hetty leaped up from her chair and thrust Georgie, whom she had been feeding, at Sarah, before rushing into the hall. 'Don't go yet,' she implored. 'I've bin bakin' a few cakes fer the children this mornin', an' it would be a shame fer 'em to go to waste. You'll stay an' have a cup o' tea, won't yer?'

Barry looked decidedly reluctant, but at the mention of homemade cakes the children whooped with delight. They only ever got them now when Grandma Daisy made them, and this was an unexpected treat. Realising that it would be rude to refuse, Barry silently followed the children into the kitchen. He stopped abruptly when he saw the baby in Sarah's arms, but then remembering his manners he averted his eyes and perched uncomfortably on the edge of a chair while Hetty fussed over the children. Once they had eaten their fill of Hetty's delicious cakes the children turned their attention to the child. Crossing to her they both stared down at her in awe.

'Blimey, she's little, ain't she?' Simon commented.

Wendy reached out to stroke the child's tiny hand and when Georgie's little fingers gripped hers she squealed with delight.

'Look, Daddy, she likes me! Come and see her, she's lovely and—'

'I think it's time we were going now.' Barry stood up so suddenly that the children's faces fell.

295

'Oh *please*, we don't have to go yet, do we?' the two chorused in unison.

'Yes, we do. Now come along. We've imposed on Mrs Brambles quite enough for one day.' Something in his voice quieted the children's arguments and meekly they followed him to the door. Hetty led them back along the hallway and once at the front door she smiled at Barry sadly.

'Bless yer, lad, fer what you've done this day.'

His face hard, he nodded at her and extended his hand, which she shook warmly.

'Thank you for your hospitality, Mrs Brambles.' He ushered the children before him but as he was about to follow, Hetty put her hand on his arm. 'Yer will come again, won't yer? *Please*, lad. Shall we say the same time next week?'

He opened his mouth to say: 'No, we won't say the same time next week!' The visit had been painful for him and had awakened feelings that he had hoped were long dead. But then he looked at the children's expectant faces and slowly nodded. 'Very well, the same time next week.'

Hetty watched him walk away down Edward Street with the children hanging on each hand then closing the door softly she hurried back to where Sarah was waiting for her in the kitchen.

'Phew, I can't say as I'm sorry that that's over,' she remarked. 'It got a bit nerve-wrackin' fer a time back there when he first set eyes on the babby, didn't it?'

'Actually, I thought he handled it very well considering,' Sarah remarked. 'I mean, think how hard it must have been for him to even come here in the first place. I think he's a very brave and kind young man.'

'Well, I won't argue wi' that, but now I'd better get up there an' see how the madam upstairs has took it.' So saying she bustled away, leaving Sarah to change Georgie's nappy.

Chapter Twenty-Nine

As she stood in the kitchen of what she still considered to be her aunt's house, Grace slowly looked around her. It was over a year now since Emily had died, and since then the place had stood empty, exactly as her aunt had left it. This was the first time that Grace had felt able to enter it and now the memories rushed back – terrible memories that still came to haunt her in the night and caused her to have recurring nightmares. Yet strangely now, although the memories were still strong, they held no fear, for now Grace could see Emily for the lonely, bitter woman who had died as she had lived for so many years – all alone.

Grace now had a very healthy bank account, as well as owning this house, which had enabled her to make sure that she and Georgie were not a drain on Hetty. However, soon now she would have to find a place of her own, not because Hetty didn't want her any more – in fact, she would have been more than happy for Grace and Georgie to make their home with her permanently – but because Grace had her pride. She had made her mistakes and paid for them and now it was time for her to stand on her own two feet again.

Georgie was progressing remarkably well and was now a beautiful little girl, who to everyone's amazement, only this week had falteringly taken her first steps. Barry had been marvellous over the last year, allowing her access to Wendy and Simon almost whenever she wanted it; he had even allowed them to stay for a few overnights at Hetty's, which had only gone to reaffirm what Grace had always known, that he was a truly remarkable, kind man. Time and again she cursed herself for a fool for letting him slip through her fingers, and she tortured herself when she remembered the time she had seen him in the town with the young woman at his side. He had never as yet mentioned his new partner to Grace, but the children frequently spoke of her and always with affection, which was like a knife twisting in Grace's heart. Only the day before, Wendy had told her excitedly about a present that Marion had brought her. 'It's a dolly that cries,' she had enthused. '*An*' she made me a cake with icing an' candles on for me birthday.'

'Yes, she did, but she *still* made us go to bed at the right time when she went out wi' Daddy,' Simon had grumbled. 'Grandma always has to babysit fer us when she goes out wi' Daddy,' he had finished, and the knife cut even deeper in Grace's heart.

Just the week before, Grace had listened to the Divorce Reform Bill's third reading on the news with a sinking heart. From now on, couples who had been apart for two years could divorce with mutual consent, which meant that very soon Barry might be asking her to end their marriage. Of course, if – or when – he did, she would agree. That was the least she could do for him after how she had treated him, but she dreaded hearing the words.

With an effort, she pulled her thoughts back to the present. Following her aunt's death, she had begged the solicitor to put the house up for sale, but he had encouraged her to wait until she was quite sure that this was what she wanted. After all, he had pointed out, it *was* an extremely desirable house. Grace supposed that it was, but somehow she could never quite imagine Georgie growing up there; it would always feel like Emily's house – and now that she had entered it again, she knew that she wouldn't change her mind. First thing tomorrow she would get an estate agent to come and value it, and then put it on the market, then she would look around for somewhere that she could make her own home. *Her own home*; her thoughts flew back to the house that she had shared with Barry. That had once been home, but some other woman would soon be living there in her place now. Serves me right, she told herself sternly, and crossing to the tiny desk that stood in one corner she ran her hands along the smooth grain of the wood. This was the only thing she would keep; everything else could stay for the new owners, whoever they might be, to do with as they saw fit. She took a last look around the room and for an instant she had the uncanny feeling of someone watching her.

'It's all right, Aunt Emily,' she whispered softly. 'The house is still yours, I'll not darken the door again, but . . . I forgive you. Rest in peace.' Turning, she left her childhood home for the very last time.

'Come here, you little beauty,' Daisy giggled as Georgie tottered unsteadily towards her. 'Come an' give yer Granny a kiss.'

When Grace stared at her incredulously, Daisy flushed. 'Sorry, love, it just sort of slipped out.'

Thankfully, Grace and Daisy had become close again over the last months and Grace now visited her regularly. It had been somewhat strained in the early days but now they were once more at ease in each other's company, although there was an unspoken pact that meant they neither of them ever mentioned Barry, unless it was about anything to do with the children.

'So where were you thinkin' of movin' to then, when you've sold the house?' Daisy asked to break the uncomfortable silence that had settled between them.

'I'm not too sure yet,' Grace admitted. 'It will have to be somewhere with at least three bedrooms though. There'll be a room for me, one for Simon, and Wendy can share with Georgie when they stay over. That's if Barry and his new girlfriend will let them, of course.'

As Daisy stared at her quizzically, Grace felt her colour rising. She hadn't meant to say that. After all, it was nothing to do with her who Barry saw, but it had just sort of slipped out.

'Barry's girlfriend! Who would that be then?'

'I . . . um . . . Well, I saw him with a young woman in town – oh, it must have been well over a year ago now, and as the children often mention her I just assumed—'

'You ain't talkin' about Marion, are you?' Daisy asked. When Grace nodded sadly, Daisy threw back her head and laughed aloud. 'Why, you daft ha'porth, you! Marion ain't Barry's girlfriend, she's a happily married woman. She childminds for him when his shifts fall awkward at work, that's all. Oh, an' she's also . . .' She suddenly clamped her lips shut and turned as red as a beetroot.

Grace's heart began to thump and seeing her confusion, Daisy became serious. 'You still love him, don't you, Grace?'

Grace scooped Georgie onto her lap as her eyes filled with tears. After a moment she nodded miserably. 'Yes, I do, but a fat lot of good that will do, won't it? How could Barry ever forgive me after what I've done to him? She . . .' She nodded at Georgie. 'She must be a constant reminder of how bad I am every time he looks at her,' she muttered.

Daisy sighed deeply. If it were up to her she would bang both of their silly bloody heads together, because from where she was standing a blind man on a galloping horse could see that they still had feelings for each other, even if they couldn't see it themselves. Still, this time she couldn't interfere. This was something they would have to sort out for themselves. She just wished they would get on with it, that's all.

'All I can say is, Grace, if I can forgive you, then perhaps in time Barry will. This little one here didn't *ask* to be born, an' she's a little darlin'. Between you an' me, she puts me in mind of our Barry when he were a nipper, but then perhaps that's just wishful thinkin' on my part. But if you *do* still love him, then why don't you bloody tell him so?' Oh dear, her and her big mouth!

'I can't.' Grace trembled at the thought and suddenly feeling totally out of her depth she carried Georgie across to her pushchair and started to strap her in. 'I'd better be off, anyway. I promised I'd nip into the butcher's for Hetty, and if she hasn't got the meat in time to cook it for when Will gets in, it will be *me* that gets the roasting.'

Daisy chuckled as she followed her to the door. 'Well, mind how you go, love. I'll see you in the week, eh?'

Grace pecked her cheek and nodded, then she was off with a spring in her step. So Marion *wasn't* Barry's partner, she was just someone who helped out with the children. The warm feeling suddenly seeped away as she came back down to earth with a bump. But what else had Daisy been about to tell her? She shrugged. What difference did it really make? Whether this Marion was his new girlfriend or not, Barry obviously didn't have feelings for Grace any more, and who could blame him?

'Strewth! The full askin' price, eh? Didn't you do well? I dare say as you'll be lookin' round fer somewhere else now then.'

'Actually, Hetty, I have somewhere I have my eye on already,' Grace confided. 'There's a nice terraced house up for sale in Tomkinson Road that would just do me. It's got three bedrooms and a good big garden for Georgie and the others to play in, overlooking the recreation ground. There's a football pitch on the rec too, so on Saturday Simon could watch Fife Athletic practising there. I think I might put an offer in now that the house in Oaston Road has sold.'

Hetty looked crestfallen. 'Happen you know best, but I'll miss yer both. Still, Tomkinson Road is only a stone's throw away, ain't it? It ain't like I won't get to see yer.'

'Of course you'll get to see us,' Grace quickly assured her. 'I don't know what I would have done without you and that's the truth, Hetty. You've been like a mother to me and I'll never forget it. But now, come on, we're both getting tearful and Barry will be bringing the children round soon. We don't want them to see us all upset, do we?'

'No, o' course not!' Hetty dried her eyes on her apron and sniffed. Like Daisy, she had hoped and prayed over the last months that Grace and Barry would become reconciled. Sometimes she would watch them together when they were playing with Wendy and Simon, and they looked such a lovely family that it almost broke her heart, but then Georgie would waddle over to join in and the closed look would come down across Barry's face. Oh, she'd be the first to admit that he was gentle to the child, kind even, but in all the time he had been visiting she had never seen him so much as touch her. Still, she supposed she could understand it. Georgie could only ever be a constant reminder to Barry of how Grace had betrayed him, and as much as she would have liked to take on the role of match-maker to get the two back together, she knew that it would be useless to even try. This was something they were going to have to work out for themselves.

'How would you feel about taking the kids for a walk along to Riversley Park for an hour?' Barry asked tentatively.

Grace, who was laughing at Wendy and Simon as they played with Georgie, flashed him a smile that lit up her face and set his pulse racing. 'Don't you have to get them to bed ready for school tomorrow?' she asked.

Barry looked out of the open back door at the beautiful summer's evening. 'I dare say half an hour won't hurt, just for one night. But of course, if you'd rather not . . .'

'Oh, I'd love to!' Grace spluttered before he could change his mind. 'There are some ducks on the River Anker, I could perhaps take some bread for the children to feed them. But . . .' Her eyes moved anxiously to Hetty, who had been feeling rather unwell all day. 'I . . . er . . . I'd have to bring Georgie. Hetty's not been too grand – she's got this summer flu bug that's going around – and I wouldn't like to impose on her.'

Barry shrugged, keeping his eyes studiously diverted from the child in question. 'As you like, though if we are going to go we ought to be off soon. As you pointed out, Wendy and Simon do have to get up for school in the morning and I don't want them to be too late.'

Grace leaped up and, grabbing a flannel, started to wash Georgie's pudgy little face. This was the first time that she and Barry would have taken the children out together since their separation, and her eyes were alight at the prospect. In no time at all she had Georgie strapped into her pushchair and they were ready to go.

'Are you quite sure that you'll be all right, Hetty? We'll only be gone for a short time, I promise,' she said anxiously as she stared into her friend's pale face.

From her position on the settee, Hetty waved an impatient hand at her. 'You get off, I'll be fine. It's a shame to waste such a lovely evenin', an' the fresh air will do yer the world o' good. It might even put a bit o' colour into yer cheeks.'

Grace shepherded the children towards the door and soon they were walking along Edward Street towards the Coton Arches.

'We'll take 'em for a walk through the Pingles Fields first.' Barry grinned. 'We may as well tire 'em out while we're at it, an' then at least they'll sleep tonight.'

Grace trundled along with the pushchair, laughing at Wendy and Simon who were skipping ahead full of the joys of spring. It felt good to be out as a family again, and she realised in that moment just how much she had missed it. Every now and again she saw Barry glance at the child in the pushchair, and her heart went out to him as she tried to imagine how she would feel if the roles had been reversed. Would she have been able to stroll along at his side with him pushing the child of another woman? She had to admit that she doubted it, and suddenly some of her pleasure seeped away. It would always be this way, because it was more than obvious that Barry would never be able to take to Georgie.

Grace's eyes settled on the fair-haired child strapped tightly into the pushchair and the urge came on her to cry there and then. Georgie was a lovely child, beautiful even, for all her disabilities. As she grew they had become more apparent, starting with her eyes, which were slanted, though a lovely shade of blue. She was short for her age, which was yet another sign of Downs syndrome, and her little legs were thick and podgy. She was also slow to talk, and up to now, the only word she had been able to utter was *Mamma*, and yet for all that Grace adored her, as did everyone who came into contact with her, for she had the nature of a little angel. Everyone except Barry, that was, but then Grace supposed that was to be expected.

They stayed silent now until they had gone though the tunnel that linked the Pingles Fields with Riversley Park. It was as they were strolling towards the river that Barry said, 'Why don't you let the little 'un out of her pushchair? It won't hurt her if she falls over on the grass.'

Nodding, Grace fumbled with the straps that held Georgie secure, suddenly all fingers and thumbs. The second that she'd set her on the ground, Georgie's little legs went like pistons as she tried to catch up with Wendy and Simon, who had raced ahead. Twice she stumbled and fell in her haste, but before Grace could reach her she was up and running again with no complaint.

'Determined little thing, ain't she?' Barry commented, and unsure how to answer, Grace merely nodded. In no time at all they had joined the children at the water's edge, and Grace kept a watchful eye on Georgie as she fished for the stale bread she had brought to feed the ducks.

302

Passing a slice to each of the children, she stared at the graceful weeping willow trees whose branches trailed into the water. The rowing boats that were tied to the side of the boathouse bobbed gently in the slowly flowing water and the sounds of children laughing and playing as their indulgent parents looked on floated to her on the air. By now a family of ducks were quacking around their feet as the delighted children tossed them their treats.

'So,' Barry said, bringing her thoughts back to the present. 'I hear as your aunt's house has been sold.'

'Yes – yes, it has.'

'What will you be doin' now then? Will you be stayin' at Hetty's or movin' on?'

'Well, I suppose I'll be moving on,' Grace said quietly. 'Hetty's been marvellous to me, but she's not getting any younger, and I think Georgie's getting a bit much for her now. Not that she doesn't love her,' she hastened to add, 'but I don't want to become a burden. I think it's time I stood on my own two feet again now, don't you? I've actually seen a house in Tomkinson Road that might just suit us.'

Barry was just about to answer when suddenly Wendy let out a piercing scream that rent the air. As they both turned towards the noise, Grace froze. In just the few seconds that she had given her attention to Barry, Georgie had gone dangerously near to the water's edge as she gleefully chased the little ducklings. Just two more steps and she would be over the steep riverbank and . . . the thought was too terrible to contemplate, but Grace was rooted to the spot with terror. Suddenly, Barry seemed to catapult into the air and with a speed that would have done justice to an Olympic runner, he was pelting across the soft grass towards Georgie. Her heart in her mouth, Grace watched as Georgie tottered unsteadily on the riverbank, and then lost her footing. For seconds that seemed to be passing in slow motion she seemed to hover in the air and Grace was convinced that the river would claim her, but then Barry suddenly snatched her into his arms just in time, and swung her into the air before gripping her to his chest.

'Don't *ever* go near the water again without me or Mammy holding your hand. *Do you hear me?*' he scolded. Suddenly realising what he had said he flushed, and as Grace flew across to him he thrust the now-sobbing child into her arms. 'Here,' he muttered. 'Sorry I shouted at her. It was just reaction, I suppose.'

Grace could say nothing as she clutched the child to her. Tears were raining down her face as a little crowd gathered around them.

'Is the child all right?' a tall dark-haired man asked sympathetically.

He banged Barry on the shoulder without waiting for an answer. 'Well done, mate. It's surprising what we dads can do when our little 'uns are at risk, ain't it?'

If Barry had been flushed before, now he was bright red with emotion, although the shock had rendered him temporarily speechless.

'She's fine, thank you,' Grace told the man as she pulled herself together with an enormous effort. 'Wendy, Simon. Come on, I think it's time we were going now. Georgie and your dad have had quite a shock, so I think we should get them home.'

'What – to *our* home?' Wendy asked hopefully as she swiped the tears from her cheeks with the back of her hand. By now the little crowd was dispersing as Grace struggled to find words to answer her.

'What I should have said is, I'll get Georgie back to Hetty's, and your dad will take you two back to your home,' she said in a voice filled with pain.

'But Mammy, *why* can't you come back to our home too?' Wendy wailed, her voice heavy with tears. 'You used to live at our home, why can't you again – and Georgie too?'

'Because I . . .'

'Come along.' Sensing Grace's distress, Barry quickly took control of the situation. 'Like your mam said, Georgie has had a nasty shock and she needs to get home.'

With leaden feet and drooping head, Wendy silently fell into step with the solemn procession that marched through the park. Barry pushed the pushchair as Grace clutched Georgie to her, almost as if she were afraid of what could happen, should she dare to let her go again. They took the short cut home across Coton Road and then went through Riversley Road, and in no time at all they were at Hetty's door.

'Will you come in?' Grace asked hesitantly, but Barry scowled and shook his head. The incident with Georgie had shaken him more than he cared to admit, and now all he wanted was some time on his own to think.

'No, thanks all the same but I think I'll get these two home and tucked in,' he said abruptly.

Wendy, who had not uttered so much as a single word since they had left the park, suddenly threw herself at Grace and began to sob uncontrollably, and Simon, almost as if he didn't want to be outdone, did the same.

'*Please*, Mammy. Come home with us. We miss you *so* much,' she beseeched. Grace felt as if her heart were breaking all over again as she clutched Georgie to her with one hand and the other two children with the other. Deeply embarrassed and obviously very upset, Barry managed to prise them away.

'Come along now, you two. Can't you see you're upsetting your mam and Georgie?' he scolded. It seemed that there was nothing to say that would ease the situation and Grace watched helplessly as Barry led them away before wearily traipsing into Hetty's.

Much later that night when the children were fast asleep in bed, Barry paced up and down the living room reliving in his mind over and over again the feel of Georgie in his arms. It had felt nothing at all like he had expected; in fact, he had quite enjoyed the feel of her sturdy little body nestling against him. Something Daisy had said to him suddenly sprang to mind. 'I wonder where the little 'un got that shock o' fair hair from, don't you, what wi' Grace an' the bugger she took off wi' being so dark? An' them eyes, you must admit they could charm the ducks off the water. The exact same colour as yer dad's, ain't they?'

With a little shock, he now suddenly realised what she had been trying to tell him. Georgie really could be his child. Sinking into a chair, Barry buried his face in his hands as he tried to put his thoughts into some sort of order. Of course, he would never know for sure. But could he accept her as his own? If the answer was no, then there was no future for him and Grace. But if the answer was yes, then perhaps, just perhaps . . . He stopped his thoughts from the path they were taking. This was something he was going to have to sleep on.

Chapter Thirty

The following day on his way home from work, Barry paused at the end of Edward Street and stood there for some time wrestling with his conscience. Then, deciding to throw caution to the winds, he strode up the street and rapped sharply on Hetty's door before he had the chance to change his mind. When Grace opened the door to find him standing on the doorstep, her face lit up and his heart did a somersault in his chest. Peeping over his shoulder she said, 'This is a nice surprise. I wasn't expecting you. Are the children with you?'

'No. I . . . er . . . they're not with me. I've not been home from work yet. But the thing is . . . I wondered if you might like to come out with me tonight?'

Grace was so shocked that for a moment she was speechless, but then she suddenly babbled, 'I'd love to!' before he could change his mind.

'Right. I'll . . . er . . . call round fer you about seven then. An' Grace . . . put yer dancin' shoes on, eh?'

She stood there watching him stride away down the street with a look of amazement on her face before slamming the door shut and running down the hallway to tell Hetty about her unexpected visitor. The old lady beamed like a Cheshire cat. 'About bloody time too. Now you go up an' get yerself ready. Me an' our Will will see to Georgie, won't we, son?'

Grace skipped away like a teenager about to go on her first date as Hetty and Will exchanged a smile that spoke volumes.

When Barry arrived on the doorstep promptly at seven o'clock, Grace was ready and waiting for him, looking positively radiant. She had chosen to wear a dress she had made some time ago that happened to be one of his favourites. It was the exact blue of her eyes, and he looked her up and down appreciatively, then offering his arm, he told Hetty, 'I promise not to keep her out too late.'

'Yer can keep her out all night fer me, lad,' Hetty told him in her usual forthright manner and Grace was so embarrassed that she almost dragged him through the door.

Once out in the street they walked along in a self-conscious silence for a while until Grace plucked up the courage to ask, 'Where are we going?'

'Courtaulds ballroom,' he answered shortly as her mouth gaped open in surprise.

The band was already playing a waltz when they entered, and the old magic immediately stirred deep inside her. Knowing how Barry hated to dance, Grace was looking around for an empty table when he suddenly asked, 'May I have this dance?'

She had no time to answer for he suddenly took her elbow and led her to the dance-floor. Then, to her utter amazement, he took her in his arms and began to sweep her around the floor with an ease that put many of the men there to shame.

'My God, Barry! I didn't know you could dance like this,' she gasped.

He grinned as he looked down at her. 'I couldn't,' he admitted sheepishly. 'Marion has been teaching me for months.'

So *that* was what Daisy had been about to tell her, she thought, on the day she had suddenly clammed up. And that was where Barry and Marion must have been going on the nights when Daisy babysat for the children. Grace felt a lump growing in her throat as he whirled her effortlessly around the floor.

'But *why* . . . ?'

Seeing the tears that were glistening on her lashes, he cleared his throat and said, 'Me mam pointed out to me that I should have made more of an effort when we were together. I always knew how much you loved to dance. I'm sorry, Grace.'

'No, Barry,' she whispered. 'It's *me* that's sorry.'

'Well, let's just try an' enjoy ourselves, eh?' He smiled, and for the rest of the night that's exactly what they did.

By the time the music finally ended, Grace was deeply impressed with his newfound dancing skills. 'I never *dreamed* you could dance like that – you're a real natural,' she told him as he walked her back to Hetty's through the balmy summer night. They had barely sat down all night and she felt as if she was floating.

He grinned self-consciously. 'I actually began to enjoy it once I started to get the hang of it,' he admitted. 'It's just a shame as I didn't try sooner, then . . .'

Suddenly the awkwardness was back between them and he wished that he could have bitten his tongue off. What did he have to go and say that for when everything had been going so well?

At Hetty's door they stood feet apart as Grace fumbled in her bag for her key.

307

'Would you like to come in for a cup of coffee?' she asked for want of something to say, but he hastily shook his head and once again they were strangers.

'No, thanks. I don't want to be too late back 'cos of me mam. She's babysitting.'

'Of course. Well, thanks for tonight then. I really enjoyed it. Perhaps we could do it again?'

'Perhaps.' Turning abruptly, he thrust his hands deep in his jacket pockets and strode away. Grace sighed and let herself into the dark hallway.

Epilogue

It was a glorious Sunday afternoon and they were all in Hetty's garden enjoying the picnic she had prepared for them. Wendy and Simon, who were sitting on a blanket that Hetty had spread out for them under the branches of the apple tree, were still somewhat subdued following the incident in the park earlier in the week. Barry and Grace also seemed ill-at-ease with each other after their night out and Daisy and May, who had become regular visitors and firm friends of Hetty's, glanced at her in exasperation.

'What say we go an' make a cuppa?' Daisy suggested.

'That's a good idea,' Hetty agreed, glad of an excuse to escape the gloomy atmosphere. 'Let's go an' put the kettle on, eh? Are yer going to join us, May?'

Barry watched the three women waddle away up the garden together before asking, 'You went to look at the house in Tomkinson Road, then?'

Dragging her eyes away from Billy and Georgie, who seemed to be the only ones in a happy mood, Grace nodded. 'Yes, I went to look.'

'*And*, did you put an offer in?'

Grace shook her head. 'No. Not yet I haven't.'

'Why's that then? Wasn't the house up to scratch?'

'Well, yes – yes, it was, but . . .' Grace struggled to find the right words. 'The house was actually very nice. It doesn't need that much doing to it and there's a lovely garden at the back for Georgie to play in, but . . .'

'Ah – there's that *but* again. But what?'

'I don't know really.' Grace shrugged disconsolately. 'I suppose it just didn't feel like . . .'

'Like what?'

'Like home, I suppose,' Grace muttered miserably.

Barry had to fight the urge to snatch her into his arms there and then. Could this mean that there might still be a chance for them? But he had to be sure. He couldn't take any more heartache, he had suffered enough of that to last him a whole lifetime. He had been forced to admit to himself that despite all that had happened he still loved Grace, had always loved her, *but* – and now it was his turn for buts – what if she didn't feel the same way?

They both turned to look at Georgie, who was tottering up the garden path at breakneck speed pushing a little trolley full of wooden building bricks in front of her with Billy close on her heels. The trolley was picking up speed and suddenly it shot into the air, throwing bricks in all directions, and Georgie sprawled her length on the cold hard concrete.

Both Barry and Grace leaped from their seats as one, and as they ran side-by-side to pick her up, Georgie started to howl.

Her startling blue eyes settled on Barry and as he approached her she held her arms up to him beseechingly, sobbing, *'Dadda.'*

Grace stopped dead in her tracks as Barry swung her into his arms and murmured words of comfort into her fair curls. 'It's all right, sweetheart. Daddy's got you,' she heard him say, but she dared not let herself believe that she had heard aright. Georgie sucked on her thumb and nestled against him as he turned to face Grace.

'She's all right now,' he assured her with a tentative smile on his face. 'But I think it's about time she came home now, don't you?'

'You mean . . . home to *you*?'

Barry grinned, that lop-sided grin that had haunted her in the lonely time they had been apart. 'Well, that *was* the general idea.'

'But – but Georgie . . . ?'

Planting a gentle kiss on the child's head, he set her on the ground and turned to Grace.

'I think it's time this family was back together again, and that includes Georgie now, doesn't it?'

'Oh, Barry.' Grace's eyes betrayed all the love she felt for him and all the pain she was feeling. 'I can't be a hundred per cent sure that Georgie is—'

'Shhh.' He drew her into his arms. 'Enough said. She's *mine* from this moment on, whatever.'

'Oh, Barry. *I love you so much.* I realise now that I've *always* loved you.'

It was said; the words that he had always longed to hear her say, and they were like a salve on his broken heart.

Billy, Wendy and Simon pounded away up the garden with huge smiles on their faces. The women raised startled eyebrows as they burst into the kitchen.

'Grandma, Hetty!' Wendy gasped in her excitement. 'Look out o'

the window, quick. Mammy an' Daddy are kissin', an' Daddy said it's time as Mammy an' Georgie were comin' home to us.'

The three women exchanged satisfied glances as they quickly crossed to the kitchen window to peep past the pretty gingham curtains. Sure enough, there were Grace and Barry clasped in a loving embrace as Georgie, now fully recovered from her tumble, bent to pick up her bricks.

'Well, all I can say is – about time too.' Hetty beamed 'I was beginnin' to think as I'd have to bang their bloody daft heads together!'

'I'll second that,' grinned Daisy, and the women returned to their well-earned cup of tea.

Author's Note

The recent 'Strictly Come Dancing' programme on TV awakened many happy memories for me. When my mum was younger, she loved to dance, as did my aunt and uncle, and these memories inspired me to write this book.

I was absolutely elated back in October when my editor asked me if I would now consider writing two books a year for Headline. Of course, I jumped at the chance, and so I can now promise another book this year that will be released early in December. The title of the next one is *Moonlight and Ashes*, a wartime saga set in Coventry. During research for this novel I was humbled to learn of the bravery of the people who lived through the Second World War, and of those who died defending our freedom. I hope you will all enjoy reading it as much as I enjoyed writing it.

It's been a wonderful year in many ways, though our family did suffer a huge loss when our little Westie, Holly, died shortly before Christmas. We all still miss her every single day, but I like to think she will remain with us as I put her in my last book, *No One's Girl*. Whenever I look at that book now, I will remember her as she was when I wrote it: happy and full of mischief. Thankfully I still have my two little Shihtzus, Sophie and Yasmin, to keep me company when I am working.

I am now thoroughly enjoying being locked away in my study doing one of the things that I have always loved to do best, which is to write. I have also loved meeting some of the people who have read my books, and it makes my day when they tell me how much they enjoyed them and ask, 'When is the next one out?' I promise to keep them coming and thank you all so much!